BREWED ITALIAN ROMANCE

A TALE OF NAPLES, ART, AND SUSPENDED COFFEE

SEEMA SHENOY

For my parents, Dr. Anant and Sudha Bhadri,

*Your beautiful partnership
showed me what real love
looks like. Not in grand
gestures, but in a lifetime
of devotion, kindness,
and quiet moments that
spoke louder than words.*

"In Naples, coffee is suspended, time is suspended, and between these suspensions, love finds its eternal moment."

- ANONYMOUS

PREFACE

Italy changes you in subtle but permanent ways. After three visits over the years with my husband, I've found myself drawn to its particular cadence of life, its unapologetic celebration of beauty in everyday moments, and its remarkable ability to blend the ancient with the present. The quality of light there is different, sharper, clearer somehow, revealing details in architecture and landscape that might go unnoticed elsewhere. This clarity extends beyond the visual; Italy has a way of bringing important things into focus.

Through our travels across various regions, I've developed a deep appreciation for Italian culture that goes beyond the typical tourist experience. I've enjoyed watching locals debate politics over coffee that lasts for hours, observed family dinners that unfold like beautiful cere-monies, and experienced the genuine warmth of shopkeepers who remember your face after just one visit. These aren't the postcard moments of Italy, but they're the ones that stay with you.

During one of our trips, I learned about "caffè sospeso" (suspended coffee), a tradition that originated in Naples where someone pays for two coffees but drinks only one, leaving the second "suspended" for someone else to claim. The practical generosity of this custom struck me immediately. There was something compelling about this connection between strangers who would never meet, this small act of faith in humanity.

The concept remained with me long after returning home to the San Francisco Bay Area. I found myself thinking about it during quiet moments, considering its implications and of stories it might generate. That's when I decided to write this novel.

I decided to do this against the backdrop of Naples, for its resilience through centuries of challenge, its vibrant artistic tradition, and of course, its renowned coffee culture.

This novel represents both my admiration for Italian culture and my fascination with how small gestures can create profound connections. It explores themes of trust after heartbreak, the healing power of art, and finding belonging in unexpected places. While the romantic elements are central to the story, I've tried to ground them in the realities of two people with complicated pasts and uncertain futures.

My hope is that these pages offer you a thoughtful journey through a culture I've come to deeply respect, and perhaps prompt reflection on the unexpected ways we might touch one another's lives.

With appreciation,

Seema Shenoy

PROLOGUE

aples, Italy - Ten Years Before

The rain had been falling for three days straight, turning Naples' ancient cobblestones into glistening rivers of reflected light. Inside Caffè Sereno, the storm created a sanctuary of sorts, a warm haven of coffee-scented air and gentle conversations while water drummed against centuries-old windows.

Signore Rossi wiped down his beloved espresso machine with the reverence of a priest tending an altar. Decades behind this counter had polished his movements to a perfect economy of grace, each gesture honed by crafting the perfect extraction every single time. His wife Lucia emerged from the kitchen, bringing with her the comforting aroma of almond biscotti still warm from the oven.

"Only four customers today," she said, arranging the fresh-baked treasures in their glass display. Her voice held no disappointment, only simple observation. "This rain keeps everyone close to home."

Signore Rossi nodded, his eyes drifting to the small glass jar beside the register. For generations, it had held the receipts for caffè sospeso (suspended coffees) purchased by customers who pay for an extra coffee that remains available to anyone in need. It was a beautiful tradition, born in post-war Naples when poverty was widespread but generosity even more so.

The jar sat half-empty, its contents slowly diminishing in recent years. The world was changing, becoming more isolated despite all its claims of connection. Signore Rossi had watched as the tradition withered, not from lack of generosity but from the growing chasm between people who no longer looked into each other's eyes when they spoke.

"I've been thinking," he said suddenly, his voice carrying a weight that made Lucia look up from her work. "About caffè sospeso."

She moved to stand beside him, her hand finding his with the ease of rivers joining. "What troubles you, amore mio (my love)?"

Signore Rossi gestured toward the quiet café, the empty chairs that usually held animated conversations, the spaces between people growing wider with each passing year. "The tradition is beautiful, paying forward kindness to strangers. But it has become... transactional. Clinical. The giver and receiver never meet, never see how their simple act touched another soul."

Lucia squeezed his hand, patient, allowing his thoughts to unfold in their own time.

"What if," he continued, his voice gathering strength with each word, "we created something different? Something that honored the spirit of caffè sospeso but brought connection back into its heart?"

Outside, lightning illuminated the rain-soaked street, briefly painting dramatic shadows across the worn wooden floor. The thunder that followed seemed to underscore the importance of this moment, a rumble of ancestral approval for thoughts not yet fully formed.

Signore Rossi led Lucia to the empty wall near the entrance, a space that had remained oddly bare despite decades of accumulated memories adorning every other surface of their beloved café. His hands framed an invisible canvas, eyes alight with vision.

"A cork board," he said, turning to meet her gaze. "When someone buys a caffè sospeso, they don't just pay. They write something; a message, a wish, a fragment of their heart on the receipt. The receipts are held in the jar on our counter."

Understanding dawned in Lucia's eyes as she picked up the thread of his idea. "And when someone claims the suspended coffee..."

"They respond," Signore Rossi finished, his face transforming with joy. "They write back on that same receipt and pin it to the board for the original giver to find." His hands became animated as the vision crystallized. "Not just a transaction, but a conversation. Connection between souls who might never have met otherwise."

Lucia's eyes misted with emotion as she recognized the brilliance in its simplicity. "Messages in bottles, sent across an ocean of humanity."

"Exactly," Signore Rossi breathed, putting his arm around her shoulder. "Some people need coffee to survive the day. But everyone needs connection to survive a lifetime."

The rain continued its symphony against the windows as husband and wife stood before the empty wall, seeing not what was but what could be. The traditional caffè sospeso would become something new in their hands; a bridge between hearts, a lifeline across the growing isolation of modern existence, a chance for strangers to recognize themselves in one another.

"We'll need a bigger jar," Lucia said finally, practical even in moments of inspiration.

Signore Rossi laughed, the sound rich with affection and hope. "And a beautiful cork board, something worthy of the stories it will hold."

As if in response, the rain began to ease, and a tentative sunbeam pushed through the clouds and windows, sending a shaft of golden light across the empty wall. It illuminated the space as if anointing it, transforming humble plaster into sacred ground where futures would unknowingly intersect.

Neither Signore Rossi nor Lucia could have imagined, in that moment of creation, how their reinvention of an ancient tradition would one day bring together two wounded artists seeking redemption. They couldn't have known that a decade later, coffee-stained receipts would become the silent messengers between souls who had forgotten how to trust. They couldn't have seen the beautiful unfolding of lives transformed by words written on the most ordinary of papers, by connections forged in the delicate space between giving and receiving.

But perhaps some part of them sensed it, felt the whisper of destiny in that shaft of sunlight, in the suddenly quieting rain, in the perfect silence that followed, a silence filled with all the possibility of stories yet to be written, of hearts yet to be healed, of love yet to find its way home through something as simple and profound as caffè sospeso.

1

YOU'VE GIVEN ME NOTHING BUT SHATTERED DREAMS

The morning light crept across Claire Bennett's kitchen floor like a timid houseguest, unsure of its welcome. It traced the edges of the granite countertops she and Mark had spent three weekends picking out, for the home they had built in Mayfield Heights, a suburb of Cleveland, Ohio. The light illuminated the copper-bottomed pots hanging above the island where they used to make Sunday breakfasts together, and finally came to rest on her half-empty mug of chamomile tea, now gone cold.

6:47 AM. The digital display on the microwave blinked its green numbers into the silence, marking another morning in what Claire had begun to think of as "the after." After Mark's confession. After the fights and tears and desperate attempts to understand. After the word "divorce" had transformed from an abstract concept to a reality spelled out in courier font on heavy legal paper.She wrapped her cardigan tighter around herself, though the April morning wasn't particularly cold. It was one of her older sweaters, a soft gray thing with slightly frayed cuffs that she'd had since graduate school. Mark had always hated it, suggesting more than once that she replace it with something more "appropriate". Now she wore it like armor, finding comfort in its familiar imperfection.

The stillness in the house pressed against her eardrums. No sounds of Mark's coffee maker gurgling to life. He'd taken it with him when he moved out, along with his collection of hand-ground coffee beans from around the world. No morning news playing softly in the background, no gentle clink of his wedding ring against his favorite ceramic mug as he stirred his coffee with absent-minded precision while reading emails on his phone.

Just silence, broken only by the occasional chirp of early spring birds outside and the soft hum of the refrigerator, a sound she'd never noticed when the house was full of life and conversation, but now seemed to mock her with its persistent drone.

She moved to pour out her cold tea, watching the pale liquid swirl down the drain. How many cups had she dumped out these past months? How many mornings had she stood here, caught in this liminal space between what was and what would be? The drain swallowed her tea with a final gurgle, indifferent to her contemplation.

Her gaze drifted to her reflection in the window above the sink. The early morning light wasn't kind, emphasizing the shadows under her eyes and the slight downturn of her mouth that seemed permanent these days. At forty-two, she wasn't old, but she felt ancient this morning, as if the weight of her failed marriage had somehow seeped into her bones.

A cardinal landed on the bird feeder outside the window. A splash of brilliant red against the pale early spring morning. Claire watched it peck at the seeds, so brilliantly alive it almost hurt to look at. She remembered the day she and Mark had hung that feeder, how he'd balanced precariously on a ladder while she held it steady, both of them laughing as they argued about the perfect height and angle. That had been in the beginning, when they were still creating their shared life with eager hands and hopeful hearts.

Now the feeder hung slightly crooked, the paint beginning to peel. She should take it down, she supposed. Add it to the growing list of things that needed to be undone, unmade, unmarried from her life with Mark. But something kept stopping her, the same something that had kept her from taking down the framed photos still hanging on the walls.

These were the moments frozen in time that now felt like scenes from someone else's life.

The cardinal took flight suddenly, startled by something Claire couldn't see. She watched it disappear into the sky, carrying its brightness away with it. The morning stretched before her, empty and uncertain, filled with the particular kind of loneliness that comes from waking up in a house full of memories you're trying to forget.

The memory ambushed her like it always did, slipping past her defenses with devastating precision. Six months ago, in this very kitchen, on what had started as a regular Tuesday evening. She'd been chopping vegetables for a stir-fry. She could still remember the exact sound of the knife against the cutting board, the sharp green scent of sliced bell peppers in the air. The recipe had been new, something she'd found on one of those cooking blogs she'd started following in an attempt to rekindle their relationship through shared meals.

Mark had come home early, which should have been her first clue. He never came home before seven, his role as senior partner at the accounting firm demanding long hours that she'd grown accustomed to over the years. But there he'd been, standing in the doorway at 5:43 PM, still in his crisp blue button-down shirt, his reading glasses tucked into his breast pocket. Looking more like a man about to discuss quarterly reports than one about to shatter fifteen years of trust.

"We need to talk, Claire."

Five words. How could five simple words carry such weight? She'd known, somehow, even before he'd spoken again. Known in the way he wouldn't quite meet her eyes, in the slight tremor in his usually steady hands, in the careful distance he kept between them as he stepped into the kitchen.

She'd put down the knife, wiped her hands on the dish towel embroidered with lemons that his mother had given them last Christmas. "About what?" Her voice had sounded strange to her own ears, as if it were coming from very far away.

"I've been..." He'd paused, adjusting his tie. It was the dark blue one she'd given him for their anniversary three years ago. "I've been..." He'd hesitated. "I've been seeing someone."

The world seemed to have stopped spinning. She looked down. The bell pepper she'd been cutting had still been on the cutting board, its inside exposed, seeds scattered like tiny tears across the wooden surface. She remembered staring at it, focusing on its bright red flesh while her world tilted on its axis.

"Her name is Jessica," he'd continued, his voice soft, as if gentleness could somehow cushion the blow. "From the Denver office. I didn't mean for it to happen, Claire. It just... did."

Jessica. The name had lodged in her throat like a sharp-edged stone. Jessica from the Denver office, who she'd met at last year's Christmas party. Young, vibrant Jessica with her MBA from Harvard and her perfectly highlighted hair, who had laughed at all of Mark's jokes and touched his arm when she talked. Jessica, who had asked Claire about her graphic design work with what now seemed like calculated interest.

"How long?" The question had escaped before she could stop it, though she wasn't sure she wanted to know the answer.

"Three months." He'd looked down at his hands, at the wedding ring he was already twisting on his finger. "It started during the Denver project. We were working late, going over the merger documents, and..."

"Stop." The word had come out sharper than she'd intended, slicing through his explanation like the knife she'd been using on the peppers. "I don't need the details."

But the details had come anyway, unbidden and unwanted, filling her mind like smoke: late nights at the office, business trips that had suddenly required longer stays, text messages that had made him smile at his phone during dinner. All the little moments she'd dismissed, explained away, refused to examine too closely.

From next door, the familiar sound of Mr. Peterson's vintage record player drifted through the open window. He was playing that old Johnny Hates song about shattered dreams again, the one from the eighties that he seemed to love so much. Claire almost laughed at the bitter appropriateness of it, the way the melancholic melody perfectly captured this moment of realizing how thoroughly her own dreams had been shattered. The music floated through the kitchen like a soundtrack to her unraveling marriage, its lyrics about broken promises and empty hearts hitting far too close to home.

"... So much for your promises ... They died the day you let me go ...

Caught up in a web of lies ... But it was just too late to know ... I thought it was you ... Who would stand by my side ... And now you've given me, given me ... Nothing but shattered dreams, shattered dreams ... Feel like I could run away, run away ... From this empty heart"

The stir-fry ingredients had sat abandoned on the counter as their marriage took a nosedive. The ginger root she'd peeled earlier had filled the air with its sharp, clean scent. Even now, six months later, that smell could bring her right back to that moment.

"I never meant to hurt you," Mark had said, and the worst part was that she believed him. In fifteen years of marriage, he'd never been cruel, never deliberately caused her pain. Even now, he was breaking her heart with the same careful consideration he applied to everything else in his life.

"But you did." Her voice had been steady, surprising her. "You are."

He'd taken a step toward her then, one hand slightly raised as if to touch her, but she'd backed away. Her hip had hit the counter, sending the dish towel floating to the floor. The lemons embroidered on it had seemed to mock her with their cheerful yellow brightness.

"Claire..."

"Don't." She'd wrapped her arms around herself, creating a barrier between them. "Just... don't."

The silence that followed had been deafening. Outside, a neighbor had been mowing their lawn, the distant drone of the mower providing a surreal soundtrack to the collapse of her marriage. The late afternoon sun had streamed through the kitchen window, oblivious to the way her world was shattering.

Standing in that same kitchen now, six months later, Claire could still feel the phantom weight of that moment pressing against her chest. The vegetables had rotted in the refrigerator. She hadn't been able to bring herself to cook for weeks afterward. She'd thrown away the dish towel with the lemons, but sometimes she still caught herself looking for it when she needed to dry her hands.

The worst part wasn't the betrayal itself, though that cut deep enough. The worst part was how it had changed everything that came before it. Every memory, every shared moment, every photograph on the walls; all of it was now tainted by the knowledge of how it would end.

Fifteen years of love and trust, dissolved in an instant into a prelude to heartbreak.

She moved to the sink, turning on the tap and letting the water run cold. The pipes groaned slightly, another sound she'd never noticed before the hush took over. She filled a glass and drank deeply, as if she could wash away the memory with the cool water. But it lingered, like the aftertaste of something bitter, like the echo of words that couldn't be unsaid.

Dr. Sullivan's office always smelled of lavender and old books, a combination that Claire had come to associate with the painful process of putting herself back together. The therapist's space occupied the second floor of a converted Victorian house, where afternoon light filtered through stained glass windows, casting kaleidoscope patterns on the worn hardwood floors. During their sessions, Claire would often find herself tracing these colored shapes with her eyes, watching them change as clouds passed overhead. It was like the way her own emotions seemed to transform from moment to moment these days.

"Healing isn't linear," Dr. Sullivan had told her in their first session, her voice carrying the gentle authority of someone who had guided countless others through their own darkness. She was an elegant woman in her sixties, with silver hair swept into a loose bun and eyes that seemed to see straight through to the heart of things. "Some days you'll feel stronger, and others will knock you back to the beginning. Both are valid. Both are necessary."

Claire had nodded, clutching a throw pillow to her chest like a shield. The pillow's tassels had been slightly uneven, and she'd found herself trying to straighten them, needing to fix something, anything, when her entire life felt so hopelessly tangled.

Now, three months into their sessions, she sat in the same spot on the plush blue couch. The maple tree beyond the window was filled with leaves that whispered secrets in the soft zephyr.

"You mentioned last week that you've been watching that movie again," Dr. Sullivan said, her fountain pen poised above her notepad. She never used ballpoints or modern pens, preferring the scratching sound of nib against paper. The sound had irritated Claire at first, but now she found it oddly comforting. It was like the ticking of an old clock, marking time's steady passage.

"Eat, Pray, Love." Claire smiled slightly, feeling almost embarrassed by her growing obsession with the film. "I know it's probably a cliché, divorced woman finding herself through travel. But there's something about it that keeps drawing me back."

"Tell me about that something."

Claire shifted on the couch, tucking one leg beneath her. The leather was warm from the sun, creaking softly as she moved. "It's not just about the travel, though that part is..." she paused, searching for the right words. "It's compelling, obviously. But it's more about the permission she gives herself. To be lost. To not know what comes next. To blow up her whole life because the old one doesn't fit anymore."

She thought about how many times she'd watched the movie in the past months. She'd seen it enough that she could recite entire scenes from memory. The way Elizabeth Gilbert's journey from brokenness to wholeness played out against backdrops of Italian streets and Indian ashrams and Balinese beaches. But it was always the Italy scenes that captured her imagination most completely.

"There's this moment," Claire continued, her voice softening with emotion, "where she's sitting in this pizzeria, enjoying her pizza margherita, and she describes it as 'having a relationship with her food.' And it sounds silly when I say it out loud, but it's about so much more than the food. It's about pleasure, about joy, about remembering how to want things again, how to hold onto a single moment, and how to live in that moment."

Dr. Sullivan's pen moved across her notepad, with the scratching sounds of muffled rainfall. "And what do you want, Claire?"

The question hung in the air between them, heavy with possibility. Through the stained glass window, a beam of cobalt blue light fell across

Claire's hands, making them look almost ethereal. She studied them, the slight calluses from hours of working with her graphics tablet, the bare ring finger still marked with a faint tan line where her wedding band used to be.

"I want..." Her voice caught, and she had to start again. "I want to feel something other than this. Something other than hurt or angry or numb. I want to wake up in the morning and not have my first thought be about what I've lost. I want to remember who I was before I was Mark's wife, before I was someone's other half. I want..."

She trailed off, surprised by the force of emotion behind her words. A car passed on the street below, its shadow briefly dimming the colored light in the room.

"Go on," Dr. Sullivan encouraged softly. "What else do you want?"

Claire closed her eyes, letting herself imagine it fully for the first time. "I want to walk down streets I've never seen before. I want to eat food I can't pronounce. I want to see art that makes my heart stop and sunsets that make me believe in magic again. I want to feel alive instead of just surviving."

Opening her eyes, she found Dr. Sullivan watching her with a slight smile. "That sounds like more than just a movie influencing you. That sounds like your own voice coming through."

"Maybe." Claire reached for the glass of water on the side table, taking a sip to steady herself. "But it also sounds impossible. I have a job, a mortgage. I can't just run away to Italy like Julia Roberts in the movie."

"Can't you?"

The question was simple, but it hit Claire like a physical force. She set the water glass down with trembling fingers, leaving a ring of condensation on the wooden table.

"That's not..." she began, then stopped, really considering it. "People don't actually do that, do they? Just... leave?"

"People do all sorts of things when they're rebuilding their lives," Dr. Sullivan said, setting her notepad aside. "The question isn't what other people do. The question is what you need to do to find yourself again."

Find yourself. Such a common phrase, almost a cliché, and yet it resonated in Claire's chest like a bell being struck. When was the last time she'd really known herself, separate from her roles as wife, as responsible adult, as the person others expected her to be?

The afternoon light was changing now, the shadows lengthening across the floor. Soon she would leave this safe space and return to her empty house with its walls full of memories. But something had shifted inside her, like a key turning in a lock she hadn't known was there.

That evening, she found herself in her living room, laptop open to flight searches, Elizabeth Gilbert's journey playing out on the TV screen for the hundredth time. But now, instead of just escaping into the story, she was beginning to imagine her own. The cursor blinked on the airline website, waiting for her to enter a destination.

The memory of that song hit her suddenly. "Shattered Dreams" playing from Mr. Peterson's vintage record player the very moment her marriage crumbled. Now, sitting alone in her dimming living room, the words "Feel like I could run away, run away from this empty heart" echoed in her mind with new meaning. Maybe that's what she needed, not to escape forever, but just long enough to piece herself back together.

Naples

She typed, her heart beating faster with each letter. The ancient city called to her in a way that Rome or Florence didn't. Perhaps it was because it was less polished, more raw, more like her own unfinished state. She could almost smell the salt air, hear the chaos of its streets, feel the weight of its history pressing against her skin.

The search results populated her screen: flights, dates, possibilities. Each one a potential door opening onto a new chapter of her life. Her fingers hovered over the keyboard as Elizabeth Gilbert's voice drifted from the TV: "I wanna go someplace where I can marvel at something. Language, gelato, spaghetti, something...."

Claire closed her eyes, letting herself feel the full weight of this moment. Behind her closed lids, she saw cobblestone streets winding into unknown adventures, felt the warm scent of the ocean breeze, heard the musical cadence of a language she didn't yet speak but somehow understood in her bones.

When she opened her eyes again, the cursor was still blinking, waiting for her decision. Outside, the spring evening was settling over her neighborhood like a soft blanket, the familiar sounds of suburban life drifting through her windows. Lawn mowers, children's laughter, cars pulling into driveways. The sounds of a life she had known, a life that no longer seemed to fit.

Her hand moved to her chest, feeling the steady beat beneath her palm. Each beat seemed to whisper: Now. Now. Now.

Time passed. She moved from the living room to her home office. The soft glow of the laptop screen illuminated her face in the darkness of her home office, casting shadows that danced across the walls like memories trying to vanish. It was well past midnight, that hour when reality seemed to blur at the edges, when impossible things suddenly felt within reach. A half-empty glass of red wine sat beside her, the same bottle she and Mark got on their last anniversary, before everything fell apart. She'd found it hidden in the back of the wine rack, dust gathering on its label like the years they'd spent together.

The email to her boss, Susan, sat open on her screen, cursor blinking at the end of a sentence she'd rewritten twelve times:

"I need to take some time..."

Time. Such a simple word for such a complicated request. Claire ran her fingers through her hair, catching them in the tangles she hadn't bothered to brush out after her shower.

The house creaked around her, settling into its nighttime rhythms. From somewhere in the darkness came the soft tick-tick-tick of the antique wall clock Mark's parents had given them as a wedding present. A sound that had once been comforting but now felt like a metronome counting down to... what?

She looked around the home office, at the carefully curated space she'd created for her graphic design work. The vintage art prints she'd collected over the years hung in perfect alignment on the pale gray walls.

Her awards from the Ohio Advertising Association sat on floating shelves, catching what little moonlight filtered through the gauzy curtains. Everything in its place, everything controlled, everything safe.

And she was suffocating.

With trembling fingers, she began to type again:

"Dear Susan,

I've been thinking a lot about our conversation last month regarding remote work opportunities, and I find myself at a crossroads that requires more than just a change of scenery.

The truth is, I need to take some time away, not just from the office, but from everything familiar. The divorce has left me feeling disconnected from myself, from my creativity, from the passion that once made me excited to open Illustrator each morning and create something new.

I'm planning to spend some time in Italy. Not a vacation, but a temporary relocation. I know this might sound impulsive..."

She paused, fingers hovering over the keys. Impulsive. The word brought back a memory, sharp and clear as broken glass:

"You're being impulsive, Claire," Mark had said seven years ago, when she'd suggested they try for a baby. They'd been in their backyard, the summer air heavy with the scent of blooming hydrangeas. "We need to think about this logically. The market's unstable, and with the new partnership track at the firm..."

Always logical. Always careful. Always later.

Until later became never, and never became Jessica from the Denver office with her fresh MBA and her perfectly timed laugh.

Claire took a long sip of wine, letting the bitter warmth of it ground her in the present moment. On her second monitor, she pulled up the research she'd been compiling obsessively: apartment listings in Naples, Italian language courses, cost of living calculations. Each open tab represented a way forward that didn't involve sitting in this house full of ghosts of the past.

Her eyes caught on a photo of a small apartment in the historic center of Naples. The listing showed a tiny balcony overlooking a maze of narrow streets, with glimpses of the Mediterranean beyond. The walls were sun-washed yellow, and the description mentioned original tile floors from the 1920s. It wasn't perfect; the kitchen was smaller than her current bathroom, and the furniture looked like it had seen better days. But something about it called to her, like a song heard from a distance that you strain to catch.

The apartment was above a bakery, the listing noted. She could imagine waking up to the aroma of fresh bread, to the sound of Italian voices rising from the street below, to a life that didn't feel like it was happening to someone else.

A notification popped up on her screen. It was an email from her divorce lawyer with yet another document requiring her signature. The sight of it made her chest tight, but not in the same way it had before. Now the tightness felt less like grief and more like the tension before flight.

She minimized the lawyer's email and turned back to her letter to Susan:

"I know this might sound impulsive, but I believe it's necessary. I've always given everything to this job; my creativity, my time, my full commitment to our clients' success. Now I need to give something back to myself, to rediscover the designer and woman I was before life took some unexpected turns.

I'm not looking to leave the company. In fact, I'm proposing to maintain my key accounts remotely, working on a contract basis until I figure out my next steps. The time difference between Ohio and Italy would actually allow me to provide extended coverage for our European clients..."

Her fingers flew across the keyboard now, the words flowing more easily as she outlined the practical aspects of her plan. She'd always been good at this part, making the improbable sound reasonable, packaging dreams in the language of logistics and solutions.

But beneath the carefully crafted professionalism, her heart was pounding. With each word she typed, the fantasy of escape became more real, more possible, more terrifying in its potential to actually happen.

She reached for her wine glass and found it empty. Standing to refill it, she caught her reflection in the window, a pale ghost against the darkness outside. But there was something different in her eyes now, a spark she hadn't seen in months. Maybe years.

The wall clock continued its steady tick-tick-tick, but the sound had changed. Instead of a countdown, it now felt like a heartbeat, like anticipation, like hope.

Returning to her desk, she opened a new tab and pulled up flight searches again. Her cursor hovered over the "Book Now" button for a one-way ticket to Naples departing in three weeks. The price was displayed in bold numbers. It was more than she should spend, less than she'd expected. Just like the apartment, just like this whole idea, it wasn't perfect. But perfect wasn't what she needed anymore.

Perfect had gotten her fifteen years in a marriage that had crumbled like a sandcastle at high tide. Perfect had gotten her a house full of carefully chosen furniture that now felt like museum pieces preserving a life that no longer existed. Perfect had gotten her exactly where she was: alone at midnight, staring at flight prices and wondering when she'd stopped being brave.

She thought of Dr. Sullivan's question: "Can't you?"

Two simple words that had cracked open the shell of her careful life, letting in possibilities that both thrilled and terrified her.

Her phone buzzed. It was a text from her hard-working real estate agent: "Just checked on your house listing. Three showings scheduled for next week."

She'd listed the house for sale two days ago, another piece of her plan falling into place. The agent had taken photos yesterday, capturing rooms that already felt more like memory than reality. Seeing her life staged and photographed for strangers had been surreal, but also strangely liberating.

"Thanks", she typed back. "It's really happening, isn't it?"

The agent's response was immediate: "Yes, the adventure has begun."

Adventure. The word glowed on her phone screen like a beacon. When was the last time she'd had an adventure? When was the last time she'd done anything that wasn't carefully planned, thoroughly researched, safely executed?

She turned back to her laptop, to the email still waiting to be finished. The wine hummed softly in her veins, not enough to blur her judgment but just enough to quiet the voices of doubt that had been her constant companions these past months.

"I know this is an unusual request," she continued typing, "but I believe it will make me a better designer, a more valuable asset to the company, and most importantly, a whole person again.

I'm happy to discuss this in detail at your convenience. I've attached a preliminary proposal outlining how we can make this work."

Her finger hovered over the send button, trembling slightly. One click and it would be real. One click and she would be committed to this path, this descent into the unknown.

In the darkness beyond her window, a cat yowled, a lonely sound that echoed through the quiet street. Claire pressed send before she could change her mind.

The email swooshed away into the digital ether, and she sat back in her chair. On her screen, the flight booking page still waited for her decision. The apartment listing showed its sun-washed walls and imperfect kitchen. Her future waited in those images, in the space between what was safe and what was possible.

She reached for her phone again, opening her photos. Scrolled back through months of memories until she found what she was looking for. A selfie from her last happy day with Mark. They were at their favorite winery, his arm around her shoulders, both of them smiling at the camera. She looked at her own face in the photo, at the woman who had no idea what was coming.

"I'm sorry," she softly uttered to that woman. "But I'm going to make it right. I'm going to find us again."

Then she deleted the photo.

On her laptop screen, the "Book Now" button seemed to pulse endlessly. Claire positioned her cursor and clicked.

The next page loaded: "Confirm Your Booking."

Outside, the night held its breath, waiting for her answer.

The confirmation email arrived at 3:47 AM: "Your flight to Naples has been booked." Claire stared at the words until they blurred, her heart drumming an erratic rhythm against her ribs. The soft pre-dawn darkness pressed against her windows like velvet, and somewhere in the distance, the first birds were beginning to stir, their tentative songs heralding another spring morning.

"I did it," she announced to the empty room, her voice catching on the words. "I actually did it."

Sleep was impossible now. She wandered through her house like a ghost, trailing her fingers along familiar walls, touching doorframes and picture frames and the smooth surface of her kitchen counter. Everything looked different at dawn, as if her decision had already begun to transform the space from home to memory.

In the guest bathroom, she found a bottle of Mark's aftershave still tucked behind the mirror. It was Acqua di Parma, the one she'd given him for Christmas three years ago. The scent had always reminded her of summer thunderstorms and expensive wool suits. Now, as she held the heavy glass bottle in her hands, it reminded her of all the small ways a person could leave pieces of themselves behind, like breadcrumbs marking the path of their departure.

She set the bottle in a box labeled "Mark's Things". It was a box she'd started months ago but never quite finished filling. It made a clinking sound as it settled among his old music CDs and the leather watch case she'd bought him for their tenth anniversary.

Her phone buzzed on the counter, making her jump. A text from her boss, Susan: "Got your email. Can we talk? Coffee at 9?"

Claire's stomach tightened. Of course Susan would be awake at this hour. She had always been an early riser, attacking each day with the kind of energy that made Claire feel inspired and exhausted.

"Yes," she typed back. "Usual place."

She looked at herself in the bathroom mirror, really looked, taking in the shadows under her eyes, the slight tremor in her hands, the way her hair curled wildly around her face in the humidity of the spring morning. She looked exactly like what she was, a woman who had stayed up all night buying a one-way ticket to a new life.

The sun had fully risen by the time she pulled into the parking lot of The Daily Grind, the local coffee shop where she and Susan had been meeting for weekly check-ins since Claire had started working at the agency seven years ago. The familiar smell of coffee and freshly baked scones wrapped around her as she pushed open the door, the little bell above it clanged harshly that suddenly felt like goodbye instead of welcome.

Susan was already there, occupying their usual corner table by the window. She looked exactly as she always did, impeccably dressed in a tailored blazer, her silver hair cut in a sharp bob that emphasized her striking cheekbones. But there was something soft in her expression as she watched Claire approach, something almost maternal.

"Oh, honey," she said as Claire sat down. "You look like you haven't slept."

"I haven't." Claire managed a weak smile. "I was up all night..."

"Booking flights to Italy?" Susan raised an eyebrow, sliding a steaming mug across the table. "I ordered your usual, vanilla latte with an extra shot. I figured you'd need it."

The kindness in the gesture nearly undid Claire completely. She wrapped her hands around the warm mug, anchoring herself in its solidity as tears threatened to spill.

"I know it seems crazy," she began, but Susan cut her off with a gentle wave.

"It doesn't seem crazy at all." She leaned back in her chair, studying Claire with those sharp eyes that had always seen straight through every design presentation, every excuse, every attempt at hiding. "If anything, I'm surprised it took you this long."

Claire blinked, caught off guard. "What do you mean?"

"Claire, honey, I've watched you dim yourself for years. Even before the divorce, even before everything with Mark, you've been playing it safe, making yourself smaller, fitting yourself into spaces that were never meant to contain you." Susan took a sip of her own coffee. Black, no sugar, like her approach to life. "Your work is brilliant, but lately... lately it's been technically perfect but missing that spark. That thing that makes it uniquely yours."

The tears Claire had been holding back spilled over, tracking silent paths down her cheeks. She wiped them away quickly, but Susan pretended not to notice, giving her a moment to compose herself.

"So you'll let me work remotely?" Claire asked finally, her voice barely above a whisper.

"Better than that." Susan reached into her briefcase and pulled out a folder. "I spent the morning drafting a new contract. Independent contractor status, retainer for our key accounts, freedom to take on other clients if you want. And..." she paused, a slight smile playing at the corners of her mouth, "a commission to redesign our European marketing materials. What better way to understand that market than to be immersed in it?"

Claire stared at the folder, unable to speak. Outside the coffee shop's window, a young couple walked past, hand in hand, laughing at some private joke. The sight sent an unexpected pang through her chest. It wasn't of regret or longing, but of possibility.

"I don't know what to say," she finally managed.

"Say you'll send me photos of all those gorgeous Italian doorways I know you'll be obsessing over." Susan's voice was light, but her eyes were serious. "Say you'll remember that running away and running toward aren't the same thing. Say you'll use this time to find that spark again."

Claire nodded, words still stuck in her throat. The morning light streaming through the window caught her silver bracelet, the one her mother had given her two birthdays ago. It sent little rainbows dancing across the table, reminiscent of the stained glass windows in Dr. Sullivan's office, where she'd learned that beauty could emerge from the way light broke and reformed itself.

"I should warn you," Susan continued, her tone becoming more businesslike, "Miranda's going to be upset. She was hoping to get you on the Cleveland account."

The mention of her colleague's name brought Claire back to the present moment, to the practical realities of her decision. Miranda, with her perfect PowerPoint presentations and her habit of scheduling 7:00 AM meetings. Miranda, who had been not-so-subtly positioning herself for the creative director position that everyone assumed would eventually be Claire's.

"Miranda can handle Cleveland," Claire said, surprising herself with the firmness in her voice. "I need to handle me for a while."

Susan smiled, a real smile that illuminated her usually serious face. "There she is," she said softly. "There's the Claire I hired seven years ago."

The rest of the meeting passed in a blur of practical details like contract terms, project timelines, technical requirements for remote work. By the time Claire left the coffee shop, the morning sun had burned away the last of the spring mist, leaving the world sharp and clear.

She sat in her car for a long moment, letting the reality of the morning settle over her. Her phone buzzed again. It was a text from her younger sister Kate:

"Hey sis, coming over to help you sort through things. Bringing boxes and wine. Non-negotiable."

Kate. With whom Claire shared everything. Who had been an important part of her support system. Kate had talked her through the nights when sleep was nowhere to be found, had coaxed her out of the house when getting out of bed seemed like climbing a mountain, and at times had helped her focus on just taking one breath at a time when panic threatened to overwhelm her.

Claire smiled, feeling the first genuine lightness in her chest she'd experienced in months. She turned the key in the ignition, the car humming to life beneath her. As she pulled out of the parking lot, she caught a glimpse of herself in the rearview mirror. Still tired, still a little broken, but somehow more real than she'd felt in years.

The street stretched out before her, leading home to a house that was already becoming a memory. She had three weeks to dismantle a life fifteen years in the making. Three weeks to sort through the physical evidence of a marriage that had defined her for so long. Three weeks to decide what to keep, what to leave behind, what to carry with her into whatever waited across the ocean.

But for the first time since Mark had shattered her world with five simple words, the future didn't feel like an empty page she was afraid to fill. Instead, it felt like a door slowly opening, letting in light and air and something new.

She turned onto her street, the familiar houses sliding past like a flip book of memories. The Anderson's maple tree where she and Mark had taken their first Christmas card photo. The corner where they'd kissed in the rain after closing on the house. The spot where she'd stood countless mornings, waving goodbye as he left for work.

But today, these landmarks felt less like wounds and more like the closing pages of a chapter that had run its course. Ahead of her, the story waited to be written, blank pages ready for new words, new memories.

Her house came into view, the pale blue shutters she'd insisted on painting herself, the garden boxes where her tulips were just beginning to fade. It looked smaller somehow, as if it too understood that its time as her home was coming to an end.

Kate's car was already in the driveway, and as Claire pulled up, she could see her sister unloading the folded boxes from the trunk. Her hair, so similar to Claire's own, was caught in the spring breeze. The sight made her throat tight with emotion. Some things would never change, never need to be left behind. Some loves were constant, unbreakable, true.

"Hey, sis," Kate called out as Claire stepped from her car. "Ready to pack the hell out of this place?"

Claire laughed, the sound surprising her with its authenticity. "Ready or not," she said, walking toward her sister and whatever waited on the other side of this endless morning, "here we go."

The late morning sun painted honeyed stripes across Claire's living room floor, where she and Kate sat surrounded by the physical artifacts of a life being dismantled. The air was thick with memories. Three empty moving boxes sat waiting, labeled in Kate's decisive handwriting: "Keep," "Donate," and "Storage." A fourth box, smaller and unmarked, waited for the things that belonged to neither past nor future, the things that needed to be let go completely. And there were more folded boxes beyond them, awaiting their turn.

"Okay," Kate said, uncorking a bottle of rosé with practiced efficiency. It was barely noon, but some tasks required liquid courage. "Where do we start?"

Claire surveyed the room, feeling suddenly overwhelmed by the sheer volume of memories each object held. The vintage record player

Mark had surprised her with on their third anniversary, convinced they needed to experience music "the way it was meant to be heard." The Moroccan throw pillows they'd haggled for in a Marrakech market during what was supposed to be their second honeymoon. The silver-framed wedding photos arranged on the mantel like an altar to a faith she no longer possessed.

"Maybe..." She took a steadying breath. "Maybe we start with the easy stuff?"

Kate handed her a glass of wine, the pale pink liquid catching the light like liquid amber. "Honey, none of this is going to be easy. But I'm right here with you."

They began with the bookshelf, which seemed safer than photo albums or jewelry boxes. Claire ran her fingers along the spines, each book a chapter in the story of who she'd been. Art history textbooks from college, their pages dog-eared and highlighted, filled with the aspirations of a younger version of herself who believed creativity could change the world. Travel guides for trips they'd planned but never taken, their pages still crisp with future promises that didn't matter any longer.

"Oh my God," Kate exclaimed, pulling out a worn paperback. "Remember this?"

Claire looked up to see her sister holding a copy of "Love in the Time of Cholera," its cover faded and spine cracked from multiple readings. The sight of it hit her like a physical blow, transporting her instantly to a summer evening years ago.

"That was the book I was reading when I met Mark," she said softly, accepting it from Kate's outstretched hand. "At that coffee shop near the flower shop."

"Where you spilled your latte all over his book," Kate finished, a gentle smile playing at her lips.

She opened the book, and a pressed flower fell into her lap. A dried violet, its purple faded to the color of twilight. She'd been using it as a bookmark when she'd first met Mark, and he'd insisted she keep it there, calling it their good luck charm.

"Keep or donate?" Kate asked softly.

Claire stared at the delicate flower, so fragile it might crumble at her touch. How many hopes had she pressed between these pages? How many dreams had dried and faded along with this violet?

"Neither," she said finally, placing the flower and book in the unmarked box. Some memories needed to be released, not preserved.

They worked their way through the bookshelf methodically, each volume a decision to be made, each choice feeling somehow more significant than it should. The afternoon light softened, casting longer shadows across the floor as they moved from books to the collection of framed photographs that lined the walls.

"Oh, Claire," Kate breathed, carefully lifting down a large black and white photo from their parents' forty-third anniversary party. In it, Claire and Mark stood with their arms around each other, both laughing at something just outside the frame. "You were so happy here."

Claire moved to stand beside her sister, studying the photograph like an artifact from an ancient civilization. She remembered that day with vivid clarity. The way the summer air had smelled of roses from their mother's garden, how the champagne had tasted like starlight, the feel of Mark's hand warm and steady against her waist.

"I was," she said simply, because it was true. The happiness captured in that photograph had been real, which somehow made its loss even more profound. "But maybe that's not the point anymore."

Kate looked at her questioningly, the photograph still cradled in her hands like something precious and breakable.

"Maybe," Claire continued, choosing her words carefully, "the point isn't how happy I was then, but how happy I could be again. Just... differently." She took the photograph from Kate.

"Naples," Claire said quietly, tracing the outline of the photograph with her fingertip before placing it gently in the storage box. Not letting go completely, but not carrying it forward either. A middle ground. "I've rented a small apartment in the historic center there, above a bakery." She looked up to meet her sister's gaze, half-expecting to see judgment or concern reflected there.

Instead, Kate's eyes lit up with that familiar spark of adventure. "God, that sounds perfect for you. The colors, the art, the food." She reached across the scattered memories between them to squeeze Claire's hand. "You know Mom and Dad are going to completely freak out, right? Dad will start listing crime statistics, and Mom will tell you about everyone who ever faced a setback abroad."

Claire laughed softly, the sound catching in her throat. "I know. But I can't stay here, suffocating in the remnants of what was supposed to be forever. I need... space to breathe again."

"Then breathe you shall," Kate said with such fierce conviction that Claire felt tears spring to her eyes. "I'll handle the parental crisis. You just promise to eat enough pasta for both of us." Claire nodded in agreement.

They moved through the house like archeologists, unearthing layers of life lived and love lost. In the kitchen, she found the pasta maker they'd bought after getting inspired by their romantic dinner at Giovanni's, a local Italian eatery. Still in its box, plans of homemade ravioli never realized. In the guest room closet, she saw the ukulele Mark had bought when they were vacationing in Hawaii and had sworn he'd learn to play someday, its small wooden body with four strings still waiting silently in its case. Each object a promise unfulfilled, a future that had never arrived.

As the afternoon wore on, the unmarked box filled with the weight of discarded parts of her life. There were movie ticket stubs saved from forgotten date nights, birthday cards with messages that no longer rang true, the silver bracelet Mark had given her the Christmas before Jessica from Denver.

In her bedroom, Claire opened her jewelry box, a Victorian piece she'd found at an antique store on one of their vacation trips. The hinges creaked softly, releasing the scent of aged wood and remembered joy. Her wedding ring lay in the center compartment, a perfect circle of platinum.

"You don't have to decide about that now," Kate said gently, noticing her sister's hesitation.

Claire picked up the ring, feeling its familiar weight one last time. In the late afternoon light, the diamond caught and fractured the sun, sending tiny rainbows dancing across the walls like escaped dreams.

"Actually," she said, surprising herself with the steadiness of her voice, "I do."

She placed the ring in the unmarked box, the soft thud it made against the bottom somehow both an ending and a beginning.

Kate squeezed her shoulder, understanding without words. Outside, a spring storm was rolling in, the air heavy with approaching rain. Thunder rumbled in the distance like applause for her courage.

They ordered pizza as the sky darkened, sitting cross-legged on the floor among the boxes of their sorting. The wine was long gone, replaced by cold beer and the kind of bone-deep exhaustion that comes from emotional labor.

"You know what I just realized?" Kate said, wiping pizza grease from her fingers with a paper napkin. "We haven't found a single thing that's just yours. Everything we've sorted has been about you and Mark, about the marriage, about the life you built together. But what about before? What about just Claire?"

The question hung in the air like the electricity from the approaching storm. Claire looked around at the boxes, not just the original four, but multiplied like gremlins carrying the same set of choices. Keep, donate, storage, let go. Each one containing carefully curated pieces of a shared life, but nothing that spoke solely of her own heart.

"Maybe that's what Italy is about," she said slowly, the truth of it unfurling in her chest like a flower reaching for sunlight. "Maybe it's about finding myself again, or..." she paused, considering, "maybe it's about discovering who I am for the first time, without building myself around someone else's life."

Kate raised her beer bottle in a toast. "To Claire," she said firmly. "Not Mark's wife, not the good girl who always played it safe, not the woman who put everyone else first. Just Claire."

"Just Claire," she echoed, clinking her bottle against her sister's.

Outside, the storm finally broke. Rain drummed against the windows in a steady rhythm that sounded like permission, like freedom, like the first notes of a new song beginning to play. Lightning flickered, illuminating the boxes that contained fifteen years of memories, each flash a reminder that endings and beginnings often looked remarkably similar in the right light.

Claire stood and walked to the window, pressing her palm against the cool glass. Her reflection was ghostly in the darkness. A woman between worlds, between stories, between lives. Behind her, Kate began humming softly, "twinkle, twinkle little star", an old lullaby their mother used to sing during thunderstorms.

The rain continued to fall, washing away the dust of the day, making everything look new in the gathering darkness. In three weeks, she would be on a plane to Naples, carrying nothing but carefully chosen pieces of her past and the trembling possibility of her future.

Time has a way of moving differently in the days before a great change. For Claire, her final week in Mayfield Heights felt like watching sand slip through an hourglass, each moment precious and fleeting.

The spring air held the first whispers of summer when she walked into Dr. Sullivan's office for her last session. Honeysuckle vines climbed the Victorian home's weathered trellis, their sweet scent drifting through the open windows and mingling with the familiar lavender and old books. Claire paused in the doorway, trying to memorize every detail. The way the afternoon light painted watercolor shadows through the stained glass, the creak of the hardwood floors beneath her feet, the ticking of the antique clock that had kept time for so many of her tears and breakthroughs.

Dr. Sullivan waited in her usual chair, elegant as always in a dove-gray dress that matched her silver hair. But today, instead of her notepad and fountain pen, she held two bone china teacups.

"I thought we might do something different for our last session," she said, gesturing to the steaming cups. "This is a special blend with herbs from my garden. Lavender for peace, mint for courage, rose petals for the heart."

Claire sank into the familiar blue couch, accepting the offered cup. The porcelain was warm against her palms, and the tea's aroma wrapped around her like an embrace. "It feels strange," she admitted, "knowing this is the last day of my therapy."

"Is it?" Dr. Sullivan's eyes held that knowing gleam that had guided Claire through so many moments of clarity. "The last time in this room, perhaps. But healing isn't confined to these four walls, Claire. It happens everywhere. In Italian cafès, on cobblestone streets, in moments of solitude and connection. You're not ending therapy; you're taking its lessons with you into the world."

Tears pricked at Claire's eyes as she sipped the tea, letting its warmth spread through her chest. Through the window, a pair of cardinals danced through the honeysuckle vines, flashes of brilliant red against the green leaves. "I'm scared," she admitted, the words falling like pebbles into a still pond. "Not of going. I'm scared of how much I want to go. Is that strange?"

"What you're feeling is the tension between your old self and your emerging self," Dr. Sullivan said carefully. "The old Claire was defined by caution, by meeting others' expectations. She's afraid of this wild wanting, this hunger for life. But the new Claire?" She smiled, setting her teacup down with a gentle clink. "She's afraid of not wanting enough, not reaching far enough, not living fully enough."

The truth of these words resonated in Claire's chest like a bell being struck. She thought of all the hours she'd spent in this room, unraveling the tangled threads of her marriage, her self-worth. "How do I reconcile them? These two versions of myself?"

"Perhaps they don't need reconciliation," Dr. Sullivan suggested. "Perhaps they need integration. The careful planner who makes sure you have travel insurance and knows which adapter you'll need for Italian outlets; she has her place. But so does the woman who books a one-way ticket to Naples on a midnight impulse. Both are you, Claire. Both are valuable."

A shaft of late afternoon sunlight broke through the clouds outside, sending prismatic colors dancing across the floor from the stained glass. Claire watched them shift and change, thinking how light could be both broken and whole.

"I have something for you," Dr. Sullivan said, reaching into her desk drawer. She withdrew a small leather-bound journal, its cover soft. "I give these to those who are embarking on significant journeys, physical or emotional. It's not for therapy notes or daily records. It's for moments of transformation, for those times when you feel yourself growing. Write down what you discover about yourself in Naples, Claire. Write down who you become."

Claire took the journal, running her fingers over its supple cover. The leather was the color of well-loved saddles, of ancient church pews, of stories waiting to be told. "Thank you," she managed, her voice thick with emotion. "For everything."

"Thank yourself," Dr. Sullivan replied. "You did the work. You found the courage. I just helped you clear away the debris so you could see what was already there."

They sat in comfortable silence for a while, finishing their tea as the sun continued its slow descent toward evening. The antique clock ticked steadily, marking moments that would never come again. When Claire finally stood to leave, her legs felt both heavy and light.

At the door, Dr. Sullivan surprised her with a warm hug. It was the first time they'd ever touched beyond handshakes. She smelled of herbs and wisdom and something indefinable that made Claire think of her mother.

"L'chaim," Dr. Sullivan said enthusiastically. "To life."

"To life," Claire echoed, and stepped out into the gathering dusk.

The drive home took her past all the familiar landmarks of her life in Mayfield Heights. The coffee shop where she'd met Mark, the park where she'd spent countless lunch breaks sketching, the electronics store where she'd bought her first professional design tablet. But in the golden light of evening, everything looked different, as if she were seeing it all through the lens of memory already.

Her phone buzzed with a text from Kate:

"Last dinner at Giovanni's tonight. The whole gang's coming."

"I'll be there. Save me a spot by the window," Claire texted back, her fingers lingering over the send button before finally pressing it.

She smiled, even as her heart squeezed with the bittersweetness of it all. Giovanni's had been their go-to celebration spot for years for birthdays, promotions, engagements. It seemed fitting that it would also be the place for goodbyes. The small Italian restaurant had witnessed every significant moment of her family's lives. Its warm terracotta walls had sheltered them through heartbreaks and triumphs alike. The owner knew their orders by heart and kept their corner table reserved. Giovanni's wasn't just a restaurant; it was where they had become a family.

The restaurant was warm and noisy when Claire arrived, filled with the clinking of glasses and the rich aroma of garlic and tomatoes. Her friends had pushed together tables in the back corner. Her mom, Barbara Bennett and dad, David Bennett, Kate and her husband Tom, Susan from work, her college roommate Rachel who'd driven in from Cincinnati, even her neighbor Mrs. Chen who'd kept an eye on her during the worst days after Mark left.

"There she is!" Kate called out, raising her wine glass. "Our very own Elizabeth Gilbert!"

Claire laughed, sliding into the empty chair they'd saved for her. The table was already crowded with appetizers; bruschetta glistening with olive oil, calamari perfectly crispy, fresh mozzarella drizzled with balsamic reduction.

"Speech!" Rachel demanded, her eyes bright with both wine and emotion. "You can't run off to Italy without giving us a proper speech!"

"Oh God," Claire protested, but they were all looking at her with such love, such genuine joy for her adventure, that she found herself standing, wine glass in hand. The words came surprisingly easily, rising from some deep place that had been waiting for this moment.

"You all know exactly when," she began, "I thought my life was over. Not literally, but in all the ways that seemed to matter. My marriage had ended, my sense of self was shattered, and I couldn't imagine ever feeling whole again." She paused, looking at each beloved face around the table. "But you all refused to let me disappear into my grief. You held space for my pain while consistently reminding me that pain wasn't the end of my story."

She took a shaky breath, feeling tears threaten. "Kate, you showed up with boxes and wine when I needed to sort through my old life, and you've been my guiding star through all of this. Tom, thank you for supporting Kate when she had to change plans to be with me. Susan, you didn't just give me permission to chase this dream; you helped make it possible. Rachel, you've listened to me cry and rage and doubt myself, and you never once told me to just 'get over it.' Mrs. Chen, your weekly deliveries of dumplings, herbal teas, and quiet wisdom kept my entire being nourished"

The tears were flowing freely now, but she didn't try to stop them. "Mom and dad, thank you for being there for me. I don't know what I would have done without your unconditional love," she continued, "I'm not running away to Italy. I'm running toward something, toward myself, toward a life that feels like my own. And I couldn't have found the courage to do that without all of you believing in me, sometimes more than I believed in myself."

She raised her glass, the red wine catching the light like liquid garnets. "So this isn't goodbye. It's thank you, and I love you, and save room for all the Italian wines I'm going to introduce you to when you come visit."

The rest of the evening passed in a blur of laughter and tears, stories and memories, plans to video chat and demands for daily photos of her adventures. The food was delicious as always, but it was the love around that table that fed something deeper in Claire's soul.

Later, as she sat at the back of an Uber, driving through the quiet streets of her soon-to-be former hometown, the moon hung low and full in the sky like a blessing. Her house, no longer really hers, with the closing scheduled for two days after her departure; it waited in darkness.

Inside, most of her furniture had already been sold or donated, the rooms echoing with emptiness. Her suitcases stood ready by the door, one large one for checking in, one carry-on, her life distilled to what could be carried across an ocean.

In her bedroom, she changed into her favorite pajamas, cotton worn to softness, and settled on the floor with Dr. Sullivan's journal. The leather cover seemed to glow in the moonlight streaming through her uncurtained windows.

Picking up a pen, she opened the first blank page. For a moment, she just sat there, listening to the familiar creaks and sighs of the house, feeling the weight of all the farewells and dawns contained in this single moment.

Then, slowly, she began to write:

"Dear Future Self,

Tonight is my last night in the house where I thought I'd spend the rest of my life. Tomorrow, I'll be staying with Kate and Tom. Tomorrow will be my last day in the town where I grew up, fell in love, had my heart broken, and found the courage to begin again. Soon, I'll board a plane to Naples with nothing but two suitcases and hope I'm only beginning to let myself feel.

I don't know who I'll be when you read these words. I don't know what adventures you'll have had, what loves you'll have found, what parts of yourself you'll have discovered or rediscovered. But I want you to remember this moment, sitting on the floor of an empty house, surrounded by moonlight and possibility, feeling equal parts terrified and exhilarated.

Remember that you were brave enough to begin again. Remember that you were loved enough to be let go. Remember that sometimes the most beautiful chapters of our story start with the words "Once upon a time, she bought a one-way ticket..."

Claire closed the journal, holding it against her chest like a sacred vow. Outside, a car passed, its headlights sweeping across her ceiling like shooting stars. In the distance, a train whistle sounded, long and low and lonely, calling to all the travelers of the world.

Soon, she would be one of them.

Claire woke before her alarm on her final morning in Mayfield Heights, roused by the first hints of dawn seeping through her bedroom windows. She lay still for a moment, watching the ceiling evolve from shadow to silver as the time held its breath between night and day. The house felt different in these last hours, less like the tomb of her married life and more like a cocoon she was finally ready to emerge from.

She'd slept on a borrowed air mattress, her bed having been sold the week before. The slight give of the mattress beneath her body reminded her of camping trips with her family as a child, that feeling of adventure and temporary shelter that made every morning feel like the start of something magical. Now, at forty-two, she was embarking on her own adventure, one that began with letting go of everything familiar.

The morning air carried the fresh, green scent of early summer through her open window. Grass wet with dew, honeysuckle in bloom, the earthy sweetness of her neighbor's garden coming alive. These were the scents of home, of childhood, of every morning she'd ever known. Tomorrow, she would wake to different scents like Italian coffee and sea air, ancient stones and new somethings.

Her phone buzzed softly: a text from Kate. "You awake, wandering woman?"

Claire smiled, typing back: "Aren't I always?"

"Coming over with breakfast. Dad insisted on making his famous pancakes. Mom's handling the coffee, her special blend in that copper thermos she guards with her life."

Tears brimmed at Claire's eyes, but they were different from the tears she'd shed so often these past months. These were tears of fullness rather than emptiness, of love rather than loss. "Tell them I love them," she wrote back, then added: "And tell Dad extra blueberries in mine."

She rose slowly, savoring each sensation. The cool hardwood under her bare feet, the soft cotton of her old pajamas against her skin, the way the growing light painted her empty walls in shades of renewal. Her suitcases stood ready by the door, watchful sentinels containing the carefully curated remains of her life: clothes chosen for their ability to mix and match and a few precious books that felt essential to who she was becoming.

In the bathroom, she went through her morning routine one last time in this space. The familiar chips in the tile around the sink caught the light differently now, like old scars that had finally healed. She studied her reflection as she brushed her teeth, noting how her hair curled wild and free in the morning humidity, how her eyes seemed brighter somehow, more alive than they'd been in years.

The doorbell chimed just as she was finishing getting dressed. She'd chosen her outfit carefully, a blue sundress that made her feel both comfortable and brave, like armor made of sky. The sound of voices drifted up the stairs, her family letting themselves in with the key they'd always had.

"Claire-bear!" her father's voice called out, using the childhood nickname that usually made her cringe but today felt like a benediction. "These pancakes aren't getting any warmer!"

She descended the stairs slowly, drinking in the scene before her. Her parents had set up an impromptu breakfast picnic on the living room floor, using an old quilt her grandmother had made as a tablecloth. The morning sun streamed through the windows, catching the steam rising from the coffee being poured from the copper thermos and making it dance like spirits being released into the air.

David Bennett stood at the center of this domestic tableau, still in his cooking clothes, worn jeans and the faded University of Michigan sweatshirt he'd had since before Claire was born. His silver hair caught the light like a halo, and his eyes, so like her own, crinkled with love and pride as he watched her approach.

"There's my girl," he said lovingly, opening his arms.

Claire walked into her father's embrace, breathing in the familiar mixture of coffee and Old Spice that had meant safety and love for as long as she could remember. He held her tight, as if trying to pour enough affection into this one hug to last across an ocean.

"My brave girl," he voiced with tender conviction, his voice rough with emotion.

"Don't make anyone cry," Barbara said, but her voice was thick too. Her mother had always been the practical one, the steady one, but today her eyes shone with unshed tears as she arranged plates and silverware with unnecessary precision.

"Come on," Kate called from her spot on the quilt. "The pancakes really are getting cold, and Dad outdid himself this time."

They settled onto the quilt like children at a picnic, passing plates and syrup, pouring coffee into the china cups her mother had brought. "Because your last breakfast at home should be civilized, darling." The pancakes were perfect, fluffy and studded with fresh blueberries that burst like tiny pockets of summer in each bite.

"Remember when you used to make these for my sleepovers?" Claire asked her father, savoring each mouthful. "All my friends thought you were the coolest dad because you'd make pancakes in funny shapes."

"I offered to make a plane-shaped one today," he grinned, "but your mother thought that might be kind of cheesy."

They laughed, and for a moment it was like every other family breakfast they'd ever shared. Comfortable, warm, safe. But there was an undercurrent now, an awareness that this was an ending as much as it was a celebration.

"I found something yesterday," Barbara said suddenly, reaching into her large handbag. "I thought... well, I thought you might want to take it with you." She pulled out a small, worn leather case that Claire recognized immediately.

"Mom's travel journals," Kate sighed. "Really?"

Claire accepted the journals with reverence. Her hands trembled slightly as she opened the case. Inside were three small notebooks, their pages yellowed with age and adventure. The scent of distant places seemed to rise from the pages with hints of exotic spices, salty air, and possibilities that had once called to her mother. Claire ran her fingertips along the faded ink, feeling connected to a version of her mother she had never truly known.

"I started keeping these when I was young," Barbara said, looking at Claire. "Before I met your father, before I became a mother, when I was just trying to figure out who I was meant to be."

She'd heard stories about her mother's years abroad like teaching English in Japan, backpacking through Europe, working as a photographer's assistant in Morocco. But she'd never seen these private records of that time.

"I always wondered," her mother continued softly, "if I did you girls

36

a disservice by becoming so... settled after I married your father. If I somehow taught you that adventure and stability were mutually exclusive."

"Oh, Mom," Claire reached for her mother's hand. "You taught us that love is an adventure all its own."

"And now you're teaching us about second chances," Kate added, "by supporting Claire's leap into the unknown, despite your worries and concerns."

David cleared his throat, emotion written across his face. "Speaking of support," he said, pulling an envelope from his pocket. "Your mother and I want you to have this."

Inside the envelope was a key on a delicate silver chain. "What's this?"

"It's to our little house in Maine," her mother explained. "The one we bought last year as our retirement project? We want you to know that you'll always have a home to come back to, not the home you had, but a new one. Somewhere you can rest and recover when you need to, then go back out into the world when you're ready."

Claire stared at the key, understanding the deeper message her parents were sending: We trust you to go, and we'll be here when you return, but we're not holding you to who you used to be.

The rest of the morning passed in a blur of precious moments she tried desperately to memorize: Kate helping her double-check her packing list; David hefting her check-in suitcase to confirm it was under the fifty-pound limit; and Barbara quietly slipping extra euros into the hidden pocket of Claire's carry-on "for emergencies only, dear."

As the sun climbed higher in the sky, the quality of the light changed, becoming more insistent, more now than then. Claire's flight wasn't until the next morning, but this was her last day in this house; she'd be staying at her sister's tonight, closer to the airport.

"It's time, isn't it?" David said finally, looking at his watch with the air of someone trying to be strong for everyone else.

Claire nodded, unable to speak. They each took one last walk through the empty house, her parents remembering the day they'd helped her move in as a newlywed, Kate recalling sleepovers and sister talks whenever Mark was out of town on business, Claire touching doorframes and windowsills like she was saying goodbye to old friends.

In the kitchen, she paused at the window over the sink. The cardinal she'd seen so many times was there, bright against the green of spring, as if it had come to wish her farewell. "Thank you," she said, to the bird, to the house, to the life she'd lived here.

David carried her suitcases out to Kate's car. Barbara fussed with her collar and hair, the way she had on Claire's first day of school, at her graduation, at her wedding. "You're doing the right thing," she said firmly, holding her daughter's face between her palms, seemingly reassuring herself more than Claire. "Following your heart is always the right thing."

On the front porch, Claire turned for one last look at the house. The morning glory vines she'd planted her first spring here still climbed the porch railings, their purple blooms, always reaching for the sun.

Claire embraced her parents one last time, breathing in her mother's familiar scent as Barbara whispered, "Be brave, my girl." Her father squeezed her shoulder, his eyes glistening. "We love you," he said simply. With final kisses and promises to call upon landing, they walked to their car. Claire watched them drive away, her father's hand waving through the window until they disappeared around the corner.

"Ready?" Kate asked softly from beside her.

Claire took a deep breath, letting it fill her lungs completely. Then she exhaled, releasing the last threads of hesitation. "Ready."

As they drove away, she watched in the side mirror as the house grew smaller. It seemed to shimmer in the afternoon light, as if it too was transforming into memory.

Kate reached over and squeezed her hand. "You know what Hemingway said about Paris?"

Claire smiled, tears tracking silently down her cheeks. "That it's a moveable feast?"

"Exactly. And so is love, sister mine. So is family. So is home. We'll all be right here," she glanced at Claire, "while you're out there finding yourself in Naples."

The car turned a corner, and just like that, her old house disappeared from view. But instead of the grief she'd expected, Claire felt something else unfurling in her chest: anticipation, wonder, the wild thrill of beginning.

She was ready for her feast to begin.

Kate's apartment smelled of jasmine and fresh-baked cookies when they arrived, the afternoon sun streaming through the wall of windows that had always made Claire just a little envious. Tom had clearly been busy; the guest room awaited with a crystal vase of dusty pink peonies on the bedside table. Claire's favorites. The crisp white sheets released a soothing fragrance of lavender. On the kitchen counter, Tom had arranged a thoughtful spread of Claire's favorite comfort foods.

"Hope you're hungry. I figured your last dinner in Ohio should be all the things you'll miss," he explained, pulling her into a warm hug. "Mac n cheese from that little place downtown, naan and saag paneer that you're obsessed with from Lotus Palace, and yes, I got the chocolate cake from Marie's."

The timer on his phone rang. "And, I baked you these cookies that you had loved at one of our holiday parties," he said warmly while retrieving the cookie sheet from the oven.

Claire felt tears threatening again. She'd cried more in the past week than she had in years, it seemed. But these were sweet tears, tears of being known and loved so completely. "You're too good for my sister," she teased, though they all knew it wasn't true. Kate and Tom had the kind of love that made other people believe in soulmates, in happy endings.

They spent the evening on Kate and Tom's balcony, enjoying the food, watching the sunset paint the sky in shades that Claire didn't remember seeing before. The air was warm with the promise of summer, carrying the sounds of the town getting ready for night.

Distant hum of traffic, children's laughter from the park across the street, the melody of wind chimes from a neighbor's balcony.

"Tell me about Naples," Kate said, curled up in her favorite chair with a glass of wine. "Tell me everything you're excited about."

Claire closed her eyes, letting herself imagine it fully for the first time. "The light," she said softly. "Everyone talks about how different the light is there, golden and thick, like honey. And the colors, all those sun-washed buildings in shades of yellow and pink and orange. The narrow streets with laundry strung between buildings like prayer flags. The way history is just... there, in every stone, every corner, every ancient church."

She opened her eyes to find both Kate and Tom watching her with knowing smiles. "What?"

"Nothing," Kate said, but her eyes were shining. "It's just... you sound like yourself again. Like the Claire who used to spend hours in art museums, who could talk about color and light like they were living things."

"They are living things," Claire said, surprising herself with the certainty in her voice. "Or at least, they're things that make you feel alive. That's what I want, to feel alive again, to see the world with artist's eyes again."

"To fall in love again?" Tom asked gently.

Claire looked out at the darkening sky, where the first stars were beginning to appear. "Maybe," she said thoughtfully. "But first I need to fall in love with myself again. To remember who I am when I'm not being someone's wife or someone's ex-wife. Just... Claire."

They stayed up late into the night, talking and laughing, sharing memories. Kate brought out old photo albums, and they spent hours reminiscing about childhood adventures, college mishaps, the people they used to be and the ones they were becoming.

When Claire finally went to bed, she lay awake for a long time, listening to the quiet sounds of the apartment and the distant symphony of the town at night. Her phone buzzed with one last text from her mother:

"Sleep well. Tomorrow you begin. Love you."

Morning came too soon and not soon enough, the first rays of dawn finding Claire already awake, her heart beating a rhythm of wild hope and fear. But mostly wild hope. She showered and dressed with careful attention, choosing clothes that would be comfortable for the long flight but also made her feel confident. Soft black leggings, a flowing tunic in deep blue, the comfortable but stylish walking sandals she'd bought specially for Italian cobblestones.

Kate made coffee and toast, though neither of them could eat much. They moved around each other in comfortable silence, both aware that words would only complicate the precarious balance of emotions filling the morning air.

The drive to the airport felt somehow both endless and too short. The city was just waking up, streets quiet except for early morning joggers and delivery trucks. Claire watched familiar landmarks slide past one last time.

But today, these places didn't hurt to look at. They felt like pages in a book she'd finished reading; loved, appreciated, but ready to be closed so a new book could be opened.

At the airport departure drop-off, Kate put the car in park and turned to face her sister. In the early morning light, they could have been looking in a mirror. Same curls, same eyes, same mixture of strength and vulnerability in their expressions.

"I have something for you," Kate said, reaching into her bag. She pulled out a small package wrapped in tissue paper.

Claire unwrapped it carefully to find her silver compass locket on a chain, the one her grandma had given her years ago, the one that always pointed to North. Kate had borrowed it from her some time back.

"Open it." Kate insisted. When Claire opened the familiar compartment that she had always left empty, she was surprised to discover that Kate had placed a tiny photograph inside. It showed their entire family from when they were children - their parents, their grandma, Kate and Claire as kids, all of them smiling together.

"So you remember," Kate said thoughtfully, "that no matter which direction you go, love always points home." Claire slipped the chain over her head, the locket settling against her collarbone as she remained silent.

Both got down from the car, got the luggage out of the trunk, and then held each other. For a long moment, sisters who had shared every-thing from clothes to secrets to broken hearts. No words were necessary; their heartbeat had the same rhythm of love and loss and hope.

"Go find yourself," Kate said with finality, pulling back to wipe tears from her cheeks. "And then come tell me all about that new Claire."

Claire nodded, unable to speak. As she started walking toward the airport entrance, Kate called out one last time:

"Claire!"

She turned back.

"I love you," Kate said simply. "All of you, who you were, who you are, who you're becoming."

"I love you too," Claire managed, her voice thick with tears and grat-itude and the bittersweetness of this moment.

Inside the airport, everything moved with perfect efficiency. Check-in, security, the long walk to her gate. She bought a bottle of water and a magazine she knew she wouldn't read, going through the motions of being a traveler while her heart thundered with the reality of what she was doing.

At her gate, she found a quiet corner with a view of the runway. Planes took off and landed in a graceful dance of metal and momentum, each one carrying its own cargo of dreams, fears, and unknowns. Soon she would be part of it, flying toward a future she could barely imagine.

She took out Dr. Sullivan's journal and began to write:

"Dear Future Self,

I'm sitting at Gate B7 at Cleveland Hopkins International Airport, watching the sun rise over the runway. In a little over two hours, I'll board a plane that will take me away from everything I've ever known, toward everything I hope to discover.

I'm terrified. I'm exhilarated. I'm ready.

The thing about broken hearts is that they create space for new love to enter. The thing about leaving home is that it teaches you home was never just a place; it was a feeling you carried inside you all along.

So here I am, carrying broken pieces that are already beginning to reform into something new, carrying dreams that finally feel bigger than my fears.

Naples is waiting. Life is waiting. I'm ready to begin."

When they called her boarding group, Claire stood on legs that felt surprisingly steady. She walked down the jet bridge with measured steps, each one taking her further from who she had been and closer to who she might become.

Finding her seat by the window, she settled in and watched through the small oval of glass. The morning sun caught the edge of the wing, making it gleam like a blade of light cutting through her past toward her future.

As the plane began to move, Claire touched the compass locket around her neck, feeling her family's love like a talisman against her skin. She thought of Elizabeth Gilbert writing about the courage it takes to walk away from a life that no longer fits. She thought of Dr. Sullivan talking about integration rather than reconciliation. She thought of her parents, watching her go with pride battling worry in their eyes. She thought of Kate's unwavering belief in her ability to begin again.

The plane gathered speed, pressing her back against her seat. Through her window, she watched her homeland blur and tilt as they left the ground. Up they climbed, through layers of cloud and consciousness, until Ohio was nothing but a patchwork memory below.

Claire closed her eyes. When she opened them again, they were above the clouds, and the sun was rising on the first day of her new life.

2

THE MISSING MUSICAL SCORE FOR MY GREAT ESCAPE

T he plane descended through clouds that looked like spun sugar, catching the golden light of an Italian afternoon. Claire pressed her forehead against the cool oval window, longing for the sweeping orchestral music that should have been accompanying this moment. In all the times she'd imagined arriving in Italy, she'd heard Dario Marianelli's musical score from 'Eat Pray Love' playing in her mind. Those heart-wrenching notes that had made Julia Roberts' journey feel so profound, so cinematic, so life-changing.

Below, the Bay of Naples stretched out like a sheet of polished sapphire, its waters dancing with diamond glints of sunlight. Mount Vesuvius loomed in the distance, a sleeping giant wrapped in a haze of purple shadows, its presence both magnificent and slightly menacing. This was supposed to be when the music would swell, when those same strings that had carried Elizabeth Gilbert through her transformation would tell the world that something extraordinary was happening to Claire Bennett too. Instead, a baby cried somewhere in the plane, and the flight attendant announced their descent in two languages.

Claire closed her eyes, feeling the subtle shift in cabin pressure that made her ears pop. Seventeen hours and two flight changes later, she was finally here. Now, adrift between sky and earth, she felt herself hovering between two lives; the safe, predictable existence she'd left behind, and whatever waited for her in the chaos of Naples. She found herself humming the theme from her favorite scene in the movie, when Elizabeth Gilbert finally lets herself feel joy again. But the melody felt hollow without Marianelli's lush orchestration behind it, without that perfect musical companion that knew exactly how to translate heartbreak and hope into sound.

The landing gear deployed with a mechanical groan that sent a shiver through the cabin. Claire's fingers tightened around her armrest, her knuckles white against the worn fabric. A memory flashed unbidden: Mark's voice, dripping with condescension. "Naples? Really, Claire? You've never even traveled anywhere within the country by yourself before. This is just another one of your impulsive reactions."

Then she realized that this is not a memory, but something she imagined Mark would have said, if she had shared her plans with him.

The words still stung, but beneath the pain, she felt something else stirring. A fierce determination she hadn't known she possessed. Yes, Naples. Yes, really. Yes, she was terrified and yes, this might be the biggest mistake of her life, but at least it would be her mistake to make.

"First time in Napoli (Naples)?"

The voice startled Claire from her thoughts. She turned to find the elderly Italian woman who'd been her seatmate on this last sector watching her with eyes the color of aged amber. The woman's face was a map of laugh lines and wisdom, crowned by a perfectly coiffed head of silver hair. A delicate gold cross nestled in the folds of her elegant silk scarf.

"Is it that obvious?" Claire attempted a smile, aware of how shaky it must look.

The woman, who had introduced herself as Valentina when they'd taken off, reached over and patted Claire's hand. Her skin was soft as worn velvet, her fingers adorned with rings that spoke of a lifetime of love stories. "You have the look of someone trying to discover something that's invisible. Naples, she has that effect." Her accent wrapped around the words like silk, making even simple English sound like poetry. "But don't worry. The city, she will take care of you."

"Everyone keeps telling me I'm brave," Claire confessed, her voice barely audible over the roar of the engines. "But I don't feel brave. I feel..." She trailed off, unable to find the right words.

Valentina's smile deepened, creating new constellations of wrinkles around her eyes. "Ah, but that is exactly what courage is, no? Feeling afraid but doing the thing anyway." She squeezed Claire's hand. "Besides, you choose a good time to come. Spring in Naples; the air smells of orange blossoms."

The plane touched down with a jarring bump that sent Claire's stomach lurching into her throat. As they taxied toward the terminal, Valentina leaned closer, her voice dropping to a conspiratorial whisper. "Let me tell you a secret about Naples. She is like a beautiful woman who knows exactly how gorgeous she is. She will not try to impress you with perfect makeup or designer clothes. Instead, she will seduce you with her realness like her loud laugh, her passionate arguments, her ability to find joy in simple moments. Give her time. Let her work her magic."

The seatbelt sign dinged off, and the cabin erupted in the usual chaos of deplaning. As Claire stood to retrieve her carry-on from the overhead compartment, Valentina pressed something into her hand. It was a small card with an address written in elegant script for 'Ristorante Italiano Fresco' (Fresh Italian Restaurant).

"My daughter's restaurant," Valentina explained. "The best seafood in Naples. You tell them Valentina sent you, yes? They will take good care of you."

Before Claire could properly thank her, Valentina had disappeared into the stream of passengers, leaving behind only the lingering scent of expensive perfume and the card that felt like a charm in Claire's palm.

The customs hall at Naples International Airport was a cathedral of uncertainty, its high ceilings amplifying every echoing footstep, every rolling suitcase, every rapid-fire announcement in Italian that made Claire's self-study language lessons seem like humming a tune in a hurricane. She joined the queue for non-EU passengers, clutching her passport like a lifeline, watching other travelers who seemed to move through the space with the easy confidence of those who belonged.

The fluorescent lights cast everyone in a slightly greenish pallor, making Claire achingly aware of how she must look after seventeen hours of travel. Her chestnut hair escaping its once-neat bun, her carefully selected "arriving in Italy" outfit wrinkled beyond salvation. She caught her reflection in the polished surface of a nearby pillar: a woman hovering somewhere between who she was and who she might become, her eyes wide with a mixture of exhaustion and barely contained panic.

The customs officer, a man with salt-and-pepper hair and reading glasses perched low on his nose, barely glanced at her passport before stamping it with a decisive thunk that echoed through her bones. Just like that, she was officially in Italy. No fanfare, no moment of profound metamorphosis, and definitely no musical score. Just another tired traveler shuffling through another airport.

But then she stepped outside, and Naples hit her with the force of a summer storm.

The air was different here. Thick and alive, carrying a thousand stories on its breath. Salt from the nearby Mediterranean mingled with exhaust fumes, coffee, garlic, bread baking somewhere nearby, and something indefinable that made her think of sun-warmed stone and centuries of lives lived passionately. The cacophony of sounds overwhelmed her senses: car horns blaring, motorcycles weaving through traffic with death-defying precision, voices calling out in cascading Italian.

A group of teenagers passed by, their laughter bouncing off the airport's facade like musical notes. They moved with that distinctly Italian grace that seemed to say they knew exactly who they were and where they belonged in the world. Claire watched them disappear into the crowd, remembering how she'd felt at their age. Before marriage, before betrayal, before life had taught her to second-guess every decision.

Her hands trembled slightly as she fumbled with her phone, trying to connect to the international plan she'd activated before leaving. The screen flickered to life, immediately flooding with delayed notifications. Two texts from Kate: "Call me when you land!", "Claire, I'm getting worried and mom keeps calling me to see if I heard from you." and one from her mother: "Just want you to be happy". And nothing from Mark. The absence of his name in her notifications shouldn't have hurt anymore, but it did, a phantom pain, like pressing on a bruise to see if it still ached.

She opened the Uber app, having to retype her destination twice before getting it right. The address, Via dei Tribunali, in the midst of Naples' historic center, looked both exotic and terrifyingly real on her screen.

While waiting, she quickly messaged Kate: "I reached safely. Waiting for Uber at the airport. Tell mom I love her."

Standing there, she watched the dance of vehicles around the airport: cars that seemed to operate on their own mysterious rules of physics, Vespas that wove between them like needles threading silk, all of it somehow working as an organized chaos that contained its own peculiar harmony.

The Uber driver who picked her up introduced himself as Giuseppe, his smile as warm and welcoming as the afternoon sun that gilded everything in sight. He was perhaps in his early sixties, with laugh lines around his eyes and hands that moved expressively as he spoke, somehow managing to gesture enthusiastically while steering through Naples' notorious traffic with casual expertise.

"First time Naples?" he asked, his eyes meeting hers in the rearview mirror. They were kind eyes, the sort that made you feel like you'd known him for years rather than minutes.

"Is it that obvious?" Claire found herself asking for the second time that day, wondering if she had some sort of neon sign floating above her head: AMERICAN TOURIST, POSSIBLY HAVING MIDLIFE CRISIS.

Giuseppe laughed, a rich, melodious sound that seemed to fill the entire car. "Obvious? No, no. You have... come si dice... fresh eyes. Like a painter seeing a beautiful model for the first time." He weaved through traffic with the grace of a dancer, his car a partner in an intricate choreography of metal and motion. "Naples, she is not pretty like Roma or Firenze, I mean Rome or Florence. She is beautiful like a real woman, passionate, honest, sometimes a little bit crazy." He laughed heartily.

Claire pressed her forehead against the cool glass of the window, drinking in the city as it unfurled around her like a love letter written in stone and light. She closed her eyes briefly, remembering how in 'Eat

Pray Love', moments like these were always perfected by musical score. Those sweeping violins that could make even a stranger in a strange land feel like she was exactly where she belonged. But Naples wasn't giving her that orchestrated perfection.

Naples wasn't conventionally beautiful. Instead, she was beautiful the way a thunderstorm was beautiful, the way a first kiss was beautiful, raw and real and absolutely unforgettable. No composed score could capture this authenticity, this unfiltered life force that pulsed through the streets. Laundry fluttered between ancient buildings, each piece telling its own story: a child's sundress dancing in the breeze, sheets bleached white by the sun, a red blouse that caught the light like a splash of wine against weathered stone. The city wrote its own music, a symphony of real life that made Claire wonder if perhaps she'd been looking for the wrong kind of soundtrack all along.

Street vendors called out to passersby, their voices rising and falling in musical notes that made Claire's heart ache with their earnest poetry. An old woman arranged blood oranges in perfect pyramids, some whole and some cut, their flesh gleaming like sunset. A young man with rolled-up sleeves kneaded dough at an outdoor counter, his movements hypnotic and sure. Two elderly men played chess at a tiny table outside a cafè, their concentration absolute, while life swirled around them like a river around rocks.

"You see that church?" Giuseppe pointed to a dome that rose above the surrounding buildings like time frozen in stone. "Built in thirteen hundreds. Here everything is old. My wife's family, they have lived in the same building since before America was even a country." He chuckled, shaking his head. "In Naples, even stones have memories."

The car turned down a street so narrow that Claire held her breath, certain they wouldn't fit. But Giuseppe navigated with the confidence of someone who had done this a thousand times before, bringing them to a stop in front of a building that made her gasp softly. The facade was the color of pale honey, weathered by centuries of sun and rain. A riot of bougainvillea cascaded over its balconies like a waterfall of fuchsia flames, and the massive wooden door was painted a shade of blue that reminded her of the sky just before dusk.

"Your home in Naples," Giuseppe announced proudly, already

moving to help her with her bags. He insisted on carrying the heavier one despite her protests, treating her not as a customer but as an honored guest in his city.

Claire checked the address against her Airbnb confirmation with trembling fingers. This was it. Her home for the next month, at least. The thought made her stomach flutter with a kaleidoscope of butterflies, each wing painted with equal parts terror and exhilaration.

The building's owner, Maria, was standing in the entrance hall, a vision that immediately put Claire at ease. She was tiny, barely reaching Claire's shoulder, with silver hair swept up in an elegant twist and eyes that sparkled with the kind of wisdom that comes from a life well-lived. Before Claire could say a word, Maria enveloped her in a warm hug that smelled of basil, fresh bread, and something indefinably, perfectly Italian.

"Benvenuta, Claire!" she exclaimed, her voice musical with genuine joy. "Come, come. You must be exhausted, poverina (poor thing)." She reached for one of Claire's bags despite her protests, her small frame belying surprising strength.

As they began their ascent, "No elevator, mi dispiace (I'm sorry), but the view, ah, the view will make you forget all these stairs!" Claire felt something shifting inside her, like tectonic plates realigning to create a new landscape of possibility. Each step took her further from the woman who had lived a careful, controlled life and closer to... who? That was the question that had brought her here, wasn't it?

Four flights of stairs later, each step echoing through centuries of marble, Maria unlocked a door that opened into what could only be described as a poem written in light and space. The apartment stretched before them, its terra cotta tiles catching the late afternoon sun like fallen stars. The ceiling soared overhead, crossed by ancient wooden beams that had witnessed countless lives unfold beneath them.

"Your home," Maria announced with the pride of someone sharing a treasured secret. She threw open the shutters with practiced ease, and Naples rushed in like a lover's embrace. Warm air carrying the pulse of the city, the distant sound of church bells weaving through the symphony of street life below.

But it was the balcony that stole Claire's breath entirely.

"Go, go," Maria urged, giving her a gentle push toward the weathered French doors. "See your kingdom."

Claire stepped out onto the small iron-wrought balcony and felt the world tilt beneath her feet. The view spread before her like a living painting. A maze of sun-washed rooftops in shades of ochre and sienna, church spires reaching toward heaven, and beyond it all, the Bay of Naples glittering like scattered diamonds beneath Mount Vesuvius's watchful gaze. The late afternoon light painted everything in hues of gold and rose, gilding even the graffiti-covered walls into something profound.

A warm current of air carried the sound of distant music. Someone practicing piano, the notes drifting up like bubbles in champagne, mingling with the calls of swallows as they swooped between buildings. The scent of jasmine from a neighbor's plant wove through the air, along with the mouthwatering aroma of tomatoes and garlic from somewhere below.

"I make you caffè?" Maria's voice floated out from the kitchen where an ancient-looking stovetop espresso maker sat like a small copper sculpture. "And you must try my sfogliatelle, fresh from this morning!"

"Oh, no, thank you," Claire started to say, but Maria was already busy, her movements precise and practiced. The kitchen came alive with small sounds: water running, the clink of cups, the melodious tap of the espresso maker being settled onto the burner.

Left alone for a moment, Claire stood in the middle of the apartment, letting the reality of her situation wash over her. The space was simple but elegant. Whitewashed walls adorned with black and white photographs of Naples through the ages, comfortable furniture that invited relaxation, windows that seemed designed to catch every possible breeze off the Mediterranean. A small writing desk sat in one corner, positioned to capture the perfect view of the bay. Above it, someone had painted a quote in flowing script: "La vita è un'avventura audace o non è niente" (Life is a daring adventure or nothing at all).

The words caught in Claire's throat. How many times had she read similar quotes on Instagram, double-tapping them absently while sitting in her safe, predictable life back in Ohio? Now here she was, living them. The thought sent a tremor through her hands as she unpacked her phone charger, the familiar object looking somehow foreign against the Italian electrical outlet.

Maria returned bearing a small silver tray set with an espresso cup that looked like a doll's teacup, steam rising from its dark depths in almost invisible spirals. Beside it sat what appeared to be small seashells made of pastry, dusted with powdered sugar that caught the light like morning frost.

"Sfogliatelle (shell-shaped flaky pastry)," Maria explained, settling the tray on a small table near the balcony doors. "You eat, then sleep. Tomorrow..." She made an expansive gesture that somehow encompassed the entire city. "Tomorrow, you begin your adventure."

After Maria left, the apartment seemed to exhale, settling into a different kind of quiet. Claire sank onto the bed, her body heavy with the kind of exhaustion that seeps into your bones after too many hours of running on nothing but adrenaline and hope. The mattress was firmer than she was used to, the sheets smelling of lavender and sunshine. So different from the sterile, department store scent of the bedding she'd left behind back home.

She should unpack. Should shower away the stale airplane air that clung to her skin. Should eat something more substantial than airplane food and Maria's pastries. Should, should, should... The list of responsibilities stretched out like a chain, trying to tether her to the person she'd been before stepping onto that plane.

Instead, she found herself drawn back to the balcony, pulled by some instinct deeper than thought. The sun was beginning its slow descent into the ocean, painting the sky in impossible shades of pink and gold that made her fingers itch for paints and canvas. When was the last time she'd felt that urge? The last time she'd created anything purely for the joy of creation?

Below, Naples was transitioning from day to evening, the rhythm of the city shifting like music changing tempo. Shop owners pulled down their metal shutters with a sound like distant thunder. The aroma of dinner preparations drifted up from nearby windows; garlic being chopped, crushed tomatoes bubbling, the sharp note of fresh basil. Somewhere, a woman called out "Antonio!" and received a chorus of responses from different directions, followed by laughter that bounced between buildings like light.

Claire closed her eyes and took a deep breath, letting the sounds and scents of Naples wash over her. The air tasted different here. Salt and stone and centuries of stories she hadn't learned yet. For the first time since stepping off the plane, she felt something inside her relax, just slightly, like a fist unclenching one finger at a time.

In the distance, church bells signaled the hour, their deep tones spreading across the neighborhood. Seven o'clock. In Ohio, it would be around two in the afternoon. Mark would be at work, probably sitting in his corner office with its view of the parking lot, typing emails with his habitual two-finger precision. Would he even think where she was right now? Would he care?

The thought didn't hurt as much as it usually did. Perhaps distance was already working its magic, or perhaps it was simply not possible to hold onto old pain in a place that felt so full of life.

She didn't unpack her suitcases that night. Didn't shower, though her skin felt grimy from traveling. Instead, she sat on her balcony until the stars emerged, watching the city transition from day to night like a woman changing from work clothes into evening wear. She ate one of Maria's sfogliatelle, the delicate layers of pastry dissolving on her tongue, sweet and rich and unlike anything she'd tasted before. She ate another one. Each bite felt like a small act of rebellion against her old life, where dessert was something to be earned through deprivation, where pleasure itself was something to be rationed carefully.

When Claire finally crawled into bed, the sheets cool against her travel-worn skin, the distant sounds of the city had become almost musical. A lullaby in a language she was just beginning to learn. Through the half-open balcony doors, the night air carried beautiful stories of lives being lived in full color: the clatter of plates from a late dinner, a burst of laughter that sparkled like champagne in the darkness, the purr of a Vespa winding through narrow streets, a snatch of an old Italian love song played on a radio somewhere close by.

She lay there in the soothing darkness, watching shadows from passing headlights dance across her ceiling like memories of dreams she'd forgotten how to have. In the quietness of this foreign room, thoughts she'd been holding at bay began to surface like letters rising from the depths of a dark sea.

Fifteen years of marriage, dissolved like sugar in bitter coffee. Fifteen years of building a life with someone who had turned out to be a stranger. The signs had been there, hadn't they? In the way Mark's kisses had become perfunctory, mechanical things. In how he'd stopped asking about her day, stopped sharing his own. In the growing silence at their dinner table, heavy with words they'd forgotten how to say.

A tear slipped from the corner of her eye, tracking a warm path into her hair. But this tear felt different from the ones she'd shed in Ohio. Less like grief and more like release, like letting go of a breath she'd been holding for too long.

Through her open window, she could see a sliver of the moon hanging over Naples like a benediction. The same moon that had witnessed countless love stories unfold in these ancient streets, that had watched generations of women find their way back to themselves in this city that seemed to pulse with feminine energy.

Claire's fingers traced along her collarbone, finding her grandma's compass locket. Originally when her grandma had given it to her, she had said: "Sometimes you have to get lost to find yourself." Back then, Claire had dismissed it as just another cryptic saying from an old woman. Now, lying in a bed in a foreign city, those words felt prophetic, resonating with unexpected clarity.

Sleep began to steal over her in lulling waves, softening the edges of her thoughts. The mattress that had felt so foreign began to cradle her like an old friend. The distant sounds of Naples merged with the rhythm of her breathing, creating a symphony that seemed to whisper, "Welcome home, Claire, welcome home."

Her thoughts were no longer of Mark, or Ohio, or the life she'd left behind. Instead, she found herself wondering about the hands that had built this room, the other souls who had slept here, perhaps even fallen in love here. How many others had lain in this same spot, looking up at these same beams, feeling terror and hope and what else?

The night air seemed to wrap around her like a tender embrace, carrying the promise of tomorrow, of new beginnings, of adventures yet to unfold. Somewhere in the distance, a Vespa buzzed past, its sound fading like the last notes of a song. Claire pulled the thin blanket up to her chin and let Naples sing her to sleep, her dreams already beginning to paint themselves in the vivid colors of her new reality.

This was just the beginning. Tomorrow, she would begin exploring. Tomorrow, she would start figuring out who Claire Bennett could be in this new world she'd chosen. Tomorrow held infinite wonders, each one glittering with potential like stars scattered across the Neapolitan night sky. She thought of how she'd watched 'Eat Pray Love' countless times, letting Dario Marianelli's score wash over her in waves of orchestrated emotion. How many times had she imagined her own journey would unfold to the same perfect soundtrack?

But as she lay there, listening to Naples breathe around her, she realized something profound. The city was offering her something better than a carefully composed score; it was giving her life in its purest form, a symphony more authentic than anything Hollywood could create.

She let herself float in that space between sleeping and waking, where the line between reality and dreams blurred like watercolors bleeding together on paper. And in that dreamy state, she finally understood. She didn't need violins to tell her when to feel. She didn't need a soundtrack to validate her journey. Naples would teach her a different way to listen, not for the swelling crescendos of a manufactured moment, but for the raw, unscripted music of a life being truly lived.

The city's nocturnal chorus wrapped around her like a blanket, and for the first time since landing, she felt completely, utterly at peace with where she was. As sleep finally claimed her, Claire smiled, knowing that tomorrow would bring its own unique melodies, its own perfectly imperfect score, written in the language of real life and genuine moments. And that was exactly what her soul had been searching for all along.

3

THE MAGIC OF CAFFÈ SOSPESO

D awn crept into Claire's apartment like a shy lover, painting the walls in watercolor washes of rose and orange. Sleep had done little to ease her restlessness; jet lag had kept her tossing through the night, her nightmares and dreams a kaleidoscope of faces and places, of Mark's betrayal bleeding into the allure of Naples' unknown streets. She woke to sunlight streaming through the lace curtains that danced in the morning breeze, her body caught in that strange limbo between time zones.

The distant chime of church bells called the faithful to morning mass. Claire lay still for a moment, letting the unfamiliar sounds of Naples wash over her: the musical cadence of Italian voices rising from the street below, the clatter of cups and saucers from neighboring apartments, the passionate honking of impatient drivers that somehow managed to sound more like a symphony than chaos.

Rising from bed, she padded barefoot to the balcony, the terra cotta tiles cool beneath her feet. The morning air carried a bouquet of scents that made her heart ache with their beauty. Fresh bread from the bakery downstairs, coffee from a dozen cafés, the salt-ringed caress from the ocean, and something else, perfectly Italian that spoke of age and beauty and lives lived without apology.

In Ohio, mornings had become a carefully choreographed dance of avoidance. She and Mark moving around each other like planets in separate orbits, the silence between them heavy with unspoken words. Here, in this sun-drenched apartment with its high ceilings and stories written in its ancient beams, even silence felt alive.

Drawn by the allure of the vintage clawfoot tub, Claire ran a bath, easing into the steaming water with a sigh that originated from somewhere deep within her soul. As she lay there, the worn porcelain cradling her like an understanding friend, she felt the true weight of her journey settle upon her. The seventeen hour flight had transported her body to Naples, but it was this moment, submerged in the ancient tub with the sounds and scents of the city drifting through the open window, that carried her spirit to this place of new beginnings. She closed her eyes, letting the warmth envelop her, washing away not just the grime of travel but the lingering doubts and fears she'd carried like heavy baggage from her old life. In the embrace of the perfumed water, Claire felt herself begin to unfurl like a flower too long in the shade, reaching for the sunlight of her own becoming.

She dressed carefully, deliberately, like an artist preparing for an important showing. The flowing sundress in pale blue had been an impulse buy before leaving. Something the old Claire would have talked herself out of. Too impractical, too romantic, too... much. But here, among the colorfully dressed Neapolitans, it would feel right. The soft fabric rustled against her skin as she moved, its color reminiscent of the bay she could glimpse from her balcony.

Her reflection in the antique mirror looked familiar yet somehow different. Perhaps it was the way the Mediterranean light softened her features, turning her normally mousy brown hair into a cascade of amber and honey. Or maybe it was something in her eyes; beneath the uncertainty and traces of sadness, there was a glimmer of something she hadn't seen there in months. Hope. Adventure. Life.

Running a brush through her hair, she saw a message from Kate flash on her phone screen: "You're having an Eat, Pray, Love moment, aren't you?" The words tinged with equal parts concern and envy. But this didn't feel like a moment. It felt like waking up from a long sleep, like colors becoming sharper, like the first breath after being underwater too long.

Claire's stomach growled, reminding her that airplane food and Maria's pastries from yesterday weren't enough to sustain a person. The thought of navigating a Naples cafés with her rudimentary Italian sent butterflies dancing through her stomach. But wasn't that why she'd come? To face the unfamiliar, to learn who she could be when nobody was watching, when nobody had predetermined who she was supposed to be?

The stairs creaked beneath Claire's feet as she descended, each soft groan like sighs from the past. How many other lost wanderers had these steps carried? The stairwell carried the signs and scents of time itself. Wrought iron railing with patina, polished marble worn smooth by countless footsteps, and the lingering ghost of someone's morning coffee.

As she reached the bottom, Claire paused, her hand resting on the cool metal of the railing. Through the ancient door, she could hear Naples awakening. A symphony of life that made her own existence from the past seem like it had been lived on mute. Here, every sound carried emotion, every scent told a story, every moment felt like a page waiting to be written.

The massive blue door required her whole body to push it open, and when it finally yielded, Naples rushed in to greet her like an enthusiastic lover. The morning light had turned the narrow street into a corridor of gold, transforming even the crumbling stucco walls into something magical. The air wrapped around her like a warm embrace, carrying the mingled aromas of fresh cornetti, coffee, and the sea.

A young mother passed by, her dark hair caught up in a messy bun, guiding a small boy whose cute Italian made Claire smile despite not understanding a word. The woman caught her eye and returned the smile. A moment of silent understanding between two strangers that somehow contained more warmth than any conversation she'd had with Mark in their final months together.

Naples in the morning was a feast for every sense, overwhelming in its intensity. Vendors were already setting up their stalls, arranging produce with the careful precision of artists creating installations. The tomatoes, oh, the tomatoes! They looked nothing like the pale, perfect spheres she'd bought at the supermarket back home. These were proudly imperfect, deeply red, so ripe they looked ready to burst with sunshine. Claire found herself reaching out to touch one before she could stop herself, earning a knowing grin from the vendor.

"Bella, bella," he said, picking up the tomato she'd touched and pressing it into her hand. The fruit was warm from the morning sun, its weight in her palm somehow more real than anything she'd held in months. When she tried to pay, he waved her money away with an elegant flick of his wrist. "Un regalo (a gift)," he insisted.

She cradled the tomato as she walked on, its presence in her hand a reminder that she was really here, really doing this. Old men gathered at tiny tables outside cafés, their animated conversations punctuated by expansive hand gestures that seemed to paint pictures in the air. They spoke not just with their voices but with their entire beings. Eyebrows rising and falling, shoulders shrugging, hands conducting symphonies of emotion. The tiny cups of espresso before them sent aromatic tendrils of steam into the morning air, like incense in a temple dedicated to the art of living fully.

A girl on a Vespa wove through the narrow street, her dark hair streaming behind her like a banner of youth and freedom, talking loudly with her pillion passenger. The sound of her laughter lingered in the air long after she'd disappeared around a corner, and Claire found herself touching her own lips, trying to remember the last time she'd laughed like that. Without self-consciousness, without restraint, without wondering who might be watching or judging.

Every corner she turned revealed something new, something that made her heart catch in her throat. A hidden courtyard filled with potted lemon trees, their fruit glowing like small suns among the dark leaves. A craftsman carefully restoring an ancient door, his weathered hands moving over the wood with the tenderness of a lover. A cat sleeping regally on a sun-warmed windowsill, its copper-colored fur turned to flame in the morning light.

The time slipped by like sand running through fingers. The morning turned to early afternoon and the heat started to build, making Claire's skin prickle with a sheen of perspiration that caught the light like dewdrops. Her sundress clung to the small of her back, and wisps of hair escaped to curl around her face in the humid air. She should find somewhere to rest, somewhere to gather the scattered pieces of herself that seemed to be floating free in this city.

The tomato in her hand had warmed to her body temperature, its weight a reminder of unexpected kindnesses. Back home, strangers didn't give gifts. They didn't smile without reason. They didn't reach across the careful boundaries of politeness to touch another soul. But here... here everything was different. Here, life spilled over its edges like wine from an overfull glass, staining everything it touched with color and meaning.

As if in answer to her unspoken yearning, she turned a corner and felt time slow, the way it does in moments when fate shifts its weight from one foot to the other. There, nestled between a bookshop and what appeared to be an antique store, stood a café with a faded green awning that fluttered in the gentle morning currents. Sunlight caught the gold lettering above the door, making it shimmer like a message written in starlight: "Caffè Sereno."

Sereno. Serene. The word itself felt like a promise, like hands cupped around a flame protecting it from the wind.

Claire stood still, absorbing every detail of the scene before her as if she were preparing to paint it from memory. The windows glowed with warm light that spilled onto the cobblestones like honey. Brass fixtures gleamed softly, polished by years of hands reaching out in welcome. A small chalkboard easel displayed the day's specials in elegant Italian script that danced across the slate like musical notes.

Through the windows, she could see figures moving in the diffused light, their gestures and expressions suggesting stories she longed to know. An elderly couple sat at a corner table, their hands clasped together with the easy familiarity of decades shared. A young woman bent over a notebook, her pen moving across the page as if taking dictation from her dreams. A man, maybe in his mid sixties, stood behind the counter, his movements as he worked the espresso machine reminiscent of a conductor leading an orchestra.

The small bell above the door chimed softly as she pushed it open. Not the harsh jangle of American cafès, but a gentle sound like laughter muffled by kisses. The interior air wrapped around her like a silk scarf, cool against her sun-warmed skin, rich with the aroma of coffee and something sweet that made her think of childhood mornings in her grandma's kitchen.

The café wasn't large, but it felt spacious somehow, as if the walls understood the importance of leaving room for imaginings to expand. High ceilings disappeared into shadows above, crossed by wooden beams that had witnessed countless meetings, partings, beginnings, and endings. The walls were the color of marigolds, adorned with black and white photographs that captured moments of Naples. Streets filled with life, lovers embracing, children playing in fountain spray, all preserved in silver and shadow.

Small tables dotted the room like islands in a calm sea, each topped with a tiny vase holding a single fresh flower. Claire recognized some like daisies, roses, sprigs of lavender, but others were mysterious blooms that seemed to have sprung from someone's imagination of what a flower should be. The marble-topped counter gleamed softly, its surface marked with the patina that comes from years of elbows leaned, hands rested, stories shared.

Behind the counter, a man with kind eyes and a salt-and-pepper beard looked up as she entered, his gaze holding the sort of warmth that made Claire think of winter fires and comfortable silences. Laugh lines radiated from the corners of his eyes like sunbeams, speaking of a life lived in pursuit of joy rather than mere passage of time. His white shirt, rolled up at the sleeves, revealed forearms tanned by the Italian sun and marked with the occasional coffee stain. Badges of honor in his chosen profession.

"Buongiorno!" he called out, his voice rich and melodious as aged wine, carrying notes of welcome that transcended language barriers. The word seemed to expand in the space between them, blossoming from a simple greeting into an invitation to belong.

Claire approached the counter, drawn as much by his friendly demeanor as by the intoxicating aroma of freshly ground coffee beans. Her heart fluttered like a caged bird; even the simplest interactions felt monumental here, weighted with either embarrassment or serendipity.

"Buongiorno," she replied, the word still feeling foreign on her tongue, like a piece of exotic candy she wasn't quite sure how to savor properly. "Um... could I have a cappuccino, please?" The question almost evaporated into the coffee-scented air, barely a thread of sound, carrying echoes of the timid woman who'd learned to make herself smaller to accommodate Mark's expanding ego.

The man's eyes twinkled with affectionate amusement, but there was nothing mocking in his expression. Only the warm understanding of someone who had witnessed countless travelers finding their way. "Ah, American!" He pressed a hand to his chest in a gesture that somehow managed to be both theatrical and entirely sincere. "I am Signor Rossi. Welcome to my little corner of paradise."

He gestured at the clock on the wall, an ancient timepiece that seemed to measure moments rather than minutes. It showed 12:30 in the afternoon, though Claire's jet-lagged body insisted it was still somehow morning. "Cappuccino is for morning only, until 11:00," he explained, his accent wrapping around the words like a caress. "The cappuccino curfew," he smiled warmly, "Try an espresso instead. It will wake your senses."

Heat rose to Claire's cheeks, painting them with the blushing peony at dawn. "Oh, right. Sorry. I read about that rule, but I forgot." The words tumbled out, tasting of embarrassment and the lingering fear of doing everything wrong in this new world she'd chosen.

"Non ti preoccupare (don't worry)," Signor Rossi said, already moving to the gleaming espresso machine that stood like a copper and brass altar to the art of coffee. His movements were precise and practiced, a dance learned through years of devotion to his craft. "Here, you will drink it standing at the bar, like a true Italian. It's cheaper this way, and you'll feel the energy of Napoli."

As Signor Rossi worked his mastery at the espresso machine, Claire found herself mesmerized by the ritual unfolding before her. His hands moved with the practiced grace, each gesture imbued with meaning accumulated through countless repetitions. The machine itself seemed to respond to his touch like a well-loved instrument, its chrome surfaces reflecting the afternoon light in patterns that danced across the walls.

The sound of coffee being ground filled the air. Not the harsh mechanical whir she was used to from chain cafès, but a gentle purring that reminded her of far away thunder or waves breaking on a distant shore. Steam rose in spirals, carrying with it an aroma so rich and complex it made her previous coffee experiences seem like pale shadows of the real thing.

As she watched, she became aware of how time moved differently here. Back home, coffee had been fuel. Something grabbed hastily on the way to somewhere else, drunk without thought or pleasure. But here, in this sun-dappled sanctuary with its marigold-colored walls and ancient beams, coffee was a transformation. It was a conversation. It was life itself, distilled into a tiny porcelain cup.

"You see," Signor Rossi said as he worked, his voice taking on the tone of someone sharing precious secrets, "making coffee is like expressing love." His eyes crinkled at her startled expression. "It requires patience, passion, and perfect timing. Too rushed, and you lose the enchantment. Too slow, and the moment escapes you. It must be..." he paused, tamping the grounds with exactly the right pressure, "...precisely right."

The espresso began to flow into the waiting cup, dark as night and crowned with crema the color of roasted hazelnuts. The aroma intensified, wrapping around Claire like a forgotten embrace, making her think of velvet and caramel and chocolate. Yes, definitely chocolate.

"Watch," Signor Rossi instructed, indicating the perfect crema forming on top of the espresso. "See how it blooms? Like a flower opening to the sun. This is how you know it's perfect." He slid the tiny cup across the counter to her with the flourish of a maestro completing his finest symphony. The cup itself was a work of art. Dainty porcelain the color of cream, decorated with hand-painted flowers in faded blues and golds.

It was then, as she reached for the cup, that Claire noticed something unusual near the entrance. A large cork board covered in what appeared to be a collage of colorful notes and tiny sketches. They seemed to be written on the backs of coffee receipts, creating a patchwork of words and images that called to her with an irresistible gravity, as if the stories pinned there had been waiting for her discovery alone.

But before she could ask about it, Signor Rossi gestured to the tiny cup before her. "First, we drink. Then, I will tell you about the magic board." His eyes held a knowing look, as if he could see the questions forming in her mind like clouds gathering before rain.

Claire lifted the cup to her lips, inhaling deeply. The aroma was intoxicating. Notes of chocolate and hazelnuts, yes, but also something deeper, more complex. Like the difference between reading about love and feeling it course through your veins for the first time.

The first sip of espresso blossomed on Claire's tongue like a revelation, and for a moment, the world around her ceased to exist. This wasn't coffee as she had known it. This was poetry in liquid form, a story told in flavors that unfolded like chapters of a beloved book. Rich and complex, with none of the bitter harshness she'd come to associate with espresso, it tasted of sunshine and dark earth, of traditions passed down through generations, of moments stolen from the rush of life to simply be.

Her eyes must have widened because Signor Rossi's face split into a smile that could have lit all of Naples. "Ah," he said gently, "now you understand."

In that moment, she did understand; not just about coffee, but about why she had come here, why she had needed to break free from the careful confines of her former life. Everything from before had been diluted, hadn't it? Watered down to make it safer, more palatable, less likely to stain or leave marks. Her marriage had become like that too, all the intensity carefully strained out until what remained was merely warm and listlessly brown and mostly tasteless.

As the flavors lingered on her tongue, Claire found her gaze drawn again to the cork board near the entrance. She walked to stand in front of the board. Now she could see that it was covered in a tapestry of human experiences. Dozens of coffee-stained receipts reborn into canvases for thoughts and confessions.

"What are all these notes?" she asked, unable to contain her curiosity any longer. The question emerged soft and wondering, like a child asking about stars.

Signor Rossi's face lit up with the particular joy of someone about to share a treasured secret. He moved from behind the counter with the ease of a man completely at home in his domain, coming to stand beside her before the board, his presence steady as a lighthouse. The scent of coffee and something warmer, perhaps cinnamon or vanilla, clung to him like a subtle cologne.

"Ah, that is the magic of Caffè Sospeso," he said, his voice dropping to match her wondering tone. The words rolled off his tongue like music.

"Caffè what?" Claire leaned closer to the board, drawn by the variety of handwriting styles that covered the receipts. Each one as unique as a fingerprint.

"Caffè Sospeso, as in suspended coffee," he explained, his eyes taking on a wistful quality, as if seeing beyond the physical board to something deeper, more meaningful. "It's a beautiful tradition born right here in Naples, in the years after the war when so many had so little. Someone pays for two coffees but drinks only one. The second coffee is 'suspended', waiting for someone to claim it. A small act of kindness between strangers, a thread connecting souls who may never meet."

Claire felt something catch in her throat. Not quite a sob, not quite a sigh, but something in between. How long had it been since she'd experienced kindness without an agenda? Since she'd felt connected to anything larger than her own careful routines?

"But here at Caffè Sereno, we do it a little differently," Signor Rossi continued, his voice carrying the warmth of afternoon sun on ancient stones. "In the original concept of caffè sospeso, the person who buys the suspended coffee and the one who claims it, both remain anonymous." He looked at Claire, and she nodded to confirm understanding. "But at Caffè Sereno, we encourage them to communicate with one another to the level they feel comfortable."

Being an artist, Claire tried to visualize the concept. "How do you keep track of the paid receipts on this board, filled with so many things?" she asked curiously.

"The person who buys the coffee writes a message on their receipt," Signor Rossi explained. "Do you see that big jar next to the cash register?" He pointed at the huge glass jar sitting on the counter. "The caffè sospeso receipts are stored in that jar until they are claimed by someone else," he continued. "The person who claims the suspended coffee picks a receipt, gets a free coffee, and while enjoying the coffee, they write their response on the receipt, and pin it to the board."

"So it becomes a conversation between strangers. A little piece of their story shared with the world," a voice like warm honey and summer twilight came from behind them. Claire turned to find its source.

There stood a woman whose presence seemed to fill the cafè with an additional layer of warmth and grace. She moved with fluid elegance as she approached, her silver-streaked dark hair swept up in a classic chignon that emphasized the timeless beauty of her face. Though she must have been in her mid sixties, age had only enhanced her allure, etching fine lines around her eyes and mouth that spoke of a life filled with laughter and love. Her dress, in shades of deep burgundy that reminded Claire of aged wine, moved like water as she walked.

"Ah, meet Lucia Rossi, the love of my life and the most talented chef and baker in all of Naples," Signor Rossi said proudly, his face glowing with the kind of love that only grows deeper with each passing year. The way he looked at his wife made Claire's heart ache with a sudden, sharp longing. Not just for romance, but for that kind of enduring connection that elevates an ordinary life into something extraordinary.

Claire shook hands with both. "I am Claire. It's so nice to meet both of you." The couple's welcoming smiles enveloped her like a warm blanket.

Signor Rossi gestured to the board with a flourish that somehow managed to encompass not just the physical object, but the entire concept of human connection. "Take a closer look at the board."

Claire stepped closer to the board, drawn by the kaleidoscope of emotions captured on those simple receipts. Some notes were written in elegant script that danced across the paper like music made visible, others in hurried scrawls that spoke of urgent needs to be heard. Many were accompanied by small sketches like flowers that seemed to bloom right off the paper, stars that appeared to twinkle in the cafè's gentle light, abstract designs that wove between the words.

"Each one tells a story," Lucia said tenderly, coming to stand beside Claire. Her eyes held the same warmth as her husband's. Her presence carried the comforting warmth of freshly baked bread and mother's wisdom. "Some seek love, others seek healing. Some are simply reaching out to remind others they're not alone."

"In our cafè," Signore Rossi said proudly, "we have turned around the concept of caffè sospeso from a mere free coffee to a conversation and a connection between people."

Claire's eyes traced the messages, each one a window into someone else's heart. "To the stranger who finds this: May your day be as bright as your smile," one read, accompanied by a sketch of a smiling sun. Beneath it, in different handwriting: "Your kindness was the sun I needed today. Thank you for helping me remember how to smile."

"That one," Signor Rossi said, pointing to another note, "was written by a young man who had just lost his mother." His voice carried the compassionate weight of shared grief.

Lucia touched the note beneath it, her fingers delicate as butterfly wings. "And this was the response from a grandmother who had lost her son. Two strangers, connecting through their pain, helping each other heal."

Another caught Claire's eye: "Life is short. Drink the good coffee first." The response below made her feel something that she could not label: "I've been playing it safe for so long, I forgot how to taste anything real. Today, I choose courage."

Tears pricked at her eyes, blurring the words until they became watercolor impressions of hope and connection. When was the last time when she'd felt this kind of simple human connection? In the final years of her marriage, she and Mark had lived in the same house but inhabited different emotional universes, each orbit growing more distant until even their morning coffee ritual had become a silent choreography of avoidance.

Claire realized she had not paid for her espresso yet. She had read that in Italy you pay for the coffee first. She apologized for not paying earlier and made her way to the cash register. Lucia followed her, moving behind the counter with the grace of a dancer despite her years.

As she paid for her espresso, Claire felt a curious mixture of fascination and hesitation stir within her. The caffè sospeso tradition touched something deep in her soul. The idea of reaching out to a stranger, of creating connections across the void of anonymity. But a small voice inside her whispered cautions, reminders of why she had come to Naples in the first place: not to forge new relationships, but to redis-cover the person she had been before her marriage had slowly erased her.

"It's beautiful, what you've created here," she said sincerely to Lucia and Signor Rossi, her eyes drawn once more to the board with its patchwork of human experiences. "I've never seen anything quite like it."

Lucia studied Claire with those perceptive eyes that seemed to read souls rather than expressions. "The best traditions," she said gently, "are the ones that help us remember who we truly are." Her elegant hand rested briefly on Claire's hand, a touch that somehow conveyed both blessing and understanding.

Claire extended her other hand toward Lucia, the tomato nestled in her palm like a small, fragile heart. Lucia's eyes softened as she accepted the offering. No words were needed between them. The simple gesture carried within it a universe of understanding. Lucia's smile bloomed across her face, warm and genuine, a silent acknowledgment of the unspoken connection they shared.

Before Claire left, Lucia pressed a small package into her hands. A cornetto (crescent-shaped Italian pastry) still warm from the oven, its buttery scent rising like a benediction. "For later," she said with a maternal warmth that made Claire's throat tighten unexpectedly. "A little taste of Naples to accompany you." The cornetto seemed to pulse with life against her palm, a small heart of flour and butter bearing the imprint of Lucia's gentle hands, or that's how it felt.

The gesture, so simple yet so deeply nurturing, touched something fragile within Claire. As she stepped back into the golden afternoon light of Naples, the wrapped pastry warm against her palm, she felt herself walking taller, as if Lucia's kindness had somehow strengthened her spine. The city suddenly felt less foreign, its ancient stones and chaotic rhythms whispering secrets she might someday understand.

That night, sitting on her balcony with the distant lights of fishing boats dotting the bay like fallen stars, Claire thought about the caffè sospeso board. The courage it must take to reach out with words across the void, to offer a piece of yourself to a stranger. She wasn't ready for that, not yet. She had come to Naples to find herself, not to be found by someone else. But the seed of possibility had been planted, taking root somewhere deep in the soil of her soul. She recalled how each suspended coffee represented a story untold, a connection deferred, and it felt like it was waiting like the tide to pull her toward some unknown shore.

She broke off a piece of Lucia's cornetto and let it dissolve on her tongue, the sweetness a counterpoint to the salt air, wondering if the act of receiving might require its own kind of courage.

The next morning found Claire at her laptop, the balcony doors thrown open to welcome the symphony of Naples awakening. As she checked the emails, she sipped her hastily made coffee, nothing like Signor Rossi's espresso, but it would have to do. Her boss, Susan, had sent over a new project brief, a rebrand for a tech company with offices in Ohio and California.

"Perfect timing," Susan had written. "Since you're working remotely, this client shouldn't care what time zone you're in. Just make the deadlines. Your Italian adventure doesn't mean vacation from billable hours. :-)"

Claire smiled wryly. Susan's brusque manner had always concealed a genuine fondness, and she had been surprisingly supportive of Claire's decision to spend time in Naples.

Working methodically through the morning, Claire created mood boards and initial sketches for the rebrand. The company wanted something "innovative but approachable," that corporate-speak that often meant "we don't know what we want until we see it." By noon, her eyes were tired and her mind was drifting from gradient swatches to the memory of espresso crema the color of hazelnuts.

Almost without conscious decision, she found herself retracing her steps to Caffè Sereno. The small bell above the door sang its gentle welcome as she entered, and Signor Rossi looked up from his work with a smile that seemed genuinely pleased to see her.

"Bella Claire returns!" he exclaimed, his hands already moving toward the espresso machine.

"I couldn't stay away," she admitted, settling onto one of the worn wooden stools at the counter. "Nothing I make comes close to your coffee."

"The secret," he confided, leaning close as if sharing classified information, "is love. You must love the beans, love the water, love the person who will drink it." His eyes softened with the profound warmth that comes only from decades of nurturing others. "Even the machine can tell the difference. It responds to the hands that truly care."

As Claire savored her perfectly crafted espresso, her gaze wandered again to the cork board. New notes had appeared since yesterday, new connections formed between strangers who might pass each other on Naples' streets without ever knowing how their words had touched one another.

The thought both thrilled and terrified her. How long had it been since she had truly opened herself? The final years of her marriage had been exercises in withdrawal, in protective isolation. Even before Mark's betrayal, they had stopped truly seeing each other, becoming instead performers in a carefully choreographed play about a marriage rather than partners in the messy, beautiful reality of one.

Lucia's dark eyes studied Claire with the careful insight of a woman who had spent decades reading the unspoken needs in others. Perhaps it was the slight pallor beneath Claire's sun-kissed cheeks, or the way she seemed to sway ever so slightly, like a flower too long without water. But Lucia saw what Claire herself had ignored.

"Cara mia (my dear)," Lucia said, her voice carrying the warmth of fresh bread just pulled from the oven, "Perhaps you need some lovingly prepared comfort food?" The observation flowed with such gentle grace that Claire felt tears welling in her eyes, touched by this near-stranger's ability to see and nurture with such intuitive precision.

Without waiting for an answer, Lucia exchanged a look with her husband, their decades of marriage allowing them to communicate volumes in a single glance. The love between them seemed to fill the space like golden light, washing over Claire with its healing warmth.

"You must try Lucia's eggplant parmigiana," Signor Rossi declared, his voice filled with the particular pride of a man who had spent a lifetime watching his wife create miracles in their kitchen. "The best in all of Naples." His eyes sparkled with joy as he added, "And perhaps a little plate of tiramisu? It makes the angels themselves weep with envy."

Before Claire could protest, Lucia had disappeared into the kitchen, trailing the scent of warmth and comfort in her wake. She returned moments later bearing a large and a small plate that seemed to contain all the love and nurturing Claire had been missing in her life, without even knowing it. The tiramisu glistened in the afternoon light, its delicious layers promising sweetness and comfort, while the eggplant parmigiana released an aroma that made her core ache with a longing she couldn't quite name.

"No, no," Lucia insisted when Claire reached for her wallet, pressing her hand back with warm firmness. "This is not for paying. This is for nourishing." Her eyes held Claire's with understanding that went soul-deep.

The eggplant parmigiana tasted of Italian summers and family gatherings, of traditions passed down through generations of men and women who understood that food was just another way to say 'I love you,' 'I see you,' 'You are not alone.' The first bite of tiramisu melted on Claire's tongue like butter kissed by sunshine.

Watching her eat, Lucia and Signor Rossi shared another of their silent conversations, their faces glowing with the particular joy of those who understand what the greatest act of love is. In their warmth, Claire felt something inside her unlock. Another door opening, another wall crumbling, another step toward becoming whole again in this city where strangers could become family in the space of an afternoon, over shared food and understanding.

As Claire finished the last bites of her meal, she noticed Signor Rossi gesturing emphatically, his voice raised in passionate Italian as he pointed to something in the pastry case. Lucia responded with equal fervor, her elegant hands painting elaborate punctuation in the air between them.

Claire blinked, startled by this sudden storm in the usually serene café. Other patrons merely glanced up, then returned to their conversations or newspapers with the casual indifference of those accustomed to such displays.

The argument, if that's what it was, continued to escalate, neither party showing signs of yielding. Though Claire couldn't understand the words, the emotional cadence was unmistakable. Finally, Signor Rossi threw up his hands in a gesture of exaggerated despair and turned to Claire.

"You," he declared, switching to English, his finger pointing directly at her. "You must be the judge. My wife insists that the sea salt should be sprinkled on the chocolate torte only at the moment of serving. Never before! I say that for busy times, we can add it an hour in advance, just one small hour! Who is right?"

Claire was caught off-guard by being suddenly thrust into the role of culinary arbiter. Both Rossis were looking at her expectantly, their argument momentarily suspended in anticipation of her verdict.

"I, um..." She glanced from one to the other, buying time. "I don't think I'm qualified to..."

"Nonsense!" Signor Rossi interrupted. "You have taste, no? You have eyes? You can judge!"

Lucia appeared beside her, depositing two identical slices of chocolate torte on a small plate. "Taste," she commanded. "The left one has salt from this morning, sprinkled by him. Right one, I just now sprinkled with love, as it should be." Her stern expression was belied by the affectionate glance she cast at her husband.

Claire obediently took a bite of each, considering carefully. The difference was subtle but unmistakable. On the freshly salted slice, the delicate crystals retained their crunch against the velvet chocolate, creating a perfect harmony of textures and flavors. On the other, though still delicious, the salt had begun to dissolve, its brightness slightly dimmed.

"They're both delicious," she began diplomatically, "but the freshly salted one is definitely superior. The salt crystals still have their perfect texture."

Signor Rossi threw his hands up again, this time in defeat, while Lucia bestowed a triumphant smile upon Claire. "You see?" she crowed to her husband. "She understands quality!"

To Claire's surprise, Signor Rossi's melodramatic despair vanished in an instant, replaced by a look of such adoration directed at his wife that Claire had to glance away, feeling as if she'd intruded on an intimate moment. He captured Lucia's hand, pressing a fervent kiss to her knuckles. "My queen of the kitchen," he declared, "as always, you are right."

Lucia's laughter bubbled up like music. "I don't know why, but he still thinks he needs to provide me instructions in cooking," she confided to Claire with a wink.

Claire couldn't help smiling at the beautiful choreography of their marriage, disguised as an argument but revealing itself as love. It was so different from the cold silences and carefully modulated discussions that had characterized her final years with Mark.

"Will you return tomorrow?" Lucia asked as Claire prepared to leave. "We have Torta Caprese tomorrow. It's a flourless chocolate almond cake that melts in your mouth."

"I wouldn't miss it," Claire promised, realizing with a small start of surprise that she meant it. In just two days, this warm café with its passionate proprietors had become something of an anchor in her new Neapolitan life.

True to her word, Claire returned the next day, and the next, Caffè Sereno becoming a daily ritual in her new Naples rhythm. Each day, Lucia presented her with some new delight from the kitchen. A slice of gattò di patat (a savory potato cake made with eggs and cheese), a perfect piece of Torta Rustica (Italian savory pie), a miniature babà (Neapolitan dessert with yeasted sponge cake soaked in a sweet rum syrup). Each offering came with a story of the dish's origins, of the particular region of Italy from which it hailed.

Each day, too, Claire found her gaze drawn to the caffè sospeso board, watching as new notes appeared and disappeared. She studied the handwriting, the choice of words, the small sketches that sometimes accompanied the messages. Some were playful, others deeply philosophical; some seemed to be reaching for romance, others for simple human connection in a disconnected world.

And each day, she considered, but did not yet act on, the possibility of participating herself. The thought simultaneously thrilled and terrified her. She had come to Naples to find herself, not to lose herself in new connections before she had even reestablished who she was on her own.

As the days passed, Claire found herself falling into a new rhythm, her life in Naples taking on shape beyond mere tourism. Mornings were for work; answering emails, creating designs for Susan's clients, participating in video conferences where her colleagues marveled at the ancient beams visible in her apartment's ceiling. Afternoons often found her wandering the streets of this vibrant city that was slowly working its magic on her wounded spirit.

At the beginning of her second week in Naples, Claire found herself once again at Caffè Sereno, savoring her afternoon espresso while working on her laptop. The familiar warmth of the café had become a comfort in this still-strange city, and Signor Rossi's friendly presence behind the counter made her feel less adrift in her new life.

"Bella Claire!" Signor Rossi called, waving her over as she prepared to leave. His weathered face creased with a smile that reached his eyes. "There is someone you must meet."

He gestured toward a young woman sitting at a corner table surrounded by stacks of papers. "This is Daniella Esposito, daughter of my good friends. Daniella, this is Claire, the American designer I told you about."

The woman rose gracefully, a cascade of black curls framing a face that transformed completely when she smiled. She was perhaps in her mid-twenties, with intelligent dark eyes that sparkled with immediate interest.

"So you're the graphic designer Signor Rossi has been praising!" Daniella extended her hand, her English accented but fluent. The enthusiasm in her voice seemed to flow through their handshake like an electric current. "He mentioned you're working remotely while living here."

"That's right," Claire replied, somehow finding it easy to meet the younger woman's gaze despite her usual reserve with strangers. "I'm taking some time to..." she hesitated, unsure how to explain her divorce, her need to rediscover herself, her impulsive decision to restart her life in a foreign country.

"To reinvent yourself?" Daniella suggested softly, with such intuitive understanding that Claire found herself nodding.

"Then we have something in common," Daniella said, gesturing for Claire to join her. "I'm trying to reinvent something too." She swept her hand across the papers on the table. There were photographs of storefronts, spreadsheets, and handwritten notes. "My family owns eight flower shops across Naples and the surrounding areas. Beautiful flowers, terrible branding." She rolled her eyes affectionately. "My parents are wonderful florists but terrible at business?"

"I've just completed my business degree, and they've finally allowed me to take over operations. Everything needs modernization like website, logo, unified design across all locations. But every designer I've met wants to make it all..." she waved her hands expressively, "...too stereotypically Italian. Too cliché. I need someone with fresh eyes!"

Before Claire quite knew what was happening, she had agreed to meet Daniella the next day to discuss the potential project further. She recalled Susan mentioning she would have independent contractor status with freedom to take on other clients if she wanted. As they exchanged contact information, Daniella's enthusiasm was as warming as the Naples sun.

"This is perfect timing," she declared. "You need to find yourself, I need to find a new direction for my family business. We help each other, yes?"

That night, as Claire created a preliminary mood board for Daniella's family business, she realized that she hadn't thought about Mark all day. The realization came with a startling lightness, as if a weight she had been carrying for so long had begun to dissolve without her even noticing its departure.

The following days brought a whirlwind of activity as Claire and Daniella collaborated on reinventing the Esposito family flower business. The work was challenging and satisfying in equal measure. A welcome change from the sometimes soulless corporate rebrands that had dominated her portfolio in recent years. Daniella's family embraced her with typical Italian warmth, her father presenting her with a fresh bouquet every time she visited their flagship shop, her grandmother insisting she stay for meals that stretched for hours, filled with laughter and stories she could only partly understand.

Through Daniella, Claire found herself introduced to a wider circle of Naples' citizens. Young entrepreneurs at a busy crossroads between honoring traditions and embracing innovation. They gathered at cafés and wine bars, at family dinners and impromptu rooftop gatherings, their conversations flowing between Italian and English with the easy cadence of those accustomed to living between cultures.

"You must meet Alessandra," Daniella declared one evening, introducing Claire to a woman with an elegant silver bob and penetrating eyes. "She owns the most beautiful ceramics shop in Naples, and her website is practically ancient history! She needs your magic touch."

And so Claire found herself with a second client, then a third. Small businesses owned by people who quickly became more than clients, who invited her into their homes and their lives with an openness that both startled and healed her. With each new connection, each successful project, she felt herself growing stronger, more assured, remembering the woman she had been before marriage had slowly eroded her confidence.

Through it all, her daily visits to Caffè Sereno remained a constant, a touchstone in her rapidly evolving life. Signor Rossi and Lucia greeted her each day as if her arrival completed their happiness, feeding her both physically and spiritually with their food and their unconditional acceptance.

"You look different today," Lucia observed one late afternoon during Claire's third week, as she placed a slice of crostata di albicocche (apricot jam tart) before her. "Something has changed in your eyes."

Claire smiled, realizing the truth in Lucia's words. "I think," she said slowly, "I'm starting to remember who I am."

Lucia nodded sagely, as if this was exactly what she had expected. "Naples has this effect," she said. "This city, she does not allow you to hide from yourself for long. Too much life, too much history, too much beauty and pain all mixed together. It demands that you live authentically."

Signor Rossi, polishing glasses behind the counter, added his own observation. "When you first came in," he said, his hands never stilling in their work, "you had the look of someone who had forgotten how to feel the sunlight on your skin. Now, I see the warmth beginning to return to your eyes."

His words struck Claire with their simple truth. When had she started accepting diluted experiences, watered-down emotions, a life lived in the muted tones of compromise rather than the vivid colors of authenticity?

As the third week of her Naples sojourn drew to a close, Claire found herself once again standing before the caffè sospeso board, studying the dance of connections between strangers brave enough to reach each other. Her fingers traced the edges of one particularly beautiful exchange. A note about feeling lost in a familiar city, accompanied by a sketch of a labyrinth, and the response below it that spoke of finding unexpected treasures precisely when one was most thoroughly lost.

Claire paused for a moment, recognizing that something had shifted within her, a subtle but profound realignment of her inner compass. The woman who had arrived in Naples three weeks ago, raw with betrayal, uncertain of her place in the world, seeking only to lick her wounds in private, had begun to transform. Naples, with its unapologetic embracing of life in all its messy glory, had worked its magic on her battered spirit.

She turned to find Signor Rossi watching her with knowing eyes, as if he had been waiting for this moment all along.

"Today," she said, her voice stronger than she had expected, "I think I'd like to buy caffè sospeso (a suspended coffee)."

His smile bloomed slowly, like a father's watching his child graduate high school after years of struggles. "I was wondering when you would be ready," he said simply, moving to the register with the proud bearing of one who witnesses small victories every day and understands their significance.

Lucia appeared as if conjured by the moment's importance, her elegant hands already producing the fountain pen that Claire had admired during her first visit. "The heart knows when it is time to reach out," she said softly. "Not before, not after."

The receipt felt different in Claire's hand now. No longer just a piece of paper, but a bridge waiting to be built, a connection waiting to be forged. The café had quieted, as if holding its breath in anticipation of this moment, the late afternoon sunlight streaming through the windows.

Claire's hand moved across the paper with a certainty born of redis-covered self-knowledge:

"To the stranger who finds this coffee waiting: I'm learning to believe in second chances. In the way light finds its way through even the smallest cracks in our carefully constructed walls. Maybe you're also learning how to believe that sometimes the bravest thing we can do is simply take that first step toward connection and hope someone responds. This coffee comes with permission, to dream, to believe, to begin again, Claire."

The words glistened on the paper, still wet, as Claire read over what she had written. They felt both deeply personal and somehow universal, like a song that belongs to everyone who's ever felt its truth in their bones.

Lucia accepted the receipt with reverence, her eyes meeting Claire's with understanding that transcended words. She placed the receipt in the glass jar with ceremonial gravity, as if adding a precious gem to a collection of treasures.

"Now," Signor Rossi said softly as Claire's note settled among its companions in the glass jar, "we wait. And we trust that the right reader will find their way to your words."

The walk back to the apartment through Naples' labyrinthine streets felt different now, as if her small act of courage at Caffè Sereno had shifted something fundamental in the universe. The early evening light painted everything in shades of promises. The weathered stones glowing like aged gold, the shadows between buildings holding secrets just waiting to be discovered, the sky above a watercolor masterpiece of rose and lavender.

When she reached her apartment building, she paused before the massive blue door, looking up at her balcony where the bougainvillea spilled over the railing like a cascade of fuchsia stars. Four flights up, but it felt like she was ascending to more than just a temporary home. Each step carried her further from the woman who had lived a careful, measured life in Ohio, and closer to someone new. Someone who left notes for strangers and drank espresso standing at bars and believed, just maybe, in the possibility of magic.

The evening breeze carried the sound of distant church bells as she unlocked her door, their bronze voices counting moments that felt heavy with potential. Inside, the apartment welcomed her with the golden warmth of sunset streaming through the lace curtains, turning mundane objects into things of beauty. The simple white cups in the kitchen catching fire like alabaster, the terra cotta tiles glowing like embers, the mirror reflecting back a woman she was just beginning to recognize.

She moved to the balcony, drawn by some instinct deeper than thought. In the distance the bay stretched out like liquid sapphire, catching the last rays of sun in diamonds of light that seemed to wink conspiratorially, as if the sea itself knew secrets about her future that she had yet to discover. Mount Vesuvius brooded on the horizon, a shadowy colossus draped in evening mist, while below, Naples throbbed with vitality, brimming and spilling over with energy.

Her hands still carried the phantom sensation of writing that note, of putting her heart on paper for a stranger to find. Would they understand what those words had cost her? Would they feel what's beneath the careful script, the desire to believe in second chances and new beginnings?

"To the stranger who claims this coffee..." she voiced to the evening air, tasting the words again like the lingering notes of that perfect espresso. Somewhere out there, her message waited in Caffè Sereno's glass jar. Tomorrow, or the next day, or the day after that, someone would read those words and...

As twilight draped its violet shawl across Naples, Claire curled into the antique chair on her balcony, letting the evening embrace her like a lover's arms. The city below had changed into its nighttime rhythm. A slower, more sensual tempo that made her think of dancers swaying to music only they could hear. The air was thick with the mingled scents of jasmine, sea salt, and a hundred different dinners being prepared in the apartments and restaurants around her.

She closed her eyes, letting the day's memories wash over her like waves on the shore. The warmth of Signor Rossi's smile, the way his eyes had crinkled at the corners with generations of accumulated kindness. The nurturing expressed without words in Lucia's actions. The perfect bitter-sweet kiss of that espresso on her tongue. The feel of that fountain pen in her hand as she'd poured herself onto paper, each word a small act of defiance against the careful, controlled existence she'd left behind.

"I'm starting over," she announced to the gathering darkness, the words carrying a weight she hadn't felt when writing the note. Starting over. Such simple words for such an enormous thing. Like diving into deep water without knowing its true depth. Or like stepping onto a path without seeing where it leads, trusting only that each step forward takes you somewhere new, somewhere waiting just for you.

A shooting star streaked across the darkening sky with a brief flash of silver. In her past life, she would have made a wish. Something safe and sensible, the kind of wish that wouldn't disappoint when it didn't come true. But here, in this city where enchantment seemed to seep from the very stones, she found herself wanting more. Wanting everything.

From somewhere in the warren of streets below came the sound of a man's laughter, rich and deep, followed by a woman's musical response. The sounds twined together in the evening air like lovers' hands clasping, making Claire's heart twist with a longing she hadn't allowed herself to feel in so long. Not just for romance, though yes, that too, but for connection. For the kind of love that made you laugh like that, as if joy was something too big to keep inside your body.

The moon had risen now, its silver turning the bay into a magical mirror. Claire watched its light paint the world in shades of pearl and shadow, transforming Naples into something out of a fairy tale. Maybe that's what she was living now. Her own fairy tale, not the kind with guaranteed happy endings and prince charmings, but the older, wilder kind, where metamorphosis came at a price.

In the velvet darkness of her new bedroom, Claire lay awake, her body still humming with the electricity of the day's small brave acts. The sheets conspiring quietly against her skin, cool cotton that smelled of lavender, as she turned to watch the play of moonlight on the ancient walls. Each beam seemed to paint pictures in the darkness: here a face, there a flower, now what looked like words in a language too beautiful to read.

Through her half-open balcony doors, she could hear the distant sound of someone singing. A man's voice, rich and unself-conscious, serenading the night with what sounded like an old Neapolitan love song. The melody wrapped around her like silk, making her skin prickle with awareness of all the love stories unfolding in this ancient city, beating with their own complex rhythms of desire and fear, aspiration and hesitation.

She pressed a hand to her own heart, feeling its steady pulse beneath her palm. How long had it been since she'd really listened to its rhythms? Since she'd allowed herself to want something wilder and more beautiful than the careful contentment she'd settled for?

The last time she'd written a love note, she'd been in her mid-twenties, slipping it into Mark's jacket pocket during their first year of dating. She'd spent hours crafting those words, trying to capture the dizzy joy of new love. Now she wondered if that note still existed somewhere, folded and forgotten in a box of memories neither of them had wanted to claim in the divorce.

But today's note felt different. More honest, somehow. She'd written it not from a place of certainty, but from that tender space between broken and healing, where hope feels like both a gift and a risk. "This coffee comes with permission, to dream, to believe, to begin again," she'd written, and in the darkness of her Naples bedroom, she finally allowed herself to fully feel the weight of those words.

The morning after leaving her the note in the suspended coffee jar, Claire woke to sunlight painting golden patterns on her bedroom wall, the distant sounds of Naples already rising into a symphony of life. For a fleeting moment, she thought of checking Caffè Sereno immediately to see if anyone had claimed her note, but she pushed the impulse aside. She had work to finish for Daniella's family business; the first round of logo concepts was due for review, and she wanted to give them the attention they deserved.

The morning passed in a blur of creative focus, her computer screen filling with variations of floral imagery rendered in contemporary styles that honored the Esposito family's history while pointing toward a fresh future. By early afternoon, she had sent the concepts to Daniella and stretched, feeling the satisfying ache of work well done.

Her phone chimed with a message from Daniella almost immediately: "These are PERFECT! Papa is dancing around the shop! Can we meet at 4 to discuss next steps?"

The validation warmed her more than she had expected. Not just for her work, but for her growing sense that she was building something real here in Naples, something that extended beyond the temporary escape she had initially planned.

Before her meeting with Daniella, Claire found herself drawn once again to Caffè Sereno. The small bell above the door sang its familiar welcome as she entered Caffè Sereno. Signor Rossi looked up from where he was arranging cups, his face breaking into that now-familiar smile.

"Ah, Bella Claire! You return!" His eyes twinkled with knowing mischief. "Perhaps to check if there is news from your note?"

Heat rose to her cheeks as she nodded, unable to deny her curiosity. Her gaze went immediately to the glass jar, searching for the receipt with her handwriting. A small thrill coursed through her when she couldn't spot it among the other waiting notes.

Signor Rossi's smile deepened as he gestured toward the cork board. "This morning," he said, his voice dropping to a conspiratorial whisper, "very early, before even the sun was fully awake. Someone claimed your coffee."

Claire's heart performed an unexpected somersault beneath her ribs as she approached the board. And there it was. Her note, pinned in the center of the board. Beneath her words, in an elegant handwriting that somehow managed to look both strong and vulnerable at once, was a response written in ink the deep blue of the Mediterranean at twilight. Beside the words, in the margin, was a small sketch of a sunflower seeking light not yet visible in the frame, its petals unfurling with a yearning that made Claire feel an ache deep within her.

"To the stranger seeking second chances," the note began, the words seeming to pulse with their own heartbeat. "Your words found me in a moment when I too was searching for courage to begin again. They say Naples has no patience for half-measures; this city demands that we either dive deep or stay on shore. Thank you for diving first. The water feels less frightening knowing someone else is already swimming. I drew this sunflower because, like you, I'm learning to turn my face toward light I cannot yet see. May we both find the courage to bloom, even when the sun hides behind clouds. - L"

A single tear splashed onto the paper before Claire even realized. In L's carefully crafted response, in the vulnerable courage of that reaching sunflower, she found an echo of her own longing for renewal, for connection, for the chance to become something beautiful again.

"L," she whispered, tracing the initial with a fingertip. One letter, containing the beginning of a story, perhaps, or merely a moment of connection in a city that seemed to specialize in weaving together the breakable threads of chance and courage.

Claire wasn't sure how long she stood there, absorbing the words and the artistry of that simple sketch, before Lucia appeared at her elbow with an espresso that she hadn't ordered.

"For moments of discovery," Lucia said simply, her dark eyes warm with understanding, "a little celebration is necessary, no?"

After savoring both the perfect espresso and the words of her mysterious correspondent, Claire accepted a blank paper from Signor Rossi and the antique fountain pen Lucia offered. The note flowed from her heart:

"Dear L, Your sunflower speaks to something in my soul that's been waiting to be named. I understand Naples demands courage from those who seek her embrace. The courage to feel deeply, to live fully, to love without reservation. Your art touches places in me I thought had gone silent, like finding music in rooms I'd forgotten existed. Perhaps we're both learning to bloom again, like your sunflower, turning our faces toward warmth we can only yet imagine. In this city where every shadow holds enchantment and every ray of light carries magic, maybe we can remember together how to spread our wings. With growing courage, Claire"

Beside her words, her hand moved with newfound certainty, creating an image that seemed to flow effortlessly through her fingers. A bird taking flight from an open window, its wings spread wide against a sky filled with stars. Each line she drew felt like truth, like confession, like a revelation.

Signor Rossi handed her a pin with a knowing smile. "The dance begins," he said simply as she posted the new note along with the original coffee receipt on the cork board.

The weeks that followed took on a rhythm new and yet somehow familiar, like a song heard long ago that suddenly returns to memory. Throughout these days, Claire called home to her parents, grandmother, Kate, sharing vivid snippets of her new life while carefully stepping around any mention of L. Each omission left a hollow ache in her chest, this precious secret too fragile for their well-intended but uncomprehending ears.

Claire's life expanded to fill the space Naples offered her. Mornings of work at the sun-drenched desk in her apartment, afternoons meeting with her growing roster of clients or exploring the city's hidden corners, evenings spent on her balcony, enjoying the changing light on ancient buildings.

And woven through it all, like a silken thread binding her days together, was the correspondence with the mysterious L.

Their notes were not exchanged daily; sometimes several days would pass before Claire found a response waiting on the board, or before she had time to return to Caffè Sereno to check for one. But each message deepened the connection, each exchange revealing a little more of the souls reaching toward each other through words and art.

From L's notes, Claire gleaned fragments of a life: someone creative, thoughtful, who had known both joy and sorrow; someone who, like her, was in the process of rebuilding, of remembering how to trust in possibilities. The art that accompanied each message spoke volumes. Small, exquisite sketches of doors standing ajar, of stars emerging after storm clouds, of hands reaching across empty space.

In turn, Claire found herself sharing more than she had intended. Not just hopes and philosophical musings, but small, specific details of her days. She wrote about the colors of sunrise over the bay, about the elderly tailor who had stopped her on the street to compliment her dress, about the stray cat that had adopted her balcony as an afternoon resting spot. She surprised herself with the candor of her words, with how easily vulnerability flowed through her pen onto those simple coffee receipts.

"I wonder who you are," she wrote in one note, accompanied by a sketch of a masquerade mask half-lifted. "Not your name or what you do, but who you are in those quiet moments when no one is watching. The person beneath the roles we all play. I'm still discovering who I am when I'm not being someone's daughter, someone's colleague, some-one's friend. Just me. Just Claire."

The response, found three days later when she returned from a day trip to Pompeii, carried a sketch of a person looking at their reflection in a pool of water, the reflection showing not a face but a constellation of stars:

"Dear Claire, Identity is such a curious thing, isn't it? We think we know who we are, and then life removes a piece, a relationship, a job, a home, and suddenly we're strangers to ourselves. I've been relearning who I am beyond the labels and roles that once defined me. Perhaps we're not meant to be any one fixed thing, but rather a constant becom-ing, like Naples herself, ancient and new in the same breath. I find comfort in that thought. Looking for the stars within, L"

Another time, after Claire had spent a frustrating day dealing with one of Susan's clients who wanted endless revisions to her design work, she poured her exasperation onto the receipt:

"Dear L, Do you ever have days when it feels like the world is determined to misunderstand you? When your vision seems so clear in your mind, but translating it for others feels like trying to describe color to someone who's never seen it? Today was such a day. I'm learning that sometimes the gap between what we imagine and what others perceive might never be fully bridged. And yet, we keep trying, don't we? Because the alternative is silence, and that seems far worse. Seeking clarity, Claire"

The answer came swiftly, appearing on the board the very next morning:

"Dear Claire, Your words about the gap between vision and perception resonated deeply. As an artist, I live in that space of translation, trying to make visible what exists first only in my mind. Perhaps the beauty lies not in perfect understanding, but in the attempt itself. In reaching across that void between minds, between hearts. Like what we're doing here, with these notes. Not perfect communication, but authentic trying. And isn't that the most human thing of all? In solidarity, L"

This time, the sketch showed two hands almost touching across a divide, reminiscent of Michelangelo's Creation of Adam, but with something luminous flowing between the fingertips despite the gap.

As their correspondence continued, Claire found herself looking for L everywhere she went in Naples. Was it the distinguished man sketching at a café near the harbor? The brooding artist with charcoal-smudged hands arranging his paintings at the weekend market? The middle-aged professor-type browsing art books in the small bookshop near her apartment? Each possibility brought a flutter of curiosity, but also a strange contentment with the mystery. There was something pure about knowing someone only through their words and art, untainted by the complications of the physical world.

The ebb and flow of their correspondence was interrupted when Daniella's family asked Claire to accompany them to Rome for three days to meet with a potential investor in their expanded business. She agreed readily, excited by both the opportunity and the change of scene.

Rome was magnificent, overwhelming in its layered history and grandeur in ways that differed from Naples' more chaotic charm. But throughout her time there, Claire found herself thinking of Caffè Sereno, wondering if L had left a new note, if they were perhaps wondering about her absence.

On her return to Naples, she went directly from the train station to the café, her small overnight bag still in hand. Signor Rossi and Lucia welcomed her as if she'd been gone for months rather than days, exclaiming over her slightly sunburned nose and insisting she sit while they prepared a special welcome-home treat.

"Someone was looking for you," Lucia said mysteriously as she placed a plate of tiny almond cookies before Claire. "They asked if the American with the beautiful notes had stopped coming."

Claire's heart performed an elaborate dance beneath her ribs. "L?" she asked, unable to keep the eagerness from her voice.

Lucia's eyes twinkled. "Who can say? They did not leave their name. But..." she gestured toward the board, "they left something."

There, pinned where their previous exchanges had been, was a new note. The sketch this time was of a calendar page with several days circled, a tiny question mark hovering above them.

"Dear Claire, The café feels different without your notes. I find myself checking the board more often than I should admit, wondering if you've returned from wherever life has taken you. Naples holds her breath, waiting for your words. Missing our conversation, L"

The simple admission of missing her, or at least missing their exchange, sent a warm current flowing through Claire's veins. She reached for a fresh paper, her pen moving swiftly across the paper:

"Dear L, I've been in Rome for a few days on a business trip that was both exhilarating and exhausting. The Eternal City is magnificent, but I found myself thinking of Naples, of this café, of our conversations. Strange how quickly new rituals become essential, isn't it? How people we've never properly met can become important to us. Rome made me think about time; how we're all just brief moments in the long story of these ancient places. And yet, those moments matter. These words matter. You and I, reaching across space and circumstance to connect, that matters. Glad to be back, Claire"

This time, her sketch showed a tiny hourglass with stars instead of sand flowing through it, each one leaving a trail of light in its wake.

Two months after arriving in Naples, Claire welcomed her first summer in the ancient city. Claire's once-pale fingers now confidently gripped her espresso cup. The pages of the journal Dr. Sullivan had given her as a parting gift, initially filled with hesitant observations and transient feelings, now brimmed with spontaneous thoughts and Italian phrases she no longer needed to double-check.

Naples had worked her magic on Claire's wounded spirit, and the woman who had arrived broken and hesitant had begun to knit herself back together into something new, something stronger. The city, with its vibrant contradictions and unapologetic embrace of life in all its messy glory, had become not just a temporary escape but a catalyst for profound transformation.

Her work had flourished as well. What had begun with Daniella's family business had expanded into a small but thriving freelance practice separate from her remote work for Susan. Word had spread among Naples' small business community about the American designer with fresh eyes and a deep appreciation for Italian aesthetics, leading to a steady stream of projects that both challenged and fulfilled her.

One afternoon, as she sat in Caffè Sereno reviewing design proofs for a local restaurant's menu, Claire's gaze drifted to the cork board where her most recent note to L was still pinned, awaiting a response. In the five weeks since her first hesitant note on the suspended coffee receipt, their correspondence had woven an intricate tapestry of thoughts, dreams, and growing trust. Though they had never met, she felt connected to this stranger in ways that defied explanation.

"Thank you," she said to Signor Rossi, her words carrying weight beyond the simple courtesies of café interaction. "For this," she gestured to the cork board, "for... everything. For creating this space where magic can happen."

His eyes held a depth of understanding. "In Naples," he said gently, "we understand that the most important connections are those of the soul. Everything else, names, faces, circumstances; these are just details."

Outside, the afternoon sun bathed Naples in amber light, turning the ancient buildings to gold and the shadows to velvet. Claire walked with the easy confidence of someone who had claimed this city as her own, no longer a tourist but someone who belonged.

Tomorrow would bring a new design project for a local gelato shop, another Italian lesson with her neighbor upstairs, perhaps another note from the mysterious L. But tonight, sitting beneath the vast Naples sky with its scattered diamonds of stars, Claire felt something she had almost forgotten how to feel: anticipation. Not anxiety about what might go wrong, but genuine excitement about what might go right.

As the first hint of dawn found Claire still awake, her body exhausted but her mind electric with possibility. She watched as night surrendered to morning, the darkness slowly dissolving, revealing Naples in shades of dusty pink and rose gold. The alchemy reminded her of developing photographs in a darkroom. The way images emerge gradually, each detail a revelation.

Rising from bed, she padded to the balcony. The air held that mystical quality unique to early morning, when the world feels newly made and anything seems possible. Below, Naples was beginning to stir. Street sweepers moving in meditative rhythm, early risers hurrying to catch trains or boats, mothers dragging children to school.

Her fingers itched to paint this moment. The way the first sunlight caught the dome of the distant church, turning its weathered copper to liquid fire. The mist rising from the bay and the shadows retreating into corners as if shy of the approaching day. When was the last time she'd felt this urge to paint so strongly? Art had been another casualty of her marriage, relegated to "someday" along with so many other dreams.

It was time to return to Caffè Sereno, to see if L had responded to her last note.

Standing in front of the cork board, she searched in vain for a response from L. She turned to where Lucia and Signor Rossi were watching her with compassionate understanding, her voice quivering like a delicate violin string.

"Tell me," she asked, the question drifting through the coffee-scented air between them, "did they... I mean, did L come here since my last note?"

Signor Rossi and Lucia shared one of their silent conversations, their eyes meeting in the mirror behind the counter, decades of love allowing them to speak without words. "Ah, the mysteries of Naples must unfold in their own time, Claire," Lucia said finally, her voice compassionate as a mother soothing her eager child.

Through the windows, the sun painted cobblestones amber and pearl, turning the ancient street into a pathway leading everywhere and nowhere at once. A young girl in a polka-dotted dress skipped past, her dark curls bouncing in rhythm with her steps, trailing a red balloon that danced against the azure sky. The sight inspired Claire with renewed purpose.

Without thinking, Claire reached for a napkin on the counter, her fingers tingling with a familiar urgency she hadn't felt in years. Before she could stop herself, she was sketching. Quick, confident strokes capturing the girl's joyful abandon, the balloon's defiant dance against the endless sky. The simple white napkin transformed beneath her touch, becoming a window into a moment of pure joy.

Signor Rossi paused in his work, watching her hands move across the napkin with the kind of reverence reserved for witnessing small miracles. "Ah," he said softly, "you have the gift."

Claire felt heat rise to her cheeks, suddenly self-conscious of this impulsive act. Her fingers stilled on the napkin, leaving the sketch slightly unfinished. "I used to," she admitted, her voice carrying the weight of years spent suppressing this essential part of herself. "Before I got married, I was an artist. I drew, painted..." She traced the edge of the napkin with a fingertip, remembering the feel of a brush in her hand, the scent of oil paints, the meditative peace of losing herself in creation.

"Used to?" Signor Rossi's voice held a gentle challenge. "No, I think the fire inside an artist never dies; it only sleeps, waiting for the right moment to ignite." He studied her sketch with knowing eyes. "Like a seed in winter soil. And now, perhaps, it is the end of winter for your art."

Looking down at the sketch, Claire felt something stir in her chest, like wings unfolding, like flowers reaching for light. The simple lines captured not just the girl's form but her essence, that pure, uncontained joy that Claire herself had almost forgotten how to feel.

"You know," Signor Rossi said, polishing a cup with careful attention, his voice taking on the tone of sharing a beautiful secret, "there is a woman, Agostina, who owns a little art supply shop just two streets over. It's called 'Bottega dei Colori' (Workshop of Colors)." His eyes crinkled with warm understanding. "Perhaps it's time to give yourself the tools to wake up the artist within you. Tell her I sent you. She will understand and will help you."

Claire somehow felt like a butterfly. The thought of holding proper art supplies again, of allowing herself to create without apology... it felt both thrilling and frightening, like standing on the edge of a cliff and finally, finally remembering she had wings.

Stepping out of Caffè Sereno, with the napkin in her hand, into the embracing warmth of the Neapolitan morning felt like emerging from a cocoon. The world seemed to shimmer with newfound vibrancy, as if L's artistic soul had somehow awakened Claire's dormant ability to see beauty in every shadow, every shaft of light, every face that passed her by.

Through the morning crowd, Claire spotted them again. The young girl in her polka-dotted dress, still trailing that red balloon like a captured star, her mother's protective hand resting gently on her shoulder. Before her mind could talk her heart out of it, Claire felt her feet moving forward, drawn by some force stronger than her usual hesitation. This wasn't the careful, controlled woman from Ohio. This was someone new, one who understood that sometimes the most profound connections begin with a simple act of courage.

Though words failed them as Claire offered the napkin sketch, something deeper than language passed between the two women. An understanding, a sharing of that perfect moment when childhood wonder had transformed an everyday street into something magical. The little girl clapped her hands in delight, recognizing herself in those simple strokes, while her mother's grateful smile confirmed that the most meaningful gifts are the ones we give without expectation of return.

Following Signor Rossi's directions, Claire wound her way through the maze of streets that seemed to reveal ancient secrets with every step. She kept returning to L. Who was this mysterious artist who reached across paper and time to touch her? The question danced in her mind like light on water, each thought more intriguing than the last.

The little art shop announced itself with a gorgeous window display. Handmade sketchbooks bound in leather the color of aged wine, pristine watercolor papers arranged like fallen clouds, pencils and brushes standing at attention like soldiers ready for creative battle. The sign above read "Bottega dei Colori" in faded gold letters that had witnessed decades of artists finding their way home.

A small bell, so different from Caffè Sereno's gentle chime, yet equally welcoming, announced her entrance. The shop's interior embraced her with the scent of paper, of graphite, of paints. Shelves lined the walls like a library of creative potential, each one holding tools that could metamorphose blank pages into windows to the soul.

"Buongiorno!" called a voice that seemed to contain all the warmth of Italian hospitality. From behind a counter appeared a woman who could only be Agostina. Silver hair swept up in an elegant twist, eyes bright with the particular wisdom of someone who had spent a lifetime helping others find their creative voice. Her flowing dress was splattered with small spots of paint that looked less like accidents and more like intentional acts of creativity.

"Signor Rossi sent me," Claire said, her voice catching slightly on the words, as if even her throat understood the magnitude of this moment. "I need... I want to start drawing again."

Agostina's smile deepened, creating a map of joy lines around her eyes that made Claire want to capture them in charcoal and light. "Ah," she said softly, coming around the counter and giving Claire a warm hug, "you have the eyes of someone who has found their way back to themselves."

The morning light filtered through Bottega dei Colori's dusty windows, catching motes of creativity that danced in the air between ancient wooden shelves. Agostina moved through her domain with the grace of a priestess tending a sacred temple, her hands hovering over various supplies with an almost mystical certainty.

"For you," she murmured, selecting a leather-bound sketchbook that seemed to hum with something that Claire couldn't put her finger on, its pages thick and cream-colored like petals of some exotic flower, "I think we need something that can hold both delicacy and strength." The leather was buttery beneath Claire's fingers, the color of dark honey touched by sunset.

Claire's breath melted as she opened the book, the spine crackling with destiny. The pages seemed to glow in the morning light, each one a blank canvas waiting to capture moments of beauty, of pain, of transformation.

"And these," Agostina continued, producing a set of pencils that ranged from ghostly pale to midnight deep, their wooden barrels smooth as sea-worn stones. "For capturing the shadows between thoughts, the light between imaginings."

As Agostina gathered more supplies like a pencil sharpener that looked like an antique treasure, compressed charcoal, kneaded eraser, chamois for blending, Claire drifted back to L's sketches once again. Those confident yet vulnerable lines that had somehow captured not just the form of hope, but its essence. Would their paths cross any time? For how long would the artists inside them continue this dance of recognition?

"When you draw," Agostina said mellifluously, arranging the items before Claire like offerings on an altar, "remember that every line you make is a truth you tell yourself. Be mindful of these truths, but be brave in telling them."

The morning sun had moved, painting long shadows across the shop's worn wooden floors, each one a story waiting to be captured. Through the window, Claire could see Naples flowing past. Young apprentices sweeping the steps of centuries-old workshops, old women haggling over fresh vegetables, children chasing pigeons with equal enthusiasm. Every scene a painting waiting to happen, every moment alive with the kind of beauty she'd forgotten how to see.

"How much do I..." Claire began, reaching for her wallet, but Agostina waved away the question with an elegant gesture.

"First," she said, her eyes twinkling with shared secrets, "you must promise to show me what you create. Art is not meant to live alone in sketchbooks. Like love, it must be shared to truly live."

After thanking Agostina with a warm hug, Claire stepped from Bottega dei Colori into the embracing warmth of midday, her new treasures cradled against her chest like precious gems. The leather sketchbook seemed to pulse, its presence both terrifying and exhilarating. Like standing on the edge of a cliff with wings you're not quite sure will work, but feeling the wind beneath them start to stir.

Three days passed without a sign from L. The cork board remained unchanged, Claire's last note sitting there like an unanswered question. Each time the bell above the door chimed, she found herself glancing up, wondering if this might be the mysterious correspondent whose words had become as essential to her days as the Italian sun.

On the fourth morning, as she nursed her cappuccino and sketched the profile of an elderly gentleman reading his newspaper in the corner, Lucia approached with a knowing gleam in her eyes.

"Someone came very early today," she whispered conspiratorially, nodding toward the board. "Before the dawn even stretched her fingers across the sky."

Claire's heart performed an intricate dance beneath her ribs as she moved to the board. There, pinned on the top of all previous notes, was a new response. The paper seemed more worn somehow, as if it had traveled a great distance to reach her. The sketch this time showed a silhouette standing before the Eiffel Tower, a thought bubble containing the cork board of Caffè Sereno.

"Dear Claire," the note began in that now-familiar elegant script, "Please forgive my silence. I was unexpectedly called to Paris for an assignment that couldn't wait. The demands of making art for others rather than for oneself. But even as I stood beneath the iron lace of the Eiffel Tower, my thoughts kept returning to Naples... to our correspondence... to you. There's something about the quality of light in Paris that makes everything appear more romantic than it is, and yet I found myself missing the honest brilliance of Neapolitan sunshine and the even more honest words we've shared. I rushed back to Naples this morning, coming straight here before even unpacking my suitcase. Have you continued drawing? I hope the artist in you is awakening. Until your reply, L."

The admission of L's hurry to return to their dialogue sent rills of warmth cascading through Claire's body. She imagined L, still faceless, still nameless, yet somehow known, rushing through morning-quiet streets, propelled by the same inexplicable urgency that had drawn her to this board day after day.

Without hesitation, she retrieved a blank paper from her journal and uncapped Lucia's fountain pen:

"Dear L, What a joy to find your words waiting! Paris must have been beautiful, though I confess there's something gratifying in knowing you thought of Naples, and our small exchange, while surrounded by such splendor. Yes, I've been drawing again. After years of silence, my hands remember their purpose. I visited Bottega dei Colori on Signor Rossi's recommendation and met Agostina, who seemed to understand what I needed before I could articulate it myself. Now I find myself seeing Naples through an artist's eyes once more. Each shadow, each weathered doorway, each face telling stories I feel compelled to capture. It's as if your art has awakened mine. I wonder if creativity is contagious, passed from soul to soul like a sacred flame? Grateful for your return, Claire."

Her sketch showed an open hand releasing a butterfly, its wings patterned with tiny sketches of Naples' landmarks.

The first week of July unfurled like the pages of Claire's new sketch-book, with each day a fresh canvas of possibility. Her work for Daniella's family business blossomed into something neither of them had initially envisioned. What had begun as a simple rebranding transformed into a comprehensive visual identity system that honored the Esposito family's generations of floral expertise while positioning them firmly in the contemporary market.

"Claire, you've captured the soul of our business," Daniella's father declared during the final presentation, his hands gently touching the mockups for the new storefront signs. The logo, a stylized bouquet where traditional Italian flowers intertwined with modern geometric elements, embodied precisely the balance they had sought.

"My grandfather would have approved," he added, his eyes glistening with emotion that transcended language barriers. "It respects where we come from while showing where we're going."

Daniella beamed with pride as she unveiled the response from their potential investor. "They've committed to funding the expansion to two more locations," she announced, her voice pitched with excitement. "They specifically mentioned how impressed they were with the cohesive vision conveyed through your designs."

The success of the Esposito project rippled outward, bringing Claire new opportunities with businesses throughout Naples. Alessandra's ceramics shop received a website that showcased her artistry in a digital gallery that felt as intimate as her physical storefront. A family-owned restaurant that had been serving traditional Neapolitan cuisine for four generations now had menus and signage that told their story through design elements that evoked both heritage and innovation.

With each project, Claire felt herself standing more firmly in her own artistic identity. A creative force capable of connecting with the heart of what made each business unique. The careful, hesitant woman who had arrived in Naples seemed to belong to another lifetime.

Between client meetings and design work, Claire made time for her correspondence with the still-mysterious L. Their notes grew longer, more intimate. Not in the sharing of personal details, but in the revelation of inner landscapes usually kept hidden from view. L described the particular quality of sunlight that woke Naples each morning, the recurring dream of flying over Naples Bay, the childhood memory of believing that stars were holes poked in the night sky to let heaven's light shine through.

Claire responded with her own revelations; how she'd once believed creativity was selfish indulgence rather than essential nourishment; how Naples had taught her that beauty and decay could exist simultaneously without diminishing either; how sometimes, in quiet moments alone, she felt herself becoming someone new, someone truer to herself than she'd ever dared to be before.

Each exchange deepened their connection, though neither suggested meeting. There was something precious about this disembodied friendship, uncomplicated by physical presence, unburdened by the expectations that came with knowing someone's name or face or circumstances.

After completing her final local project, a complete identity system for a bookseller whose shop had been in his family for six generations, Claire made a decision. She had earned enough from her Naples clients to allow herself a luxury she hadn't permitted in years: time dedicated solely to her art.

"I'm taking two weeks away from client work," she announced to Lucia and Signor Rossi one golden afternoon as she savored a slice of torta della nonna (grandmother's custard tart). "Simply to capture Naples with my art."

"Bravissima (Excellent)!" Signor Rossi exclaimed, his hands

conducting an imaginary orchestra of approval. "The artist must sometimes create only for herself, or she forgets why she creates at all."

Lucia's knowing eyes studied Claire's face with maternal perception. "You look lighter," she observed, "as if you've set down a burden you didn't know you were carrying."

With her sketchbook as her constant companion, Claire embarked on a love affair with Naples itself. Each morning found her in a different corner of the city, her pencils dancing across paper as she captured moments that might otherwise have passed unnoticed: an ancient doorknob carved with mythology figures, its brass worn to silk by centuries of hands reaching for home; a grandfather teaching his granddaughter to make pizza dough, their four hands working in perfect harmony; fishermen mending nets, their fingers performing intricate ballet passed down through generations.

She sketched the theater of daily life; women hanging laundry from balconies, their movements graceful as dancers; street musicians whose faces revealed lifetimes in each crease and fold; children playing calcio (historical Florentine football) in narrow alleyways, their bodies expressing joy in every motion. Each drawing became not just a record of what she saw, but a testament to what she felt; her gratitude for this city that had pulled her from the margins of her own life back into its vibrant center.

One afternoon, she found herself back at Bottega dei Colori, her sketchbook nearly full of Naples' treasures. Agostina's face blossomed with delight as Claire shyly showed her the collection.

"You see with your heart," Agostina declared, her fingers hovering reverently over a drawing of two elderly men playing chess in a sunlit piazza. "Not just with your eyes." She turned the pages with the care one might give to sacred texts. "This is what I hoped for you, that you would remember how to translate feeling into form."

When she reached a series of sketches inspired by L's notes, a sunflower reaching for invisible light; hands almost touching across empty space; a bird taking flight from an open window, Agostina paused, her expression softening with recognition.

"Ah," she said gently, "these speak of something else, no? Not just what you see, but what you feel." Her eyes held a question she was too discreet to ask aloud.

Claire nodded, unable to articulate the strange connection she felt to someone whose face she'd never seen, whose name she didn't know, whose presence in her life consisted entirely of words and drawings exchanged through Signor Rossi's cork board.

"It's complicated," she admitted, her fingers tracing the outline of L's sunflower that she had recreated from memory.

Agostina's laugh was melodious as wind chimes. "All the important things are, cara mia (my dear). All the important things are."

That evening, Claire shared her artistic renaissance with L:

"Dear L, These past days have been a revelation. I've been drawing Naples, not just its landmarks and vistas, but its soul. The vegetable vendor's hands, gnarled as olive roots but impossibly gentle with his tomatoes. The way afternoon light transforms ordinary doorways into portals to other worlds. The conversations told through gestures between neighbors across narrow streets. I feel as if I've been sleep-walking through life and suddenly opened my eyes to find myself surrounded by beauty I'd forgotten how to see. Your art helped awaken mine. Thank you for that unexpected gift. With gratitude, Claire."

Her sketch showed a woman with her eyes closed, colorful images swirling around her head like a brilliant storm. A visual representation of creativity reawakening.

One moonlit evening as July drew to a close, Naples found Claire on her balcony, the city spread before her like an elaborate tapestry woven from light and shadow. Her sketchbook lay open beside her, the day's drawings capturing moments that had caught her artist's eye. An old woman's hands twisting pasta dough with practiced precision; a young couple stealing a kiss beneath a flowering trellis; the intricate pattern of cobblestones after a brief shower had polished them to gleaming.

The transformation that had begun with that first espresso at Caffè Sereno felt complete somehow, though Claire understood that transformation is never truly finished; it's a continuous unfolding, a perpetual becoming. She was not the same woman who had stepped off the plane almost three months ago, wounded and uncertain. Naples had worked its particular magic on her, teaching her to embrace the beautiful disorder of authentic living.

A breeze from the bay carried the scent of jasmine and salt, ruffling the pages of her sketchbook, caressing her face like a lover's gentle touch. Tomorrow, she would return to Caffè Sereno to check for L's response. Tomorrow, she would begin a new commission for a small art gallery that contacted her after seeing her work for Alessandra's ceramics shop. Tomorrow held possibilities she couldn't yet imagine.

But tonight, tonight belonged to this moment of perfect contentment. Claire lifted her glass of local wine in a silent toast to Naples, to Signor Rossi and Lucia, to Daniella and Agostina, to all the strangers who were now woven into the fabric of her new life. And yes, to L, whose words and art had reached across the void to touch something essential in her soul.

Naples glittered below her like a reflection of the heavens above, and Claire felt perfectly poised between them. No longer falling, but flying.

4

THE FACE BEHIND THE ART

I t had been about three and a half months since Claire's arrival in Naples, yet her fascination with the early morning light remained as strong as ever. So when dawn broke over Naples like a lover's whisper, painting the city in shades that had no names in any earthly language, Claire couldn't admire it enough.

Claire headed to Caffè Sereno, sketchbook and pencils in hand, while Naples streets lingered in that sacred pause between night and morning. A few early risers moved through the purple-shadowed lanes. Bakers carrying the first bread of the day, fishermen returning with their silvery catch, lovers reluctantly parting after night-long embraces. Each scene begged to be captured in her sketchbook, but Claire's feet carried her forward with singular purpose, her heart keeping time with the distant sound of church bells announcing the birth of another day.

She arrived at Caffè Sereno just as Signor Rossi was turning the sign from "Chiuso (Closed)" to "Aperto (Open)," the morning glow catching the brass handle like a wink of conspiracy. His eyebrows rose in surprise at her early arrival, but his smile held understanding that went beyond words.

"Ah, the early bird seeks her morning song, no?" he said warmly, holding the door open with a flourish that transformed the simple gesture into something almost ceremonial. The cafè smelled of freshly ground coffee, of bread just emerging from the ovens, and hopes yet unnamed.

The interior of Caffè Sereno held that quality unique to spaces caught between night and day, when shadows still clung to corners like reluctant dreams hiding from the first rays of sun. Today for some reason, Claire's pulse quickened as she stepped inside, her skin tingling with anticipation that felt almost electric.

There, on the cork board, nestled among all paper inhabitants was a fresh note, its edges crisp and new, bearing a flowing calligraphy that she had come to recognize instantly.

Her fingers reached for the note, its paper still warm as if it carried traces of the hand that had written upon it. The morning light caught the subtle watercolor wash that decorated its edges. Shades of dawn painted with such delicate precision that they seemed to glow from within.

In the center of the page, L had painted a single moth drawn to a distant flame, its wings detailed with patterns that spoke of midnight gardens and starlit wisdom. The image seemed to breathe with the sacred rhythm that captured that eternal dance between desire and fear, between staying safe and risking flight.

Beneath it, L's words flowed across the paper:

"Dear Claire, In the quiet hours before dawn, when the world is between darkness and light, I find myself thinking of courage; yours, which sparked like a match in darkness, illuminating something I'd forgotten existed. Mine, which grows stronger with each word we exchange, each artistic confession we share.

Last night, I watched a moth dance with moonlight, its wings carrying stories written in silver and shadow. It made me think of us. These fragile souls of ours, drawn to light we can't quite name but recognize in each other's art, each other's words.

Tell me, do you also feel this strange gravity pulling us toward something that feels both terrifying and inevitable? With growing wonder, L"

The words seemed to shimmer on the page like dew catching first light. This was more than their previous notes. More intimate, more daring, more real.

On her favorite table near the window, Claire spread her artistic tools like weapons in a battle for her own becoming. She selected her finest pen, its nib catching light like a tear about to fall. The blank paper before her seemed to ripple with potential, each fiber waiting to carry words that felt too big, too raw, too real for the delicate vessel of paper and ink.

Around her, the café was beginning to stir with its first patrons. The early morning wanderers, the night shift workers seeking solace in caffeine, the solitary seekers looking for connection in cups of perfect cappuccino. But Claire existed in a bubble of crystallized time, where nothing existed except the pressure of words building in her chest like a symphony searching for its first note.

Finally, her pen touched paper, and the words flowed like water breaking through a dam:

"Dear L, your moth speaks to something in me that I've never dared name. This wild, nocturnal part of my soul that's drawn to dangerous beauty. Just like you, I lie awake in these velvet hours before dawn. Yes, I imagine the hand that creates such exquisite art, the mind that shapes such impactful words, the heart that seems to beat in time with my own.

Here's my confession: I find myself studying every face I pass on these ancient streets, wondering if eyes will meet and recognition will spark like lightning between storm clouds. I examine every artist's hands, searching for traces of ink that might have shaped your intricate drawings.

Is it strange that I feel I would know you? That something in me would recognize my counterpart, even in a city of thousands?

Here's my offering in return..."

Her hand moved with certainty as she began to sketch, this time creating a constellation of fireflies dancing through a midnight garden. Each tiny light she drew held a different emotion: hope glowing like a pearl, desire burning like amber, fear flickering like distant stars. The image seemed to emerge from some deep well within her, where truth lived in shapes and shadows rather than words.

"These fireflies are my heart's lanterns, each one carrying a different fear, a different hope. Like your moth, they dance with light; but they carry their own fire, their own risk, their own reason to fly.

Shall we be moths and fireflies together, daring to dance with flame in the darkness?

Yours in growing courage, Claire"

The hours after pinning her note on the board stretched like honey dripping from a spoon, sweet with expectancy yet agonizingly slow. Claire wandered Naples' labyrinthine streets in a daze of heightened awareness, every sense attuned to the chance of connection.

A violinist played in a hidden piazza, his music weaving through the morning air like silk threads of longing. Claire stopped to listen, recognizing in the melody's rise and fall the same yearning that filled her own chest. The musician's eyes were closed, his entire being surrendered to the music flowing through him, and she found herself wondering if L approached art with that same absolute abandon.

She settled on the piazza's worn steps, her sketchbook open on her lap, and began to capture the scene. Not just the violinist with his instrument, but the way his music transfigured the space around him. On the page, she drew sound waves visible in the air, turning notes into tangible things that curved around objects and people in the vicinity. Each stroke of her pencil felt like a prayer, reaching across the void toward someone who might understand this need to make the invisible visible, to capture the ephemeral in permanent lines.

An elderly couple dropped a coin in the violinist's case and began to dance, their movements speaking of decades of love worn smooth like stones on a riverbank. The woman's silver hair caught sunlight as her partner spun her gently, their bodies remembering steps practiced over decades together. Claire's hand moved quickly now, trying to capture not just their dance but the space between them where a lifetime of love resided.

"Mi scusi (excuse me)," a voice said softly beside her, making her heart leap before she registered its feminine tone. A young woman with dark curls and artist's hands stained with paint had paused to look at Claire's sketch. "You capture the music itself, not just the people. Bellissimo (beautiful)!"

Claire's insides clenched with an emotion she couldn't name. The thought kept coming back. Was L out there right now, perhaps watching her from some sun-dappled café corner? Would they recognize each other's artist souls if they passed on these ancient streets? The questions buzzed in her mind like bees drunk on summer flowers, sweet yet somehow raw.

The violinist's song reached its crescendo, notes climbing toward heaven like birds taking flight. Claire closed her eyes, letting the music wash over her like waves, like possibility, like love's first tentative touch. When she opened them again, the world seemed sharper, more vivid, as if the melody had cleaned her vision like rain washing a window.

In the far corner of the piazza, Claire noticed an outdoor café surrounded by ancient lemon trees, their fragrant branches swaying gently in the afternoon breeze. The name stirred something in her memory, 'Ristorante Italiano Fresco', and as her eyes traced the elegant script on the façade, realization washed over her like a warm tide. This was the place from Valentina's card, the one pressed into her palm as they parted on the plane. How could she forget the Neapolitan woman's knowing smile, the way her eyes had crinkled at the corners when she'd insisted Claire visit her daughter's restaurant? That first genuine connection since landing on Italian soil had felt like a sign, a whispered promise of belonging.

She claimed a table nestled in the dappled shadows of the lemon trees, settling into the wrought-iron chair as summer itself filtered through the glossy leaves above. The pages of her sketchbook lay open before her, filled with today's artistic confessions. The violinist and his visible music, the dancing couple with the space between them shaped by decades of love.

But in the margins of each drawing, almost unconsciously, she'd sketched moths and fireflies, their wings carrying messages she hadn't meant to write. It was as if L's presence had seeped into her art like water into parched earth, transforming everything it touched.

A gust of wind stirred the lemon blossoms overhead, releasing their perfume into the air like secrets finally spoken. Claire closed her eyes, inhaling deeply, and in that moment of suspended time, she allowed herself to acknowledge the truth that had been growing inside her like a vine seeking light; this connection with L had become more than an artistic exchange. It had become something that made her dreams deepen, something that painted her world in colors she'd forgotten existed.

"Signorina," the waiter's voice broke into her reverie, "this was given for you."

Her heart stopped, then resumed beating at double time as she saw what he held. A folded heavy artist's paper, its edges deckled like waves catching moonlight. Her name was written on the outside in that achingly familiar script that had come to mean everything.

With trembling fingers, she unfolded it to find an intricate ink drawing of a labyrinth, its paths decorated with tiny flowering vines and scattered stars. At its core, two lights glowed; one a moth with silver-dusted wings, the other a firefly carrying its own flame. They were drawn as if caught in the moment just before meeting, creating a single radiance in the maze's center.

Beneath it, words flowed like water over stones:

"Claire, I saw you today. You were drawing in the piazza, lost in capturing the violin's song. Your hair caught the morning light like copper wire conducting electricity, and your hand moved across the page as if you were writing spells instead of making art..."

Claire's world tilted on its axis as she read L's words, each one striking her like lightning finding earth. Her fingers traced the elegant script as if she could absorb their meaning through touch alone, as if she could feel the echo of L's presence in the pressure of ink against paper.

"...You didn't see me. How could you? You were lost in that space artists go when the world falls away and only beauty remains. I watched your face as you captured the dancing couple, saw how your lips moved silently as if you were tasting the moment before committing it to paper. Your entire being seemed to glow from within, like a lantern holding the last light.

I almost approached you. My feet took three steps in your direction before courage failed me. How do you tell someone that you've been witnessing their metamorphosis through paper butterflies of truth? How do you explain that their art has become the lens through which you see the world anew?

So I stood in the shadow of the church and watched you work, feeling like a character in a story I never thought I'd be brave enough to live. You wore a dress the color of wild roses, and when the wind caught it, I couldn't help but sketch you. Here, see?"

Below was a quick study that made Claire's breath catch in her throat. There she was, captured in swift, sure strokes of ink; bent over her sketchbook, hair falling forward to veil her face, dress dancing in invisible wind. But L had drawn her surrounded by an aura of light, as if she were some kind of modern-day saint communing with divine inspiration. The image showed her not as she saw herself, but as L saw her; luminous, enchanted, enchanting.

"Now you know: I'm real. Not just words on paper. I'm here, walking these same streets, breathing this same air, carrying your words and art in my heart like talismans against loneliness.

The question is: are we brave enough for what comes next? Yours, L"

A teardrop fell onto the paper, making the ink bloom like a flower opening in fast motion. Through the blur of unshed tears, she raised her eyes to scan the café's perimeter, her heart suddenly hammering against her ribs. Could L still be here somewhere? The thought sent electricity racing through her veins; that L might have lingered after delivering the note, perhaps watching her reaction from some shadowed corner or behind the curtain of hanging vines. Her gaze darted from table to table, searching for a familiar silhouette, a pair of eyes she might recognize even across a crowded café, someone who might be pretending not to watch her world unravel and reform around these words he'd written.

In that piazza, beneath the blessing of ancient lemon trees and afternoon light, Claire felt every molecule of her being rearrange itself around this new reality. L had seen her. L had watched her. L had captured her essence in strokes of ink that spoke of something deeper than mere observation; they spoke of recognition, of understanding, of a connection that transcended the ordinary boundaries of stranger and friend, of artist and muse.

The café around her continued its eternal dance; waiters gliding between tables, couples sharing secrets over tiny cups of espresso, sunlight painting lattices across worn stone floors. But Claire existed in the moment where the world around her vanished completely, leaving nothing except the weight of L's confession in her hands.

With fingers that trembled like leaves in an autumn wind, she reached for her own artist's paper; a sheet from her premium sketch-book, torn out with deliberate care. This moment demanded more than rushed words on borrowed paper. It demanded permanence, intention, courage.

Her pen hovered above the pristine surface for a heartbeat, two, three, then descended like a bird coming home to roost:

"Dear L,

You saw me today, but what you couldn't see was how your art has taught me to look at the world differently. That violinist's music became visible to me because you showed me how to capture the intangible. Those dancers moved through space made sacred by your influence on my artist's eye.

You stood in the church's shadow and watched me draw, while I've been inspired by your talent, learning to trust my own spark again. You say you lacked courage to approach, but don't you know, your very exis-tence has become an act of courage in my world.

Here's my truth, drawn in ink and starlight..."

Her hand moved across the page with fierce certainty now, creating an image of two artists separated by a paper-thin veil. On one side, she drew herself lost in creative fever. On the other, she drew a shadowed figure holding a sketchbook, their outline purposefully undefined except for hands marked with ink stains and eyes that held all the wisdom of the ancient city itself. Between them, the veil rippled as if caught in a current of certainty, threatening to tear at any moment.

"The time for shadows and veils has passed, don't you think? Meet me at Caffè Sereno tomorrow at sunset. Let's be brave enough to step out of the shadows together. Awash with terrified hope, Claire"

Leaving her half-finished ravioli and a hastily paid bill behind, Claire rushed from Ristorante Italiano Fresco with an urgent rhythm drum-ming against her ribs. Caffè Sereno beckoned like a lighthouse in the gathering dusk, and she knew L would be waiting for her response, their connection pulling her forward through Naples' winding streets like an invisible thread of fate.

Lost in the whirlwind of her thoughts, she barely registered the moment she pushed through Caffè Sereno's door and pinned her note to the cork board. It wasn't until Signor Rossi's warm greeting broke through her reverie that the world snapped back into focus, and she found herself enveloped in the café's familiar embrace. With just enough presence of mind to share quick hugs and a breathless account of the day's revelations with Signor Rossi and Lucia, she left the café.

Her next stop was Bottega dei Colori, the charming art supply shop. Among the dozen carefully curated easels, Agostina's gentle guidance led her to one that resonated deep within. A wooden masterpiece that folded gracefully, promising to accompany her wherever inspiration beckoned. Together they gathered the essential tools of her craft: pristine canvases yearning for color, oil paints that seemed to hold entire oceans in their tiny wells, some brushes with tips as fine as eyelashes and others whose bristles seemed to quiver with impatience. Claire splurged on a leather portfolio that can hold her creations. As a parting gift, Agostina pressed into her hands an ancient palette, its surface marked with the remnants of countless paintings of the past. A cherished keepsake of good fortune from one artist's heart to another.

Embracing Agostina goodbye, she cradled her precious easel and newfound treasures, turning homeward, her body heavy with exhaustion but her spirit soaring on wings of possibility.

The sun began its descent over Naples like a conductor drawing the day's symphony to a close, painting everything in shades of strawberries and raspberries in a fleeting beauty. She stood in her apartment, watching day surrender to evening through her balcony doors.

Tomorrow at sunset. The words echoed in her awareness like the trembling certainty finally understanding itself. Tomorrow, the mystery that had captured her imagination and reshaped her world would take solid form. Tomorrow, L would become more than elegant script and exquisite sketches, more than a soul reaching across the void to touch her own.

The thought sent shivers dancing along her spine like piano notes climbing toward crescendo. She moved to her wardrobe, fingers trailing across fabrics that suddenly seemed inadequate for such a momentous occasion. How does one dress for the moment when fantasy becomes reality? What does one wear to meet the person who has been reading your core through ink-blessed confessions and midnight whispers?

A knock at her door startled her. Opening it, she found Maria, her landlady, holding a package wrapped in brown paper and tied with twine that had seen better days.

"For you, bella," Maria said, her eyes twinkling with the wisdom of one who had witnessed countless love stories unfold beneath Naples' eternal sky. "It was left at Caffè Sereno for you; Signor Rossi brought it here himself."

Claire's entire being seemed to vibrate with anticipation as she accepted the package, which somehow felt like holding a bird in cupped palms. Maria squeezed her hand once, a gesture that spoke volumes about understanding and warmth, then disappeared down the stairs humming an old Neapolitan love song.

With trembling fingers, Claire undid the twine, letting the brown paper fall away. Inside was a book. Not just any book, but a vintage collection of Italian love poetry, its leather binding worn smooth by decades of hands seeking wisdom in its pages. The poetry book lay open in Claire's hands, its pages releasing the scent of aged paper and remembered loves into the purple-shadowed evening air.

A piece of art paper marked one of the selections, and as Claire opened to it, her breath tangled. L had marked a passage with what appeared to be an original painting. A watercolor bookmark depicting two paper boats navigating a storm-tossed sea, their tiny lanterns glowing and pulsing against the darkening waters.

The marked poem was Montale's "Ho Sceso, Dandoti il Braccio (I Have Gone Down, Giving You My Arm.)" L had translated it in that now-beloved handwriting, each word seemingly chosen with the care of someone selecting precious stones:

"I have gone down millions of stairs at least, giving you my arm, not already certain whether you were there with me; the centuries, the moments tumbled, and at the bottom was what I do not know: the key, the code..."

Below the translation, L had written:

"Dear Claire,

Some poets capture what simple words cannot contain. Montale wrote of descending countless stairs with his beloved, uncertain if she was truly there; yet taking each step in faith, in hope, in love. Tomorrow at sunset, we'll finally see each other clearly, no longer separated by the whispers through papers.

I've sent you this book because every poem inside reminds me of what we're creating together, this vulnerable bridge between souls, this dangerous dance of hearts learning to trust again. Each page holds the hopes of lovers who came before us, who also stood on the edge of something magnificent and terrifying and chose to leap.

I wish for these poems to remind you that what we're doing, this slow unveiling of souls through art and confession, has been happening since humans first learned to love, to hope, to reach across darkness toward another reaching hand.

Until tomorrow, when faith becomes sight, L"

Claire traced L's words with reverent fingers, feeling the slight indentations where pen had pressed into paper, as if she could absorb their meaning through touch alone. Outside, Naples was painting itself in twilight colors, each shadow a pledge, each glimmer of light a new possibility.

The evening wrapped around Claire like silk as she curled into her balcony chair, the poetry book cradled in her lap like a sleeping child. Each page she turned released tales of other loves, other hopes that had stood where she now stood, on the precipice between what was and what could be.

The distant church bells marked the hour, their resonant tones flowing over the cityscape. A crescent moon hung low over the distant bay, its reflection fracturing into a thousand silver shreds on the dark water. The city below had transformed into its nighttime self. More intimate, more mysterious, alive with the kind of magic that only exists in spaces between streetlights and stars.

Claire's fingers found another poem, this one marked with a pressed flower. A tiny sprig of lavender that still held its scent, as if L had tucked summer itself between these pages. Her composure dissolved at the intimacy of it, this shared secret pressed between pages that had held other lovers' dreams.

She found herself speaking to the night air: "Who are you, L? Who leaves pressed flowers in vintage poetry books and draws moths dancing with fireflies? What kind of heart sees mine so clearly through nothing but ink and paper?"

The questions hung in the shadowed air like unsung notes in a lover's serenade. Below her balcony, a young couple passed, their laughter floating up like bubbles in champagne. The man pulled his companion close, said something that made her throw her head back in delight, the sound of their joy a counterpoint to Claire's exquisite ache of restlessness.

She pulled her sketchbook from the nearby stool and opened it, its pages now a chronicle of her awakening. Each drawing seemed to glow with new meaning; the violinist and his visible music, the dancing couple with their lifetime of love held in the space between them, L's moth meeting her firefly in a maze of what could be. Her hand moved across a fresh page, creating without conscious thought; this time drawing herself standing at a crossroads, one path leading back to the careful, contained life she'd left behind, the other spiraling into unknown territory marked only by moths and fireflies lighting the way.

"Tomorrow," she whispered to the star-scattered sky. "Tomorrow everything changes."

In the deepest part of night, when even Naples' eternal symphony had softened, Claire found sleep impossible. The poetry book lay open on her bed, its pages catching pale moonlight like fish with silver sheen in a midnight stream, while L's watercolor bookmark seemed to glow with its own inner luminescence.

She moved to her new easel, the purchase made that afternoon at Bottega dei Colori with help from Agostina. The blank canvas loomed before her, pristine and terrifying, much like tomorrow's promised meeting. Her hands trembled as she squeezed paint onto the ancient palette, colors she hadn't dared to use in years: crimson like first love, gold like dawn breaking over new horizons, midnight blue like secrets kept between kindred spirits.

The first brush stroke felt like breaking a spell, like stepping through a doorway she couldn't return from. Colors erupted beneath her fingers as if they'd been waiting years for this moment of release. She painted with the fever of revelation; not planning, not thinking, just letting her heart guide her hands across the canvas.

What emerged surprised her; not a literal scene, but an emotional landscape. Two figures woven from yearning, reaching toward each other across a space filled with swirling things; moths and fireflies, yes, but also pages of poetry torn free from their bindings, musical notes escaped from their staffs, drops of paint liberated from their tubes. Every flying thing carried its own light, creating a constellation of hope between the reaching figures.

"This is what you've done to me," she said to the absent L, her voice catching on emotions too new to name. "You've turned my world into this, this riot of light, this dance of things breaking free from what contains them."

A shooting star streaked across the night sky beyond her window, its brief illumination painting her canvas in otherworldly light. Claire stood back, brush still dripping color onto the palette like moments spilling down. The painting wasn't finished; couldn't be finished until tomorrow, until the mystery of L took solid form, until possibility became reality.

But it was true. Every stroke spoke of this transformation taking place in her soul, this awakening that had begun with a simple note left in a café and had grown into something that made her previous life seem like a single candle flame compared to the infinite starlit sky.

The first hints of dawn found Claire still at her easel, her hands stained with colors that matched the bruised purple of the nascent sky. She'd painted through the night like an artist rediscovering her voice after years of enforced silence. Around her, empty coffee cups and discarded sketches told the story; each attempt bringing her closer to capturing the ineffable connection that had bloomed between two people through beautiful paper gardens.

The painting before her pulsed with raw emotion; no longer just two figures reaching to one another, but an entire universe of connection. She'd added layers through the night: veils of translucent color that suggested the passage of time, texture that spoke of barriers broken, of walls crumbling beneath the persistent touch of understanding.

"You've made me brave again," she whispered to the canvas, to L, to the dawn breaking over Naples like an oath about to be sealed. Her voice held the roughness of someone emerging from a reverie too beautiful to leave.

The morning air drifting through her open window carried the usual combination of scents. Fresh bread from the bakery below, coffee from a dozen cafès, salt from the eternal Mediterranean, and then, there was something else. Something new, like never before. It was the scent of change, of renewal, of butterflies emerging from chrysalises they'd outgrown.

She turned from the painting to face her reflection in the vintage mirror, barely recognizing the woman who gazed back. Paint streaked her cheeks like war paint, her hair wild from running passionate fingers through it as she worked. But it was her eyes that caught and held her attention; they blazed with a light she hadn't seen in them since before her marriage, before she'd learned to make herself small, before she'd forgotten how to burn with creative fire.

"Today," she told her reflection, the word carrying all the weight of certainties and some things yet unnamed. "Today, L becomes real."

The sun climbed higher over Naples as Claire stepped out of the shower, steam rising from her skin like mist from sacred waters. Each movement held the deliberate grace of a pianist before her solo performance as she opened her wardrobe, fingers trailing across fabrics that told stories of their own.

She chose a silk dress she'd bought her first week in Naples, in a moment of uncharacteristic daring. The color of storms gathering over the Mediterranean, that precise shade between grey and blue when the sky held its breath before releasing rain. She laid it carefully across her bed, ready for the evening that awaited her.

Out on her balcony, Naples spread before her like a living canvas. The sky had morphed to that perfect shade of blue and purity. Every color seemed sharper, more vibrant, as if the world itself was dressing up for this moment of revelation. Even the air felt different, charged with the kind of electricity that precedes life-changing moments.

"L," she whispered to the wind, tasting the letter on her tongue like a new wine, trying to imagine the face, the voice, that someone who would soon materialize from dream to reality. Would she recognize L instantly, like planets remembering their ordained orbits? Would there be a moment of hesitation, of uncertainty before recognition?

Time moved strangely in the hours before sunset, each minute stretching like winter frost melting on a windowpane, then suddenly rushing like water over falls. She looked at her painting from the night before, now drying in the summer heat. The figures reaching across seemed to move when she wasn't looking directly at them, as if fragments of her soul were rearranging themselves into new stories. She'd tried to sketch, to read, but she had hard time focusing and the poetry book's words blurred before her eyes like watercolors in the rain. Every glance at the clock sent butterflies racing through her stomach, threatened to soar and shatter in the same breathless moment.

She paced her apartment, her pulse keeping time with the ancient church bells that marked each passing hour. Then she decided to get ready. Satisfied with her choice, she slipped into the dress, its silk charmeuse flowing like water, transforming once-mechanical movements into dance. The neckline dipped just low enough to reveal her grandmother's locket.

Her hands trembled as she applied makeup with an artist's precision; not to hide, but to enhance, to celebrate. A hint of rose on her lips, like stolen petals from a forgotten garden. Each gesture felt like painting the last strokes on a masterpiece, preparing it for an ultimate unveiling.

"You're really fussing over this small thing," she told her reflection, but she herself ignored that comment. Because this wasn't a small thing; this was magnificent and terrifying and exactly as monumental as it felt.

The storm-colored dress rippled around her as she moved to the balcony one last time, needing to breathe in the essence of Naples before everything changed. Her hand found her grandma's locket, warm from resting against her skin. "Was it like this for you?" She asked her grandma thousands of miles away, who had taught her to believe in second chances and in looking for magic in the ordinary. "Did your heart feel too large for your chest? Did your skin feel too thin to contain all the hope, all the terror, all the wild imagination?"

The last rays of sun ignited the city's windows, turning each pane of glass into flames of crimson and gold. Claire knew that somewhere in this labyrinth of ancient streets, L was watching the same sunset, feeling the same exquisite anticipation, preparing to step into the same transformative moment.

She picked up L's poetry book one last time, letting it fall open where it would. The page it chose held a single line: "Some loves are so large, they need a whole city to contain them."

"Yes," she said to herself and to the beautiful city. It was time.

Claire descended the stairs from her apartment for the last time as a woman who knew L only through art and words. Each step felt momentous, as if she were walking not just down worn marble stairs but through a threshold in time itself. The silk of her dress whispered against the ancient stones like secrets finally ready to be spoken.

Naples had prepared itself for this moment of revelation, the golden hour painting everything in the tender light. The cobblestones beneath her feet gleamed like buried treasure, each one holding memories of countless others who had walked this path toward destiny. The air wrapped around her the history and hope all woven together into an intoxicating symphony for the senses.

Her path to Caffè Sereno had become as familiar as the lines on her palm, but tonight every corner held a new mystery, every doorway thrummed with potential. A woman singing to her baby on a balcony above became an aria of promise. The clash of pots and pans from a restaurant kitchen sounded like percussion for her heart's wild symphony. Even the evening swallows seemed to dance differently against the watercolor sky, as if they too understood the magnitude of what was about to unfold.

She passed the violinist's piazza, now empty save for scattered rose petals from a wedding party long dispersed. Had L stood in these same shadows yesterday, watching her draw? Had those artist's hands, marked with ink stains, gripped the edge of ancient stones of the church to keep from reaching out too soon?

The questions pulsed in her blood like lightning trapped beneath still waters, each step bringing her closer to answers that would reshape everything. Her portfolio, clutched against her chest like a shield, held one last painting. Created in that suspended hour between decision and destiny. Not for the cork board this time, but for L alone. A gift of truth, of revelation, of her essence finally ready to be seen in all its magnificent vulnerability.

Claire paused at the last corner before Caffè Sereno. One more turn, and everything would change. One more step, and the mystery that had captured her imagination would take solid form.

"I'm ready," she confided quietly to the universe that had orchestrated this elaborate dance, finding their way to each other through art and courage and the magical space between coffee cups and providence.

A flock of white doves took flight from the piazza nearby as Claire stood before Caffè Sereno's weathered green awning, her heart a wild thing beneath silk and skin. The familiar bell awaited her touch. Through the windows, she could see the interior that looked like when ordinary spaces turn into catalysts for serendipity. She could see that the evening had drawn other people to the cafè. Couples sharing conversations over tiny cups of espresso, solitary visionaries bent over notebooks filled with hope, artists capturing the unremarkable moments to turn them into something otherworldly. But Claire saw them as if through a veil, her entire being focused on one question: Which of these souls was L?

Her hand trembled as she reached for the door, fingers hovering over the handle like a musician about to strike the first note of a love song. Inside, Signor Rossi stood behind his copper altar of connection, his eyes holding all the wisdom of one who had witnessed countless beings finding their way to each other across cups of perfect espresso and whispered confessions. As Claire entered, he gave her a smile that contained multitudes. Understanding, encouragement, and something that looked suspiciously like joy.

"Ah, Bella Claire," he said lovingly, his voice carrying the weight of moments about to transform everything. "You are ready?"

Was she ready? Ready to step through this threshold between fantasy and reality? Ready to discover if the connection that had flourished could survive the transition to flesh and blood? Ready to risk everything for the chance at something magnificent?

Her hand found her grandmother's locket once again, her fingers tracing the silver compass with emotions too vast to name. The metal caught the day's final light, gleaming like a key to doors long sealed.

"Yes," she said, the word felt like her promise to herself to finally complete the unfinished melody. "I'm ready."

Inside Caffè Sereno, time seemed to slow, each second stretching like the last notes of a lover's serenade as Claire's eyes adjusted to the delicate play of shadow and light. The café had prepared itself for this moment of revelation, or perhaps she was seeing it differently now, standing on the threshold between who she had been and who she was about to become.

Each table held its own story; a young couple sharing tiramisu with two forks, their fingers touching 'accidentally' between bites; an elderly man reading Dante, his lips moving silently as if tasting each word; a man with paint-stained fingers sketching in a leather-bound journal...

Claire thought... Could it be...?

But before she could take a step forward, movement from the corner caught her eye. A man rose from his seat by the window, his hands bearing the unmistakable ink stains of an artist. His eyes held the same mixture of hope and terror she felt, as he took one hesitant step in her direction.

And then, from the back of the café, another figure came forward from the shadows. Tall, elegant, with a sketchbook clutched against their chest like a shield.

Claire's pulse roared in her ears like waves breaking against ancient shores. Which one was L? Which of them had been reaching across paper to touch her heart? Or was L someone else entirely, watching from another corner, gathering courage to step into the light?

The moment stretched like a string pulled too tight, vibrating with potential energy. One wrong move and everything could shatter. One right move and everything could transform into something more beautiful than she'd dared to dream.

"Courage, Bella Claire," Signor Rossi's voice came as a father's embrace behind her. "Trust yourself to know what you cannot yet see."

The air in Cafè Sereno seemed to condense around Claire. Her storm-colored dress caught the last rays of sun like waves catching starlight, while her heart orchestrated a symphony that threatened to drown out all other sound.

Three pairs of eyes met hers in the golden twilight; each holding questions, each carrying the potential to move her world. And everything started moving in slow motion. She saw a woman with midnight hair bent over her sketchbook, an elderly man by the window stood frozen mid-step, and then... in a flash... she saw him.

He emerged from the shadows at the back of the cafè, his mid-thirties lending a seasoned grace to his tall frame, elegant in a paint-stained linen shirt rolled up at the sleeves, revealing strong forearms marked with the beautiful scars, or maybe she thought they were beautiful. Dark curls fell carelessly across his forehead, and his face, oh, his face held all the classical beauty of his Italian heritage combined with something deeper, something that spoke of passion barely contained.

A gust of wind from the opening door stirred the papers on the nearest table, sending a single sheet floating through the air like a leaf caught in the graceful tumble of seasons changing. Without thinking, Claire reached out to catch it.

Her fingers closed around the paper at the very moment another hand reached for it. A hand belonging to the man from the back of the café. A hand she knew intimately, though she'd never touched it before. A hand marked with ink stains in precisely the patterns she'd imagined during countless nights of wondering. A hand that had crafted moths and sunflowers and doors standing ajar, that had written words that made her soul unfurl like flowers reaching for light.

She looked up, and the world stopped spinning.

Dark eyes met hers, eyes that held all the wisdom and fervor she'd sensed in every sketch, every soul-baring truth. Eyes that saw her not as she had been, but as she was becoming. Eyes that widened with recognition, with wonder, with a joy so pure it made her throat ache.

"Claire," he breathed, his voice carrying all the music she'd imagined, rich with an Italian accent that made her name sound like mystical poetry.

"I'm Luca Castellano," he introduced himself.

And just like that, the pieces of her world aligned into place. L was Luca; the presence who had walked through her dreams, whose words had wrapped around her heart like moonlight around shadows. Her pulse sang his name, a melody she had known before she knew its meaning. She stood perfectly still, afraid that even a breath might shatter this moment, might scatter it like stars at dawn. "Luca Castellano," she whispered back, her voice carrying all the weight of waiting, all the lightness of finding. For a moment she wondered if she said his name out loud or only in her own mind. In either case, those two words lived every letter she had read, every moment that had led her here.

Reality crystallized into a single heartbeat as Claire and Luca stood frozen in that moment of recognition, their hands still touching over the floating paper that had brought them closer at that moment. The last light of day painted them in unusual shades, remaking the modest café into a cathedral of connection.

Luca was everything Claire had sensed through paper and ink, and nothing she could have imagined. Tall and striking, with eyes the color of aged whiskey that seemed to hold entire universes of creativity and understanding. His dark curls fell rakishly across his forehead, and his strong, elegant hands bore the beautiful marks of his craft. Paint stains and calluses that spoke of years devoted to capturing beauty. He wore a simple white linen shirt, rolled at the sleeves, with an artist's scarf knotted carelessly at his neck, managing to look both perfectly disheveled and devastatingly handsome.

"I've been waiting," he said, his voice a melody of longing finally finding its resolution. "For the right moment. I wanted to speak to you, to bridge the distance, but some moments demand their own perfect timing." His smile held the warmth of a thousand Italian summers.

"Your hands," Claire managed, her voice catching on words too big for any speech. "They're exactly as I imagined when I looked at your moth, your sunflower, your..." She trailed off, overwhelmed by the reality of finally speaking words that had lived so long in her being.

"And your eyes," he breathed, the Italian lilt in his voice making the words sound like music. "I tried so many times to capture their color in my sketches. Like the Mediterranean just before a storm, holding all the wild emotions of sky and sea and..."

He paused, a soft laugh escaping that held equal parts joy and wonder. "Listen to us, two artists trying to capture the impossible with words, holding brushes dipped in forgotten dreams."

He guided her to a table near the window, her favorite spot, where countless sketches and notes had flowed from her hands onto paper. "This table..." she said, with wonder dancing in her eyes as she turned to him. "How did you know?" His smile held a touch of shy warmth as he shook his head. "I didn't," he admitted softly, "but I thought you might want to watch the city lights come alive." A smile curved across Claire's face as she settled into her familiar place, now somehow seemed different by his presence.

Around them, Caffè Sereno had morphed into an intimate cocoon of mellow light and shadow, as if the universe itself had drawn a veil around this moment of revelation. The familiar sounds of the café faded to a distant symphony, serving only to underscore the exquisite tension crackling between them.

"I have something for you," they both said simultaneously, then laughed; the sound of their mingled voices creating a new kind of music. "You go first," Claire said softly.

Luca reached for his portfolio, a battered leather one that bore the beautiful scars of a life dedicated to art. His hands, those magnificent instruments of creation, trembled slightly as he withdrew a canvas, wrapped in brown paper and tied with twine. "I painted this for you," he confessed, his accented voice carrying that vulnerable quality unique to artists sharing their work. "When sleep felt like betrayal to the magnitude of what was coming."

Claire unwrapped the painting, each layer of paper falling away like rose petals scattering across marble floors. When the last barrier fell, her voice abandoned her, leaving only the thunder of her heart to fill the silence.

There on the canvas was her own image, but not from any moment she recognized. Luca had painted her standing at the edge of a moonlit lake, her silhouette ethereal against the star-scattered sky. But what rendered her speechless was how he had captured the dream-soft expression she'd never seen on her own face. Around her, water lilies floated on the lake's surface, their petals glowing with an inner light that matched the gleam in her painted eyes. And rising from the water like prayers were countless paper boats, transforming into stars at the canvas' edge. As if her very presence was enough to turn everything sacred and beautiful.

"How did you..." Claire began, but words failed her as emotion closed her throat.

"I painted what I saw with my inner eyes," Luca said simply, his dark eyes holding a depth of understanding that redefined perfection. "Not just your physical presence, but the way you create. The way the universe seems to hold its cadence in silence when you're lost in capturing beauty. The way you..."

He trailed off as Claire reached for her own portfolio, withdrawing the painting she'd created during her sleepless night of fervor.

The café lights had begun to glow softly as twilight deepened outside, casting intimate shadows that danced across their faces. Claire's hands trembled as she revealed her own canvas, her heart thundering with such force she was certain Luca must be able to hear it.

"I couldn't sleep either," she whispered, the words carrying all the weight of confession. "Every time I closed my eyes, colors exploded behind my lids like fireworks, demanding to be set free."

As the wrapping fell away, Luca's sharp intake of breath set butterflies dancing in Claire's stomach. His eyes, those expressive Italian eyes that seemed to hold centuries of artistic passion, widened as he took in her work. The painting showed two figures composed of light and shadow, reaching across a universe of their own creation. Where she had started with moths and fireflies, the space between the figures had evolved into something more profound; a galaxy of artistic souls finding each other across time and space.

"Claire," Luca breathed, his fingers hovering over the canvas, not quite touching, as if afraid the images might dissolve like morning mist. "You've painted my thoughts. The ones I never dared to speak aloud, the ones that felt too wild, too wonderful to exist outside my imagination."

Their eyes met across their paintings, across the space that had grown smaller with each passing moment, each shared breath. Luca's eyes held flecks of gold that caught the café's diffused light like captured stars, and Claire found herself wanting to paint them, to capture that exact shade of wonder.

"From that first note," Claire said softly, her voice carrying the rawness of absolute truth, "when you drew that reaching sunflower... something in me recognized something in you. Like finding a door in your heart you didn't know existed until someone knocked from the other side."

Luca's hand found hers, their fingers intertwining with the natural grace of elements finding their perfect combination. His touch was warm, certain. "And now?" he asked, the question floating between them like a violin's final note. "Now that we're real to each other, now that we're more than ink and paper?"

Claire felt the world shift and realign around this single perfect moment. Luca's question hung in the air between them, fragile as a soap bubble catching rainbow light, heavy as destiny finally finding its path.

"Now," Claire began, her voice carrying all the music of discovery, "now we begin the real dance. Not just those who reached across paper and possibility, but the ones who want to learn each other's rhythms in flesh and blood." Her fingers tightened slightly around his, feeling the answering pressure that spoke of understanding too deep for words.

Luca leaned forward, close enough that Claire could breathe in his scent. Oil paint and sandalwood, creativity and masculine warmth melding together. The slight stubble on his jaw caught the evening light like bronze dust, and this close, she could see the tiny flecks of amber in his dark eyes. "I've drawn you a thousand times in my mind," he confessed, his free hand rising to hover near her cheek, not quite touching, as if asking permission. "But no sketch could capture this; the way your pulse flutters here," his finger hovered, tracing an invisible line of her throat where her heartbeat danced beneath skin, "or how your eyes hold entire galaxies."

His almost-touch sent anticipation shivering along Claire's nerves, making her lungs seize with delicious suspense. Around them, the café had faded to a melodic blur of sounds and shadows. Their paintings leaned against the window frame beside them, mirror images trying to recognize their counterpart across time and space.

"I'm afraid," Claire confessed, the words falling from her lips like the first drops of summer rain. "Afraid that this is too perfect, too beautiful to be real. That I'll wake up in my apartment with nothing but my dreams."

Luca's smile held all the tenderness of forgotten melodies suddenly remembered. "Then we'll have to make it more real," he uttered softly.

Claire's voice trembled slightly as she voiced the question that had danced in her head for some time. "Yesterday, when you saw me there in the piazza... how did you know it was me?" The words hung between them like threads of fate, waiting to be woven into understanding.

Luca's eyes softened as he gazed at her, the artist in him painting truth in every word. "I knew you through your art first. When I saw you yesterday, your essence matched every line you'd drawn and shared. My soul recognized yours, Claire. Some things," he professed, taking her hand, "our intuition sees long before the mind understands."

Then Luca reached into his portfolio to withdraw a small leather-bound sketchbook, its cover worn smooth as river stones by years of artistic devotion. The café's gentle light caught the gold leaf of its edges, making them shimmer like the horizon line where sea meets sky at dawn.

"Il mio diario del cuore (my heart's diary)," he offered in a hushed tone, his native Italian slipping out in a moment of raw emotion. "Every sketch I couldn't send, because it was too raw to share through paper chronicles." His voice carried the vulnerability of someone offering their most precious truth. "Would you..." he paused, gathering courage like an artist selecting their finest brush, the slight tremor in his hands betraying his nerves, "would you look at them with me?"

Claire's hands hesitated slightly as she accepted the book, feeling its weight. Not just physical, but emotional. She moved her chair next to his, their shoulders touching in a way that sent sparks dancing along Claire's skin. She was acutely aware of his warmth beside her, the subtle scent of his cologne, that sandlewood, mingling with turpentine and coffee.

The initial sketch made tears spring to her eyes. There she was, but not as she existed in reality; rather, as she existed in Luca's dreams. He had drawn her sitting by an ancient fountain, her hands trailing in the water as if seeking stories hidden in its depths. Though he hadn't known her face then, he had somehow captured her essence; the one caught between worlds, seeking something that sparkled just beyond reach.

"I drew this the day I first imagined you," he whispered against her ear. "Not your physical form, but the feeling of you; someone who would understand the language of art that Naples speaks. I didn't know your face then, only that somewhere in this city, there is a beacon that would recognize me."

Each page revealed new treasures of his imagination, each sketch a window into his longing. Her fingers traced the lines he'd drawn, feeling the passion in every stroke. He had created scenes of the woman he wanted to meet; sometimes just hints of a presence: hands reaching for morning light, hair caught in wind off the Mediterranean, a silhouette framed in an ancient doorway.

"Here," he said softly, his voice rough with emotion as he turned to a particular sketch; a woman whose face he had left deliberately undefined, standing among the ruins of Pompeii at twilight, her dress becoming one with the shadows that held centuries of love stories. "I drew this when I imagined you to be a woman who would understand why an artist needs to capture not just images, but feelings."

Their fingers had somehow become entwined as they turned the pages, each sketch revealing new layers of his yearning. Near the end of the book, Claire found something that silenced her world momentarily. A series of studies that had been drawn just yesterday, after he saw her. Now her real features emerged from the pages, but transformed by his artist's eye into something magical: her smile carrying echoes of Mona Lisa's mystery, her eyes holding the same spark he'd been trying to capture in all his imagined sketches.

"I've never shown anyone this book," Luca said, vulnerability raw in his voice. "These pages held someone who would understand both art and the heart. And yesterday, when I saw you..." He paused, gathering words like a painter gathering perfect colors. "Reality proved more beautiful than all my imaginings."

Luca shifted to face Claire fully, their knees touching in a way that sent wild roses blossoming beneath her skin, each petal of sensation unfurling with dangerous sweetness.

"Now," he said, his voice carrying the quiet certainty of an artist who has found his perfect subject, "now we create something new. Something that isn't just treasured notes and midnight confessions, but real and solid and..." He paused, his free hand rising to trace the air near her cheek, as if sketching her features from memory. "And terrifying in its beauty."

From his position behind the counter, Signor Rossi began to hum softly. An old Neapolitan love song that seemed to wrap around them like silk, like the persistent rhythm of ocean waves against weathered stone, like permission to believe.

"Since we're finally meeting in person," Luca said with a warm smile, "would you like to stay for dinner? I know Caffè Sereno doesn't usually serve dinner, but Lucia told me earlier that she's making something special tonight, and she would love to serve it to us."

Signor Rossi, who had been polishing glasses nearby, stepped forward with a knowing twinkle in his eye. "For our artists, we make exceptions. Tonight, we have something prepared, if you would honor us by staying."

Claire looked between the two men, touched by the gesture. "I'd love to."

Signor Rossi disappeared momentarily and returned with a bottle of wine, its label worn with age. "A special Aglianico from my brother's vineyard," he explained as he uncorked it with practiced ease. The rich aroma of blackberries and spice filled the air as he poured two glasses, the deep ruby liquid catching the café's warm light.

As they clinked glasses, Lucia emerged from the kitchen carrying a basket of bread still steaming from the oven. "To start," she said warmly, placing it between them along with a small dish of golden olive oil flecked with herbs. "From our family's olive grove in Sorrento."

The bread was crusty on the outside and pillow-soft inside. Claire dipped a piece into the oil, savoring the peppery, grassy flavor that spread across her tongue.

By now, the café had emptied of other patrons, leaving them in a cocoon of privacy. When Lucia returned, she carried two earthenware plates of what Claire recognized as gnocchi, the potato dumplings nestled in a vibrant tomato sauce and topped with melted mozzarella that stretched in tempting strings as she set the plates down.

"Gnocchi alla Sorrentina," Lucia announced proudly. "Hope you enjoy it."

Claire took a bite and closed her eyes involuntarily. The gnocchi were soft pillows that seemed to melt in her mouth, while the sauce had a brightness that spoke of sun-ripened tomatoes plucked directly from the vines. The basil added freshness, and the mozzarella brought a creamy richness that balanced everything perfectly.

"This is incredible," she said honestly, looking up to see Luca watching her with a smile.

"In Naples, food is never just sustenance," he said, his voice warm. "It's family, history, love, all served on a plate."

As they finished their meal, the soft murmur of a friendly disagreement drifted from the kitchen. Moments later, Signor Rossi emerged with Lucia, both engaged in animated discussion.

"Cannoli would be perfect," Signor Rossi insisted, his hands gesturing expressively. "Crisp shells with sweet ricotta filling. A classic!"

Lucia shook her head firmly. "No, no. Cannoli are individual desserts. For tonight, we need something they can share." She turned to Claire and Luca with a knowing smile. "Pastiera (Neapolitan cheesecake) is better. It requires two forks, one plate."

Signor Rossi considered this, crinkling his eyes thoughtfully before nodding. "You're right, as always, Lucia. Pastiera it is."

When the dessert arrived, Claire found herself looking at a golden-crusted pie with a creamy filling. The subtle scent of orange and cinnamon rose from the warm slice.

"Pastiera Napoletana," Lucia explained, setting down a single plate with two forks. "We normally make it for Easter, but some moments deserve celebration."

The first bite revealed a delicate sweetness, the creamy ricotta complemented by the bright notes of candied orange and the warmth of cinnamon. What struck Claire most was how the flavors seemed to unfold gradually, each bite revealing new dimensions.

"Now you've tasted a true Neapolitan secret," Luca said, his eyes never leaving hers as they shared the dessert. The simple act of taking turns, watching him enjoy the same sweetness from the same plate, felt surprisingly intimate.

Signor Rossi approached with two tiny cups of espresso, each bearing a perfect crema the color of caramel. The cups were mismatched. One blue-and-white ceramic, the other painted with tiny yellow flowers, yet somehow perfectly complementary, like two different voices harmonizing in song.

"My special blend," he said proudly, setting them down with a flourish. "For special occasions."

The espresso was velvet on the tongue; bitter and sweet in perfect measure, strong enough to anchor Claire to the moment when everything else felt dreamlike. She watched as Luca savored his, his expression one of simple reverence for life's perfect small pleasures.

When the last of the coffee was gone, Luca reached for his wallet, prompting an immediate protest from Signor Rossi, who waved dismissively at the gesture.

"No, no, no, for the artists, there is no charge," he insisted, his hands moving expressively through the air as if erasing an invisible bill.

"Please, I insist," Luca countered with gentle firmness, pressing several bills into Signor Rossi's reluctant hand. "Your kindness and Lucia's genius deserve proper appreciation."

Claire reached for her own purse, American practicality asserting itself. "Let me split it with you," she offered, already calculating her share.

Luca's hand covered hers, warm and certain. "Not tonight," he said softly, that slight Italian accent making even this simple refusal sound like poetry. "I asked you to stay for dinner. Here, the one who extends the invitation has the honor of paying. Next time...," his eyes held a question, a hope. "Perhaps you will invite me?"

The possibility of "next time" hung in the air between them like the sweetest promise. Outside, Naples had dressed herself in evening splendor with streetlights casting gold against ancient stones.

"I should walk you home," Luca offered as they stepped from the warmth of Caffè Sereno into the gentle embrace of the Neapolitan night. The street had quieted somewhat, though music still spilled from open windows, and somewhere distant, someone was singing an aria that seemed to give voice to the swelling emotion in Claire's chest.

"I'd like that," she replied, surprised by the steadiness in her voice when everything inside her felt like watercolors bleeding into each other, creating new shades she had no names for.

They walked side by side through streets that seemed transformed by their shared presence, neither rushing nor lingering, finding a rhythm together that felt both new and achingly familiar. Occasionally their hands brushed, each accidental touch sending sparks dancing along Claire's nerves.

At the entrance to her building, they paused. The moment stretched between them, fragile as spun glass, heavy with unspoken possibilities. Above them, stars punctuated the velvet sky like an artist's deliberate brushstrokes of light against darkness.

"Tomorrow?" Luca asked, the single word carrying the weight of invitation, of hope. "Sunset at Caffè Sereno? I have something I'd like to show you."

"Sunset," Claire agreed, her voice softening around the promise. "I'll be there."

His goodbye was a kiss placed gently on each of her cheeks, the traditional Italian farewell between friends, yet somehow transformed into something that left her skin tingling long after his lips had departed. As he stepped back, his eyes held a depth of emotion that stole her breath more effectively than any passionate embrace could have.

"Buona notte (Good night), Claire," he said, her name in his mouth sounding like something precious, something rare.

"Good night, Luca," she replied, the name still new on her tongue, yet feeling like a word she'd been waiting her whole life to speak.

She watched him walk away, his tall figure gradually blending with the shadows and light of the ancient street until he turned a corner and disappeared from view. Only then did Claire realize she'd been holding her breath, as if afraid exhaling might dispel the magic of the evening like dandelion seeds scattered by a careless wind.

The next day unfolded for Claire in a dreamlike state of creative energy. She woke with the first light, something inside her vibrating with inspiration that wouldn't be contained. Setting up her easel in the balcony, she lost herself in color and form, painting scene after scene from her growing collection of Neapolitan moments, a blend of vistas from her balcony and treasured glimpses captured during her wanderings through the streets.

Each brush stroke felt more confident than any she'd made in years, as if something within her had been freed by last evening's connection. The morning light gave way to afternoon's golden glow, and still Claire painted, existing in that sacred space where time loses its ordinary meaning.

Only when the light began to shift toward evening did Claire set down her brushes, suddenly aware of how the hours had flown. The realization that sunset, and Luca, awaited sent her heart racing as she rushed to clean herself.

In the shower, she let hot water wash away paint from her hands, watching swirls of color disappear down the drain. Standing before her wardrobe afterward, Claire selected a dress the color of ripened peaches, its silken fabric flowing around her like sunset clouds.

As she applied a touch of makeup, Claire studied her reflection. Something had changed, not just in how she looked, but in how she carried herself. Her eyes held a light that had been absent for too long, and her smile came more easily, as if remembering its purpose.

The walk to Caffè Sereno felt like a journey through Naples she was seeing with new eyes; each familiar corner revealing fresh beauty, each moment charged with anticipation. The evening light turned ordinary streets into paintings waiting to happen, and Claire found herself mentally mixing colors that might capture this exact quality of golden hour.

She paused at the corner before the café, gathering herself. Through the windows, she could see the familiar interior, Signor Rossi behind the counter, regulars at their usual tables, and there, at her favorite spot by the window, sat Luca.

Even from this distance, the sight of him quickened her pulse. He wore a linen shirt the color of sand, his dark curls catching the evening light.

Taking a deep breath, Claire pushed open the door, the familiar bell announcing her arrival like the opening notes of a symphony about to unfold. As if sensing her presence, he looked up, his eyes finding hers across the distance with unerring precision. The smile that bloomed across his face sent warmth spreading through her chest.

Hours melted away as Claire and Luca shared stories and laughter over Lucia's lovingly prepared delicacies and Signor Rossi's masterfully crafted espressos, until finally they emerged from Caffè Sereno into the star-strewn Neapolitan evening, their silhouettes merging into one against the ancient cobblestones. With each step forward into the moonlit streets, with every shared glance that contained volumes of unspoken understanding, Claire felt the manuscript of her life turn to a fresh, unblemished page, one waiting to be filled with colors more vibrant, with emotions more profound than any she had known before. And that's when the next chapter in Claire's life began.

5

THE COLOR OF US

Two weeks had passed since that magical evening at Caffè Sereno when Claire and Luca's souls had finally found each other beyond the paper-winged confessions they'd exchanged. Each evening unfolded like a treasured gift, revealing new dimensions of connection neither had dared imagine possible.

Their courtship bloomed with the passionate intensity unique to Naples, a city where love was never a timid thing but rather an art form practiced with the same devotion as creating masterpieces. Their separate days and shared evenings wove their artistic lives into a tapestry of moments that seemed to exist outside ordinary time.

Days found Claire immersed in her work, balancing Susan's demanding projects with her growing roster of local clients. The Esposito flower shop rebrand had led to three more commissions as word spread through Naples' small business community. Luca, too, kept busy with his commissioned paintings and restoration work that filled his daylight hours.

But evenings, evenings belonged to them alone. They became a sacred ritual of shared meals at Caffè Sereno, where Signor Rossi and Lucia watched over their blossoming romance with the tender pride of surrogate parents. The caffè sospeso board, once their only means of connection, now bore witness to their physical presence as they sat together, hands intertwined across the worn wooden tables, speaking in the dual language of words and touches.

With each setting sun, Claire felt herself transforming, her American reserve gradually yielding to the intoxicating freedom of Italian passion. Luca taught her to experience life as art; to savor each moment like the first brush stroke on pristine canvas, to find beauty in imperfection, to embrace the wild unpredictability of a heart fully awakened.

They shared their first kiss on the third day, standing beneath the ancient lemon tree in the piazza near her apartment. The fifth day brought their first argument, a passionate debate about color theory that ended with laughter and reconciliation beneath a twilight sky streaked with precisely the shade of violet they'd been disputing. After dinner each night, they would walk through the hidden piazzas and intimate courtyards near Caffè Sereno, discovering the magic of Naples that tourists rarely witnessed; ancient fountains that whispered centuries of secrets, tiny chapels with frescoes that glowed in twilight, hidden corners where time seemed to stand still.

Their loyalty to Caffè Sereno never wavered. Though Naples offered countless restaurants and cafés, they returned each evening to the warm embrace of Lucia's cooking and Signor Rossi's perfect espresso, drawn as much by their affection for the owners as by the sense that the café had become the heart of their unfolding story.

Yet for all the ways their artistic souls had entwined around each other like vines seeking sunlight; there remained one threshold they hadn't crossed. Luca's studio, his most private creative sanctuary, remained a mystery Claire had glimpsed only in her imagination, a sacred space he'd yet to share with her.

Until tonight.

They sat at their favorite table at Caffè Sereno, the twilight hour painting everything in shades of lavender. Lucia had just served them her magnificent torta di cioccolato e lamponi; layers of rich chocolate sponge, delicate raspberry cream, and fresh berries that glistened like jewels beneath a glossy chocolate ganache. Luca watched Claire take her first bite, his dark eyes reflecting the flickering candlelight as her expression melted into pleasure.

"I have a studio," Luca said suddenly, his voice carrying the weight of invitation. His gaze held hers with an intensity that made the bustling café disappear around them. "Not just the one where I close my eyes and draw, but a real working space. With windows that catch the perfect northern light, and enough room for two easels, and..."

He stopped, color rising beneath his olive skin, making him look younger, more vulnerable. After two weeks of growing closer, this invitation carried emotional significance that transcended a simple visit to his workspace. "Dio mio (my god), I'm getting ahead of myself, aren't I? These past two weeks have been like living inside a dream, and here I am, already imagining..."

"No," Claire interrupted softly, reaching across the table to take his hand. "You're not getting ahead. These two weeks have shown me more about love and art than I've learned in my entire life before Naples." She squeezed his hand gently. "Show me. Show me your studio, show me where your art is born."

Luca's smile bloomed like the sun breaking through clouds after a storm, elevating his classical features into something almost divine. He rose, pulling Claire gently to her feet, their half-finished desserts forgotten in the wake of this new anticipation. Then both of them glanced down at their plates and simultaneously had the same thought. "You know what? It can wait for a few minutes," Luca said with a grin, already sitting back down. Claire laughed, nodding in agreement. "Lucia's desserts deserve our full attention," she replied, savoring another bite of the chocolate-raspberry confection. They shared a conspiratorial laugh, finishing every last morsel before finally getting up to leave.

The evening air embraced them as they stepped out of Caffè Sereno, the sky painted in shades of deep purple that made Claire's artist's soul ache with their fleeting beauty. The street lamps were just beginning to flicker to life, transfiguring corners into settings for enchanting moments.

Their hands remained linked, Luca's strong fingers interlaced with hers, his thumb occasionally brushing across her knuckles in a way that made her tremble like the first stars emerging in twilight's tender hour. They entered a piazza and approached a gleaming Vespa parked there.

Claire's eyes widened in surprise when Luca released her hand and moved to the scooter's side, his movements fluid as he opened a hidden compartment. From within, he produced two helmets, offering one to her with that same mesmerizing smile that had first captured her attention at the café two weeks ago. The helmet felt cool and smooth against her palms, and she found herself caught between laughter and disbelief at how quickly this evening was evolving into something straight out of an Italian romance film.

Threading through Naples' labyrinthine streets, Claire found herself pressed against Luca's back, the warmth of him seeping through his linen shirt as they navigated the city's beating arteries. The Vespa climbed higher, weaving through narrow alleys that opened suddenly to breathtaking glimpses of the bay below, its waters shimmering like scattered diamonds in the darkening sky. Over the purr of the engine, Luca's voice carried back to her, rich with pride as he spoke of Capodimonte, describing it as a sloping hill cradling the artistic essence of Naples where his studio was located. The wind whipped playfully through Claire's hair, carrying with it the intoxicating scents of exotic flowers and sea salt, and she found herself surrendering to the moment's wild beauty.

A voice of caution spoke; despite these two weeks of growing closer, here she was in an unknown part of the city, embracing a stranger who had transformed her world, racing through streets she'd never walked, toward a destination she couldn't pronounce. What was she doing?

But was Luca truly a stranger after these two weeks of shared meals and conversation, of learning the geography of each other's souls through art and words? Their connection had deepened with each passing day, proving that some people were never really strangers at all, but destined souls waiting patiently across time and distance for that perfect moment of serendipity. And so, Claire chose to silence that cautionary voice, letting herself flow into the moment, her arms tightening around Luca's waist as they curved around another ancient corner, climbing ever higher toward whatever destiny awaited them in his studio above the bay.

"Just a little further," Luca said, his voice carrying notes of anticipation and something deeper, more profound. Each word fell from his lips like a caress, the Italian lilt rendering simple English into poetry. "Through this alley, past the church with the copper dome, and..."

They emerged into a small piazza where he parked his scooter. A fountain played at its center. The palazzo rising before them was the color of aged honey, its walls telling stories in layers of weathered stones and climbing vines.

"The entrance is around back, through the courtyard," Luca explained, leading her through an arch draped with wisteria. His hand at the small of her back sent warmth spreading through her entire body.

The courtyard was a world unto itself, sheltered from the city's eternal symphony by high walls covered in vines. Ancient orange and lemon trees stood like sentinels, their fruit glowing like tiny moons in the gathering dusk. The air here was different, slower, sweeter, heavy with the perfume of flowers.

"This is where I come to sketch when the world feels too loud," Luca confessed, his free hand gesturing to a worn stone bench beneath the largest orange tree. In the fading light, his profile could have been carved by Michelangelo himself. "Sometimes I think these trees have seen more love stories than all the poets in Naples combined."

They approached a door painted in the exact shade of midnight blue that Luca had used in his moth drawings. "Ready?" he asked softly, producing an ancient key that looked more like an heirloom than a mere tool.

The door opened with a creak of aged wood, releasing the scent of turpentine, oil paint, and something yet unnamed. Luca reached inside, and warm light spread from a collection of mismatched lamps, revealing a space that made Claire take a deep breath.

The studio was everything an artist's sanctuary should be, and nothing like the sterile spaces she'd known back home. Enormous windows stretched nearly from floor to ceiling, their panes divided into squares. Easels of various sizes stood like patient sentinels, some holding works in progress draped in cloth, others bare and waiting. The walls were a patchwork of inspiration; sketches, photographs, dried flowers, all pinned up in seemingly random patterns that somehow created their own artistic harmony.

"This is where I've been drawing you," Luca said softly, his hand finding the small of her back as he guided her to a corner where a wall was dedicated entirely to studies of her; quick sketches on small pieces of paper, detailed drawings on proper artist's stock, even a few attempts in watercolor that caught the exact shade of copper in her hair when morning light struck it. Each piece was a love letter written in graphite and paint, a chronicle of his growing fascination since her first note at Caffè Sereno, capturing not just her form, but her essence.

Claire's fingers trembled as she reached out to touch one of the sketches, herself laughing, her head thrown back in abandon. Though they'd spent many hours together, this particular image was born from Luca's imagination rather than direct observation. "You've made me beautiful," she whispered.

Luca's hand found her chin, turning her gently until their eyes met. In the warm lamplight, his dark eyes held depths that made her heart stutter. "No," he said with quiet intensity, his voice deepening with emotion. "I've simply drawn what I see when I look at you. You carry beauty within you, Claire. I just caught its reflection on paper."

The studio held other treasures; shelves lined with art books and journals, a collection of paint-splattered brushes arranged meticulously in vintage ceramic jars, and a worn leather sofa positioned perfectly to catch the morning light. But what caught Claire's attention most was a space that seemed to be waiting; an empty easel positioned next to his own, a clear section of wall ready for new work, a small table that looked perfect for holding coffee cups and shared aspirations.

"I may have been..." Luca paused, color rising on his cheeks. "I may have been hoping. Planning. Dreaming."

The confession hung in the air between them like paint dissolving in water, beautiful in its raw honesty. Claire moved through the studio slowly, her fingers trailing over surfaces that held stories in every scratch and stain. A palette crusted with dried paint spoke of passionate creations.

The space itself seemed to echo with masculine energy; Luca's presence infused in every corner, from the carelessly draped linen cloth over an easel to the coffee cup still bearing the imprint of his lips.

"Show me," Claire said softly, her voice carrying a confidence that surprised her. "Show me what you've been working on these past two weeks."

Luca's eyes lit with an inner fire that made her heart skip. He moved to the largest easel, his strong hands hesitating on the paint-splattered cloth that covered the canvas. The muscles in his forearms flexed slightly with the movement, drawing Claire's attention to the beautiful contrast of olive skin against his rolled white linen sleeves. "This is... different from what I usually do," he admitted. "It started the night after our first note exchange, evolved through all the notes we shared over two and a half months, and has taken on new dimensions with each day we've spent together these past two weeks."

The cloth fell away like a curtain rising on epiphany. And Claire forgot to breathe. The painting was an ancient forest captured at that magical moment when day surrenders to dusk. Towering trees with bark rendered in deep carmines and burnished golds stretched toward a sky bleeding hues of indigo and amber. But what made Claire's heart stutter was how Luca had painted the light; thousands of fireflies suspended between the trees, their glow illuminating hidden paths that wound through the woodland in intricate, overlapping patterns.

"It's us," Claire breathed, recognition blooming in her chest like flowers opening to sunrise. "Not just how we found each other, but all the beautiful, unexpected moments that led us here."

"Yes," Luca whispered, moving to stand behind her. The heat of his body radiated against her back. "I've been trying to capture how it feels when you discover someone whose path seems destined to cross with yours again and again, like these fireflies lighting the way through darkness we didn't even know surrounded us."

Claire turned to face him then, drawn by something deeper than thought or reason. His eyes held galaxies of emotion. The evening light filtering through the studio's grand windows painted him in shades of purple and shadow, sculpting him into something almost mythical, a Renaissance master in his temple of creation.

The studio seemed to hold its breath as they stood there, suspended in a moment between what had been and what could be. Luca's skin was warm beneath Claire's fingertips, alive with the same electric energy that pulsed through her own veins. Beyond the windows, Naples had donned her evening jewels, the city glowing like scattered moonstones against darkness.

"I have an idea," Luca said suddenly, his voice dropping to that velvet baritone that made Claire's soul stumble. Rising with fluid grace, he strode to the space where the two easels stood quietly. With deliberate care he shifted them closer until they touched, their wooden frames kissing like shy lovers. From behind his workstation, he produced an enormous blank canvas, pristine white and full of unsaid promises. His strong hands positioned it carefully across both easels, bridging the gap between the separate creative spaces. The graceful power in his movements reminded her of a dancer, an athlete, an artist in complete command of his body and his craft. "Create with me. Right now. Not separately, but together. One canvas, no planning."

The invitation sent shivers dancing along Claire's spine. This was different from exchanging notes and sketches, different from sharing completed works. This was raw, immediate in a way that made her heart race with the wild abandon of someone skydiving, opening of parachute, or falling, awaited with equal magnificence.

Luca was already gathering supplies; tubes of paint, brushes of various sizes, palettes that bore the beautiful scars of previous artistic battles. His motion spoke of years mastering his craft, each movement precise yet passionate. Claire found herself mesmerized by his hands, those magnificent instruments of creation that had drawn her into his world through letters born in candlelight.

"No rules," he said, squeezing rich colors onto the palettes; emerald green like wishes straight from secret gardens, amber like honey caught in late summer light, violet like the depth of dreams just before waking. "No expectations. Just us, creating something new together." The Italian accent in his voice made even simple words sound like seduction.

Claire felt something unlock inside her chest as she accepted a brush from his paint-stained fingers. Their hands touched in the exchange, and the contact sent sparks of creativity dancing along her nerves. The blank canvas before them seemed to sing with potential, like a page of music waiting for its first notes.

They began slowly, tentatively. Luca making the first mark, a sweeping line of gold that caught the studio's gentle light. Claire responded with a curve of midnight blue that wrapped around it like an embrace. Their movements grew more confident as they found their rhythm, dancing around each other in the space before the canvas, brushes meeting and parting like stars in a celestial dance, their orbits perfectly aligned in the infinite canvas of space.

Colors erupted beneath their hands; not just paint, but emotion made visible. Where their strokes met, new shades emerged, imperfect, yet surprisingly perfect. Neither led, neither followed. They created as they had connected, with hearts open to possibility, reaching across space to touch, to transform, to become something entirely new.

Paint spattered their clothes as they worked, each drop a badge of artistic abandon. The studio filled with their shared energy, the space between them charged with creativity and something deeper, more primal. The soft sound of brushes against canvas mingled with their breathing, punctuated by moments of breathless laughter when their strokes collided in unexpected ways.

Claire had never painted like this before. Before her marriage, her art had been careful, controlled, each stroke planned and measured. But now, with Luca's presence beside her like a flame drawing her toward light, she found herself creating from some deeper place, a well of passion she'd forgotten existed. She was acutely aware of him, the way his body moved with athletic grace as he reached across the canvas, the subtle scent of his cologne mingling with paint and turpentine, the occasional brush of his arm against hers.

"Look," Luca spoke in hushed tones, stepping back slightly. His voice had grown husky with emotion, wrapping around the single word like silk warmed by summer sun. "Look what we're making."

The canvas pulsed with life and movement. Their individual styles had merged into something entirely new, Claire's tendency toward structured beauty weaving through Luca's wild expressionism like order dancing with chaos. The result was breathtaking. At the center, a vortex of pure emotion emerged from the maelstrom of color, a cosmic heartbeat made visible, pulsing with the raw energy of creation itself. Ribbons of light spiraled outward from this luminous core, dancing between shadow and brilliance like memories too profound for words. It was as though they had captured the very moment when inspiration first ignites, that sacred, invisible flash when something that never existed suddenly becomes inevitable.

"It's perfect," Claire breathed, her voice catching on emotion too big for any words. "It's exactly what this feels like. This thing growing between us. This..."

She trailed off as Luca reached out with a paint-stained hand, gently turning her to face him. A smudge of gold paint across his cheekbone somehow made him even more magnetically handsome.

"Claire," he said intimately, her name on his lips sounding most exquisite in his accented English, "I need to tell you something. From that first note you left at the café, I've been falling in love with your soul. With the way you see beauty in shadows, the way you capture hope in simple lines, the way you..."

He never finished the sentence. Because Claire, moved by something deeper than thought or reason, closed the distance between them. Their kiss tasted of chocolate and creativity and courage finally finding its reward. Luca's hands, still wet with paint, came up to frame her face, leaving traces of color that marked her like an artist signing his masterpiece.

Around them, Naples began to sing its evening song, the melodic calls of gelato vendors and the hum of Vespas from the streets. But in the studio, they created something new, a love story written not in words, but in color and courage, perfectly aligned.

When they finally drew apart, both were painted in more ways than one, colors from their creative passion marking their skin and clothes like beautiful battle scars. The studio had grown dimmer as evening deepened outside, but neither moved to turn on more lights. The mellow glow from the mismatched lamps created an intimate atmosphere that wrapped around them.

"Stay," Luca whispered, the word carrying the weight of more than just an evening's invitation. His voice had grown deeper with emotion, making even this simple word sound like a love song. "Stay and watch how the moonlight changes the colors on our canvas. Stay and let me sketch you in this light that makes you look like something from a Botticelli dream. Stay and..."

"Yes," Claire breathed, the single syllable contained her whole universe. "To all of it. To everything."

Their painting was still wet, colors blending and shifting like a living thing. They settled on the worn leather sofa positioned perfectly for viewing both their work and the Naples skyline beyond the studio's magnificent windows. Luca pulled a paint-splattered blanket around them both, and Claire found herself fitting perfectly against his chest, her head tucked beneath his chin as if they'd been designed by some cosmic artist with this moment in mind.

His heartbeat beneath her ear was steady and strong, a rhythm she could imagine painting to for the rest of her life. His hand found hers beneath the blanket, their fingers intertwining with the ease of brush strokes meeting on canvas.

"Sometimes I feel like I'm floating inside my imagination," Claire confessed softly, watching the scene from the windows. "As if all of this beauty is too much for one person to hold without spilling over."

Luca's laugh rumbled in his chest, rich and warm as aged wine. His free hand came up to stroke her hair, the gesture so tender it made her throat ache. "Then we'll have to keep painting ourselves into reality. Keep creating things too beautiful, too real to be just imagination." His lips brushed her temple, leaving a trace of a kiss. "Though I must say, if this is an imagination, it's the most exquisite one I've ever had."

Through the windows, they could see the stars, the Naples sky, that seemed to mirror the tiny sparks of white paint scattered across their canvas. Outside, the orange trees in the courtyard released their evening perfume, mixing with the scents of turpentine and oil paint to create a fragrance unique to this moment, this beginning.

"Tomorrow," Claire said, the word feeling like a promise of the first stroke on a fresh canvas, "we'll create something new again."

"Tomorrow," Luca agreed, pressing a kiss to her temple that left a small smudge of blue paint.

Claire woke to sunlight painting unfamiliar constellations across a ceiling she'd never seen before. For a moment, disorientation swept through her like waves disturbing still water, then memory flooded back, bringing with it a joy so profound it felt almost like pain. She'd fallen asleep on Luca's studio sofa, their shared painting still on its easel, speaking softly of art until exhaustion had finally claimed them both.

The first thing she became aware of was warmth, Luca's solid presence beside her, his arm draped protectively around her, his steady breathing stirring her hair, her back pressed against his chest, their bodies fitting together as perfectly as complementary colors on an artist's wheel.

She lay still, savoring this moment between sleep and full waking, memorizing every sensation: the gentle rise and fall of his chest against her back, the subtle scent of him, sandalwood and paint and something uniquely, intoxicatingly male, the way his fingers had curled possessively around her hip even in sleep. There was something profoundly intimate about this shared vulnerability, this unguarded moment before the world fully awakened.

The morning light streaming through the enormous windows recast the studio into something almost mythical. Their painting had dried overnight, its colors settling into permanence. Scattered art supplies lay where they'd abandoned them, brushes standing in jars like bouquets, palettes crusted with the evidence of their shared creation.

Claire felt the moment Luca woke, a subtle change in his breathing, a slight tightening of his arm around her waist. His lips brushed the sensitive spot behind her ear, and when he spoke, his voice was rough with sleep but rich with happiness.

"Buongiorno, mia bella artista (good morning, my beautiful artist)," he crooned, the words vibrating against her skin like music. "I was afraid that you were not real."

Claire turned in Luca's arms, her throat constricting with tender surprise at the sight of him bathed in morning light. Sleep had softened his features, making him look more vulnerable, a striking contrast to his usual confident presence. His dark curls were charmingly mussed, and a streak of dried paint still marked his jaw like a brushstroke of adventure. His eyes, when they met hers, held the kind of warmth that made her think of Italian summers and endless horizons.

"I keep thinking the same thing," she whispered, reaching up to trace the line of his cheekbone where golden sunlight painted his olive skin. "That any moment I'll wake up alone in my apartment, and all of this, you, us, this perfect moment, will fade like watercolors in rain."

Luca caught her hand, pressing a kiss to her palm. "Then let me prove how real this is," he accepted the challenge. Moving with the fluid grace that never failed to captivate her, he rose from the sofa and pulled her gently to her feet.

Their shared painting from the night before seemed to be more radiant in the dawn light, with the colors that looked deeper, richer, grander. But what caught Claire's breath wasn't the art, it was the way Luca was looking at her, as if she were a masterpiece he couldn't quite believe he'd been allowed to discover.

"Your hair," he said softly, reaching out to touch a strand that had caught the light like a captured flame, "it's the exact color of sunrise over the bay. I've been trying to mix that shade for years." His fingers trailed down her cheek, along the line of her jaw, coming to rest at the pulse point in her throat where her heartbeat betrayed its rapid dance. "And here, this is the rhythm I hear when I paint now. The tempo of new beginnings."

His other hand found her waist, drawing her closer until the space between them disappeared like mist in the morning sun. Claire could feel the solid strength of him, the steady beat against her palm where it rested on his chest. The thin linen of his shirt, wrinkled from sleep, did little to disguise the warmth of his skin beneath.

"Dance with me," he beckoned, already beginning to sway gently. "Let's waltz with the morning light."

No music played except the distant sounds of Naples awakening, yet they moved together as if hearing the same silent symphony. Luca led with the natural grace of someone born to movement, his artist's hands splayed warm and sure against Claire's back as they swayed in the morning light. The space between their bodies hummed with electricity, with surrender, with something that was yet to be spoken.

"My mother always said," Luca shared intimately, his voice vibrating against her temple, "that there are two perfect moments in Naples, sunset, when the city turns to gold, and sunrise, when she reveals her true self to those awake enough to see it." His hand moved up her spine in a caress that made her shiver. "But she never told me about this moment, when morning paints the woman you love in shades that no artist could capture."

The casual way he spoke of love, so different from American hesitancy, from the careful dance of saying too much too soon. She pulled back just enough to see his face, finding in his dark eyes a certainty that took her breath away.

"You say it so easily," she said in a fragile cadence, her fingers curling into the soft linen of his shirt. "Love. As if you're not afraid of its weight."

Luca's smile bloomed delicate and fierce, a contradiction that stole her breath, elevating his features from merely handsome to something that belonged in Renaissance frescos. "Ah, mia Claire (my Claire)," he said, one hand coming up to cup her cheek, his thumb tracing the line of her lower lip in a way that made coherent thought impossible. "In Italy, we know that love is like art, the more afraid you are of it, the less beauty you create. We embrace it, celebrate it, let it transform us completely or not at all."

Their dance had carried them into dawn's embrace, where sunlight spilled through the windows, bathing them both in nature's own luminescence. In this ethereal glow, Claire found herself mapping the beloved terrain of his features, the rugged shadow of stubble along his jaw, the mesmerizing flecks of amber scattered through his dark eyes, and that wayward curl at his nape that beckoned her fingers like a siren's call.

"And what about you?" she asked. "Are you ready to be transformed completely?"

Luca's response was to draw her even closer, one hand sliding into her hair while the other pressed against the small of her back, as if he couldn't bear even the whisper of space between them. When he spoke, his voice carried the raw honesty.

"Claire," he began, her name floating between them like a fragile wish carried on autumn wind, "I was transformed the moment I read your first note at Caffè Sereno. Before you, my art was technically perfect but emotionally safe. I painted what I saw, not what I felt." His fingers trembled slightly where they cradled her face. "But that morning, reading your words over and over... something in me broke open. Suddenly colors had new meaning, shadows held different secrets, and every blank canvas became a chance to capture not just beauty, but hope."

The morning sun streaming through the windows caught tears in his dark lashes, turning them to precious stones. Claire reached up to brush them away, but he caught her hand, pressing a kiss to her palm that felt like a vow.

"Every sketch I've made since meeting you," he continued, "every line I've drawn, they're all different now. Because I'm no longer just creating art..." His voice caught, and he had to pause, swallow hard before continuing. "I'm creating love letters. To you. To us. To this magnificent thing growing between us that makes everything else I've ever felt before seem like mirages compared to this masterpiece."

Claire felt tears spill over her own cheeks, but these were different from any she'd shed before, they carried not sadness but the exquisite ache of finding something so perfect it hurt to look at it directly. Like staring at the sun, like touching beauty too pure to be contained in moments.

"Last night," she said, her hands coming up to frame his face, "watching you paint, seeing how your whole being comes alive when you create... I realized I'd forgotten how to feel anything deeply enough to paint it. But you..." She had to pause, overcome by the intensity of emotion rising in her chest like a tide. "You make me feel everything so deeply I can barely contain it. Every color is brighter, every shadow holds meaning, every moment feels like art waiting to happen."

Luca's response was a kiss that seemed to gather all the morning's golden glow and pour it directly into Claire's soul. His lips moved against hers with passionate reverence, as if he were both worshipping at an altar and claiming his heart's deepest desire. One hand tangled in her hair while the other pressed her closer, his artist's calluses catching slightly against the silk of her dress that left trails of sweet fire wherever his fingers brushed.

When they finally parted, both breathless, he rested his forehead against hers. "I have something to show you," he revealed. "Something I've been working on since that first day, something I've never shown anyone."

Taking her hand, he led her to a corner of the studio she hadn't noticed before, hidden behind a heavy velvet curtain that seemed out of place in the otherwise informal space. His fingers found the edge of the fabric, hesitating for just a moment before drawing it aside.

The morning light flooded the space, revealing a series of canvases that left Claire awestruck. Each one captured a moment of their unfolding story, but not in conventional portraits or scenes. Instead, Luca had painted pure emotion, each canvas expressing a different facet of falling in love through abstract forms and colors that somehow managed to be more real than reality.

"This one," he said softly, indicating the first canvas, "was the morning when I found your first note on the caffè sospeso receipt. See how the colors are tentative, reaching toward each other but not quite touching? And here," his hand moved to the next piece, "this was the day you left your second note. Look how something in my heart starts to take form."

Each successive painting showed their connection growing stronger, deeper, more certain. The final canvas, blazed with such passionate intensity that Claire felt tears spring to her eyes. Gold and crimson danced together like flames, while underneath, deeper colors spoke of foundation, of permanence, of love that had roots as well as wings.

"I've titled the series 'Il Risveglio del Cuore' (The Awakening of the Heart)." Luca whispered, his arms sliding around her waist from behind, drawing her back against his chest.

Claire moved through the series of paintings in reverent silence, each one revealing another layer of their unfolding love story. Her fingers hovered near the canvases, not quite touching, as if she could feel the emotions radiating from them like heat from a flame. Luca remained behind her, his presence both anchor and inspiration, his hands resting lightly on her shoulders as if he couldn't bear to break contact completely.

"Here," she breathed, stopping before a canvas that seemed to shimmer with the liquid grace of moonlight on midnight waters. The painting captured the exact moment they had first truly recognized each other, not through physical meeting, but through art and words pieced together with ink-blessed wishes and midnight serenades. Sweeping lines of indigo and gold spiraled together like DNA strands, while smaller marks of brilliant white danced around them like sparks from a cosmic forge. "You've painted exactly how it felt, reading your notes, seeing your sketches. Like stardust settling in my veins."

Luca's hands tightened slightly on her shoulders, and when he spoke, his voice carried the rough edge of emotion barely contained. "You see it, then? How even before we met, we were creating something remarkable?" His lips brushed her temple, the gesture achingly beautiful. "In all my years of painting, I've never experienced anything like this. This need to capture not just what I see, but what I feel. What you make me feel."

She turned around, needing to see his face. The morning light caught his features at an angle that emphasized their classical beauty; the chiseled curve of his cheekbone, the artistic sensitivity on his lips, the depths in his dark eyes that seemed to hold centuries of Italian passion and poetry.

"Show me how you paint what you feel," she demanded gently, the words emerging with more courage than she knew she possessed. "Show me how to translate emotion into art the way you do."

A slow smile curved Luca's lips, transforming his face from merely handsome to devastating. Without speaking, he led her to a blank canvas already mounted on an easel. Standing behind her, he took her hand in his, wrapping his fingers around hers as they gripped a brush together.

"Close your eyes," he instructed with endearment. The music of Naples lived in his speech, turning everyday phrases into serenades against her ear. "Don't think about technique or rules. Just feel. Feel this moment, this connection, this..."

His other hand settled on her waist, drawing her back against his chest until she could feel his heartbeat against her spine, strong and steady as waves against Naples' ancient shores.

With her eyes closed, Claire's other senses heightened; the solid warmth of Luca against her back, the way his breath stirred her hair, the subtle tremor in his hand where it covered hers on the brush. His presence enveloped her like a celestial embrace, all-encompassing.

"Now," he resonated softly, "let the brush become an extension of you. Don't paint what you think love should look like. Paint how it feels in this exact moment."

Their joined hands began to move across the canvas, and Claire gasped softly at the sensation. It was unlike anything she'd experienced before; as if Luca's artistic soul was flowing through her, guiding her hand while simultaneously following her lead. Each stroke felt both deliberate and instinctive, like steps in a dance they'd somehow always known.

The scent of paint mingled with his cologne, creating an intoxicating blend that made her head spin. His other hand had slipped beneath the hem of her dress to trace spirals on her hip, each touch igniting every dormant nerve ending until her whole being hummed with an exquisite awareness of his presence. The intimate contact forged their painting into something more sensual, more primal, colors flowing across the canvas like lovers' caresses.

"Open your eyes," Luca suggested after what could have been minutes or hours. "See what we've created together."

Claire's eyes fluttered open to a vision that filled her with sunlight and immense joy. The artwork pulsed with raw emotion; broad, confident strokes of royal purple interweaving with sun-kissed coral, while accents of turquoise and warm bronze created unimaginable layers. Each color spoke its own love language, yet together they sang a harmony that touched something deeper. But what overwhelmed her completely was how their distinct artistic voices had woven together like twin flames merging into a single brilliant light, the precision of her careful brushstrokes now flowing seamlessly into his bold, passionate gestures, creating a visual symphony that spoke of two of them finding their perfect counterpoint in each other.

"It's us," she breathed, leaning back against his chest. "Not just what we look like or what we do, but who we are together. What we become when we..."

"When we love," Luca finished for her, turning her in his arms, his paint-stained hands coming up to frame her face. His dark eyes held an intensity that made her knees weak. "This is what love looks like mia Claire (my Claire). This is what we're painting together, not just on canvas, but in life."

Like the artists they were, they'd left their marks on each other; traces of paint that mapped their shared passion across skin and clothing. A streak of warm ivory painted Luca's jaw where Claire had touched him, while his fingers had left impressions of deep indigo and burnished rose gold on her waist. These beautiful battle scars of creation made Claire's heart ache with their perfect imperfection.

"You're trembling," Luca observed softly, his thumb tracing the curve of her lower lip. The tenderness in his touch contrasted exquisitely with the raw passion in his eyes, creating a tension that made breathing feel like a forgotten art. "Cold?"

"No," Claire revealed, leaning into his touch. "Overwhelmed. By you, by this, by how quickly everything I thought I knew about love and art and life has changed into something entirely new."

He smiled. His smile, patient and overwhelming like dawn breaking over the endless ocean. "Ah, mia bellissima (my most beautiful one)," he expressed with gentle passion, drawing her closer until their foreheads touched. "In Naples, we have a saying: 'L'amore è come l'arte, più ti lasci travolgere, più diventa bello.'"

"Love is like art," he translated, while her palm caressed the contours of his face. "The more you let it overwhelm you, the more beautiful it becomes."

His hands slid into her hair, cradling her head with infinite sensitivity. "And you, my Claire, you overwhelm me completely. Every brush stroke, every breath, every heartbeat since you walked into my life has been a new shade of beauty I never knew existed."

Oh, that intensity of emotion in his voice... Here was a man who approached love the way he approached art, with total commitment and passionate abandon, brave enough to pour himself completely into creation. No careful American dating rituals, no measured steps of getting to know each other. Just this headlong dive into something magnificent and terrifying and absolutely necessary.

"I don't know how to do this," she confessed, her hands fisting in his paint-stained shirt. "How to feel so much, so fast, so deeply. It's like trying to contain the ocean in a teacup."

Luca's response was to gather her closer, one hand sliding to the small of her back while the other cradled her face with an artist's precious touch. The morning light bathed them both in divine radiance.

"Claire," he breathed, her name escaping his lips like a confession too precious to contain, "you don't need to contain the ocean. Let it overflow. Let it reshape the landscape of your being. In Italy, we understand that love, like art, requires courage; the courage to let beauty break you open, to let passion remake you into something new."

His thumb brushed away a tear she hadn't realized had fallen, the callus on his finger catching slightly against her skin in a way that made her shiver. Every point of contact between them hummed with electricity, with promises yet to be given but already written in their shared art.

"Look at our painting," he continued, turning her gently in his arms until she faced their creation. "See how the colors don't fight to stay within the lines? How they bleed into each other, creating new shades that couldn't exist if they remained separate?" His lips brushed her temple, sending cascades of sensation down her spine. "That's how love can be, wild and free and transformative."

Claire leaned back against his chest, feeling his heartbeat against her shoulder blades. The painting before them seemed to stir with life, with passion, with the kind of truth that could only emerge when two souls brave enough to be vulnerable created something together.

"Before you," she shared, her fingers finding his where they rested on her waist, "I painted like I lived, in careful strokes, always worried about making mistakes, about going too far, feeling too much." She turned her head to press a kiss to his jaw, tasting the salt of his skin and the lingering traces of paint. "But you make me want to be reckless. To paint with my whole self, to love without measuring the cost."

Luca's arms tightened around her and the words from his mouth floated. "Then be reckless with me, mia Claire (my Claire). Let's create something magnificent together, not just on canvas, but in life. Something that makes the angels wonder about its beauty."

"Being reckless does not come naturally to me," Claire confessed.

"The things I have done since I met you, I could've never imagined I could do anything like that."

"Take as much time as you need. And know this," Luca murmured against Claire's hair, "Sono sempre qui per te (I am always here for you)." The Italian endearment flowed from his lips like sweet syrup.

His hands, those magnificent instruments that had created countless masterpieces, trembled slightly as they traced the curve of her waist. "From the moment I saw your note in Caffè Sereno, it was as if every painting I'd ever created was just practice for capturing this, capturing you, capturing us."

She looked at him. His eyes held her captive; those expressive Italian eyes that contained worlds of passion barely contained. They watched her now with a naked adoration. This was so different from Mark's careful American restraint, from the measured affection she'd known before. This was love as an art form, desire as a masterpiece in progress.

"I don't know how to love like this," she confessed. "Everything I knew before feels pale and insipid compared to how I feel when I'm with you. It's like..." she paused, searching for words big enough to contain this truth, "like I've been painting in pale watered down muted colors all my life, and suddenly you've handed me these vibrant paints and shown me what real depth looks like."

Luca caught her hand, pressing a kiss to her palm that bloomed through her body like roses opening to morning light. "Then let me teach you," he offered. "Let me show you how we love in Italy, with our whole hearts, without holding anything back. Let me show you how every moment can be art, how every touch can be a masterpiece, how every kiss can be a prayer."

His words painted pictures in her mind, as vast and beautiful as the Naples sky spreading beyond his studio windows. The air between them seemed to crystallize with potential.

Two weeks passed in a delicious blur of creativity and connection. Claire and Luca fell into a rhythm that felt at once new and strangely familiar, as if they'd been crafting this dance together across lifetimes. Claire found herself at Luca's studio several times a week after completing her client work.

She discovered a hidden shortcut that bypassed Naples' labyrinthine streets; a secret passage known only to locals that wound through terraced gardens where ancient olive trees stood, their silver-green leaves whispering secrets in the afternoon breeze. The narrow stone steps, worn smooth by centuries of footfalls, led her through a succession of hidden courtyards where citrus trees perfumed the air with their intoxicating fragrance. Lemons hung like captured sunlight among glossy leaves, and sometimes an elderly nonna would nod to her from a window above, recognizing her now as a regular presence in their private world. This enchanted path became Claire's daily pilgrimage to Luca's studio, each step bringing her closer not just to him, but to the woman she was becoming in this sun-drenched corner of Italy.

They created side by side, sometimes working on separate paintings, other times collaborating on shared canvases that seemed to capture the essence of their blossoming relationship; bold strokes meeting delicate lines, colors merging in unexpected harmony.

Some evenings they met at Caffè Sereno, where Signor Rossi and Lucia welcomed them with knowing smiles and plates of exquisite food that appeared without being ordered.

They were learning each other slowly, deliberately, each revelation a brushstroke in a masterpiece neither rushed nor forced. When they painted together, their bodies moved in instinctive harmony, sometimes not speaking for hours yet communicating everything through shared glances and the dance of creation.

One evening, as the day's final light streamed through tall windows to cast long shadows across the paint-splattered floor of Luca's Studio, Claire stood before her canvas, lost in that sacred space where time dissolved and only creation existed. Her dress, once a pale yellow, now bore the beautiful battle scars of artistic passion: cobalt streaks across the bodice, a crimson splash near the hem, emerald fingerprints along the sleeves.

For hours, she and Luca had worked in companionable silence, broken only by occasional murmurs of appreciation or the gentle sound of brushes swirling in water. The large studio space hummed with creative energy, alive with the scent of turpentine and linseed oil, with dreams taking form beneath skilled hands.

Luca moved behind his own canvas, muscles shifting beneath his paint-stained linen shirt as he reached toward the ceiling in a luxurious stretch. His dark curls caught the dying light, burnished to bronze as he rolled his shoulders to release the tension of hours spent in focused creation.

"I think I'm finished for today," Claire sighed, stepping back to assess her work with a critical eye. The painting, a study of Naples' harbor at sunrise, had evolved throughout the afternoon, the water now shimmering with precisely the luminous quality she'd been struggling to capture. "I should head back to my apartment before it gets too late."

Luca crossed the studio to stand beside her, his presence warm and solid as he studied her canvas. "Beautiful," he murmured, his voice carrying that particular reverence he reserved for art that moved him deeply. Then he turned to her, his expression shifting to something more personal, more intimate.

"Or," he suggested, the single word hanging between them like a bridge waiting to be crossed, "you could stay."

Claire's breath caught somewhere between surprise and anticipation. In the month since their first meeting at Caffè Sereno, they had shared countless hours in the studio, dozens of meals at Caffè Sereno, long walks through ancient streets where their fingers had gradually entwined with increasing certainty. But always, they parted ways at evening's end, back to their own homes.

"Stay?" she echoed, searching his eyes.

His smile emerged slowly, transforming his face from merely handsome to breathtaking. "My apartment is just upstairs," he explained, one paint-stained hand gesturing toward a door partially hidden behind a large canvas. "It's much closer than your place, and the view of the bay is..." he paused, as if seeking words grand enough, "indescribable at night. You could see it for yourself."

The invitation carried no pressure, only simple offering, another door opening in their gradually unfolding story. Claire found herself nodding before conscious thought could intervene, drawn by both curiosity about this private space she'd never seen and the magnetic pull that seemed to exist between them, growing stronger with each passing day.

"I'd like that," she said softly.

Luca's eyes warmed with pleasure as he moved to turn off the studio lights, leaving only a single lamp glowing near the back wall. In its gentle illumination, he led her toward the hidden entrance at the rear of the studio. He pulled open the weathered wooden door, revealing the staircase beyond. He placed his hand lightly at the small of her back as he ushered her through the door.

The staircase beyond rose in a graceful spiral, each step worn in the center from centuries of footfalls. Small sconces cast pools of amber light along the way, transforming their ascent into something almost ceremonial. Claire felt her heart quickening with each step, aware of Luca's presence close behind her, of the whisper of his breath near her ear.

At the top landing, another door awaited. Luca produced an ancient bronze key from his pocket, its intricate design catching the soft light as he slid it into the lock. It turned with a sound like destiny finding its path, the mechanism yielding with a satisfying click that seemed to mark a threshold being crossed. The door swung open, revealing a space that stole Claire's breath with its perfect reflection of the man she'd come to know.

The apartment unfolded before her like petals of a night-blooming flower; soaring ceilings crossed by ancient wooden beams, walls the warm gold of Neapolitan sunshine, floors of polished terra cotta that had witnessed centuries of life. Everywhere, evidence of an artist's soul and heart: bookshelves overflowing with volumes in multiple languages, copper pots hanging in the kitchen catching the last light like captured moons, a worn leather sofa positioned perfectly to capture the view.

And what a view it was. The windows, enormous arches that dominated the far wall, framed Naples like a living masterpiece. The bay stretched vast under the shimmering sky, while the city herself sparkled with a thousand lights beginning to emerge like stars fallen to earth.

"Oh, Luca," Claire breathed, moving as if in a dream. "It's magnificent."

He joined her there, opening the french doors to reveal the balcony. His presence was both exciting and comforting as they stood together before the panorama of Naples at twilight. The silence between them felt sacred, charged with unspoken understanding as the last crimson light painted them in identical hues of anticipation.

"Would you like some wine?" he asked finally, his voice carrying that slight roughness she'd come to recognize as emotion barely contained.

Claire nodded, following him to the kitchen where he selected a bottle with the casual expertise of someone who understood that wine, like art, was meant to enhance life's beauty. His movements were sure and graceful as he uncorked it, poured two glasses, his artist's hands making even this simple task seem like choreography.

They carried their wine to the relaxing chairs in the balcony, settling close enough that she could feel the warmth of him, the subtle scent of sandalwood and paint that had become as familiar to her as her own heartbeat. Outside, night had fully claimed Naples, transforming the view into a constellation of golden lights against velvety darkness, the bay a sheet of black silk embroidered with reflections.

"Your home is beautiful," Claire said, taking a sip of wine that bloomed across her tongue with notes of sunshine and earth. "It feels exactly like you."

Luca's smile held a touch of shyness, surprising in a man usually so confident. "I've been adding pieces slowly," he explained, his free hand gesturing to the space inside. "Each one has a story, a memory."

As the night deepened around them, those stories emerged; the copper pots inherited from his grandmother who had taught him to cook as a child, the ancient olive wood table rescued from a villa being demolished, the collection of art books acquired during his travels through Europe. With each revelation, another layer of Luca revealed itself, another piece of his soul offered to her with humble generosity.

Their wine glasses emptied and were refilled as conversation flowed between them with the easy rhythm they'd established over these weeks of discovery. Before settling back on the chair, Luca excused himself to the kitchen, returning moments later with a worn wooden board laden with antipasti that he'd assembled with the same artistic precision he brought to his canvases. Aged pecorino nestled against paper-thin slices of prosciutto that gleamed like rose quartz in the low light. Plump olives glistened with a sheen of olive oil, while tiny sweet peppers stuffed with herbed ricotta added vibrant spots of crimson to the composition. Fresh bread, torn rather than cut, revealed a golden interior that seemed to capture the apartment's warm glow.

"Just a little something," he said with a modest shrug that belied the thoughtful curation of the platter. His fingers, so skilled with paint-brushes, moved with equal dexterity as he arranged plucked sprigs of rosemary and basil from his windowsill garden onto the platter.

Claire watched, entranced by this new dimension of him, how naturally he moved between artist and host, how the same hands that created breathtaking canvases could also craft such simple, perfect pleasure. The night felt different; more intimate, more charged with possibility. Perhaps it was the sanctuary of his private space, or the way Naples spread beneath them like a tapestry of shared dreams, or simply the natural evolution of what had been growing between them since that first exchange of notes at Caffè Sereno.

When Luca reached to brush a strand of hair from her face, his fingers lingered against her cheek in a tender caress. The air between them seemed to crystallize, holding them suspended in a moment of perfect potential. His eyes, reflecting the distant lights of the city, held a question that needed no words.

Claire's answer came not in speech but in movement, her hand rising to cover his where it cradled her face. Something elemental passed between them; permission, invitation, certainty. When their lips met, it felt like the final brushstroke on a canvas they'd been painting together since the beginning, completing a masterpiece that had existed first in possibility, now manifesting in exquisite reality.

The kiss deepened, transforming from gentle exploration to mutual discovery, each touch revealing new territories of sensation. Luca's artist's hands, so skilled at creating beauty, now created something even more profound as they traced the contours of her face, her shoulders, the curve of her waist with reverent appreciation.

"Claire," he whispered against her lips, her name emerging like a prayer, like gratitude for something long awaited. "My beautiful Claire."

What followed was its own kind of artistry; a composition of tenderness and passion, of discovery and recognition. They moved together through the apartment, a sanctuary separate from time, from the world beyond those magnificent windows. Moonlight painted them in silver and shadow as clothing gave way to the desire for closeness without barriers, each new revelation of skin meeting skin like colors blending on a palette, creating shades neither could achieve alone.

In Luca's bedroom, a space of calm beauty dominated by a bed crafted from ancient wood, they created their most intimate masterpiece yet. His hands mapped her body with an artist's appreciation and a lover's adoration, finding places that made her gasp, that made her bones turn to watercolor, flowing beyond their ordinary boundaries. In turn, she discovered the landscape of him; the strength in his shoulders, the vulnerability at the hollow of his throat, the places where tenderness elicited sounds that resonated through her entire being.

Their each touch was a brush stroke, each kiss a new shade of passion, each shared breath a moment of artistic perfection. In the sanctuary of his bed, beneath the ancient beams that had witnessed centuries of love stories, they wrote the beginning of their own most beautiful chapter. As they crested the peak together, it transcended mere physical union, becoming instead a conversation between souls finding perfect harmony.

Afterward, they lay tangled in Italian sheets that carried the scent of lavender and newfound intimacy, the moonlight through shuttered windows painting patterns across their skin. Luca propped himself on one elbow, his dark eyes drinking in Claire's features with wonder, as if seeing her for the first time. His free hand traced patterns on her skin that felt like sketches being drawn in light; each touch reverent, tender, memorizing.

"I've imagined this," he confessed softly, his voice carrying the raw honesty that emerged only in moments of profound connection. "Not just this..." his gesture encompassed their entwined bodies, "... but you here, in my home, in my life. It felt right from the beginning, like a painting I'd been working on in my dreams suddenly taking form in the waking world."

Claire caught his hand, pressing a kiss to his palm that made his breath catch. "I've never felt anything like this," she whispered against his skin. "It's as if every moment before you was just preparation, just learning the techniques that would allow me to create something real."

His smile bloomed slow and certain in the moonlight as he gathered her closer, her head finding the perfect resting place against his chest where his heartbeat created a rhythm as steady as waves against Naples' ancient shores. They spoke softly into the night, words flowing between them like paint diluted with perfect medium; sometimes serious, sometimes playful, always revealing new dimensions of connection.

Sleep found them still entwined, Claire's copper hair spread across Luca's chest, his arms holding her as if she were the most precious creation he'd ever encountered.

Morning arrived with gentle insistence, sunlight slipping through the shutters to paint stripes of gold across the rumpled bed. Claire woke slowly, her body luxuriating in the unfamiliar yet completely right sensation of Luca's warmth beside her. For a moment, she simply watched him sleep; the dark lashes fanned against his cheeks, the slight smile that curved his lips even in dreams, the tousled curls that begged for her fingers to smooth them.

As if sensing her gaze, he stirred, his eyes opening to find her immediately. The smile that bloomed across his face held such unguarded joy that Claire felt her heart expand beyond its ordinary boundaries.

"Buongiorno, mia bella artista (Good morning, my beautiful artist)," he murmured, his voice rough with sleep yet warm with happiness. "Did you sleep well?"

"Mmm," she hummed, stretching languidly against him. "Better than I can remember."

His hand traced the curve of her shoulder, down her arm, finding her fingers to entwine with his own. "I love waking to find you here," he said simply. "It just feels right."

The morning light revealed new details of his bedroom that darkness had concealed; a small bookshelf beside the bed filled with poetry volumes and art monographs, a chair draped with a handwoven blanket in shades of Mediterranean blue, a single perfect painting of Naples Bay at daybreak, where first light transformed the water into shimmering hues of apricot sorbet and peach mousse, hanging opposite the bed.

With gentle consideration, Luca rose first, pressing a kiss to her forehead before crossing to an antique chest. From it, he produced a soft towel, a new toothbrush still in its packaging, and one of his T-shirts, presenting them with a blend of courtly grace and shy thoughtfulness.

"This should work," he said, offering the shirt with a gentle smile. "It'll be a bit large, but comfortable." He gestured toward the ornate door. "Bathroom's through there. I'll use the one down the hall. You freshen up. And then we'll have some breakfast and coffee. Does that sound good?" Claire nodded, trying to ignore how her heart fluttered at the casual way he said 'we', as if their shared morning was the most natural thing in the world.

The bathroom, like the rest of his apartment, reflected Luca's essence perfectly; the vintage fixtures speaking of respect for history, the modern comforts seamlessly integrated, fresh flowers in a small vase suggesting appreciation for beauty in even the most private spaces. Claire showered beneath water that seemed to wash away not just sleep but any lingering doubt, any hesitation about the path she and Luca were creating together.

When she emerged, the apartment now had a symphony of morning sounds and aromas that drew her toward the kitchen. There she found Luca, moving with practiced grace through his culinary domain, his bare feet padding softly across the terra cotta tiles. The sight that stopped her breath was the simple dish towel carelessly flung over his left shoulder, a detail so mundane yet somehow devastating in its effect on her. She'd seen countless men in expensive suits and carefully curated outfits, but there was something about this, the casual intimacy of a man at ease in his kitchen, that disheveled towel draped with unconscious grace, that made her pulse quicken in ways she couldn't quite explain. Heat rose to her cheeks as she realized she was staring, wondering when exactly a dish towel had become the most attractive accessory a man could wear.

With the same focused intensity she'd witnessed in his studio, Luca was now crafting their breakfast as if it were another masterpiece. His hands moved with artist's precision as he sautéed leeks until they turned translucent as sea glass, then added fresh spinach that wilted into deeper shades of emerald. She watched, mesmerized, as he cracked eggs into a bowl, added cream and salt, whisking them with a rhythm that spoke of countless mornings spent in this kitchen. Fragments of fontina cheese melted like drops of sunlight over the frittata he was creating, while fresh basil leaves, plucked from the terracotta pot on the windowsill, released their aromatic essence into the air.

He suddenly announced, "Just one more thing!" and bounded out the door, down the stairs, all the way to the courtyard. Claire found herself drawn to the window. There, she watched him reach up into the lemon tree, its leaves dappled with morning light, to select a single perfect lemon, as if even this small detail needed to be exactly right for their first shared breakfast.

Taking her eyes off the courtyard view, Claire turned at the sound of his footsteps ascending the stairs. Luca burst back into the kitchen, lemon in hand and triumph in his eyes, as if he'd retrieved some rare treasure. The light caught the slight sheen of exertion on his forearms as he zested the lemon, his hands wielding the wooden-handled zester with the same artistry they brought to his canvases, releasing delicate yellow ribbons that fell like confetti onto their breakfast. Then he cut the lemon and squeezed some juice over the frittata.

They settled at the small kitchen island, thighs almost touching on adjacent stools, and ate straight from the skillet; an intimacy that felt both casual and profound. Steam rose from their coffee cups like dancers in slow embrace, and Claire couldn't help but notice how Luca's eyes crinkled with pleasure each time she reached forward with her fork, as if sharing this simple meal brought him as much joy as sharing his art.

The fontina cheese stretched in silken strands between their forks, creating gossamer bridges that made them both laugh, and in that moment, Claire realized that sometimes the most exquisite masterpieces weren't painted on canvas at all, but were created in quiet morning moments like this. The way he savored each bite, the fleeting brush of his arm against hers as they reached for their coffee cups; it all wove together into something far more intimate than she'd expected from a breakfast.

As they lingered over second cups of coffee, the morning light shifting through the apartment to paint new patterns across the ancient floors, Luca's expression suddenly changed, a remembered obligation surfacing in his consciousness.

"I almost forgot," he said, his free hand capturing hers across the small space between them. "My friend Alessandro is hosting a gallery opening this evening. He's featuring several of my paintings alongside his own work."

"That's wonderful!" Claire exclaimed, genuinely delighted for him. "You must be excited."

A slight shadow crossed his face as his thumb traced absent patterns on her palm. "I hadn't planned to attend," he admitted. "I thought perhaps we could spend the evening together instead."

Claire studied him with growing understanding. "You should go," she said gently. "It's important to support your friend, and to be present when your work is being celebrated." Her fingers tightened around his. "There will be more evenings for us to spend together."

His eyes brightened, the shadow lifting. "You're right, of course. But..." he hesitated, his expression turning hopeful, "would you come with me? I'd love for you to meet Alessandro, to see my work displayed alongside his. To be there with me."

The invitation touched her deeply; not just the event itself, but what it represented: Luca wanting to share his professional world with her, to introduce her to his artistic community, to stand beside her as both his personal and creative worlds merged.

"I'd love to," she said. "Let me head back to my apartment to get ready, then you can pick me up."

Luca's expression shifted to that particular intensity she'd come to recognize as inspiration taking hold. He rose from his stool, moving to kiss her with surprising fervor before pulling back with determination in his eyes.

"I have a better idea," he said enthusiastically. "There's a boutique just around the corner owned by a friend of my mother's. Let me get something for you from there. Give me an hour."

Claire caught his hand, her expression turning serious despite the smile playing at her lips. "You should know something about me," she said, mapping treasured territories on his palm with her fingertip. "I have a perfect record of hating every single piece of clothing that anyone has ever given me. Family, friends; they've all learned not to try. I'm impossibly fussy about clothes."

Instead of looking deterred, Luca's smile only grew more confident. "Ah, but they weren't looking at you with an artist's eye, were they?" He pressed a kiss to her palm that somehow managed to be both reverent and slightly wicked. "Trust me. And if you don't love what I bring, I'll return it."

Something about his absolute certainty, combined with the way he was looking at her, as if she were a masterpiece he'd already composed in his mind, made her nod. "Alright," she agreed, reaching up to brush a wayward curl from his forehead. "Show me what an artist sees when he looks at me."

Luca dressed with the kind of effortless Italian elegance that made even simple clothes look like fashion statements, then pressed a lingering kiss to her lips before heading out on his mission.

Left alone in his apartment, she wandered through the rooms, discovering new details that revealed further dimensions of the man she was getting closer to. A collection of small sculptures arranged on a windowsill, each one a different artist's interpretation of hands creating; a wall of photographs showing Luca with various people, all caught in moments of genuine connection; a small desk positioned to catch perfect morning light, covered with sketches and handwritten notes.

The apartment felt like a visual autobiography, every object selected with meaning rather than mere decoration. Moving through these rooms was like reading chapters of Luca's life, understanding him more deeply with each new discovery.

When he returned just under an hour later, his arms were laden with garment bags from what was clearly an exclusive Naples boutique. His expression barely contained excitement as he laid them carefully across the bed.

"I couldn't choose between them," he admitted, a slight flush coloring his cheeks as he watched her reaction. "Each one spoke to me of different aspects of you, like trying to capture Naples in just one color."

Claire felt her eyebrows rise in amused surprise. "How many dresses did you buy?"

"Three," he confessed, his artist's hands moving to unzip the first garment bag with ceremonial care. "But if you hate them, the boutique owner will take them back. No pressure at all."

The first dress drew a gasp from Claire's lips. The color was exactly that shade of deep Mediterranean blue that Luca had used in his paintings of their love story, the cut somehow managing to be both elegantly modest and subtly sensual. When touched, the fabric felt like water, catching the light in ways that made her think of sunset, or maybe sunrise, she couldn't decide.

The second dress was the color of Italian fresco in sunlight, with dainty details that reminded her of the architectural elements in Naples' ancient churches. It lay across the bed like a whisper of a dream, its folds creating valleys and peaks that caught the morning light streaming through the windows. The craftsmanship was evident even at rest, each embellishment positioned with intention, promising to transform whoever would eventually slide into its embrace.

And then the third dress! It was a beautiful shade of green, almost like the color of fresh sage, that Luca had used to paint hope in his abstract series, with subtle undertones of light through leaves. The cut was pure Italian sophistication, promising to make Claire feel like she belonged in this city of eternal beauty.

"Luca," she breathed, running her fingers over each dress with growing wonder. "They're all beautiful. I don't know how to choose."

His smile bloomed slow and satisfied, like sunrise breaking over the bay. "Then don't choose," he said simply, coming to stand behind her, his hands settling on her waist with warm certainty. "Keep them all."

"I can't accept all three," she protested, though her heart was already imagining how each of them would look in the gallery's light, how it would feel to stand beside Luca wearing something he had chosen specifically for her.

Luca turned her gently to face him, his expression more serious now. "Claire," he said softly, his hands framing her face with artist's precision, "in Italy, we understand that beauty should be honored, celebrated, embraced without hesitation. These dresses. They're not just fabric. They're my way of showing you how I see you, how beautiful you are to me. Please, accept them."

Put that way, as an artist's tribute rather than mere extravagance, the gifts took on a different meaning. Claire found herself nodding, her hands coming up to cover his where they cradled her face.

"Thank you," she whispered. "I'll wear the blue one today."

His smile was reward enough, but the kiss that followed, tender yet carrying undercurrents of passion barely restrained, made her grateful for all the circumstances that had led her to this moment, to this man, to this unfolding love story in the heart of Naples.

As dusk approached and preparations began, Claire found herself before Luca's mirror, hardly recognizing the woman who gazed back at her. The Mediterranean blue dress transformed her, flowing around her body like water finding its natural course, the color bringing out hidden gold in her eyes that she'd never noticed before. She'd twisted her hair into a simple updo, allowing a few strands to frame her face in a way that felt both elegant and natural.

When Luca emerged, he stopped mid-stride, his eyes widening as they took her in. For a moment, he simply stared, his expression one of such genuine appreciation that Claire felt herself flush beneath his gaze.

"Claire," he breathed finally, crossing to where she stood. "You're absolutely breathtaking."

He himself had transformed from the paint-splattered artist to something from an Italian fashion magazine; charcoal suit that fit his athletic frame with tailored precision, crisp white shirt open at the collar, his dark curls tamed into artful dishevelment. Together, they looked like characters stepping out of an Italian art film, except this was real, this was happening, this was their story unfolding.

Instead of his usual Vespa, Luca surprised her by revealing a vintage Fiat in the courtyard, a charming little car in pale yellow, matching its color to the lemons on the tree under which it was parked.

"She was my grandfather's," he explained, helping Claire into the passenger seat with old-world courtesy and carefully placing the garment bags with the two new dresses and the one she wore yesterday on the back seat. "I restored her myself over three summers. I only drive her on special occasions."

The Fiat wound through Naples' labyrinthine streets like a dancer, Luca's hands confident on the wheel as they navigated passages so narrow that Claire could almost reach out and touch the sun-warmed stones of buildings on either side. As they made their way toward the gallery, Claire found herself filled with a sense of perfect contentment.

The gallery was housed in a renovated 17th-century palazzo, its limestone facade illuminated by strategically placed lights that transformed the ancient stone into a canvas of shadows and golden warmth. As they entered, the space opened around them like a flower; high ceilings traced with original frescoes, walls painted in neutral tones that allowed the art to command attention, the gentle murmur of conversations in Italian creating a melodic backdrop.

Alessandro spotted them immediately, a man with an artist's intense gaze who moved through the crowd with magnetic presence. His face split into a grin of genuine delight when he saw Luca.

"Luca! Finalmente (Finally)!" he exclaimed, embracing his friend with typical Italian demonstrativeness before turning curious eyes toward Claire. "And you must be the American artist Luca has been telling me about."

Luca's hand settled at the small of her back, warm and reassuring as he made the introduction. "Alessandro, this is Claire Bennett. Claire, my oldest friend and occasional artistic rival, Alessandro Bianchi."

There was something in Alessandro's appraising gaze, a knowing look that suggested Luca had shared more about Claire than just her name and nationality. "The influence behind the new direction in Luca's work," he said, taking her hand in both of his. "Now I understand."

The evening unfolded like a dream sequence; champagne in delicate flutes, conversations about art that flowed between English and Italian, introductions to Naples' creative community who welcomed Claire with genuine warmth. Throughout it all, Luca remained a steady presence beside her, his hand occasionally finding the small of her back or his fingers entwining with hers, their bodies instinctively orienting toward each other even when engaged in separate conversations.

When they reached the wall dedicated to Luca's paintings, Claire's breath caught in her throat. Here was his soul laid bare for all to see; canvases that captured emotion in abstract forms, each one pulsing with the kind of passionate intensity that had drawn her to his work from the beginning. But what made her heart stumble was seeing several pieces she recognized from his studio's hidden collection, works inspired by their connection, by the transformation that had begun with coffee-stained notes exchanged at Caffè Sereno.

"This one," Alessandro said, gesturing to a particularly striking canvas dominated by shades of amber and indigo that seemed to move like ocean currents, "has already sold to a collector from Milan. He said it made him feel something he couldn't name but couldn't live without."

Claire felt Luca's eyes on her rather than on the painting, and when she turned to meet his gaze, the vulnerability there made her throat tighten with emotion. This was a different kind of intimacy; seeing how she had influenced his artistic expression, witnessing the translation of their private connection into public art.

"Do you see?" he asked quietly, just for her ears. "What you've awakened?"

As midnight approached, they made their farewells to Alessandro and his wife Sofia. The night embraced them as they stepped from the gallery's warmth, the stars scattered above Naples like diamonds flung across dark velvet. In the little Fiat, driving through streets now quieted from their daytime chaos, Claire felt a profound contentment settle over her.

"Your friends are wonderful," she said as they wound through a narrow passage that opened suddenly to reveal the bay, its waters reflecting the city's twinkling lights.

Luca smiled, the streetlights painting his profile in fleeting gold as they passed beneath them. "They liked you immediately, I could tell," he said, his voice warm with pleasure. "Sofia told me I seemed different tonight, more present." His free hand found hers across the car's small interior. "She's right. Being with you makes me feel more alive, more connected to everything around me."

Claire's heart swelled at his words, and she squeezed his hand gently in response. Their eyes met briefly in the dim light of the car, a silent acknowledgment of the deepening connection between them. She didn't need words to express how his confession touched her; her soft smile and the tender way she leaned slightly toward him said everything.

The little Fiat continued its journey through Naples' night-hushed streets, its vintage engine purring contentedly as they wound past ancient buildings and moonlit piazzas. The car seemed perfectly at home in these narrow passages, navigating them with the same easy confidence as its owner. Claire found herself admiring how the little vehicle embodied the spirit of the city; compact, stylish, resilient, and unapologetically full of character.

"Your Fiat is incredible," Claire said, running her hand appreciatively along the dashboard. "There's something so special about it, so authentically Italian, so perfectly you."

Luca smiled, his eyes briefly leaving the road to find hers. "Grazie (Thanks). She has character, doesn't she?" His fingers drummed affectionately on the steering wheel. "Tomorrow, if you're free, my Fiat and I would like to show you some places around Naples that tourists never see."

The idea of seeing these hidden places with Luca, of experiencing the landscape that had shaped him as an artist, filled Claire with a sense of anticipation she hadn't felt in years. "I'd love that," she said softly. "What time will you pick me up?"

"Early," he replied, turning the Fiat down the narrow street that led to her apartment. "The morning light is magical here; like liquid gold pouring over everything it touches."

As they pulled up in front of her building, the massive blue door stood illuminated by a single streetlight, its ancient wood telling stories of countless homecomings across centuries. Luca shut off the engine and quickly circled the car, opening her door with that old-world gallantry that seemed so natural to him.

He extended his hand, helping her from the car with a gesture that managed to be both respectful and intimate. Standing before her apartment building, they lingered in the gentle cocoon of night, neither quite ready to part.

"Thank you for tonight," he said, his voice dropping to that velvety baritone that made her heart stumble. "For sharing my work, my friends... for being there beside me."

"Thank you for inviting me into your world," Claire replied, feeling the weight of something profound that had shifted, as if the universe had rearranged itself around this new reality they were creating together.

Luca drew her close, one hand coming up to cradle her face with an artist's precise touch. The kiss began gently, a question, an offering, then deepened as Claire responded, her fingers finding his hair, drawing him closer. The world beyond their embrace seemed to disappear, leaving only this perfect moment of connection suspended in the Neapolitan night.

When they finally broke apart, both slightly breathless, Luca pressed his forehead against hers. "Until tomorrow," he whispered, the words carrying the weight of promise. Then he retrieved the garment bags from the back seat, carefully draping them over his arm. "Let me help you carry these upstairs," he offered, his eyes never leaving hers. She smiled and assured him that she could manage.

He waited as she slipped through the massive blue door, his tall figure perfectly still, a silhouette of devotion against the cobblestones. Claire climbed the ancient stairs, each step taking her further from him yet somehow bringing her closer to the woman she was becoming in his presence.

Reaching her apartment, she moved immediately to turn on the lights, then crossed to the balcony. Something told her he would still be there, waiting to see her safely home. When she stepped out into the night air, she saw him, exactly where she'd left him, his eyes raised to her balcony as if drawn by invisible threads.

Claire waved, the simple gesture carrying emotions too vast for any words. His answering wave rose through the night air between them, a promise spanning the distance. Only then did he return to his car, sliding into the driver's seat.

She watched as the little yellow Fiat pulled away, its vintage outline gradually blending into the tapestry of Naples at night, until it disappeared around a corner. Claire remained on her balcony, her fingers tracing her lips where his kiss still lingered, the Mediterranean breeze playing with her hair as she savored the perfect completion of this evening and the anticipation of tomorrow's adventure to experience the hidden treasures that tourists never see.

6

BEAUTY THROUGH ARTIST'S EYES

The morning light crept through the lace curtains of Claire's apartment, painting her bedroom walls in a way that reminded her of how Luca's hands moved when he painted; fluid, purposeful, full of commitment. She lay in bed for a moment, savoring the thrill that hummed through her veins like electricity. Today marked a new adventure in their relationship; Luca had planned a special excursion to show her the hidden treasures beyond Naples, the secret places only locals knew about in the surrounding countryside.

Her phone buzzed with a text from him: "Buongiorno, mia bella artista (good morning, my beautiful artist). Pack your sketchbook and wear comfortable shoes. Today, we begin our adventure."

Claire's heart performed a complicated dance in her chest as she read his words. Even through the simple medium of text messages, his Italian passion spilled through, making ordinary moments feel like scenes from an epic romance.

She dressed carefully in a flowing sundress the color of fresh sage, one of the three dresses Luca had picked for her the previous day. The fabric moved like wind blowing through a forest, rustling the leaves ever so softly.

She gathered her art supplies; sketchbook, pencils, the new set of paints she'd been saving for a special occasion. Each item went into her leather portfolio with the kind of care usually reserved for sacred objects.

When she heard the door knock, her skin warmed with a rush of sensation, her body responding to that now-familiar symphony that only Luca could inspire. Opening the door revealed him leaning against the frame with casual Italian elegance, looking like something stepped from a Fellini film in his white linen shirt and artfully disheveled dark curls.

"You look gorgeous!" He said looking at her. "Ready to see beauty through my eyes?" he asked.

Claire's answer was a smile that contained universes of yes.

Luca's vintage Fiat wound through the streets of Naples and beyond like a mirage in motion, each turn revealing treasures, inspiring Claire in new ways. He drove with one hand on the wheel, the other resting on her knee, his thumb tracing promises that sent shivers dancing along her skin.

"First," he announced as they climbed higher into the hills above the city, "I show you where inspiration sleeps."

The car emerged into a hidden courtyard that seemed to exist outside of time itself. Ancient stone walls rose around them, weathered by centuries of sun and rain into something that looked more like natural formations than human-built structures. Wisteria cascaded down these walls in purple waterfalls, their fragrance mingling with the morning air like nature's own perfume.

"The old monastery gardens," Luca explained, coming around to open her door with that effortless grace that made even simple movements look like choreography. "Most tourists never find this place. But artists..." His dark eyes sparkled with secrets as he helped her from the car. "Artists have been coming here for centuries to capture how nature reclaims what humans have built."

Claire's breath caught as they stepped through an archway draped with climbing roses. Before them stretched a series of terraced gardens that descended the hillside like a giant's staircase. Each level held its own magic; herb gardens that perfumed the air with rosemary and sage, citrus trees heavy with fruit that glowed like captured sunlight, hidden corners where stone benches waited beneath arbors thick with flowering vines.

"Oh, Luca," she breathed, her fingers already itching for her sketchbook. "It's like stepping into a painting."

He drew her closer, his arm sliding around her waist with possessive tenderness. "This is just the beginning, mia bella (my beautiful one). Watch how everything changes as the sun keeps moving. See how each moment creates new masterpieces?"

From the back of his car, he retrieved art supplies... and a familiar looking package. "Before coming to pick you up, I stopped at Caffè Sereno," he said with a smile. "Lucia has packed her famous breakfast sandwiches made with eggs, ham, and a local cheese." Claire watched him with awe as he gathered the food package and a thermos filled with, what Claire could guess, Signor Rossi's amazing coffee. Luca's thoughtfulness, his nurturing, his outright mothering was heartwarming.

Together they settled on a bench beneath a centuries-old olive tree, their breakfast and art supplies spread between them like offerings to the muse.

He helped her set her easel and then set his own right next to her. As Claire began to sketch, she felt Luca's eyes on her; not watching her work, but watching her face, as if her expressions while creating were the real art he wanted to capture.

The monastery gardens enveloped them in a cocoon of timeless beauty as Claire's pencil danced across paper, capturing the way light filtered through ancient olive branches to paint dappled patterns on weathered stone. Beside her, Luca sketched with an intensity engaging his entire being, his usual easy grace replaced by the focused zeal of an artist lost in creation.

Occasionally their eyes would meet over their respective sketchbooks, and in those moments, Claire felt as if her heart was learning a new rhythm, one that beat in perfect synchronization with his. She felt that in these surroundings his classical features had turned into something that belonged in ancient times.

"Look," he said suddenly, moving behind her. His chest pressed against her back as he reached around to guide her hand holding the pencil. "See how the shadows create depth here?" His fingers, warm and sure over hers, traced lines she hadn't noticed before. "And here, where the light breaks through leaves, it creates an intricate design like lace on marble."

The intimacy of the moment, his breath warm against her ear, his body cradling hers, their hands moving together across paper, dissolved Claire into liquid longing. She could feel his steady beat against her shoulder blades, its rhythm as constant as waves against Naples' ancient shores.

"You see the world differently," she melted into his embrace. "Everything through your eyes becomes art waiting to happen."

Luca's free hand slid around her waist, drawing her closer until there wasn't even air between them. "I think we both see the world as artists," he conveyed in velvety tones, his lips brushing her temple. "Sometimes we just need someone who understands to remind us how to look. Watch..."

He guided their joined hands to capture a new detail; the way a fallen blossom created a perfect shadow on sun-warmed stone, how morning light turned dew drops into diamonds scattered across ancient steps. Each stroke they made together felt like a love letter written in graphite and shadow.

And in that perfect morning moment, surrounded by centuries of beauty and the man who helped her see it anew, Claire felt herself falling even deeper into the masterpiece they were creating together. And she wasn't even thinking about the piece of art in front of her.

After their morning of sketching, Luca led Claire deeper into the monastery grounds, through an ivy-covered archway that seemed to guard mysteries centuries old. The path narrowed, stones worn smooth by countless footsteps before theirs, until it opened into a hidden courtyard that drew a soft gasp from Claire's lips.

Here, nature and architecture had merged into something that transcended both. A fountain played at the center, its gentle music a counterpoint to distant church bells. Around it, wild roses climbed ancient columns in riotous displays of dusty pink and cream, their perfume mingling with the salt breeze from the distant bay.

"This is where I come when I need peace," Luca said softly, drawing her to sit beside him on the fountain's worn marble edge. Water music played behind them as he reached into his satchel and withdrew a small package wrapped in brown paper and tied with twine. "I brought something for you."

Claire's fingers trembled slightly as she undid the simple wrapping. Inside lay a leather-bound sketchbook, its cover the exact shade of color that sunlight turned to when it caught in Luca's dark eyes. The paper within was thick, textured, the kind that made artists' hearts skip beats with its potential.

"I had it made specially," he explained, his voice carrying that slight roughness she was learning meant he felt vulnerable. "See here?" His artist's fingers traced the subtle pattern embossed in the leather, tiny moths and fireflies dancing together, an echo of their first shared artwork. "So you'll always remember how our story began."

Tears pricked at Claire's eyes as she ran her fingers over the design. "Luca, it's perfect. It's..." she trailed off.

He caught her hand, pressing a kiss to her palm. "This garden has inspired artists for centuries," he raved. "Now it will hold the beginning of your renaissance too, your return to seeing the world through an artist's eyes."

And then she saw something that made her speechless. Each textured paper inside the sketchbook had her name embossed at the bottom right corner "Claire", like an artist's signature, beautifully announcing to the viewers who created the art. She had never seen her name written so artfully. She looked at Luca. Without a single word from her he understood; everything she wanted to say, everything she wanted him to know.

The first birdsong of day orchestrated a gentle symphony around them as Claire turned to face him fully, the precious sketchbook cradled between them like their shared future made tangible. "By giving me this, you're," she paused to look for words, "you're helping me remember who I was before I forgot how to see beauty in everything. You've given me... me." She trailed off.

The fountain's melody surrounded them as Luca reached into his satchel once more. "One more thing," he said, his voice rich with anticipation. "Close your eyes."

Claire felt something cool and smooth being pressed into her palm.

Opening her eyes, she found a small glass bottle filled with deep sepia ink.

"From the monastery's ancient recipe," he explained, watching her face with tender intensity. "The monks here made their own ink for centuries. This is the last batch made in the traditional way; walnut shells, iron salts, time, and patience. The same ink countless artists used to capture this very garden."

The bottle gleamed in the morning light, its contents swirling with hints of copper and mahogany. Claire uncapped it, inhaling the complex aroma that spoke of earth and wisdom and stories yet untold.

"Now," Luca exulted, producing an elegant wooden pen from his pocket and filling it with the ancient ink, "let's make something beautiful together."

They sat side by side at the fountain's edge, sharing the pen between them. Each took turns adding elements to a single drawing, Claire capturing the graceful arch of ancient stonework, Luca adding the wild roses that embraced it, their artistic styles merging and dancing together on the page with a perfect harmony.

The morning deepened around them as they worked, adding intimate details to capture the essence of the garden. Above them, swallows darted through azure skies, their wings cutting graceful arcs that begged to be captured in ink and imagination.

"This garden," Luca said softly as they added final touches to their shared creation, "it's like what we feel about each other; familiar and new at once, wild and structured, full of surprises waiting to be discovered."

Claire looked at their drawing, at the way their distinct styles had merged into something entirely new, something neither could have created alone. "Show me more," she demanded playfully. "Show me all the places that make your artist's soul sing."

Luca's smile held mysteries as he gathered their supplies. "This is just the beginning, mia bella artista (my beautiful artist). Naples and its surroundings have so many secrets to share with those who know where to look."

The Fiat curved along coastal roads as Luca guided them away from the monastery gardens, each turn revealing new vistas that made Claire want to reach for her new sketchbook. The Mediterranean stretched endless and blue beside them, while ahead, cliffs rose in dramatic sweeps against cerulean skies.

"I love watching you see everything for the first time," Luca said, his eyes dancing between the road and her expressions of wonder. "It makes me experience it all anew."

The car slowed as they approached what appeared to be a simple turnout in the road. But when Luca led Claire through a narrow path between ancient olive trees, she discovered something magical; a small, hidden cove nestled between towering cliffs, accessible only to those who knew where to look.

"The fishermen used to shelter here during storms," he explained, spreading a blanket on a smooth expanse of rock. While her gaze lingered on the breathtaking panorama surrounding them, he slipped away to the car, returning moments later with a small picnic basket cradled in his hands. As he gently placed it between them and lifted the lid, the basket revealed a carefully arranged treasure of local delicacies; fresh figs bursting with sweetness, cheese that tasted of mountain herbs, bread still slightly warm from some hidden bakery's ovens, an ornate glass bottle with preserved lemons that captured the essence of summer itself, and chocolates filled with gooey caramel sprinkled with sea salt on top.

"A surprise picnic?" Claire smiled, accepting a perfect fig from his fingers.

"The best art comes from a well-nourished soul," he replied, arranging their feast with the same care he gave to composing a painting. They enjoyed the food and the view; vibrant blue waves dancing below, distant islands floating like dreams on the horizon, fishing boats trailing white paths across the sea.

They ate with the leisure of those who understand that some moments deserve to be savored. The sea zephyr played with Claire's hair, carrying salt spray and wonderment. Each bite of food seemed heightened by their surroundings; the figs sweeter, the cheese more complex, the bread more satisfying than any meal she'd known before. And the caramel filled chocolate; no words could describe the feeling when it melted in her mouth.

"I've never tasted anything like this," she said, sampling a slice of preserved lemon that exploded with bright flavors on her tongue.

"That's because you're not just tasting with your mouth anymore," Luca replied, reaching out to trace her lower lip with his thumb. "You're tasting with every part of you that knows how to love beauty."

The sun climbed higher as Luca gathered things spread out around them, rising with natural grace to extend his hand to Claire. "Dance with me," he said, his voice rich as aged wine. The sounds of waves and distant seabirds created nature's own music around them.

"Here? Now?" Claire laughed, but found herself already moving into his embrace, drawn by the irresistible magnetism that seemed to pulse between them whenever they were close.

"Why not here? Why not now?" His arms encircled her waist as they began to sway together on their sun-warmed rock stage. "In Naples, every moment is right for dancing, for loving, for living fully."

They moved together as if they'd been dancing all their lives, finding their rhythm in the eternal music of waves meeting shore. Claire's dress swirled around them both as Luca spun her gently, then drew her back against his chest. His white linen shirt carried the scent of sea salt and sunshine, mixing with that uniquely masculine aroma that made her head spin with wanting.

"I never danced like this out in the open before," Claire admitted softly as they turned slowly in their private ballroom of sky and sea. "So free, so..."

"Unafraid," Luca finished for her, one hand sliding up her spine to cradle the back of her neck. "That's what love should be, a dance without fear, a song without end, a painting that never stops revealing new colors."

The motion of their dance brought them closer with each turn, until Claire could feel Luca's heartbeat against her own. His dark eyes held depths that reflected the endless Mediterranean, drawing her in like a tide to shore.

When he kissed her, it felt like the most natural continuation of their dance, as if their movements had been leading to this moment all along. His lips were soft against hers, tasting of figs and chocolate, while his hands held her as if she were something infinitely precious.

Time seemed to lose its meaning as they swayed together between sea and sky, creating their own private universe where only love and art existed.

The intimate spell of their seaside dance was broken by Luca suddenly straightening, his eyes alight with inspiration. "I want to show you something special," he said, leading Claire back to the Fiat with barely contained excitement.

They wound higher into the hills above the cove, the little car handling the twisting roads with Italian flair. Each curve revealed new aspects of the coastline until Luca finally pulled onto a narrow dirt track nearly hidden by flowering oleander.

"Close your eyes," he instructed, helping Claire from the car. His hands steady on her waist, he guided her forward several steps. "Now look."

Claire opened her eyes to find herself on a natural terrace carved into the hillside. Before them stretched a panorama so breathtaking it seemed almost unreal; the entire Bay of Naples spread out like a living canvas, painted in every shade of blue possible, azure and indigo, aegean and cobalt, sapphire and cerulean. Vesuvius rose in the distance, while closer, ancient villages clung to cliffsides like jewels on a necklace.

"This is my secret place," Luca said softly, setting up his and her easels he'd brought from the car. "When the world feels too loud, too busy, I come here to paint."

He positioned their easels side by side with a single large canvas, arranging palettes and brushes with practiced ease. "Today," he continued, his eyes holding an intensity that made Claire's stomach do a little flip, "we paint together. Not just what we see, but what we feel."

As they worked side by side, Claire found herself stealing glances at Luca, watching how he painted, how his focus turned razor-sharp yet somehow remained soft around the edges. His hands moved with confidence born of years mastering his craft, yet each stroke carried a devotion that spoke of deep emotional connection to his subject.

The afternoon light caressed them both as they created, turning simple moments into memories that would last forever.

Their shared canvas enriched with colors as the afternoon hours passed. Claire found herself lost in the pure joy of creation, each brush stroke a celebration of the view before them and the man beside her. Their individual styles merged and danced across the canvas; his bold, passionate strokes complementing her more delicate touch.

"Look how the clouds cast shadows on the water," Luca professed, mixing a complex shade of blue on his palette. "It's like watching the sea dream in color." His brush moved with sure strokes, capturing the ever-changing play of light.

Claire added touches of violet to the distant mountains, watching how the color transformed the entire mood of their painting. "It's amazing," she said softly, "how changing just one shade can affect everything else on the canvas."

"Art is like that," Luca replied, his brush pausing mid-stroke. "Each element affects everything around it, creating something greater than its parts." He turned to her, his eyes reflecting the endless blue of the Mediterranean. "Working with you makes me see everything with fresh eyes."

The intensity of his gaze made her feel as if she were melting from the inside out. Around them, the afternoon painted everything in rich hues that turned their private terrace into an artist's paradise. A breeze carried the mingled scents of sea salt and wild herbs, while boats carved delicate memories into the azure canvas of the bay.

Their brushes found new rhythms as they worked, sometimes moving in perfect synchronization, other times following their own paths only to meet again in unexpected ways. With each stroke, their shared canvas became more than just a painting; it orchestrated a visual symphony of their growing love.

As the sun began its slow descent toward the horizon, their shared canvas took on a luminous quality that seemed to capture not just the view, but the essence of their afternoon together. Claire stepped back, taking in the full effect of their combined artistry.

"It's unlike anything I've ever created before," she said softly, studying how their styles had merged into something entirely new. The painting radiated with shared passion.

Luca set down his brush, moving to stand behind her. His arms encircled her waist as they both gazed at their work. "Because this isn't just a painting," he murmured against her ear. "It's our story, look here, where your violets blend with my bold blues. See how they create something neither of us planned?"

The late afternoon light bathed their private terrace in deepening shades of amber, turning the Mediterranean below into a mirror that reflected the sky. A family of swallows swooped past, their wings cutting dark silhouettes against the painted sky.

"I never want this day to end," Claire whispered, leaning back against his solid warmth. The simple admission carried layers of meaning; not just about their afternoon of shared creativity, but about everything building between them.

Luca's embrace tightened slightly. "Then let's not let it end," he said, his voice carrying notes that made her heart soar.

As they packed their supplies, Claire noticed how Luca handled their shared painting with particular care, his expressions suggesting he already knew exactly where in his studio it would hang. Each gesture, each look they shared, felt weighted with significance, as if they were not just creating art together, but crafting the foundation of their shared future.

New colors kept emerging all around them as they made their way back to the faithful little Fiat, feeling fulfilled for having shared in the magic of creating together.

The Fiat wound through Naples' streets as evening descended, the city coming alive with its particular nighttime magic. "Would you like to stay at my place tonight?" Luca asked, his eyes briefly meeting hers before returning to the road. "We could eat together, talk, and maybe paint a little more if you feel inspired."

Claire's answer was a smile that needed no words. The day had been too perfect to end with separation.

Luca's apartment welcomed them like an old friend, its familiar spaces now holding memories of shared creativity and connection. They moved together in comfortable harmony - Luca preparing a simple meal while Claire arranged their painting supplies, all with the easy rhythm of two people who had found their natural counterpoint in each other.

The evening unfolded in gentle perfection; shared food that tasted of Naples' bounty, wine that loosened tired muscles and inspired quiet conversation, and finally, the sweet surrender to each other's arms that felt both familiar and thrillingly new.

As moonlight painted silver patterns across Luca's bed, Claire traced the contours of his face with gentle fingers. "Thank you for today," she whispered. "For showing me Naples through your eyes."

His answer was to draw her closer, his lips finding hers in the darkness with unerring precision.

Morning found them entwined in Italian sheets, the early light revealing their artist's hands still bearing traces of yesterday's paint; blue beneath fingernails, violet staining a knuckle, a streak of gold along a wrist. These beautiful battle scars of creation mingled with marks of passion; a small love-print on Claire's shoulder, a faint scratch where her fingers had claimed his back.

They shared breakfast on Luca's balcony, watching Naples awaken below. Later, they savored a light salad for lunch while lounging on the sofa, planning their evening ahead.

"I have something special to show you tonight," Luca said, his eyes holding emotions Claire couldn't quite decipher. "Something even more personal than yesterday's adventures."

Late afternoon, they descended to the courtyard where the faithful yellow Fiat awaited, gleaming like a promise of adventure. Claire settled into the passenger seat, watching as Luca turned the key, bringing the vintage engine to life with a purr that seemed to express excitement. The little car maneuvered through Naples' bustle, gradually leaving the city behind as they followed winding roads into the surrounding countryside. With each passing mile, Claire felt the ordinary world receding, replaced by a landscape that seemed painted specifically for their journey together.

The Fiat wound its way higher into the hills above Naples as the sun kissed the surface of the Mediterranean. Claire watched Luca's profile against the darkening sky, marveling at how his features seemed carved from the same stuff as the ancient statues that graced their city's piazzas. His hands moved with easy confidence on the wheel, while his eyes held a glimmer of anticipation that made her wonder what new he planned to share.

"Almost there," he said, turning onto a narrow road that wound through groves of twisted olive trees. Ancient stone walls lined their path, their weathered surfaces telling stories of centuries past.

When they finally stopped, Claire found herself at what appeared to be a beautiful vintage Mediterranean-style villa, its facade warm pink in the fading light. Wildflowers pushed through cracks in the old stones, while ivy draped the walls like nature's own tapestry.

"My grandmother's old villa," Luca explained, producing a weathered key that matched the building's timeworn elegance. "I spent countless summers here with my Nonna Eleonora, learning her recipes, absorbing her stories that seemed to breathe life into the very walls. When I was a teenager, my mother passed away. After that, Nonna raised me in this villa. When she passed away a few years back, she left this treasured place to me, her final gift."

Luca pushed open the ancient oak door, revealing a world preserved in amber. The entrance hall welcomed them with faded grandeur; terracotta tiles worn smooth by generations, walls adorned with sepia photographs of stern-faced ancestors. What stole Claire's breath was the golden light bathing everything in a dreamlike glow. Hundreds of candles, some in silver holders, some nestled in alcoves, and others floating in shallow bowls, transformed the space into an earthbound constellation. Their flames danced with the evening breeze, casting living shadows that whispered secrets. "This way," Luca murmured, guiding her through the flickering labyrinth, past an arched doorway, and into the kitchen. There, copper pots hung from rustic beams and an old wood-burning stove waited like a sleeping giant, all illuminated by the ethereal candlelight that transformed the humble space into something from a fairy tale.

"When did you...? I mean how did you...?" she began, turning to find him watching her reaction with gentle intensity.

"I may have enlisted some help," he admitted with a smile that made her knees weak. "My cousin Marco set everything up while we were painting. Because tonight, mia bella (my beautiful one), I will cook for you in the place where I first learned that food and art come from the same place in the soul."

In the candlelit sanctuary of his grandmother's kitchen, Luca moved with the same artistic precision he brought to his paintings. Claire perched on an ancient wooden stool, watching as he created a different kind of masterpiece. His white shirt sleeves rolled up, he chopped fresh herbs with rhythmic certainty, the knife's motion against the well-worn cutting board creating its own kind of music.

"My nonna always said cooking is another form of love," he explained, the candlelight dancing across his features as he worked. "Each ingredient must be chosen with care, touched with respect, combined with intention." His hands moved surely as he scattered fresh basil and oregano into a sauce that already filled the kitchen with mouthwatering aromas.

She offered to help. "You're already helping, by being my inspiration," he said with a warm smile.

The space between them hummed with intimate energy as Claire watched him work. Everything about this moment felt sacred; the way the candles painted shadows on centuries-old walls, how the evening invited the mingled scents of herbs and sea air through open windows, the look of complete absorption on Luca's face as he created their meal.

"Here," he said soothingly, holding out a spoon of sauce for her to taste. "Tell me what you think."

Claire closed her eyes as flavors exploded across her tongue; sun-ripened tomatoes, fresh herbs, something deeper that spoke of tradition and time. When she opened them again, she found Luca watching her with an intensity that made her heart race.

"It tastes like summer," she said, each syllable carrying the weight of unexpected discovery. "Like love and sunlight and everything great in Italy."

His smile could have lit the kitchen without any candles at all. "That's exactly what my nonna used to say." He turned back to his work, adding a pinch of something that made the sauce's aroma deepen magnificently. "She would have loved you, you know. She always said artists see the world the way it truly is."

The kitchen filled with the sounds and scents of their developing feast as night gathered outside, wrapping their private world in layers of deepening blue.

In the glow of a hundred dancing flames, Luca set their small table with the care of a curator arranging priceless art. The ancient wooden surface gleamed with well-loved patina, while mismatched antique plates told stories of generations of family meals. A bottle of wine, opened to breathe, caught candlelight in its dark glass like captured stars.

Claire watched him place a single sprig of wild rosemary on each dinner napkin, the simple gesture somehow profound in its thoughtfulness. His movements held that particular grace she'd come to associate with him; whether he was painting, cooking, or simply existing in space, everything he did carried an artist's appreciation for beauty.

"This table has held centuries of love stories," Luca said, pulling out her chair. "My grandparents sat here as young lovers. My parents enjoyed countless feasts prepared by Nonna. Now it welcomes us, adding our story to its collection."

The pasta he served looked like art itself; handmade strands nestled in that magnificent sauce, fresh herbs scattered across the top like an artist's final touches on a masterpiece. The first bite made Claire close her eyes, overwhelmed by how flavors could tell stories as eloquently as paint on canvas.

"I don't know why. But I've never tasted pasta like this," she marveled, opening her eyes to find his gaze upon her, warm, reverent, a confession without words.

"Because it's made with love," he replied simply. "Food should be like art, created with passion, shared with joy, experienced with all the senses." He reached across the table to catch her free hand. "When one cooks with love, you can taste it in every bite."

Outside their candlelit haven, night birds began their evening songs, their melodies drifting through open windows like nature's own romantic serenade. Each moment felt weighted with significance, as if they were crafting memories that would shine forever in their hearts.

Between bites of their shared feast, stories flowed as naturally as the wine in their glasses. The candlelight painted ever-changing highlights across Luca's features as he told tales of summers spent in this kitchen, learning his grandmother's recipes, watching her hands shape pasta with the same dedication he now brought to his art.

"She taught me that creating beauty, whether on canvas or in the kitchen, is a way of showing love," he said, refilling Claire's glass with the deep red wine that tasted of Italian hillsides. "Each brushstroke, each ingredient, carries intention and emotion."

Claire found herself sharing too, stories she hadn't thought about in years, of childhood aspirations of becoming an artist, of the pure joy she'd felt the first time she'd truly captured light in watercolor. Luca listened with his whole being, his dark eyes reflecting not just candle-light but understanding that went soul-deep.

"What made you stop?" he asked softly when she spoke of how her art had gradually taken second place to safer choices.

"I think... I forgot how to be brave," she admitted, the wine and the intimacy of their setting making honesty feel natural. "It's easier to be safe than to risk creating something that comes from your deepest self."

Luca rose from his chair, coming around the table to kneel beside her. His hands found hers, warm and sure. "But look at what you're creating now," he said softly. "Your art speaks with such honesty and beauty. You found your courage again."

In that moment, surrounded by dancing candlelight and centuries of love stories held in these ancient walls, Claire could feel the final walls around her own heart were finally and gloriously crumbling.

The night deepened around their candlelit sanctuary as Claire and Luca moved to the kitchen's small stone balcony. A wrought iron railing curved like calligraphy against the star-scattered sky, while below, Naples twinkled like earthbound jewels.

The wine had left a pleasant warmth in Claire's veins, making every-thing feel soft at the edges. Luca stood behind her, his arms encircling her waist as they watched the city below. The night air carried the fragrance of jasmine and notes of distant music; somewhere, someone played a violin that spoke of love and longing.

"I never understood before," Claire said softly, "why artists always painted Italian nights. But now I see, everything here feels like magic waiting to be captured."

"Not just Italian nights," Luca confessed against her hair. "It's the way light and shadow dance together everywhere, but somehow more intensely when I paint with you," His arms tightened slightly around her. "Everything becomes clearer, more vibrant."

Claire moved in his embrace, turning her face to nuzzle his neck. The starlight caught in his dark eyes, while behind him, the candles from the kitchen cast an ethereal glow. In this light, he looked like something from a dream, but his warmth, his solidity against her, spoke of a reality more beautiful than any fantasy.

"You've taught me to see everything differently," she professed. "Not just art, but life and love and..." She placed her hand over his heart, feeling its strong, steady rhythm. "You make me believe in the kind of love I used to think only existed in poetry."

Luca caught her hand, pressing it more firmly against his chest. "Poetry, art, music, they're all just different languages for speaking truth," he said. "And sharing them with someone who understands makes everything more meaningful."

Under the vast Italian sky, Claire felt suspended in a moment of perfect clarity. Luca's words rippled through her like waves across still water, awakening depths she hadn't known existed. His nearness intoxicated her more than the wine they'd shared, while the night air carried promises in every breath.

"I never knew it could be like this," she confessed against his chest. "Everything feels heightened, more vivid, more..." She searched for words to capture the enormity of what she felt.

"Real," he finished for her, one hand sliding into her hair. "Because we're not just living moments anymore, we're creating art with every breath, every touch, every shared heartbeat."

In each other's arms they swayed together, time dissolving into a perfect night plucked from classic Italian cinema. The universe narrowed to this single point; the warmth where their bodies met, the synchronized rhythm of their hearts, the mingled breath between them. In their private universe of starlight and candlelight, time seemed to pause, holding them in an ephemeral bubble of connection.

When Luca lowered his lips to hers, the kiss felt inevitable as sunrise, natural as breathing. His mouth moved against hers with exquisite tenderness that gradually deepened into something more urgent, more demanding. Claire responded with equal passion, her hands sliding under his shirt to find warm skin, while his fingers traced pathways of desire along her spine.

The charged energy between them built like a gathering storm as their kiss deepened on the starlit balcony. Claire felt herself melting into Luca's embrace, every point of contact between them electric with shared wanting. His hands moved with an artist's devotion over her curves, while her fingers mapped the strong planes of his chest, learning him by touch as she'd learned to read light and shadow.

"Stay with me tonight," he requested against her lips, his voice carrying notes that made her inner flames dance higher. "Let me show you how artists love in Italy."

The candlelight from the kitchen spilled around them like liquid amber as Claire pulled back just enough to meet his eyes. What she saw there, raw emotion mixed with tender devotion, made any hesitation fade away. This felt right, felt inevitable, felt as natural as paint flowing onto canvas.

Taking her hand, Luca led her through the kitchen to a door she hadn't noticed before. It opened onto a sitting room where more candles cast hushed shadows. A narrow staircase wound upward, each step bathed in golden light that seemed to illuminate a path to some unspoken destination.

"My old bedroom," he said softly. "Do you want to..." His eyes held a question, giving her space to choose.

Claire's answer was to rise on tiptoe, pressing a kiss to the sensitive spot below his ear that made him shiver. "Show me," she whispered.

They ascended together, each step feeling weighted with significance. The bedroom above took Claire's breath away; more candles created pools of intimate light, while French doors opened onto a large private terrace overlooking the twinkling lights of Naples below and the stars above, the two blending together in a seamless tapestry of light. The bed, draped in Italian linens fluffy as clouds, waited like a blank canvas for their love story to unfold.

Luca drew her close, his hands sliding into her hair as he kissed her with escalating passion. Every touch between them felt sacred, every caress an art form all its own. When clothes fell away, it was with the reverence of unwrapping priceless masterpieces.

In the candlelit sanctuary of the bedroom, time seemed to move with a different frequency. Their touches spoke languages beyond words; each caress a confession, every kiss a vow. Luca's hands moved over Claire's skin as if he were sculpting her from pure light, while her fingers traced the strong lines of his body like mapping constellations in a private sky.

The night air flowing through the French doors carried the scent of jasmine and distant sea, wrapping around them like nature's own blessing. The stars watched through gauzy curtains that swayed, their shared ardor painting new masterpieces with every breath.

Luca kissed her with the dedication of an artist studying his greatest inspiration, learning the curves and planes of her body with exquisite attention. His touch ignited fires that burned away any remaining walls between them, leaving only pure feeling, pure connection, pure love.

Claire discovered new kinds of art in the way they moved together; in how their bodies found perfect harmony, merging into something greater than themselves. Each moment built upon the last like layers of paint creating depth and meaning.

When they finally reached that transcendent moment together, it was like watercolors bleeding into each other on dampened paper; boundaries dissolving, individual hues surrendering to create something entirely new and breathtakingly beautiful. The world beyond their candlelit haven ceased to exist as they created their own universe of sensation and emotion. Everything that had led them to this moment; every note exchanged, every shared glance, every artistic collaboration, seemed to crystallize into perfect clarity.

In the aftermath, they lay entwined like living art, their skin painted copper and gold by candlelight. No words were needed; their hearts spoke in touches, in shared breaths, in the way their bodies curved together as if designed by the same divine artist.

Above them, the Italian night spread its velvet canopy of stars, while below, Naples continued her eternal song. But in their private paradise, only love existed, pure, profound, and perfect as a masterpiece fresh from the creator's hands.

The first hints of sunrise found them on the private terrace next to the bedroom, wrapped in dreamy Italian linens, watching day break over their eternal city. Claire sat between Luca's legs, her back against his chest, while his arms encircled her like protective wings. Neither spoke; the moment felt too precious for words.

Below them, Naples stirred to life with the gentle persistence of waves on shore. Early morning light painted the world in subtle water-colors; rose bleeding into lavender, amber softening to pearl.

Luca's fingers lingered idly on Claire's skin, each touch carrying echoes of their night together. His other hand sketched invisible masterpieces in the air as he pointed out different views; fishing boats heading out to sea trailing silver paths across dark water, a seabird swooping past their terrace, its wing catching sunlight like polished silver.

"You paint differently now," he said tenderly, remembering their shared creation from two days back. "With more abandon, more..."

"More love," she finished for him, understanding flooding her heart. "Because that's what you've taught me, that art and love are the same thing. Both require us to open ourselves completely, to risk everything for beauty."

They dressed unhurriedly, stealing kisses between buttons and clasps, neither wanting to break the spell that seemed to hover around them like morning mist. The candles had burned down to stubs, their spent wax telling stories of passion's passage through the night.

As she freshened up, the scent of fresh coffee wafted up from the kitchen downstairs where Luca had disappeared moments before. Claire remained on the terrace, still enveloped in the lingering warmth of their night together. Her body held sweet memories of his touch that sang with profound joy.

He returned bearing two cups of steaming cappuccino, a plate of still-warm cornetti that filled the air with buttery aroma, and a tiny bouquet of wild flowers. He set their breakfast on a small table on the terrace.

"My cousin Marco delivered this morning," he answered to her surprised glance at the fresh cornetti. "And I gathered these wildflowers just outside the kitchen." Her returning smile said it all.

"I've been thinking about the art we have been creating," she said soulfully, " I never knew art could feel like this," she continued, reaching for his hand. "So free, so completely natural. It's as if everything I create now flows directly from my heart, without my mind getting in the way."

Luca pressed a kiss to the sensitive spot back of her neck that he'd discovered during their night of exploration. "That's because you're no longer afraid," he whispered against her skin. "You've learned to trust, in your art, in love, in connection."

The morning sun bathed them in its blessing as they shared breakfast on the terrace, feeding each other bites of cornetti between kisses that tasted of coffee and joy.

They didn't realize when morning became early afternoon, and then turned to late afternoon as it painted its final masterstrokes across the skyline as Luca and Claire stepped out of the villa, their hearts enlightened with shared memories. The faithful Fiat waited in the courtyard, gleaming in the sun like an eager companion ready for new adventures.

As they started to come back through a different route than the one they had taken the previous day, they wound through lanes that grew progressively narrower and more remote. But the little car handled each curve with Italian determination. Claire watched the landscape transform around them, countryside with wild stretches where nature painted her own masterpieces in swathes of wildflowers and ancient olive groves.

The road climbed higher and lower, each turn revealing new vistas. Luca drove one-handed, his other hand resting on her knee, maintaining that essential connection between them that had grown so precious. Every so often, he would squeeze her leg gently, drawing her attention to particularly beautiful views; a hidden valley, a distant church spire catching light like a beacon.

Then all of a sudden, without any warning, a sharp sound pierced their idyllic journey. The Fiat shuddered, tilting to one side as Luca expertly guided it to a stop on the narrow road's shoulder.

Luca got out of the car, trying to find the problem. When Claire tried to get out of the car, due to the uneven surface below she sprained her ankle, but considering the situation with the car, decided not to inform Luca about it.

"Flat tire," he announced after a quick inspection, running a hand through his dark curls, trying to contain his frustration. "And no spare. I kept meaning to replace it after using it a while back." He was upset not at the situation, but at his own inadequacy and carelessness.

Claire reached for her phone, but the screen showed no signal. Luca's phone revealed the same; they were too far from civilization for modern technology to reach them.

"The nearest village is over three kilometers from here," he said. Then studying the slightly confused look on her face, "Sorry, that's about two miles or so," he said quickly. "Maybe we can walk, find help..."

Claire glanced down at her feet, specifically at the sprained ankle, thinking how she can do two miles of country hiking.

Claire took a few experimental steps on the rough country road, her hurt foot betraying her with each step, while the uneven road made every movement precarious. She told Luca what had happened.

Luca watched her struggle for only a moment before making his decision. Without a word, he swept her into his arms as if she weighed nothing at all, cradling her against his chest with more care than he showed for his most precious paintings.

"What are you doing?" Claire gasped, instinctively wrapping her arms around his neck. "You can't carry me for two miles!"

His smile held all the confidence of a man who had found his true purpose. "Watch me," he said simply. "Besides, what kind of Italian man would I be if I let my love hurt her foot on these rough roads?"

And so they began their journey, Claire nestled in Luca's strong arms, her head tucked naturally into the curve of his neck. Each step he took was measured and sure, his breathing steady as a metronome. The late afternoon sun painted them in strokes of light and shadow as they moved through the wild Italian countryside.

"Tell me a story," Claire murmured against his skin, feeling that a distraction will help him take his mind off the effort of carrying her. "Tell me about the first time you knew you wanted to be an artist."

His laugh rumbled through his chest where she rested against him. "When I was young, I would watch my mother paint for hours. She had an extraordinary gift," he said, his eyes growing distant with memory. "The way her brush danced across the canvas was like magic to me." He continued, his voice as steady as his stride. "When I was six years old, my mother found me in the garden with one of her canvases, painting the roses with mud because I had no real paint..."

The story flowed between them as naturally as the breeze that carried the scent of wild thyme and sun-warmed stones.

The Italian countryside unfurled around them like a living painting as he carried her along the winding road. His strength seemed limitless, drawn perhaps from the same well of passion that fueled his art. Each step was a declaration, each steady breath a promise.

The story of his childhood artistic awakening blended with the rhythmic sound of his footfalls on ancient stone. Claire found herself enchanted not just by the tale, but by the vibrations of his voice where her cheek pressed against his chest.

"The roses weren't enough," he continued, adjusting his hold on her with infinite gentleness. "Soon I was covering everything I could reach; walls, furniture, even my cousin's favorite doll. My parents could have been angry, but instead..." He paused, both in speech and stride, his eyes distant with memory. "Instead, my father came home the next day with real paints and brushes. And my mother told me if I was going to make the world more beautiful, I should have proper tools."

Claire touched his face, feeling how the sun had warmed his skin. "They understood, even then, that art wasn't just something you did, it was something you were."

"Yes," he replied softly, resuming their journey. "Just as I understood, the moment I saw your first note in Caffè Sereno, that love isn't something that happens to you, it's something you create, stroke by stroke, moment by moment, choice by choice."

The road curved ahead of them, dipping into a valley where wild-flowers painted the fields in sweeps of purple and orange. A distant church bell tolled, its fluid sound rolling across the countryside like waves of pure beauty.

Each step brought them closer to help, but neither felt any urgency to end their serendipitous journey. Cradled in Luca's arms, Claire felt as if she'd found her true home.

After thousands of steps and a couple of breaks later, with the sun getting ready to set, they came upon an old stone building nestled against the hillside. Weathered grape vines climbed its walls, while smoke curled invitingly from a crooked chimney. A hand-painted sign proclaimed it "Trattoria della Nonna (Grandmother's Eatery)," its faded letters telling stories of decades serving weary travelers.

"Ah, La Trattoria (The Eatery)!" Luca's face lit with recognition. "I remember now, Grandma Rosa's place has been here forever. She's like everyone's grandmother." He tightened his hold on Claire, pressing a kiss to her forehead. "Let me introduce you to real Italian hospitality."

The door opened before they reached it, releasing heavenly aromas. A tiny woman with silver hair and sparkling eyes filled the doorway, her lined face transforming with delight at the sight of them.

"Luca! Mio piccolo artista (my little artist)!" She exclaimed, then took in how he carried Claire, her expression shifting to motherly concern. "Che cosa è successo (What happened)? What happened to your bella donna (beautiful woman)?"

"Claire, this is our Grandma Rosa," Luca introduced, "and this is Claire."

Inside, the trattoria felt like stepping into a living memory from another century; wooden beams darkened by decades of wood smoke, copper pots gleaming on stone walls, dried herbs hanging in fragrant bunches. Grandma Rosa fussed over them like a mother hen, or maybe grandmother hen, insisting Claire rest her foot while she served them homemade wine and dishes that seemed conjured from pure love.

"The best accidents," Grandma Rosa declared as she set down plates of handmade pasta dressed simply with local olive oil, garlic grown in her backyard, and herbs from her garden, "are the ones that bring love stories to my door."

The evening light slanted through windows warped with age. In this timeless sanctuary, surrounded by the evidence of decades of nurturing through food and warmth, Claire and Luca found themselves sharing not just a meal, but another chapter in their unfolding love story.

Claire watched Luca interact with the elderly proprietress, their rapid Italian punctuated by warm laughter and affectionate gestures. Something about seeing him here, in this place untouched by time's rushing current, made her discover layers to this gorgeous man she hadn't noticed before.

The way he listened intently to Grandma Rosa's stories, how his eyes crinkled with genuine joy at her teasing, the enthusiasm with which he translated what she was saying for Claire, the adoring way he touched the old woman's shoulder. Each moment revealed layers of his character that made Claire fall even deeper into love's endless ocean.

"She says we must stay the night," Luca translated as Grandma Rosa bustled away to check on something bubbling fragrantly on her ancient stove. "Her grandson Tony, who is a mechanic, will get a spare tire, put it on our car, and bring it here first thing tomorrow. Tonight we sleep in the room where she says all great love stories find shelter." His eyes held Claire's with intimate intensity. "Oh and she has invited both of us to her granddaughter's wedding." He continued.

Claire was overwhelmed at the informality of it all. The arms that welcomed the strangers, the nurturing that touched the soul, and the effortless vulnerability between new acquaintances, all came so effortlessly to these beautiful people of Italy.

The wine she served them tasted of sun-warmed earth and secret hopes, while her simple food spoke of traditions passed down through generations of loving hands. Each bite seemed infused with something beyond mere flavor; perhaps the essence of all the love stories that had unfolded at this very table.

"Tell me, cara mia (my dear)," Grandma Rosa said in careful English as she served them fresh figs drizzled with honey, "how did our Luca steal your heart?" Her wise eyes twinkled with knowing light.

Claire found herself sharing their story, of notes exchanged in Caffè

Sereno, of art becoming love becoming art again. She listened with her whole being, nodding at moments as if confirming some private theory about love's inevitable path.

"Ah," she said finally, reaching out to pat their joined hands. "Some loves are written in the stars. But the best ones?" She gestured to their empty plates, to the evidence of simple pleasures shared. "The best ones are written in everyday moments, in the way two hearts learn to beat as one."

She led them up creaking wooden stairs to a room that seemed crafted from moonlight and memories. Simple white linens draped over the mattress on the iron bed caught evening's first shadows, while wooden shutters opened to reveal a view that made Claire catch her breath. Rolling hills painted in twilight's shades and distant mountains fading into purple mist.

"The lovers' room," Grandma Rosa said softly, lighting a single lamp that cast mellow shadows across ancient walls. "Every couple who has slept here has found their way back to each other, no matter what paths life took them down." She pressed a key into Claire's hand, its iron surface worn smooth by countless other lovers' touches. "Dormite bene, figli miei (Sleep well, my children).”

When the door closed behind her retreating form, Claire felt the weight of all the love stories that had unfolded in this simple space. The room held a quality of timelessness, as if here, in this refuge above the rushing world, only love and truth could exist.

Luca moved to the windows, opening them wide to let in the evening air that carried hints of the herb garden. Against the deepening sky, his profile looked carved from marble and memory, while his eyes held depths that made Claire's thoughts spin with recognition of every-thing they were becoming together.

"Come here," he said intimately, extending his hand. When she took it, he drew her into his arms, swaying gently to music only they could hear. The breeze played with her hair, carried the mingled scents of their day's adventure. Sun-warmed skin, wild herbs, and traces of paint that never quite left them.

"What began as an accident," he proclaimed, "has become another gift. Another perfect moment in our story." His arms tightened around her waist as evening's first star appeared above the distant mountains. "Every step I carried you today felt like walking toward our future."

Claire pressed closer, feeling the solid strength of him, knowing in that moment that no matter what paths lay ahead, her heart had found its true home.

Dawn painted the lovers' room in shades of pearl and rose as Claire tried to open her eyes. She recalled both of them falling asleep while gazing into each other's eyes. But there were other tell-tale signs of their shared night. The rumpled sheets that told stories of tender passion, the way morning light played across their bare skin, the memories brought a shy smile to her lips and a blush to her cheeks. Luca saw that as he was just opening his eyes.

Before he could ask her anything , a gentle knock at their door announced Grandma Rosa's arrival, bearing a tray of fresh breakfast for them. She kept the tray on the small table outside their door.

Before she left, she announced, "Tony has brought your car. But first, you eat. In my house, love stories begin with proper breakfast."

When Luca brought the tray to their bed, it revealed two tiny cups of cappuccino filling the room with aromatic affirmations, still-warm bread that carried the scent of love baked into every crumb, homemade butter and strawberry jam, and local honey that could be appropriately named as 'Amber Memories'.

They shared a simple meal in bed, feeding each other bites of bread; sometimes slathered with butter and strawberry jam, other times dipped in honey, stealing sweet kisses between each savored morsel. Through the open windows, birdsong mixed with distant church bells, while the morning air carried hints of the adventures yet to come. Claire was surprised to find that her sprained ankle had almost healed completely.

Maybe it was a combination of Grandma Rosa's nurturing, Luca's love, and the resting.

As they prepared to leave, Grandma Rosa pressed a small card into Claire's hands. "Family recipe," she said with a conspiratorial wink. "When both of you want to remember this time." As if it was possible to forget what they experienced there, Claire thought to herself and gave her a big hug. Wrapping Grandma Rosa in a warm embrace, Claire knew these precious moments were already etched permanently in her and Luca's hearts.

When Luca tried to pay for all the food and the stay, "Tell me, how can you possibly put a price on grandma's love and care? " she demanded, leaving Luca and Claire speechless.

"We'll come back," Luca and Claire said, embracing the tiny woman who'd given them such precious memories.

"Of course you will," she replied with absolute certainty. "Love always finds its way home."

Their Fiat waited below, its tire now fixed, ready to carry them back to their Naples life. But as they bid farewell to Grandma Rosa, both knew they'd found more than just shelter in her ageless retreat. They'd discovered another layer of their love story, another chapter in their shared odyssey.

7

THE PLAY OF SHADOWS AND LIGHT

The days following their adventurous exploration blended together like watercolors on wet canvas. Each morning dawned with new discoveries as Luca guided Claire through hidden corners of his beloved city and its surroundings, revealing treasures that tourists never glimpsed and locals often overlooked. They wandered through forgotten courtyards where Renaissance fountains played ancient music, discovered tiny chapels with frescoes that had survived centuries of political upheaval, and found secluded viewpoints where Naples spread before them like a living mosaic.

Time became elastic in Luca's company. Hours stretched into moments of artistic wonder, then compressed into heartbeats of shared creativity. They sketched together on weathered stone benches overlooking the bay, their shoulders touching as their pencils captured the ever-changing patterns across water. They painted side by side in his studio, the afternoon sun streaming through tall windows.

"Look how the light changes everything it touches," Luca would show, guiding her attention to how shadows shaped perception, how reflection altered reality. His artist's eye found beauty in places Claire had been taught to overlook. The tarnished patina of ancient door handles, the complex geometry of shadows across cobblestones, the eloquent stories told by wrinkles on an old fisherman's face.

When not exploring or creating together, they lost themselves in each other, discovering the landscapes of their bodies with the same cherishing attention they gave to art. Every touch, every kiss, every shared breath became another brushstroke in the masterpiece they were creating together. Claire's apartment, once a temporary shelter in a foreign city, transformed into an oasis of passion and creativity, while Luca's studio became an extension of her own artistic endeavors.

In this immersion of love and art, modern trappings fell away. Claire's phone remained forgotten in her bag for days, her laptop closed and pushed aside on her antique desk. The digital world with its demands and deadlines seemed to belong to another life, one that grew more distant with each sun-drenched day in Naples.

A week after their stay at grandma Rosa's place, Claire woke alone in her bed, the indent of Luca's head still visible on the pillow beside her. A note in his flowing script rested on her nightstand: "Gone to meet with a client. Back with lunch and stories to share. Every moment away from you feels like an eternity. Ti amo con tutto il cuore (I love you with all my heart)."

The apartment seemed to lay quiet as Claire stretched, her body pleasantly sore from their passionate night. Sunlight streamed through half-drawn curtains, painting golden paths across the floor. Church bells chimed in the distance, announcing the hour as their sound drifted across the city.

With Luca's temporary absence creating space in her consciousness, Claire checked her phone. The battery power had drained out. So she plugged it into the power source. The phone started blinking insistently. How long had it been since she'd checked it? She couldn't even remember. The professional responsibility she'd temporarily set aside suddenly rushed back like a tsunami hitting the shore.

With the weight of mountains pressing upon her trembling hands, she picked up the device. The screen illuminated with notifications with seventeen missed calls, thirty-four text messages, and forty-six emails, all demanding her immediate attention. Susan's name appeared most frequently, the progression of messages evolving from professional inquiries to concerned personal outreach to crisis management.

The most recent text, sent just an hour ago, carried undeniable urgency: "Claire, Barton Worldwide is threatening to pull their account if they don't see progress by Friday. I've covered as much as I can, but they need YOU. Please call me as soon as you get this."

Barton Worldwide, her biggest client. The one whose CEO had specifically requested her for their complete rebranding after seeing her work for a competitor. The account she couldn't afford to lose, professionally or financially.

Claire's heart accelerated as she opened her laptop for the first time in days. The screen flickered to life, revealing a digital landscape of mounting obligations and missed deadlines. Three major projects sat in various states of incompletion. The Barton presentation, due in three days, remained little more than conceptual sketches. The Milano portfolio review needed final touches before their meeting next week. The website redesign for Lakeside Properties hadn't even been started.

Her professional life, carefully built over years of dedication and discipline, was unraveling while she'd been lost in the intoxication of new love and artistic awakening.

"Oh my God," she exclaimed to the apartment, scrolling through email after email, each one more urgent than the last. How had she let this happen? How had she forgotten the responsibilities that had once defined her entire sense of self?

As the reality of her professional predicament settled around her shoulders like a heavy cloak, Claire moved through her apartment in a daze of mounting anxiety. She put on water for coffee, her movements mechanical while her mind raced through potential solutions, none of them perfect.

The calendar mocked her from the laptop screen. Barton presentation, just three days away. Three days to create an entire rebranding presentation that would normally take weeks. Three days to save her professional reputation and financial stability.

She dialed Susan's number with trembling fingers, each ring increasing the tightness in her chest.

"Claire! Thank God," Susan's voice carried equal parts relief and tension. "Where have you been? I've been trying to reach you for days."

"I know, I'm so sorry," Claire began, words tumbling out in a rush of apology and explanation. "I've been caught up in... it's been..."

"You're in love," Susan stated simply, no judgment in her tone, just understanding. "I recognized the signs from your last email. The way you described your Italian artist, the life in Naples... I understand, Claire. But right now, we have a situation that needs your full attention."

As Susan outlined the crisis with Barton Worldwide, Claire felt herself splitting between the professional designer who had built her career on reliability and excellence, and the woman who had finally rediscovered her artistic soul in Luca's arms. These two selves seemed to pull her in opposite directions.

"I need three uninterrupted days," Claire said finally, the decision crystallizing. "If I work around the clock, I can deliver something exceptional for the Barton meeting."

"That's my girl," Susan replied, relief evident in her voice. "I've already told them you've been developing something revolutionary, that's why it's taking longer. Don't make me a liar, Bennett."

After ending the call, Claire stood at her window, watching Naples buzz with morning life below. The familiar streets now seemed to belong to two different worlds. One of artistic freedom and passionate discovery with Luca, the other of professional obligation and responsibility to her career.

The sound of her apartment door opening announced Luca's return. He appeared in the doorway carrying a basket from which emanated the mouthwatering aromas of fresh bread and local delicacies. His smile, that smile that transformed his entire face, faltered when he saw her expression.

"Mi amore (my love), what happened?" He set the basket aside, crossing to her in three swift strides, his hands coming up to cradle her face instinctively.

The concern in his dark eyes nearly undid her completely. How could she explain that the real world had intruded on their perfect artistic bubble? That responsibilities she'd temporarily forgotten now demanded payment in full?

"I've been negligent," she announced, gesturing toward her laptop where emails continued to accumulate like snow in an avalanche. "My work... my clients... I've let everything slip away while we've been..." She couldn't finish, the conflict between joy and obligation crushing her voice.

Luca's gaze followed hers to the computer screen, understanding dawning in his expression. Without a word, he led her to the small sofa, sitting beside her with their hands still linked. His presence, solid, patient, and unwavering, created space for her to find words for the emotional maelstrom inside her.

"I've never been irresponsible like this," she began, the words emerging with difficulty. "Never missed deadlines or ignored clients. My career has always been the one area of my life where I felt completely in control, completely capable. But these past days with you..." She raised her eyes to his, finding nothing but compassionate attention. "Everything else just faded away. All I could see was art and beauty and the way the world awakens when we create together."

Luca listened without interruption, his thumb grazing the sensitive hollow between her thumb and forefinger as she explained the precarious state of her professional obligations. When she finished, silence enveloped them. Not tense or judgmental, but thoughtful, as if the room itself were considering solutions.

"How much time do you need?" he asked finally, his voice carrying his deepest emotions.

"Three days," Claire whispered, the words feeling like glass in her throat. "Three days of complete focus. No distractions, no adventures, no..." She touched his face, fingers tracing the contours that had become more familiar than her own reflection. "No beautiful Italian artist teaching me to see the world through new eyes."

Understanding bloomed in Luca's expression, followed quickly by something that looked like admiration. "Your dedication to your work, it's part of what makes you who you are. Part of what drew me to you from the beginning."

"You're not upset?" Claire asked, relief and surprise mingling in her chest.

His smile held gentle wisdom as he brought her hand to his lips, pressing a kiss to her knuckles. "How could I be upset about something that is essential to the woman I love? Your dedication to your work, your sense of responsibility, these are facets of your beautiful soul."

He rose, drawing her gently to her feet. "Three days," he repeated, his eyes never leaving hers. "I will miss you every moment, but I understand. Your career isn't separate from who you are, it's another canvas where you create beauty."

The simple acceptance in his voice, free from resentment or pressure, made Claire's heart swell with emotions too complex for words. This was so different from her experiences with Mark, who had viewed her work as competition for her attention rather than an integral part of her identity.

"I was afraid you wouldn't understand," she admitted, leaning into his embrace. "That you might think I was choosing work over us."

Luca's arms tightened around her, his cheek resting against her hair. "Mi amore (my love), this isn't a competition. Your work needs you now, just as art calls to us both." He drew back just enough to meet her gaze. "Besides, these three days will give me time to complete a special project of my own."

Curiosity flickered across Claire's face, momentarily displacing anxiety. "What project?"

His smile carried mischief and secrets. "You will see when the time is right. For now, know that I will be counting hours, no I will be counting minutes until we're together again."

Luca began gathering the few belongings he'd accumulated in her apartment over the past days. A sketchbook, a spare shirt, and the special brushes he preferred for watercolor. Each item he collected seemed to underscore the reality of their temporary separation.

At the door, he turned back, his expression a complex mixture of longing and support. "Remember to eat," he said softly. "Remember to rest sometimes. Your brilliant mind needs fuel and recovery to create its best work."

"I will," Claire assured him, her throat tight with emotion.

"And Claire?" His voice deepened with feeling. "When your work is complete, when these three days have passed, I'll be waiting at Caffè Sereno, keeping time until you return. Until then, no calls, no messages."

After he left, Claire stood motionless in her suddenly empty apartment. The space felt larger somehow, echoing with absence. But as she turned back to her desk, a strange clarity descended upon her. A focus born from knowing that Luca understood, that he supported her completely, that their connection wasn't threatened by her need to reclaim her professional balance.

Opening her laptop, she began to work, each keystroke a step toward reclaiming the part of herself that existed beyond their shared artistic world. Outside, Naples continued its eternal symphony, while inside, Claire found herself becoming whole in a new way, integrating the woman who created beauty with Luca and the professional who built her reputation on excellence and reliability.

The three days ahead would be challenging, demanding everything she had to give. But with Luca's understanding creating a foundation beneath her, Claire found herself capable of focusing completely on the task at hand, secure in the knowledge that their connection would be waiting, undiminished, when her work was done.

Two days of intense work had cleared most of her deadlines, bringing a sense of accomplishment that lifted her spirits. She'd maintained her promise to Luca, eating on time, sort of, taking breaks, and keeping her phone silent, channeling all her energy into her projects.

For two days, Claire had survived on the bread, cheeses, fruits, and nuts Luca had brought back before their separation. She had not stepped outside her apartment, existing in a bubble of creative intensity and digital deadlines. On the third day, with most of the work under control and her presentation taking shape, she decided to venture outside, both to replenish her dwindling food supplies and to breathe the fresh air her lungs had begun to crave. Now, walking through Naples' winding streets, back to her apartment, Claire allowed herself to imagine their reunion tomorrow at Caffè Sereno. Her mind painted pictures of his smile, the way his eyes would light up when he sees her, how his hands would reach for hers across their familiar table.

The path she chose cut through an unfamiliar section of the city, where elegant shops and high-end cafés lined streets paved with ancient stones and ornate lampposts.

And then suddenly she saw him through the window of Café Milano.

Luca!

A huge smile burst on Claire's face. Her first reaction was to go in and say hi. But then her steps faltered as the scene through the window etched with devastating clarity. The café's interior glowed with under-stated luxury; brass fixtures gleaming softly in the chandelier lights, marble tables arranged with artistic precision, servers floating around in their pristine white uniforms and white gloves. And there, at a table bathed in morning light, sat Luca with a woman who embodied every Italian ideal of beauty.

Time seemed to stop, trapping Claire in a bubble of acute observation. The woman's dark hair fell in perfect waves past her shoulders, her sundress a masterpiece of elegant simplicity. But it was her face that seized Claire's breath, delicate features arranged with the kind of symmetry artists spent lifetimes trying to capture, eyes that held depths of emotion as she spoke intently to Luca.

Unable to move, Claire watched as Luca leaned forward, his expression intense with focus. The woman's hands moved expressively as she spoke, her fingers adorned with rings that caught light like captured stars. Then, in a gesture that shattered Claire's world completely, Luca reached across the table and took the woman's hand in his.

The contact wasn't casual. His fingers wrapped around hers with familiar tenderness, while his other hand came up to cover their joined hands completely. The woman's free hand moved to rest atop his, creating a moment of intimate connection that spoke of deep under-standing.

Through the window, Claire could see their lips moving in conversa-tion too private to hear. Whatever passed between them made the woman's eyes fill with tears, while Luca's face held an expression Claire had thought belonged only to their shared moments, tender, protective, full of unspoken emotion.

The ground beneath Claire's feet seemed to tilt as memories crashed. Mark's confession about Jessica, the way he'd looked when speaking about their connection, how blind she'd been until it was too late. History wasn't just repeating itself; it was mocking her with perfect symmetry.

A passing delivery truck blocked her view for a moment. When it cleared, Luca had drawn even closer to the woman, their heads bent together in profound intimacy. The morning light painted them in gentle radiance, transforming the scene into something that belonged in a romantic film, two beautiful people sharing a perfect Italian moment.

Claire's legs carried her forward without conscious thought, each step taking her further from the elegant café where her dreams lay shat-tered like broken glass. Her mind filled with a high pitch sound that might have been her own heart crying out in denial.

The streets of Naples, streets that had seemed so full of magic, now felt like a maze with no exit. She walked blindly, letting her feet carry her anywhere that wasn't here, that wasn't now, that wasn't this moment of devastating recognition.

In her mind, Luca's voice echoed with all his passionate declarations of devotion. How many other women had heard those same words? How many others had believed, as she had, that they were special, unique, irreplaceable?

Claire found refuge in a small piazza where a weathered Madonna watched over a forgotten fountain, her stone eyes holding centuries of hidden sorrows. The fountain's natural music should have been sooth-ing, but each drop of water seemed to echo the tears Claire was fighting to contain.

Her hands shook as she withdrew her phone, muscle memory finding Kate's number before conscious thought could intervene. The international rings stretched endlessly until her sister's voice, warm, familiar, and safe, wrapped around her like a childhood blanket.

"Claire? What's wrong?" Even across an ocean, Kate's protective instincts rang clear. "I can hear it in your breathing."

"I let myself believe again," Claire admitted, the words raw with pain. "After Mark... after everything... I took a vow that I'd never be so blind. But here I am, living the same story with different characters."

"Tell me everything," Kate commanded gently. "Start from the beginning."

Claire's laugh held no humor. "Which beginning? When Mark decided Jessica was worth destroying our marriage? Or when I came to Naples thinking I could outrun my own broken heart? Or when I met an Italian artist who made me believe in second chances?"

"The real beginning," Kate said pensively. "Tell me about him. Help me understand how it all began."

The fountain's steady rhythm kept time as Claire described those first magical days with Luca. The coffee shop notes they had exchanged for almost three months before meeting, the way art flowed between them like a living thing, how his passion for beauty had awakened something she'd thought forever lost. Now, six weeks into spending time together almost daily, their connection had deepened beyond what either could have imagined from those initial handwritten messages.

"He sees the world differently," Claire explained, her voice catching. "Or at least... I thought he did. Everything through his eyes became art waiting to happen. He taught me to trust creativity again, to feel deeply again, to believe that love could be..."

"Like it was before Mark?" Kate finished gently.

"No." Claire watched a young mother guide her child past the fountain, their joined hands a reminder of simple trust. "Different. Bigger. More real somehow. With Mark, I always felt like I had to make myself smaller, more contained. But Luca... he encouraged every wild impulse, celebrated every artistic urge. He made me feel like my passion was a gift, not an inconvenience."

"And now?"

"Now I've just watched him share an intimate moment with a woman who looks like she stepped from a Vogue cover." The tears finally fell, hot against her cold cheeks. "Just like Mark with Jessica. Another successful, beautiful, perfect woman who makes me feel like a pale shadow in comparison."

Kate's silence stretched for several moments. The kind of weighted pause that preceded difficult truths. When she spoke again, her voice had changed, taking on a protective edge Claire hadn't heard since high school, when Bobby Mercer had broken up with her before prom.

"Claire, I need to tell you something I have read before." Kate said with concern in her voice. "These real life stories, American women who fall for charismatic European men, especially artists and musicians. They're swept into this world of romance and grand gestures, everything feels magical and passionate, and then..."

"And then what?" Claire asked, though some part of her already knew the answer.

"And then they discover they're just one in a series. That the beautiful words, the intense gazes, the artistic connection, it's a pattern, not something unique." Kate's voice softened with compassion. "You're still healing from Mark, sweetie. Your heart is vulnerable. And this man, this artist who seems to understand you so perfectly, appeared exactly when you were most vulnerable."

"That's not fair," Claire protested, though doubt had already begun its insidious spread through her veins. "You don't know him."

"I know enough," Kate countered gently. "I know he's charming enough to make you forget your work responsibilities for the first time in your career. I know he's convinced you that your connection is something mystical and profound after knowing him what, a few months? And now I know he shares intense, intimate moments with other beautiful women while you're working yourself to exhaustion."

The fountain's steady music filled the silence as Claire struggled to find words that could defend what she and Luca shared. But each argument that rose to her lips seemed hollow against the evidence of what she'd witnessed through that café window.

"You have to understand how these situations look from the outside," Kate continued, her voice carrying years of protective instinct. "You're alone in a foreign country where you don't speak the language fluently. You're emotionally vulnerable after your divorce. You meet a handsome, charming artist who sweeps you into this world of passion and creativity... Claire, it's like a script these men follow."

"He's not like that," Claire insisted, but her voice lacked conviction.

"Maybe not. But, are you willing to risk it again on 'maybe'? Are you willing to wake up six months from now and discover you've built your entire life around someone who sees you as temporary? As interesting but ultimately replaceable?"

The words struck with devastating precision, finding every insecurity Mark's betrayal had planted. Claire's mind filled with unwelcome images. Luca and the beautiful woman, heads bent together in perfect intimacy. How many others had there been? How many others would there be?

"What should I do?" she asked, her voice small against the vastness of her confusion.

"Come home," Kate answered immediately. "Come back to where people love you unconditionally. Where you have support and a career you've worked so hard to build. This Italian adventure, it was meant to help you heal, not leave you more wounded than before."

Logic and emotion warred within Claire's chest as she considered Kate's advice. Home. The word conjured images of family Sunday dinners, of her cozy office overlooking the park, of friendships that had weathered decades of life's storms.

"I have obligations here," she said weakly. "The apartment lease, my European work arrangements...".

"All technicalities that can be handled," Kate interrupted gently. "The real question is, can you handle staying there, seeing him around town, watching him charm other women the way he charmed you? Naples isn't exactly a metropolis, Claire. Your paths would cross."

The thought of encountering Luca with another woman, perhaps the stunning goddess from the café, sent a physical pain through Claire's body.

"Pack your bags," Kate advised. "Not necessarily to leave tomorrow, but to give yourself the option. Having an escape route ready... it gives you power. Control. Meanwhile, finish your work, meet your deadlines. And when that's done, you can decide whether this Italian chapter of your life needs to close before it causes more damage."

As Claire ended the call, Madonna's stone eyes seemed to hold centuries of women's sorrows. How many others had sat by this fountain, hearts breaking over beautiful words that proved as transient as echoes after prayers have died?

The walk back to her apartment passed in a daze of emotional turmoil. Each street corner, each café, each glimpse of the bay now carried memories of moments with Luca. His hand at the small of her back as he guided her toward a perfect view, his voice rich with passion as he explained how light elevated ordinary scenes into artistic wonders, his eyes crinkling with joy when she captured a particularly difficult perspective in her sketches.

Inside her apartment, Claire moved as if underwater, each gesture requiring conscious effort. She pulled her suitcase from the closet, its familiar weight both comforting and devastating as she placed it on the bed. Mechanical movements guided her hands as she began folding clothes. The sundress Luca had said made her look like "spring personified," the dress that still carried traces of paint from their first shared canvas, the scarf he'd draped around her neck one evening when air turned cool.

Each item carried memories that cut like shattered glass, yet she continued packing, Kate's words echoing in her mind: "Having an escape route ready gives you power. Control."

With half the suitcase filled, Claire turned to her laptop. The presentation for Barton Worldwide stared back at her, awaiting final touches. Professional pride pushed through her emotional chaos. Whatever happened with Luca, she wouldn't allow her work to suffer. For the next two hours, she poured herself into completing the project, channeling her heartache into creative energy that transformed the regular rebrand into something exceptional.

When she finally hit send, attaching the files to an email for Susan, exhaustion crashed over her like a physical wave. The emotional marathon of the day, from hopeful anticipation of reunion to devastating discovery to heartbroken preparation for departure, had drained every reserve.

Claire collapsed onto her bed beside the half-packed suitcase, her body curling instinctively around the hollow ache in her chest. Tears came again, silent and relentless, until emotional and physical exhaustion finally pulled her into merciful darkness.

Morning light filtered through half-drawn curtains, painting tentative paths across Claire's bedroom floor. She lay motionless on her bed, eyes fixed on a hairline crack in the ceiling, a tiny imperfection she'd never noticed before. Her phone, deliberately silenced, vibrated on the nightstand with persistent urgency, each buzz marking another attempt by Luca to reach her. Beside her, the half-packed suitcase gaped open like a wound, clothes spilling over its edges in silent testimony to her fractured dreams.

The luminous numbers on her bedside clock marked the passing hours. Time flowing around her while she remained suspended in emotional limbo. Nine o'clock. Nine thirty. Ten fifteen. Each minute taking her further past when she should have been sitting across from Luca at Caffè Sereno, celebrating her completed work, planning new artistic adventures.

Another text notification illuminated her phone screen. Without looking, she knew it would be him, increasingly concerned, confused by her absence. Part of her, a small voice nearly drowned by pain, wondered if she should at least read his messages. But the larger part, the part shaped by Mark's betrayal and reinforced by Kate's warnings, couldn't bear to see more beautiful words that might prove as ephemeral as early morning fog in summer, there one moment, gone the next.

From afar, church bells announced the time, their melodic sounds cascading across the urban landscape. Eleven o'clock. In another life, the one she'd imagined just yesterday, she and Luca would be planning their afternoon by now, perhaps deciding which hidden courtyard to explore or which perspective of the bay to capture in paints.

Claire closed her eyes against fresh tears, wondering how many times one heart could break before it stopped attempting to reassemble itself.

The first knock came at eleven twenty-four, three gentle raps that echoed through her silent apartment like stones dropped into still water. She didn't move, couldn't move, her body weighted with despair that made even breathing feel like tremendous effort.

"Claire?" Luca's voice, muffled by the wooden door but unmistakably his, carried notes of concern that pierced her forced detachment. "Are you there? Are you alright?"

Silence stretched between them. Physical space measured in inches, emotional distance expanding like the universe itself.

The second series of knocks came with more urgency, his voice rising with undisguised worry. "Claire, please. If you're inside, let me know you're okay. I waited at Caffé Sereno... I've been calling..."

She pressed her palms against her ears, trying to block his voice that seemed designed to find all her vulnerable places. But even with the physical barrier, she could feel him there, his presence on the other side of her door was as tangible as the pain in her chest.

"I can feel you there," he said wistfully, the words somehow penetrating her defenses. "My heart knows you're here. Whatever's wrong, whatever's happened, I'm here. You can trust me to stand beside you through anything."

Trust?

The word struck like lightning, galvanizing Claire from her paralysis. She rose from the bed in a single fluid movement, emotion surging through her veins like wildfire. The suitcase tumbled to the floor as she pushed past it, clothes scattering across terra cotta tiles. Her bare feet carried her across the apartment with determined strides, each step fueled by the righteous anger that suddenly burned away her melancholy.

When she wrenched open the door, Luca's hand was raised mid-knock, his expression changing from concern to relief before registering the cold fury in her eyes.

"Trust?" The word exploded from her lips, sharp as shards of broken glass. "Do you even know the meaning of that word?"

Luca stood frozen in the doorway, his artist's eyes cataloging every detail of Claire's transformation from the woman he'd known to this avenging angel before him. Her hair tousled in wild disarray around shoulders held rigid with tension. Her eyes, usually warm as summer skies, had hardened to glacial blue. Even her voice had changed. All softness stripped away, leaving only the razor edge.

"Claire," he began cautiously, "what's...".

"I saw you," she cut him off, each word precise as a blade. "Yesterday at that fancy café. With her. And don't even think of insulting my intelligence by denying it."

Understanding dawned in his eyes, followed quickly by something that looked like desperate relief. "With Angelica, yes. But it's not...".

"Not what it appeared?" Claire's laugh held no humor, only the brittle sound of trust shattering. "I saw it. I saw everything with my own eyes."

She stepped back into the apartment, a silent invitation that felt more like a challenge. Luca entered cautiously, keeping distance between them as she continued.

"I watched you hold her hands," Claire said, her voice dropping to a dangerous softness. "I saw how you leaned close to her, how your expression held such... intimacy. The exact same way you look at me." Her voice caught on the last words, betraying the pain beneath her anger.

"You held her hands like she was precious to you. Like you couldn't bear to be apart from her." She said with effort, trying to keep her anger under control. "Then when I was about to leave, I saw you move even closer, as if sharing secrets meant only for each other." Each detail emerged with perfect clarity, the scene permanently etched into her memory. "I'm so sorry, if being with me took you away from her. Maybe that's why she was upset. Sorry, I'm still breathing, making everything so difficult for you to juggle." She said in a voice that held nothing but utmost contempt.

Luca made an abortive gesture toward her, stopping when she flinched away. "Please," he said quietly, "let me explain. Yes, I was with Angelica. Yes, I was holding her hands, comforting her. But not for the reasons you think."

"Then what reasons?" Claire demanded, wrapping her arms around herself as if for protection. "Explain to me why you were sharing such an intimate moment with a woman who looks like she stepped from a fashion magazine. A woman you've apparently never mentioned before."

Luca's eyes held steady on hers, not evading her accusations but meeting them directly. "Angelica is granddaughter of Grandma Rosa," he said quietly. "We've known each other since childhood."

Claire blinked, momentarily thrown off balance. "Grandma Rosa? The angel-like woman from the trattoria?" The tiny silver-haired woman who'd sheltered them and fed them during their car trouble flickered in front of her eyes.

"Yes. Angelica is getting married in three weeks. She and her fiancé Gregory asked me to paint their wedding portrait, to be unveiled at their rehearsal dinner."

Claire's eyes darted involuntarily to the half-packed suitcase, clothes scattered like abandoned plans across the floor. "And that explains the intimate hand-holding? How, exactly?" Claire asked half mockingly.

Luca moved further into the apartment, stopping near the window where morning light caught his features, bathing the emotional exhaustion etched there. "I was supposed to meet both of them yesterday at Café Milano to discuss the portrait. When I arrived, they were already there, arguing. Gregory stormed out just as I walked in, leaving Angelica in tears."

His voice softened with remembered concern. "She was devastated, Claire. Talking about calling off the wedding. About how maybe love wasn't worth the pain it caused." He ran a hand through his dark curls, a gesture of distress Claire had come to know well. "I stayed with her, tried to help her see that one argument doesn't negate a relationship built on real understanding."

The explanation hovered between them, plausible yet insufficient to counteract what Claire had witnessed. "You seemed very... practiced at comforting her," she said, the accusation still implicit in her tone.

Luca's expression shifted, a flash of hurt quickly masked. "Because I understand what it feels like when love seems to be slipping away. Because I've lived through my own heartbreak."

Claire pressed her fingers to her temples, trying to organize scattered thoughts. "Either way, it doesn't explain why you were being so... intimate with her."

"What you didn't see," Luca continued gently, "what you couldn't have seen because you'd probably already left, was me going after Gregory. Finding him at the bar down the street, talking some sense into him. Bringing him back to Angelica so they could actually communicate instead of letting fear drive them apart."

As he spoke, Luca carefully reached into his pocket and withdrew his phone. "I want to show you something," he said, unlocking the screen with deliberate movements. "A message from Angelica, sent last night."

He held the phone out, keeping enough distance that Claire would need to choose to step forward, to bridge the gap between accusation and understanding. After a moment's hesitation, she moved close enough to see the screen, where a text message displayed a photo of Angelica and a handsome man with sandy hair, both smiling broadly at the camera, her head resting on his shoulder.

The Italian text beneath it was unfamiliar to Claire, but Luca translated softly: "'Thank you for saving us from ourselves today. Gregory and I talked through everything. The wedding is still on. We can't wait for you and Claire to create our portrait together.'"

Claire's eyes snapped up to his. "Together?"

Something vulnerable flickered in Luca's expression. "That was the surprise I wanted to tell you about when our three days apart ended. Angelica and Gregory commissioned us both, not just me, but us as artistic partners. I wanted it to be a special thing for you, recognition of how beautifully our styles complement each other."

"Grandma Rosa has invited us both to the wedding.," he continued. "I told you that day when we were at her place. She's been asking when she'd see us again since that night at the trattoria. She calls us her 'piccoli artisti innamorati' (little artists in love)."

The phrase hung in the air between them, fragile as blown glass. Claire turned away, moving to the small kitchen table where her laptop still sat open, evidence of her late-night work session. Her thoughts whirled chaotically, trying to reconcile what she'd seen with what Luca was telling her.

"Why didn't you mention Angelica before?" she asked finally, the question emerging softer than intended.

"Because the portrait commission was meant to be a surprise. Because..." He hesitated, then continued with quiet honesty, "Because I wanted to give you the three days you needed for your work without adding any pressure or distraction."

Claire's fingers traced the edge of her laptop, focusing on the smooth surface to ground herself amid emotional turbulence. "My sister says Italian men are known for their charm. For sweeping vulnerable women off their feet, only to..." She couldn't finish, the words tasting like copper on her tongue.

Luca remained silent for a long moment, his expression unreadable. When he finally spoke, his voice carried a depth of emotion that made Claire's chest ache.

"Your sister has never met me," he said quietly. "Has never seen how my hands shake when I'm painting you because I'm terrified of not capturing your essence perfectly. Has never heard how my voice changes when I speak your name. Has never felt how my heart beats differently since you walked into my life."

He moved closer, stopping when just two feet of distance separated them. "I'm not asking you to trust me because of pretty words or grand gestures, Claire. I'm asking you to trust what you've experienced yourself, every moment we've shared, every truth we've exchanged, every piece of art we've created together."

Claire stood at the precipice of a choice that felt momentous. She could believe in the evidence of her eyes in that café window, or trust in the deeper pattern she and Luca had been weaving together since that first note in Caffè Sereno.

"I was going to leave," she revealed, glancing toward the half-packed suitcase. "Go back to Ohio, back to what's safe and known."

"I know," Luca replied softly. "I can see it in more than just the suitcase. I can see it in how you're holding yourself away, preparing for pain."

He moved to her bookshelf where a small framed sketch stood, the first drawing he'd ever given her, a sunflower reaching toward light not yet visible. With careful movements, he picked it up, holding it between them like evidence.

"This is who I am, Claire. Not some charming stereotype, not a man who collects admirers like trophies. I'm an artist who sees beauty in truth, who found his perfect creative partner in you, who cannot imagine returning to a world where your soul doesn't speak to mine through art and touch and shared vision."

His fingers traced the sunflower's reaching petals. "When I was comforting Angelica, do you know what example I used to help her understand that real love survives disagreements? I told her about us, about how you needed three days for your work, and how difficult it was for both of us to be apart, but how that separation would ultimately strengthen what we're building together."

Claire stilled completely as pieces began rearranging into new configurations. "You used us as an example of healthy love? While I was..." She gestured helplessly toward the scattered clothing and open suitcase.

"While you were demonstrating incredible professional dedication," Luca completed gently. "While you were honoring an important part of who you are, even when it was difficult." His eyes held hers with unwavering sincerity. "That's what real partnership looks like, Claire. Supporting each other's growth, not just when it's convenient, but especially when it requires sacrifice." He set the framed sketch down.

Then he moved with calm and resolve to lift the now empty suitcase from the floor and placed it inside the closet. Then he gathered the scattered clothes from the floor, one by one, and placed them inside the closet. He reached slowly for her hand, giving her every opportunity to pull away. When she didn't, his fingers entwined with hers, that familiar connection that had felt like coming home since the first time they'd touched.

Claire took a deep breath, gathering courage to share what she'd kept hidden since they met. Her eyes found a point just beyond Luca's shoulder, focusing there as she prepared to reveal her past. "There's something I haven't told you," she began hesitantly. "My marriage ended because my husband Mark had an affair. I discovered he'd been living a double life for months, lying to my face while betraying everything we'd built together." Her voice caught as she continued, "When I saw you with Angelica, holding her hands, leaning close and speaking so intimately... all those old wounds suddenly felt fresh again."

Luca's expression softened with understanding, his eyes never leaving hers. "Claire," he said, his voice gentle as he processed her revelation. "What you went through..." He moved closer, taking her hand in his with a touch so tender it made her heart ache. "Now I see why seeing me with Angelica affected you so deeply. Trust, once broken, leaves scars that take time to heal."

"I know I should have told you sooner," Claire admitted, meeting his gaze directly. "But talking about it meant reliving it, and with you, I've felt so... free from all that pain." She squeezed his hand, grateful for his patience. "I'm sorry I jumped to conclusions without giving you a chance to explain."

His fingertips brushed the sensitive hollow of her wrist, feeling the steady rhythm of her pulse beneath his touch, the simple touch grounding her in present truth rather than past trauma. "I completely understand your feelings. Because I have experienced the same." He continued. "Let me share with you what I have gone through. About Alessandra, that was the person I was in love with and Giovanni who was my best friend. Oh it hurts just to say those names."

Claire studied their joined hands, feeling the slight tremor in his fingers that betrayed the emotional cost of this revelation. "Tell me," she whispered.

Luca's eyes held shadows of old pain as he began. "Alessandra and I... we were together for three years. I thought she was my future, we'd known each other since childhood, grew up in the same neighborhood. I gave her everything, my love, my trust, my present, my future."

His voice roughened with remembered hurt. "Then I found out she'd been sleeping with my best friend for months. Giovanni had been like a brother to me since we were boys. They'd been meeting in secret, laughing about how blind I was, how naive I was, how easy it was to deceive an artist who lived in dreams."

His hand tightened briefly around hers. "It nearly destroyed me. Not just the betrayal, but the humiliation of realizing everyone had known except me. I stopped painting for two years. Couldn't bear to create when everything I thought I knew about love had been proven false."

"What changed?" Claire asked softly, hearing the echo of her own journey in his.

Luca's eyes found hers, holding depths of emotion that took her breath. "You did. Your notes in Caffè Sereno, your art, your soul reaching across paper to touch mine... you reminded me that real love isn't about possession or perfect performance. It's about seeing someone completely and being seen in return."

His free hand rose to touch her cheek with infinite tenderness. "That's why I was helping Angelica yesterday. Because I recognized the fear in her eyes, the same fear I lived with after Alessandra, the same fear I saw in you when you opened the door today. The fear that love isn't real, that trust only leads to pain."

The morning light had repositioned while they stood there, painting new revelations across her apartment floor. It was like how understanding was reshaping Claire's perception of what she'd witnessed through that café window.

"I thought..." she began, her voice catching. "When I saw you with her, all I could see was Mark telling me about his affair. The same betrayal playing out before my eyes, like some cruel echo designed specifically to break my heart again."

"I know," Luca empathised, his expression open with compassion. "But Claire, look at me. Really look. Do you see deception in my eyes? Have I ever misled you in any way? Ever asked you to be less than who you are?"

Claire studied his face, the eyes that had never learned to hide emotion, the mouth that spoke truth even when difficult, the open vulnerability that Mark had never once shown her. "No, you have never misled me," she finally admitted, feeling walls inside her start to crumble. "You've only ever encouraged me to be more authentic, more daring, more..." She met his gaze directly. "More myself than I've been in years."

"Because that's what real love does," he said with quiet intensity. "It doesn't diminish us, it expands us, challenges us, helps us become our truest selves." His eyes never left hers as he continued. "When you disappeared into silence these past days, I realized something profound. Every painting I create, every breath I take, every moment I live, they're all shaped by your presence in my life. You've awakened parts of me I thought died with Alessandra's betrayal."

Claire felt something shift in her chest, like light breaking through storm clouds. "I've been so afraid," she surrendered to the truth. "Not just of being hurt again, but of hurting myself, of running from something magnificent because I couldn't trust my own judgment."

"Then trust mine," Luca said, closing any remaining distance between them. His hands came up to frame her face with gentleness. "Trust that I would rather die than cause you pain. Trust that every beat of my heart carries your name, every stroke of my brush tells our story."

Tears spilled down Claire's cheeks as years of carefully constructed defenses melted beneath the truth in his eyes. "I do trust you," she realized aloud. "Despite everything Mark did, despite all my fears... something deep within me recognizes you. It always has."

Luca's thumbs brushed away her tears as his own eyes glistened with emotion. "Then let me show you," he whispered, "exactly how completely you own my heart."

His lips found hers with exquisite delicacy that quickly deepened into something more primal. Claire felt herself responding with equal passion, pouring years of held-back emotion into this moment of perfect understanding.

They merged like two halves of a whole finally reuniting, each touch an affirmation that transcended their past wounds and present fears.

As they moved together, each touch erased another shadow of doubt. His hands traced her features as if memorizing them anew, while her fingers mapped the familiar territory of his chest.

Their kisses deepened, carrying notes of relief and renewal, of understanding hard-won through shared truth. Claire felt herself melting into his embrace as Luca's lips traced a path from her mouth to her neck, each caress an affirmation of devotion.

"Ti amo con tutta l'anima," his lips said against her skin. "I love you with my entire being."

Time seemed to suspend as they found their way to the bed. Afternoon light filtered through the curtains, turning the simple space into something sacred now. Their coming together felt both familiar and entirely new, each touch carrying deeper meaning after the emotional tempest they'd weathered.

Later, wrapped in bedsheets that smelled of sun and passion, Claire traced lazy poetry on Luca's chest while his fingers played with her hair. The quiet between them held no tension now, only the peaceful understanding finally laid bare.

"I've never felt this way," Claire murmured, pressing a kiss to his shoulder. "This complete certainty that I can be exactly who I am, that my heart is safe in someone else's keeping."

Luca's arms tightened around her. "Because this isn't just passion or romance," he said softly. "This is recognition, two artists finding their perfect match and creating something greater than themselves."

As twilight descended over Naples, Luca reluctantly prepared to leave. An important meeting with an art collector awaited him at his studio early the next morning. He invited Claire to join him, his eyes conveying how much he wanted her presence beside him. With bittersweet regret, she declined, explaining she needed to remain at her apartment to complete the final touches on several impending projects with looming deadlines. Though they yearned to remain together, their mutual respect for each other's professional commitments prevailed, as a result of the understanding they'd fought so hard to rebuild.

He kissed Claire softly on the forehead and stepped into the warm evening air. The click of the door behind him echoed with the promise of tomorrow.

Dawn painted Claire's bedroom in watercolor washes of apricot and peach as she awakened, still feeling the weight of yesterday's misunderstanding. She had finished her work late at night. After that she still couldn't sleep soundly, she kept thinking of Luca's wounded eyes.

Rolling to her side, Claire's gaze drifted toward the half-open closet door, which served as a portal to the evidence of yesterday's emotional tempest. Inside, her suitcase rested against the wall like an abandoned escape plan, while her folded clothes told the story of Luca's tender care. Some hung from wooden hangers, their fabrics still bearing the memory of his touch, while others lay in perfect, loving folds on the shelves, each crease and arrangement a silent testimony to how he had restored order from chaos after her world had tilted back into balance. In those neatly organized garments, she could see the careful attention of a man whose artist's hands created beauty even in the most mundane tasks, a silent poem of devotion written in cotton and silk and chiffon.

How close she had come to throwing everything away, to letting fear poison the most beautiful connection she'd ever known. The realization made her chest ache with remorse.

Rising from bed, Claire moved to the window where Naples spread before her, the same city she'd viewed yesterday with eyes clouded by suspicion and hurt. Today, the sunlight bounced off ancient domes and rooftops with renewed brilliance, as if the world itself celebrated her return to clarity.

"I doubted him," she admitted, to the empty room, each word heavy with regret. "After everything we've shared, I was ready to run at the first hint of trouble."

As morning light strengthened around her, Claire reached for her phone with a sense of purpose crystallizing in her mind. Her fingers moved across the screen with newfound certainty:

"When you're finished with the art collector, come to Caffè Sereno. I'll be waiting."

The message was sent with a whoosh that seemed inadequate for words carrying such weight of intention. Three days they'd spent apart for her work, then another day nearly lost to fear and misunderstanding. No more wasted time.

Claire moved through her morning routine with deliberate care, each action infused with the significance of decision. The dress she chose, a deep teal that caught the light like Mediterranean waters at midday, felt like armor and declaration combined. Her hair, swept up with artful looseness, revealed the vulnerable curve of her neck where Luca loved to press his lips.

As she applied a touch of mascara, Claire studied her reflection, noting how her eyes held a depth that hadn't been there before Naples, before Luca. They were the eyes of a woman who had faced her deepest fears and chosen love despite them, a woman who understood that real connection requires courage.

"I love him," she avowed to her reflection, testing the words that had lived in her heart but remained unspoken between them. The simple declaration sent a shower of warmth cascading through her body, as if saying it aloud had broken some final barrier within her.

Her phone chimed with Luca's response:

"I'll be there. The collector is still here. It may be about one and a half hours before I reach Caffè Sereno. Counting minutes until I see you again."

The words brought a smile to Claire's lips and fresh determination to her spirit. One and a half hours, enough time for what she had in mind. Gathering her bag and keys, she stepped into the Naples morning with purpose and the taste of unspoken declarations sweet on her tongue.

The streets of Naples shed their morning shadows as Claire wound her way through familiar passageways that had become extensions of herself. Shop owners raised their metal shutters with metallic symphonies that echoed between ancient buildings, while the aroma of fresh bread and coffee turned the air itself into sustenance.

Claire had no specific destination in mind beyond eventually reaching Caffè Sereno, allowing her artistic instincts to guide her through streets she hadn't yet explored with Luca. Each turn revealed new aspects of the city. A hidden fountain where old women filled water jugs with practiced motions, a tiny chapel whose open door released incense-laden air into the morning, a small piazza where children jumped across stones worn smooth by centuries of footsteps.

As she rounded a corner into a narrow street lined with shops selling everything from handmade leather to antique books, something caught her eye. A glint of metal in a dimly lit window that seemed to call to her. The shop front was modest, its weathered sign announcing "Tesori

Antichi" in faded gold letters. By now Claire knew that antichi meant antiques.

The display window held an assortment of objects from the bygone eras. There were tarnished silver candelabras, porcelain figurines with dainty hand-painted features, and pocket watches that had once marked time for people.

But it was the small velvet display tucked into the corner that drew Claire forward like a magnet finding true north. A bracelet lay against midnight blue fabric, its silver surface catching morning light in ways that transformed metal into liquid poetry. Without conscious thought, she found herself pushing open the shop's heavy wooden door, a small bell announcing her arrival with gentle insistence.

The interior smelled of beeswax and history, the air itself seeming thicker with the weight of accumulated memories. Shelves lined the walls, each one bearing treasures from different eras. Art Nouveau vases alongside Renaissance-inspired picture frames, Victorian jewelry boxes nestled against ancient Roman coins.

"Buongiorno (Good morning)," came a voice from the shadows at the back of the shop. An elderly man emerged, his movements deliberate with age but his eyes sharp with intelligence. His hands bore the beautiful marks of a craftsman, slight calluses, a few small scars, nails kept meticulously clean despite the dust that seemed to coat everything else in the shop.

"Buongiorno," Claire responded, her Italian still hesitant but improving with each passing day. "The bracelet in your window..."

The old man's face creased with a smile that made his features change from merely dignified to genuinely warm. "Ah, you have a good eye, signorina. Very special, that one." He moved to the window with surprising grace, carefully retrieving the velvet display.

Up close, the bracelet revealed itself as even more magnificent than Claire had first thought. It was a wide cuff of silver, not polished to modern perfection but bearing a patina that spoke of age and authenticity. It had an intricate engraved pattern that seemed to flow like water, curves and angles meeting in perfect harmony, creating an endless design that drew the eye in circles of perpetual motion.

"May I?" Claire asked, gesturing toward it.

The shopkeeper nodded, his eyes watching her reactions with evident pleasure as she lifted the bracelet from its velvet bed. The weight surprised her, substantial without being heavy, the kind of presence that would be impossible to forget once worn. The inside curve was smooth, designed to rest comfortably against skin, while tiny hinges allowed it to open and close with precision engineering that had withstood decades of use.

"It's beautiful," Claire breathed, turning it to catch the light streaming through the shop's dusty windows.

"È stato creato nel millenovecento ventiquattro," the man said, then switched to careful English when he noticed Claire's slight confusion. "Made in 1924 by Salvatore Donati, a painter from Palermo. See here..." He pointed to a tiny maker's mark stamped inside the cuff. "His signature. Donati created very few pieces of jewelry, only for those he loved or deeply respected."

Claire's mind swirled with enchantment as her fingers traced the flowing patterns. "He was an artist?"

"Si, si (Yes, yes). Very passionate. His paintings hang in small museums throughout Sicily. But his metalwork was kept mostly private, gifts for fellow artists, for lovers, for those who inspired his creative soul." The shopkeeper's eyes twinkled. "They say he believed an artist's hands should be adorned only with pieces that understand the creative spirit."

The bracelet seemed to grow warmer in Claire's grasp, as if responding to her touch, to the artist's blood that flowed in her own veins. "Was it made for a man or a woman?"

"For a man. Donati's closest friend and fellow painter, Emilio Vazzano. They created together for many years, their styles different but complementary." He gestured to the intricate pattern. "This design represents their artistic connection, see how each line influences the next, how the patterns merge and separate but always remain connected?"

Claire's vision blurred slightly as emotion welled up unexpectedly. The parallels were too perfect to be coincidence. This bracelet created by one artist for another that spoke of creative souls finding harmony together. Just as she and Luca had done, their distinct artistic voices weaving together to create something neither could achieve alone.

"Is it for sale?" she asked, already knowing she would pay whatever he asked.

The shopkeeper named a figure that made Claire blink, not outrageously expensive, but certainly significant on her freelancer's budget. Yet she nodded without hesitation, understanding that some expressions of love rise above the financial considerations.

"A gift, yes?" he asked astutely as he moved to wrap the bracelet.

"For someone who taught me to see beauty again," Claire confirmed. "An artist who helped me remember who I truly am."

The old man nodded, understanding shining in his eyes. "Wait," he said, holding up one finger before disappearing into the back of the shop. He returned moments later with a small wooden box lined with aged velvet, bearing intricate inlay work that spoke of master craftsmanship.

"For such a special gift," he explained. "No extra charge."

As he placed the bracelet in its new home, Claire had a sudden inspiration. "Is it possible to have something engraved inside? Today, before I give it to him?"

The shopkeeper's smile deepened. "My son is a master engraver. His workshop is next door. What words would you like to preserve?"

Claire's heart swelled as she found precisely the right phrase, words that would transform silver into a declaration, metal into a promise.

On her way to Caffè Sereno, Claire paused in a quiet piazza, her heart too full to contain another moment. She called Kate, stirring her from sleep in the predawn hours of Ohio, unable to wait another second to unburden her emotions. With words tumbling like water over stones, she revealed how yesterday's shadows had dissolved into light, how Luca was exactly the man she'd known him to be, the entire misunderstanding a phantom of her own creation. Kate listened, understanding dawning in her voice as she apologized for hastily categorizing Luca as merely another "Italian man" from some worn travel stereotype. Her genuine joy for Claire resonated through the connection, along with wholehearted support for Claire's decision to remain in Italy for now.

Caffè Sereno welcomed Claire like a beloved returning home after a long absence. The familiar bell above the door chimed her arrival, its musical notes announcing her presence before she'd taken three steps inside. The aroma of Signor Rossi's perfect cappuccino blended with the subtle sweetness of Lucia's baking, creating an atmosphere that had become as essential to Claire as air itself.

"Claire! Nostra bella artista (our beautiful artist)!" Lucia said, dusting the flour from her hands. Without hesitation, she enveloped Claire in an embrace that conveyed both affection and gentle admonishment. "Where have you been hiding? Four days without seeing your smile, it's too long!"

"I know," Claire admitted, returning the embrace with genuine warmth. "I had some important work related projects and deadlines and then..." She hesitated, uncertain how to explain the emotional tempest of the past two days.

Lucia saw something on Claire's face and an understanding flickered in Lucia's wise eyes. "Ah, the challenges of intimate connection," she said thoughtfully. "They test us, right? But make the sweet moments sweeter by having earned them."

Before Claire could respond, Signor Rossi appeared from behind his copper altar, his face lighting with pleasure at the sight of her. "The prodigal artist returns!" he declared, spreading his arms wide in welcome. "Come, sit! Let me make you the perfect cappuccino, still morning, so no breaking of Italian coffee rules today."

The familiar banter wrapped around Claire like a favorite blanket as she settled at her usual table by the window. Sunlight streamed through the glass. She put her hand inside her handbag to touch the box containing Luca's bracelet, its presence both comforting and nerve-wracking, a physical manifestation of the declaration she planned to make.

Lucia joined her, settling into the chair opposite with the comfortable ease of family. "So, the work is finished? The important projects that kept you from us?"

"Yes," Claire nodded, gratitude washing through her at how easily this couple had become essential anchors in her Naples life. "Everything submitted on time, clients happy, professional reputation intact."

"And Luca?" Lucia asked gently. "He was here yesterday morning, waiting. His eyes checking the door each time the bell rang. When you didn't come..." She didn't finish, but her gaze held questions too perceptive to evade.

Claire's fingers traced wood grain on the tabletop, her eyes following their movement as she gathered courage to be honest. "I made a mistake," she admitted quietly. "I saw something I misinterpreted, let old fears cloud my judgment. But we've talked now, cleared everything up."

Signor Rossi arrived with the cappuccino, setting it before her with the flourish of a maestro presenting his finest work. The perfect heart traced in the foam seemed a fitting symbol for the day's intentions. "Mistakes between two people who truly see each other are never permanent," he said, his voice carrying the wisdom of one who had weathered many storms across decades of marriage. "They are just new paths to deeper understanding."

The simple truth in his words made Claire's eyes fill with unexpected tears. "That's exactly what we found, deeper understanding," she acknowledged. "He's meeting me here soon."

Lucia's hand covered hers, a touch both grounding and nurturing. "Good. Very good. Now drink your cappuccino before it cools." She said in a motherly tone.

The bell above the door chimed again, drawing all eyes toward the entrance where late morning light silhouetted a familiar figure. Luca stepped into the café, his dark eyes immediately finding hers across the space between them.

The world narrowed to a single focal point as Luca crossed Caffè Sereno toward Claire. Every detail of him registered with crystalline clarity, the slight dishevelment of his dark curls from running his hands through them, a habit when deep in artistic discussion, the white linen shirt with sleeves rolled to reveal forearms marked with traces of charcoal, evidence of working while waiting for the collector, the way his eyes never left hers despite Signor Rossi's enthusiastic greeting.

Lucia and Signor Rossi exchanged knowing glances before discreetly retreating to the counter, creating a private bubble around their table. The café's ambient sounds, espresso machine hissing, cups clinking, and muted conversations, formed a backdrop to this moment suspended between heartbeats.

"Claire," Luca breathed as he reached her, her name emerging from the depths of his soul. He didn't sit immediately, instead remaining standing as if unable to break the magnetic connection between their eyes.

She rose to meet him, driven by an impulse deeper than thought. "You came," she said, though there had never been any real doubt.

"I would walk through fire to reach you," he replied simply, the words carrying no hint of exaggeration, only honest truth.

The space between them vibrated with unspoken emotion. "I have something for you," she said tenderly. "Something that carries meaning beyond its form."

She reached for the box in her handbag and placed it in Luca's hands. His fingers caressed its smooth surface before carefully opening the lid. The silver bracelet nestled inside in midnight velvet seemed to capture every ray of sunlight in the café. The intricate design looked as if they had come alive with kinetic energy.

Luca's eyes widened as he took in the gift, his artist's appreciation for craftsmanship evident in his immediate reaction. "Claire," he whispered, her name containing multitudes of emotion.

"It belonged to an artist from Palermo," she explained, her voice steadying as she shared the bracelet's history. "Created in 1924 for another artist, his creative partner, the one whose style complemented his own, whose vision helped him see the world more completely." She continued. "As artists they were connected, though their techniques differed. Together, they created works neither could have imagined alone." Her eyes met his, conveying the parallel that had struck her so forcefully in the antique shop. "It reminded me of us."

"There's an inscription," she said, barely containing her enthusiasm. "Inside."

Luca lifted the bracelet from its velvet bed, the silver warm from his touch. He turned it over to read the engraving, his breath catching visibly as the words registered.

"For my Luca, Forever connected through art and heart, with love from Claire," he read aloud, each word weighted with significance.

When he looked up, his eyes shimmered with emotion too deep for ordinary expression.

The profound understanding dawned upon him as he grasped the significance beyond the physical object. Without words, he extended his left wrist toward her. An offering, a surrender, a request.

Claire's fingers trembled slightly as she opened the bracelet's clasp and placed it around his wrist. The silver looked as if it had been created specifically for him, the width and curve perfectly complementing his artist's hand. With gentle pressure, she closed the clasp, the click sealing more than just metal against his skin.

Claire took his hand, her fingers brushing the cool silver now warming against his wrist. The moment had arrived. The culmination of a journey that had begun with coffee-stained notes.

"Luca," she began, trying to keep her voice steady. "These past days have taught me something profound. Love isn't just passion or creativity or even understanding. It's a choice, choosing to believe, to trust, to see beauty even when doubts exist."

Her thumb traced the edge of the bracelet where it met his skin. "This will rest against your pulse, marking the rhythm of your heart. And I want you to feel, with each beat, what I'm telling you now." She took a deep breath, gathering courage for the most impactful words. "I love you. Not despite our shadows, but including them. Everything you are, everything we're becoming together, I choose it all."

For a moment, Luca remained perfectly still, as if her declaration had sculpted him into one of the statues that graced Naples' ancient piazzas. Then, with the fluid grace that characterized his every movement, he brought his bracelet-adorned wrist to his lips, pressing a kiss to the silver that now carried her words against his skin.

"This," he said, his voice rough with emotion, "will never leave my wrist. It will rest here," he touched the spot where the bracelet covered his pulse point, "marking every heartbeat as yours. Each pulse carrying your name through my veins, each beat a reminder that art brought us together but love keeps us that way."

He drew her closer, one hand rising to cradle her face with infinite care. "Claire, Ti amo (I love you). With every color on my palette, every stroke of my brush, every breath in my body. I love you with an artist's complete devotion, seeing all of you, the complexity and contradiction, and finding it all unutterably beautiful."

In the sanctuary of Caffè Sereno, surrounded by the scent of coffee and freshly baked pastries, they sealed their declarations with a kiss that felt like coming home after a long journey. The silver bracelet caught the light between them, transforming metal into a relic of promises made and kept, of love that metamorphosed fear into its most beautiful canvas.

From behind the counter, Lucia and Signor Rossi watched with misty eyes, bearing witness to the kind of connection they recognized from their own decades together. The rare and precious union of those who had found in each other not just passion, but true partnership.

The bracelet gleamed against Luca's wrist as he drew Claire closer, its silver reflecting fragments of light across the café walls like stars scattered across an Italian night sky, each one a declaration of creative magic yet to come.

8

THE PORTRAIT OF SOULS

The afternoon sun bathed the countryside in the hue of honey as Claire and Luca's car wound its way up the familiar narrow road toward Trattoria della Nonna (Grandma Rosa's place). Every curve revealed vistas that stirred memories for Claire. Memories of being carried in Luca's arms, of how everything transformed into one of their most treasured moments together. The small stone building material-ized around the bend, just as timelessly beautiful as when they'd first stumbled upon it with a flat tire and Claire's sprained ankle. Now they returned purposefully, to meet the enigmatic couple engaged to be married.

Angelica and Gregory had specifically requested a portrait to be created by Claire and Luca that would "capture their souls' bond," a concept that Claire and Luca understood, and at the same time could not put their arms around. That's why they arranged to meet the couple.

As Luca parked their car in the small gravel area beside the trattoria, Claire's fingers nervously tapped against her sketchbook. "Do you remember when we first came here?" Luca asked, his eyes dancing with shared memories. "Grandma Rosa said everyone who stays in the lovers' room finds their way back to each other." Claire squeezed his hand, drawing strength from the connection that had only deepened since that accidental first visit. Together they stepped toward the weathered wooden door, ready to glimpse another profound connection they were being asked to immortalize.

Grandma Rosa greeted them like returning children, her weathered hands clasping theirs with the strength of a woman who'd kneaded love into bread dough for decades. "My beautiful artists," she cooed, ushering them into the courtyard's embrace.

Beneath the ancient fig tree in the courtyard, a dappled sanctuary from the hot Mediterranean sun, sat Angelica and Gregory.

Claire's gaze lingered on Angelica's elegant profile, briefly recalling her fleeting misunderstanding from days past when she'd glimpsed Luca and Angelica at the café. How foolish those shadows now seemed in the clarifying light of today.

Beneath the fig tree's dappled light, Claire and Luca settled across from the young couple, the four of them forming a perfect square of anticipation and curiosity around the weathered courtyard table. Angelica's eyes sparkled with recognition as they made introductions, her hand extending toward Claire with the warmth of someone greeting not a stranger but a kindred spirit. Gregory, tall with shoulders that seemed built to carry responsibilities, offered a smile that transformed his scholarly features into something boyishly charming. Claire felt Luca's presence beside her, steady and reassuring, as they exchanged those first pleasantries that somehow already felt like the beginning of friendship rather than mere politeness.

The small wicker tray Grandma Rosa carried delivered treasures still warm from her oven, cantucci (almond biscotti) that crumbled like subtle memories in their mouths, alongside tall glasses of lemonade so fresh Claire could taste sunshine in every sip. "From my tree to your hearts," Grandma Rosa said, pointing to the gnarled lemon tree that stood sentinel at the courtyard's edge, its fruit hanging like small golden lanterns among glossy leaves.

"So, how did you two meet?" Claire asked, leaning forward with genuine curiosity as she accepted another cantucci from Grandma Rosa's tray.

The question hung in the fragrant air for a moment as Angelica and

Gregory exchanged a glance. One of those private communications that seemed to contain an entire conversation. Claire noticed how their expressions synchronized perfectly, a mirror of surprise followed by shared amusement.

"You know," Angelica said, turning back to Claire and Luca, "we've never told anyone the complete story." Her voice carried a warm quality, as if she were sharing a cherished secret.

Gregory laughed softly. "It started at Caffè Sereno, actually."

"Caffè Sereno?" Luca's eyebrows rose in surprise as he set down his lemonade. "Signor Rossi and Lucia's place?"

Claire felt an unexpected flutter in her chest. The very mention of the café where she and Luca had begun their own journey through notes and shared art created an immediate connection. Threads of parallel experiences weaving together in ways she couldn't have anticipated.

"The very same," Gregory confirmed, his expression warming with recollection. "I had just returned from the US. My parents had decided it was time for me to learn the family business here in Italy. I knew no one except distant relatives, and felt..." he paused, searching for the right word.

"Unmoored," Angelica supplied, her fingers finding his with instinctive precision.

"Exactly. Unmoored." Gregory nodded gratefully. "One morning, I wandered into Caffè Sereno. Signor Rossi was explaining caffè sospeso to another customer. The tradition of paying for an extra coffee that someone else could claim later."

Claire's attention sharpened, her artist's mind immediately drawing parallels between their stories. She glanced at Luca, finding in his expression the same recognition that was blooming within her. A shared understanding that needed no words.

"The concept fascinated me," Gregory continued. "This uniquely Neapolitan way of connecting strangers through small acts of generosity. So I ordered two espressos, one for myself and one suspended. Then I wrote a note on the receipt."

"And I claimed that suspended coffee," Angelica interjected, her eyes brightening with the memory. "I was there helping Grandma Rosa deliver her special bread to Lucia. It was my weekly ritual."

"Signor Rossi told me about the cork board," Gregory added, "how people who claimed coffees could leave notes, and those who bought the suspended coffees could respond."

Luca made a small sound of wonder, his leg pressing gently against Claire's beneath the table, a silent communication of all they couldn't say aloud. This revelation helped them understand the young couple before them. Not just as clients for a commission for a portrait, but fellow travelers on a remarkably similar path.

"So we exchanged a few notes," Angelica continued, a faint blush coloring her cheeks. "Nothing profound at first, just pleasantries, observations about Naples, recommendations for local spots worth visiting."

"My Italian was terrible then," Gregory laughed. "I'm sure my early notes were barely comprehensible."

"They were endearing," Angelica corrected him with affectionate firmness. "Like watching someone try to dance to music they couldn't quite hear yet."

Claire found herself holding her breath, captured by the echoes of her own experience with Luca, the tentative first communications, the gradual unveiling of selves through art and words. She felt Luca's hand find hers beneath the table, his touch conveying everything words couldn't express in this moment.

"What we didn't know was," Gregory said, "our families were connected. My parents had been in the US so long that the old Italian relationships had faded into background stories. I didn't realize that Angelica's family and mine had histories enmeshed for generations."

"The first time Gregory mentioned the Valenti name in one of his notes, I didn't make the connection," Angelica admitted. "It wasn't until I visited the Valenti Winery for a delivery that I realized who he was."

"And I had no idea that the woman whose notes were becoming increasingly important to my days was connected to Grandma Rosa, whose bread I'd grown to love almost as much as her granddaughter's words," Gregory added, his voice softening with affection.

Claire felt a delicious anticipation building. Not just for the story itself, but for what it revealed about connections that existed beyond conscious awareness, about finding counterparts through seemingly random circumstances that perhaps weren't random at all.

Gregory's expression turned reflective. "It was about one month after our first caffè sospeso notes exchange. We were still exchanging casual notes and had not met yet."

"Then one day..." He said with his expressions softening, eyes turning inward as if revisiting a sacred memory. The same expressions echoed on Angelica's face. The shift was so pronounced that both Claire and Luca instinctively leaned forward, pencils poised to capture this ephemeral change.

"I was working in the winery alone that afternoon," Gregory continued, "checking the barrels in the old stone cellar."

"And I," Angelica interjected, her fingers instinctively seeking Gregory's as she spoke, "had told Grandma Rosa I would deliver her special sourdough to Valenti family." A soft smile played at the corners of her mouth. "I had never seen a winery from the inside before. This mysterious place where regular fruit creates something sacred."

"When she appeared in the doorway," Gregory continued, his gaze now resting fully on Angelica's face, tracing her features as if memorizing them anew, "backlit by the afternoon sun, basket in hand, I remember thinking she looked like someone from mythology."

"He introduced himself and offered to show me around the winery," Angelica said, her voice softening with the warmth of memory. "Then it struck me like lightning, Valenti, Gregory Valenti, the same Gregory from caffè sospeso!" Her eyes sparkled with the wonder of recognition, hands gesturing as if catching fragments of destiny.

"The moment we finally met felt written in the stars," Gregory continued, his gaze distant with remembrance. "As we wandered through the winery, exchanging glances and stories, the clouds gathered overhead with breathless urgency, as if heaven itself was leaning in to witness our beginning, the first thunderclap shaking the ancient stone walls just as we reached the barrel room."

"The rain came in sheets," Angelica said, her free hand moving through the air like falling water. "Torrential, biblical. The kind of sudden storm that makes you understand why ancient peoples believed in vengeful gods."

"I suggested we wait it out," Gregory said, a quiet laugh escaping him. "Just for a few minutes, I thought. The main house was only a short dash away, but...".

"But then the lights went out," Angelica finished, her eyes meeting his in a look so full of love, Claire felt like an intruder witnessing it. "Complete darkness, except...".

"Except for the lightning," Gregory completed. "Every few moments, the room would illuminate, just enough to see each other's faces, these perfect flashes of the person across from you."

"We could have left," Angelica admitted. "Should have, perhaps. But neither of us moved toward the door. Instead...".

"Instead, I found an old lantern," Gregory said. "Just enough light to cast shadows across the floor. We sat between those ancient barrels, vessels that had held generations of my family's wine."

"The thunder became our soundtrack," Angelica said softly. "For hours, we just... talked. Really talked. Not the polite conversation of acquaintances, but the kind where souls recognize each other."

"I told her things I'd never told anyone," Gregory confessed, his voice carrying a hint of wonder still. "About my fears for the winery's future, my doubts about carrying on my family's legacy. Dreams I hardly admitted to myself."

"And I shared my own secret," Angelica added. "My pottery hidden away in the attic room, my desperate longing to create beauty in a world that seemed to value only practicality." She paused, eyes glistening. "In the darkness, between thunderclaps, it felt safe to be truthful."

"When the storm finally passed," Gregory said, "and morning began filtering through the windows, we realized we'd talked through the entire night."

"By the time the storm ended," Angelica said, her voice hushed as if sharing a precious secret, "I felt like I'd known him all my life. Like my soul had been having a conversation with his long before we ever met."

As they spoke, Claire's and Luca's hands moved across their respective sketchpads, not drawing literal representations but capturing impressions, feelings, the atmospheric quality of the story being shared. Claire found herself sketching barrel shapes that turned into protective enclosures, lightning becoming threads of connection, darkness rendering two silhouettes visible only to each other.

"And you, Gregory?" Luca prompted. "Was it the same moment for you?"

Gregory nodded, his expression serious now. "Almost, but not quite. For me, the absolute certainty came three days later. I'd been thinking about our conversation constantly, replaying it in my mind. Then I was walking through the vineyard at sunrise and found myself standing in a spot where I could see all the way to the village. And I had this overwhelming need to know if Angelica was awake, what she was thinking, if she was remembering our conversation too."

His hand tightened around Angelica's. "It wasn't a desire, exactly. It was... recognition. Like suddenly realizing part of me was walking around in another body, and I needed to be near it to feel complete."

The passionate honesty in his declaration hung in the air like the aftermath of music, resonating long after the notes had faded. Claire felt her eyes grow moist at the simple truth in their words, while beside her, Luca's pencil moved with increased intensity across his sketchpad.

"So, Angelica and Gregory," Claire began, pencil poised above her sketchpad, "help us understand what would you like us to capture in your portrait."

Angelica leaned against Gregory, his arm naturally finding its place around her shoulders. "We want something that is beyond our faces or bodies captured on canvas," Angelica said softly, her voice carrying the weight of something precious. "We want you to somehow capture the invisible thread that binds us, that essence that makes us *us* when we're together." Gregory nodded, his eyes never leaving her face as he added, "The portrait should show the people we were and those we've grown into because of our love, the way we hold each other's aspirations as carefully as our own."

The quiet confidence in their connection was immediately apparent, not the showy affection of new lovers, but the comfortable certainty of two people who had found their home in each other.

"Exactly," Angelica said. "We want something that, years from now, will remind us not just of how we looked, but of how we felt. How our souls recognized each other."

Claire watched the couple closely, her artist's eye cataloging the subtle ways they moved in harmony, how Gregory's hand unconsciously adjusted the cushion behind Angelica when she shifted position, how her fingers found his without looking, how their breathing had synchronized without effort.

Later that afternoon, after the couple had left, Claire and Luca spread their preliminary sketches across a worn wooden table in Grandma Rosa's kitchen. The elderly woman bustled around them, occasionally pausing to peer at their work while muttering approving phrases in Italian.

"I see it now," Claire said, pointing to complementary elements that had emerged in their separate impressions. "The barrel room as a cocoon of sorts. A protected space where transformation happens."

Luca nodded, his finger tracing the lightning bolt motifs in Claire's sketches that eerily mirrored the connection lines in his own. "And here, the way we both depicted them as partially transparent, their true selves visible only to each other."

"We need to speak with their families next," Claire mused, flipping to a fresh page. "Get different perspectives on their connection."

"And visit the places that matter to them," Luca added. "The winery and other spots where key moments in their relationship unfolded."

"But most importantly," Claire said, reaching for his hand across the sketches, "we need to capture what we just witnessed, that palpable current between them. The way they finish each other's sentences, not because they're predictable, but because they're harmonized."

Luca's eyes met hers, dark and intense in the afternoon light. "Like us," he said softly, the words carrying layers of meaning.

Grandma Rosa chose that moment to place a plate of tiny, perfect amaretti cookies between them, their almond fragrance rising like an offering. "You understand because you share the same blessing," she said matter-of-factly. "Two souls that speak the same language even in silence. This is why Angelica and Gregory chose you both for this special portrait."

As they sampled the delicious cookies, Claire felt the weight of responsibility settling across her shoulders. This wasn't merely a commission or an artistic challenge. It was an invitation to translate the most sacred human experience, soul recognition, into visual form. To create something that would hang in Angelica and Gregory's home for decades, reminding them of what mattered most when time and circumstance tested their bond.

"We'll need to work differently for this," she said thoughtfully. "Not separate styles merging, but a true collaboration from the first brushstroke."

"One vision, four hands," Luca agreed, the silver bracelet catching light as he reached for another cookie. "Creating together the way they exist together, as parts of a unified whole."

Outside the window, the ancient fig tree cast dancing shadows across the courtyard stones. Claire watched the patterns change, thinking about the generations of lovers who had sat beneath those branches, sharing stories and secrets and the simple miracle of finding one's counterpart in a world of strangers.

"Tomorrow we talk to Gregory's parents at the winery," she said, turning back to their sketches with renewed purpose. "Then to the church to understand the spiritual dimension of their union."

"And then," Luca added with a smile that still made her heart skip, "we begin to paint what cannot be seen but only felt."

As twilight descended over Grandma Rosa's courtyard, turning the ancient fig tree into a silhouette against the purple sky, Claire and Luca gathered their sketches with the careful adoration of those entrusted with something precious. Not just paper and graphite, but the first notes of a visual love song that would accompany two people through a lifetime together.

The kitchen of Caffè Sereno hummed with orchestrated chaos as Lucia moved between cooling racks and marble countertops. The pastry shells, still warm from the oven, awaited their sweet fillings while copper bowls of whipped cream and mascarpone stood at the ready. The air, perfumed with vanilla, lemon zest, and baking almonds, turning the space into an aromatic symphony that Claire could almost taste.

"No, no, no," Lucia admonished a young assistant who was piping cream with too much force. "Gentle! Like you're writing love letters, not hammering nails."

Claire and Luca had arrived at 6:00 AM as requested, to watch and capture the essence of wedding pastry preparations. The pastries that were specifically requested by Angelica and Gregory. They found themselves captivated by the master at work. Lucia had dressed for the occasion in a crisp white apron embroidered with her name, her silver-streaked hair captured in a neat bun secured with what appeared to be a pencil.

"Come, come," she beckoned to Claire, patting the marble counter beside her. "Let me show you the secret to my sfogliatelle (shell-shaped flaky pastry). It's the pastry that made Signor Rossi propose after just one bite."

Luca grinned at this familiar family legend while settling onto a stool across from them. "Be warned," he stage-whispered to Claire, "once you learn Lucia's secrets, you're officially famiglia (family). No escape."

"As if she would want to escape," Lucia sniffed, though her eyes twinkled as she guided Claire's hands to feel the gossamer-thin layers of pastry dough. "Now, watch. These must be shaped exactly like seashells, each layer distinct, each fold containing pockets that will expand in the oven."

Claire marveled at the technique, understanding now why the pastries she'd enjoyed at the café had such extraordinary texture, crisp yet yielding, substantial yet fragile. Lucia's fingers moved with practiced precision, creating edible art from simple ingredients.

"For Angelica and Gregory's wedding, we create five special pastries," Lucia explained, gesturing to a handwritten menu propped against a flour canister. "Each one tells part of their love story."

"Pastries can tell stories?" Claire asked, fascinated by the concept.

"Of course! Food speaks its own language," Lucia said with the confidence of one stating an obvious truth. "First, sfogliatelle to represent their beginning, many delicate layers coming together to create something beautiful."

As she spoke, Lucia finished shaping the pastry, its resemblance to a seashell uncanny. With practiced efficiency, she filled it with a mixture of ricotta, candied orange, and a hint of cinnamon before placing it on a waiting tray.

Claire and Luca worked to capture the pastries and the story with quick sketches, their pencils dancing across paper with the urgency of artists who recognized the ephemeral beauty unfolding before them. The soft scratch of graphite against parchment became its own kind of love language.

"Next, bomboloni (Italian cream-filled doughnuts). Sweet dough that must rise twice, testing patience but worth the wait. Like how they were separated when Gregory had to return to the US to finish his studies, but their connection only grew stronger over time."

Signor Rossi appeared with fresh cappuccino for everyone, causing a brief pause in the lesson. He placed a gentle kiss on his wife's floured cheek before returning to the café's front where early customers had begun to arrive.

"Third, cannoli siciliani (crispy ricotta-filled tubes), hard exterior protecting the sweet interior, representing how they defend each other's vulnerable hearts," Lucia continued, moving to a new station where perfectly fried pastry tubes awaited filling.

Luca and Claire exchanged knowing glances, a silent conversation rich with shared understanding, before returning to their sketchpads with renewed focus and synchrony like paired instruments in a duet. In the space between their gazes had passed volumes. Recognition of the parallels between the pastry chef's love story and their own unfolding romance, appreciation for how craftsmanship and love intertwined in this sacred Italian kitchen.

"Fourth, piccoli tiramisù (mini layered coffee desserts) in individual cups with bitter coffee and sweet mascarpone finding perfect balance, just as their different temperaments complement each other and will help them to navigate through any tough times in the future."

Claire watched, entranced, as Lucia filled tiny glass cups with lady fingers, drizzled it with fragrant espresso, piped rich sweet mascarpone filling over it, and then dusted with the lightest touch of cocoa powder. Each movement was economical yet graceful, the culmination of decades perfecting her craft.

"And the final pastry?" Luca prompted, stealing a bit of cream from a bowl when Lucia turned away.

His sleight of hand didn't escape notice. Lucia swatted his fingers with a kitchen towel, the gesture so loving it made Claire's heart swell with affection for her who had become a surrogate mother during her time in Naples.

"La piece de résistance," Lucia announced with deliberate French pronunciation. "The most remarkable thing," Luca translated for Claire. "millefoglie della promessa (thousand-layer promise pastry)," Lucia continued. "We will assemble it at the reception. One thousand layers of pastry representing one thousand promises they will make to each other, one thousand challenges they will overcome together, one thousand joys they will share."

She wiped her hands on her apron and turned to face them fully, her expression suddenly serious. "This is why I insisted on providing the pastries myself. At an Italian wedding, food is not merely sustenance. It is part of the ceremony, carrying blessings and wishes for the couple's future."

The kitchen fell silent for a moment, even the assistants pausing in their tasks as Lucia's words settled over them. Then she clapped her hands, breaking the spell. "Now, enough philosophy! Claire, those hands were made for creative work. Come knead this dough while I prepare the orange blossom syrup."

For the next three hours, Claire was initiated into the ancient alchemy of Italian pastry-making. Her fingers grew confident with the feel of different doughs, learning when to be gentle and when to be firm. Luca moved between helping his cousin Marco with precision piping and assisting Signor Rossi in the café, occasionally catching Claire's eye across the kitchen with looks of such tender pride that her cheeks warmed.

By mid-morning, the preparation area was transformed into a staging ground for edible artistry. Trays of pastries stood in various stages of completion, from the airy ladyfingers ready for the tiramisu to the cooling shells of cannoli awaiting their sweet ricotta filling on the wedding day.

"We're all done for today," Lucia announced as she supervised the careful storage of everything they'd prepared. "The final assembly happens at the venue, to ensure maximum freshness. But today..." She beamed at Claire with motherly pride. "Today you learned the foundation, the structure that holds everything together."

Claire looked down at her flour-dusted hands, realizing they now carried new knowledge. Not just techniques, but understanding of how food connected families, how traditions passed through generations, how love found expression through all forms of creation.

"Thank you," she said simply, words inadequate for the gift she'd received.

Lucia cupped Claire's flour-streaked cheek with a warm palm. "Family teaches family," she said warmly. "This is how we continue."

As they cleaned up, Claire noticed Luca watching her from across the kitchen, his expression unreadable yet somehow containing multitudes. When their tasks were complete and they stepped outside into the late morning sunshine, he took her hand, his thumb brushing across her knuckles.

"What are you thinking?" she asked, noting the pensive quality in his dark eyes.

"I'm thinking about family," he said quietly as they began walking toward their next appointment at the winery. "How it can be created through blood or through choice. How it shapes us, holds us accountable, celebrates with us, and becomes our greatest strength when we need it."

He paused, looking back at the café where Lucia was now visible through the window, arranging fresh flowers on the tables with the same care she'd given to her pastries. "I'm thinking about how quickly you've become part of mine, how naturally you fit into these traditions."

Something in his tone made Claire's heart accelerate. There was a question beneath his observation, one not yet formed into words but hovering in the air between them.

Before she could respond, his expression lightened and he tugged her forward. "Come. Gregory's parents are waiting for us at the winery, and we have souls to capture on canvas."

As the Fiat made its way through Naples' winding streets, Claire's fingers entwined with Luca's, flour still embedded in her nail beds from the morning's lessons. The simple warmth of his hand against hers stirred something profound in her chest. A bittersweet ache that caught her by surprise. Lucia's maternal tenderness had awakened memories that flooded through her with unexpected force, of her mother and grandmother in that sun-drenched Ohio kitchen, three generations of women standing shoulder to shoulder at the worn maple counter, her small hands guided by weathered ones as they worked butter into flour for apple pie crust.

"Just a moment," she murmured to Luca, who nodded with understanding as her fingers began typing a message home.

Mom, standing in Naples sunshine with flour on my hands from learning to make traditional Italian pastries. The woman teaching me reminded me so much of you and Grandma, I could almost hear your voices guiding my hands through the dough. Remember those Sunday afternoons making apple pies? How Grandma insisted the apples had to be sliced paper-thin, and you always snuck in extra cinnamon when she wasn't looking? Today I realized I've never properly thanked you both for showing me that creating something with your hands is a form of love. Missing you terribly even as I find my heart expanding in this place so far from home. Love, Claire.

She pressed send and tucked the phone away, glancing over at Luca. Their eyes met briefly, his dark gaze taking in her glistening eyes and understanding immediately the complex tangle of homesickness and discovery, of past and present colliding in her heart. A soft smile passed between them as the car wound upward, her heart lighter for having connected the family who had shaped her with the new world unfolding before her.

The winding road to Gregory's family winery climbed steadily upward, each curve revealing new perspectives of the landscape below. Claire pressed her face to the window of the Fiat, drinking in the panorama of Naples Bay spread beneath them like an azure blanket, while ahead, terraced vineyards rose in geometric precision against the hillside.

"It's incredible," she breathed, watching how the vines caught afternoon light, conjuring living art from agriculture. "How long has his family owned this land?"

"Six generations," Luca replied, navigating a particularly sharp turn with practiced ease. "The Valenti family came from further north originally, Tuscany, I think, but found this microclimate perfect for their specific grapes. The winery has remained relatively small compared to some commercial operations, but what they produce is... exceptional."

The reverent note in his voice made Claire smile. "You sound like a wine expert."

"Merely an enthusiastic admirer," he said with a quick grin. "Though I did work a harvest here during university, picking grapes from dawn till dusk, my hands stained purple for weeks afterward. It was exhausting, beautiful work." Claire admired the expressions on Luca's face.

The road narrowed as they approached massive wrought-iron gates, scrollwork forming the letter "V" at their center. As if by magic, they swung open upon their approach, revealing a gravel drive that wound between ancient cypress trees standing like sentinels.

"Gregory must have told them to expect us," Luca commented as they followed the drive to its conclusion before a villa that seemed to grow organically from the hillside itself.

The building was a masterpiece of traditional architecture updated with modern sensibility. Warm stone walls softened by flowering vines, large windows designed to capture both light and spectacular views, a broad terrace overlooking the vineyards that cascaded down the hillside like a green waterfall.

They had barely stepped from the car when a tall, distinguished man came out from the villa's massive wooden doors. Ernesto Valenti moved with the confident grace of someone accustomed to commanding attention, his silver hair contrasting with deeply tanned skin that spoke of days spent in the sun among his vines. Despite being well into his sixties, he carried himself with vigor that made him appear much younger.

"Ah! Our artists arrive!" he called, descending broad stone steps to greet them. "Luca Castellano, it has been too long since you've visited us. And this must be the talented Claire Bennett we've heard so much about."

His English carried an Italian rhythm that Claire found instantly charming. As they exchanged greetings, a woman appeared behind him, Corina Valenti, Gregory's mother, her elegant appearance softened by warm eyes that evaluated Claire with undisguised curiosity.

"Come, come," Ernesto urged, gesturing toward the villa. "We'll talk on the terrace. Corina has prepared refreshments."

As they followed the couple, Claire found herself cataloging details with her artist's eye. How Ernesto's hand reflexively reached back to ensure his wife was beside him on the steps, how Corina's fingers briefly touched a flowering vine as they passed.

The terrace proved even more spectacular up close. Massive terra cotta pots overflowed with herbs and flowers, their fragrance mingling with the distinctive scent of sun-warmed stone. A pergola covered in mature wisteria provided dappled shade over a large marble table set with wine, cheeses, bread, and fruits. A casual feast rendered sublime by its setting.

"Our Gregory tells us you're creating something unique for the wedding," Corina said as they settled around the table. Though more reserved than her husband, her interest appeared genuine. "Not a traditional portrait?"

"Not traditional, no," Claire confirmed, accepting a glass of pale wine that Ernesto insisted was "perfect for afternoon contemplation." She felt Luca's reassuring presence beside her, his quiet confidence bolstering her own. "We're attempting to capture something more essential about their connection, the spiritual and emotional bond that defines them."

"Ah, the soul portrait," Ernesto nodded, his expression thoughtful as he swirled wine in his glass. "Gregory explained the concept, though I admit I found it somewhat... abstract."

"It's quite concrete, actually," Luca interjected smoothly. "Every meaningful relationship has a unique energy, a distinctive pattern of connection. As artists, our challenge is to make that invisible current visible through color, composition, and symbolic elements."

Corina leaned forward slightly, her interest visibly piqued. "And how do you accomplish this?"

"That's partly why we're here," Claire explained. "To understand Gregory and Angelica through different perspectives, especially from those who have watched their relationship develop. The family often sees certain connections that even the couple themselves might miss."

A subtle exchange passed between Ernesto and Corina. A glance containing volumes of unspoken communication. Claire recognized it immediately as the same silent language she and Luca were developing slowly but surely, the wordless understanding that forms between two people whose thoughts and feelings align like constellations in a shared night sky.

"What would you like to know?" Ernesto asked, breaking a piece of bread from the rustic loaf before them.

"Tell us about the first time Gregory brought Angelica here," Luca suggested. "What did you observe about them together?"

The question triggered a transformation in Corina's expression. Reserve melting into reminiscence, her eyes taking on a distant quality. "It was October, harvest time. Gregory had mentioned her before, of course, but in that casual way young men speak of women when trying to seem unbothered." A small smile played across her lips. "We knew she was different because he cleaned his room before bringing her to Sunday dinner."

Ernesto chuckled at the memory. "He also changed his shirt three times. I caught him in the upstairs bathroom with every bottle of cologne he's received since his fifteenth birthday."

Claire and Luca exchanged quick glances, both recognizing the significance of these small details. The universal behaviors of someone desperately wanting to impress, to be seen favorably through beloved eyes.

"When they arrived," Corina continued, "the first thing I noticed was how she looked at him when he wasn't watching. Not with infatuation, but with... recognition. As if she was continually discovering new facets of him and finding delight in each one."

"And he kept finding reasons to tell stories that would make her laugh," Ernesto added. "Our Gregory, who has always been somewhat serious, suddenly became animated, almost playful."

As they spoke, Claire's hand moved across her sketchpad, capturing not literal representations but impressions. Flowing lines suggesting the vineyard's terraced slopes, interwoven forms that spoke of connection across generations, the circular marks of wine glasses leaving impressions on tablecloths just as relationships left marks on lives.

"There was a moment," Corina said, her voice softening, "when we were walking through the vines after dinner. Angelica asked about the winemaking process, so Ernesto was explaining how our approach differs from more commercial operations. I was walking behind with Gregory, and I saw him watching her, the intensity in his expression..."

She paused, seemingly searching for the right words.

"It was the look of a man seeing his future unfold before him," Ernesto finished for his wife. "The exact expression I recognize from our own early days together."

Luca's pencil hovered over the page, his eyes reflecting genuine curiosity. "What did you notice about Gregory after he met Angelica? Was there a moment when you realized this relationship was special?"

The Valentis exchanged a glance. A silent conversation cultivated through decades of successful marriage. Claire watched as something profound passed between them, a shared recognition of a memory that had clearly left its mark.

"It was during that first dinner here," Corina began, her voice softening with remembrance. "Gregory has always been methodical, thoughtful, measured in his reactions. But that evening, watching him with Angelica..." She paused, searching for the right words. "It was as if someone had finally unlocked a door inside him that we never even knew existed."

Ernesto nodded, leaning forward in his chair. "The next morning, he came to find me among the vines. I was checking the early growth, and suddenly he was beside me, helping as he'd done since childhood. But something was different." He gestured expansively with his hands, an Italian emphasis to his words. "Usually, Gregory speaks of the vines,

254

the business, the future of our wine. That morning, he spoke only of Angelica."

"What did he say?" Claire asked softly, captivated by the tenderness in their telling.

"He said, 'Papa, I've been living in black and white, and now everything is in color,'" Ernesto recalled, his voice rough with emotion. "He told me that when Angelica spoke about her dreams, building a small ceramic studio, her hopes to create beautiful things that would last, he could see their future unfolding together like the seasons across our vineyard."

Corina reached for her husband's hand. "We've watched Gregory build his life with such careful precision," she said. "Right from his education at Stanford, to every decision he made was weighed and measured. But that morning, there was something almost... luminous about him. As if certainty had replaced all his usual careful deliberation."

"I asked him if he wasn't moving too quickly," Ernesto admitted. "It was my fatherly duty to ask. And do you know what he said?" His eyes glistened in the afternoon light. "He said, 'Some things you don't need time to know, Papa. Some things you recognize instantly.' I knew then that this was very special."

"I've never forgotten the look in his eyes," Corina added. "It wasn't attraction or passion. It was peace. Like a man who had been searching his whole life and could finally rest because he'd found what he was looking for."

Claire felt the resonance of those words settling into her artist's heart, already seeing how this essential truth might translate to canvas, the visual representation of a soul finding its counterpart, the moment when searching ends and recognition begins.

As the conversation continued, a coherent picture began to form in Claire's mind; the unique connection between Gregory and Angelica. Their relationship had evolved from immediate recognition to mutual understanding and respect, ultimately harmonizing with family history and tradition.

"There's something else you should see," Ernesto said when they had exhausted their initial questions. He rose from the table with the natural authority of a man accustomed to guiding others. "Something that might help with your... soul portrait."

He led them from the terrace, through the villa's cool interior with its harmonious blend of antique furnishings and contemporary art, and into what appeared to be his private study. The room embodied masculine elegance; leather-bound books lining built-in shelves, a massive desk overlooking the vineyard, family photographs chronicling generations of Valenti history.

From a cabinet behind his desk, Ernesto withdrew a large portfolio bound in aged leather. With ceremonial care, he placed it on the desk's surface and opened its cover to reveal meticulously preserved botanical illustrations.

"These were created by Gregory's great-great-grandmother, Eleonora Valenti," he explained, gently turning pages to display exquisite renderings of grape vines, root systems, and fruit in various stages of development. "She was not formally trained as an artist, but she had exceptional observational skills and patience. These drawings helped her husband revolutionize their cultivation techniques."

The illustrations were breathtaking in their precision and detail. Scientific in purpose yet imbued with undeniable artistry. Claire leaned closer, noting how even the technical renderings conveyed a deep reverence for the subject matter.

"Gregory spent hours with these as a child," Corina said softly. "Fascinated by the intersection of art and agriculture, beauty and practicality. It shaped his understanding of legacy, of how one generation's work nourishes the next."

"And now we understand where his appreciation for artists comes from," Luca observed, his finger hovering just above one particularly beautiful rendering of a grape cluster.

"Precisely," Ernesto nodded. "When he told us he wanted artists, not photographers, to create a portrait, we knew immediately it was the influence of Eleonora's work. His connection to our family's artistic heritage."

"And a wonderful thing we observed recently," Corina said thoughtfully, "it was when he showed this portfolio to Angelica, she fell in love with it and spent hours just studying everything closely." That's when we knew that they were made for each other.

As they carefully examined more pages, Claire felt pieces clicking into place in her conceptual understanding of the commission. This wasn't merely about capturing two individuals in love. It was about documenting their place within a continuum that stretched backward through family history and forward into an unwritten future.

"There's one more thing we'd like you to see before you go," Corina said as they returned the portfolio to its protective cabinet. "The old barrel room where Gregory and Angelica sheltered during that fortuitous thunderstorm. It's where they'll hold their rehearsal dinner, and understanding that space might help with your portrait."

The barrel room occupied the winery's lowest level, thick stone walls maintaining perfect temperature and humidity for wine maturation regardless of external conditions. Massive oak barrels lined the walls, their wood darkened with age, brass fixtures glowing warmly in the subdued lighting. The space held a cathedral-like quality; soaring ceilings, perfect acoustics that transformed even whispers into something mystical.

"This is where wine becomes more than fermented grape juice," Ernesto explained, his voice taking on reverential tones that echoed softly against the stone walls. "Where it develops complexity, nuance, character."

"Where time becomes an invisible ingredient," Corina added. "Just as in a marriage."

Claire moved slowly through the space, imagining Gregory and Angelica here during that storm, sitting between these ancient barrels, sharing confidences as thunder rolled overhead and lightning briefly illuminated the room through small, high windows. She could almost feel the intimate atmosphere that would encourage soul-baring conversation, the sense of being cocooned within history while creating something entirely new.

"The evening before the wedding," Corina said, "they want to have a small gathering here, just family and the wedding party. Tradition suggests it brings good fortune when a couple shares bread and wine in the place where they first recognized their feelings for each other."

"We would love for you to attend," Ernesto extended the invitation.

Outside, afternoon had softened toward evening, the vineyard bathed in the honey-amber light photographers call "the golden hour." As they prepared to depart, Ernesto surprised them with a final offering; a bottle of the winery's premier vintage, its label bearing the Valenti family crest. Claire and Luca expressed their heartfelt gratitude for the Valentis' generous hospitality and invaluable insights before taking their leave, the weight of newfound knowledge as precious as the wine they carried.

As they drove back down the winding road toward Naples, the bottle of Valenti wine secured carefully in the back seat, Claire's mind buzzed with creative energy. The visit had provided not just insights for the wedding portrait, but opened doors to new artistic revelation Naples had nurtured.

"What are you thinking?" Luca asked, casting a quick glance at her pensive expression.

"I'm thinking about roots," she said slowly, watching how the vines blurred into continuous lines of green as they passed. "How Gregory and Angelica are both deeply connected to family traditions, yet creating something unique in their union. How they honor the past while growing toward the future."

Luca nodded, understanding immediately. "Like the vines themselves, rooted in ancient soil but producing new fruit each season."

"Exactly. And I'm thinking this needs to be central to our portrait concept; this tension between heritage and new creation, between being part of something larger than themselves while also being something entirely unique."

The road curved sharply, momentarily revealing a breathtaking view of Naples Bay far below, the late afternoon sun gilding water into sheets of hammered copper. Claire found herself contemplating how her own life had similar tensions; her American roots and Italian awakening, her commercial design background and fine art rediscovery, her independent spirit and deepening connection to Luca.

"Tomorrow we visit the church," Luca reminded her as they descended toward the city. "To understand the spiritual dimension of their commitment."

Claire nodded, already envisioning how the various elements of their research would merge into a cohesive concept. As the vistas kept emerging through the twists and turns the car was taking, she found herself filled with quiet certainty that this commission was more than a creative endeavor. It was an opportunity to explore visually the same questions of connection and commitment that resonated in her mind.

The Church of San Lorenzo nestled into the hillside, not too far from the Valenti Winery, its weathered stone façade blending with the landscape while its bell tower reached determinedly skyward. Built by Angelica's great-great-grandfather in 1873, the modest structure had witnessed generations of family celebrations, sorrows, and sacred transitions.

Morning light slanted through ancient cypress trees as Claire and Luca approached, casting alternating patterns of brightness and shadow across the worn stone path. A profound silence enveloped the churchyard. Not absence of sound, but a quality of stillness that seemed to exist outside of time.

"It feels different here," Claire admitted, unconsciously drawing closer to Luca as they neared the heavy wooden doors. "Almost as if..."

"As if the air itself holds memory," he finished for her, his voice equally hushed. "Many old churches in Italy have this quality, stones that have absorbed centuries of prayers and devotion."

A figure appeared in the doorway. Father Benedetto, whom they had arranged to meet. The elderly priest's lined face creased into a welcoming smile as he gestured them forward. Despite his advanced age, he moved with surprising vitality, his traditional black cassock sweeping the stone steps as he descended to greet them.

"Benvenuti, benvenuti (Welcome, welcome)," he said warmly, switching to English with only a slight accent. "Angelica told me to expect you. Come inside, where we can speak about this most unusual portrait."

The church's interior embraced them with cool dimness punctuated by pools of jewel-toned light from stained glass windows. Unlike the grand cathedrals of Rome or Florence, this church had a cozy scale that invited contemplation rather than awe. Simple wooden pews faced an altar carved from local stone, while niches along the side walls held statues of saints worn smooth by generations of devoted touches.

"Angelica was baptized here," Father Benedetto explained as he led them toward the altar. "As was her mother, and her grandmother before her. When she was a little girl, she would come after school to sit in the last pew and do her homework. She said the quiet helped her think."

Claire observed how the priest spoke of Angelica with familial affection rather than mere pastoral duty. "You've known her all her life, then?"

"Since before she drew her first breath," he confirmed with a gentle smile. "I blessed her mother's womb when pregnancy was confirmed, and have watched Angelica grow from an inquisitive child to the remarkable woman she has become."

He gestured for them to sit in the front pew while he settled onto a simple wooden chair beside the altar. "An unconventional couple in many ways," Father Benedetto continued, his eyes crinkling at the corners with fond remembrance. "Angelica has always questioned tradition, seeking the meaning beneath ritual rather than accepting practice for its own sake. When she first brought Gregory here, not for Mass, but on a quiet Tuesday afternoon, I knew something profound had shifted in her heart."

Claire opened her sketchbook, pencil poised. "What did you observe about them together?"

The priest's gaze turned inward, accessing memories with the careful precision of one accustomed to preserving sacred moments. "They moved through this space differently than most young couples. Not speaking much, but communicating constantly; a glance here, a touch there. Gregory would pause at something that caught his interest, and without words, Angelica would appear at his side as if summoned by silent call."

Luca nodded, his own pencil making swift notations. "A physical attunement."

"Precisely." Father Benedetto smiled approvingly. "But what struck me most powerfully was how they studied the older couples who came for evening prayer. I observed them watching Maurizio and Teresa Lombardi, married sixty-two years and still holding hands during the rosary. The young ones were witnessing not just love's beginning, but its endurance."

Claire found herself captivated by the priest's observations, noting how he discussed the spiritual dimension of relationship with the same practical clarity one might use to describe vineyard cultivation or pastry preparation. There was no artificial separation between sacred and ordinary in his perspective; just the continuous flow of love expressing itself through daily actions and ritual observances.

"When they asked me to perform their marriage ceremony," he continued, "Gregory had an unusual request. He wanted to know if they could help restore some of the church's older features as their gift. Not merely writing a check, but participating in the actual work. They spent weekends here for months, Gregory repairing stonework he had learned from maintaining the winery's structures, Angelica carefully cleaning centuries of candle soot from the ceiling frescoes."

The priest gestured upward, drawing their attention to beautifully painted vines that wound across the coved ceiling, connecting biblical scenes with flowing tendrils of green and gold. Though faded with age, the artistry remained evident; a visual metaphor for divine connection expressed through natural imagery.

"The frescoes were barely visible before their efforts," Father Benedetto explained. "Angelica worked from old photographs and parish records to ensure authentic restoration. Gregory built the scaffolding himself to reach the highest points."

"They were literally uncovering history together," Claire murmured, seeing deeper significance in the couple's choice of gift. "Making visible what time had obscured."

"Yes, and in doing so, discovering their complementary strengths. Gregory's practical solutions supporting Angelica's artistic vision, a partnership revealed through shared purpose." The priest's eyes twinkled with appreciation for their quick understanding.

Luca rose from the pew and moved toward the altar quietly. "May I?" he asked, gesturing toward the sacred space.

At Father Benedetto's nod of permission, he stepped closer to examine subtle details; how morning sunbeams cascaded across carved stone, the arrangement of elements creating natural focal points, the way the architecture itself guided attention upward from earthly concerns toward spiritual contemplation.

"The ceremony will begin at four o'clock," the priest explained, following Luca's observant gaze. "When the light enters through those western windows, illuminating the altar with particular radiance. A time representing transition; not yet evening, no longer full day. The threshold hour."

Claire joined them at the altar, noting how the space felt simultaneously personal and expansive. "Angelica mentioned they've incorporated some non-traditional elements into the ceremony?"

Father Benedetto's expression warmed with approval. "Indeed. Rather than being 'given away' by her father, Angelica will walk the center aisle accompanied by both parents. Gregory will do the same from the opposite side, the two processions meeting at the altar to symbolize equal commitment and the merger of families rather than transfer of the bride from one man to another."

He moved toward a small side chapel where a beautifully carved wooden table held artifacts clearly intended for the ceremony. A woven cord of three strands in white, gold, and deep burgundy; two simple clay cups; a bottle of wine from Valenti Winery; a piece of linen to wrap a loaf of bread; and an ancient-looking book bound in worn leather lay arranged with ceremonial precision.

"They've also revived some older traditions often overlooked in modern weddings," he continued, touching each item gently with respect. "The handfasting cord woven by Grandma Rosa, symbolizing their lives entwined with divine presence. The sharing of bread and wine not only as communion with God but as first nourishment offered to each other as married partners. And readings from this family Bible that has recorded Angelica's ancestors' marriages since the church was built."

As they examined these ceremonial objects, Claire felt emotion swelling beneath her breastbone; not just appreciation for the thoughtfulness evident in each choice, but recognition of how these tangible symbols created bridges between past and future, spiritual and physical, traditional and innovative. The portrait they would create needed to capture this same integration, this weaving together of seemingly separate dimensions into unified wholeness.

Father Benedetto observed their reactions with quiet understanding. "You see why photography alone cannot capture what they are creating together. The camera might freeze for a moment, but it cannot show the invisible currents connecting these symbols to their meaning, these vows to their fulfillment."

"That's exactly our challenge," Luca acknowledged, his voice carrying respectful admiration for the priest's insight. "To make visible what exists between and beyond physical appearance."

The priest's weathered hand came to rest on Luca's shoulder with surprising warmth. "You understand because you live within such a connection yourselves. This resonance between souls; it recognizes itself across different relationships."

The simple observation sent a flush of warmth through Claire's chest. Though they had come to study Angelica and Gregory's spiritual bond, she hadn't expected their own connection to be so transparently visible to others, especially someone with Father Benedetto's depth of experience witnessing human relationships.

"Come," the priest said, gesturing toward a small door beside the altar. "There is one more place that may help your understanding."

He led them through the door and up a narrow spiral staircase that wound within the church's stone walls. The passageway was barely wide enough for single-file progression, its steps worn into shallow depressions by countless feet over centuries. After climbing what felt like several stories, they emerged onto the bell tower's observation platform; a simple stone balcony encircling the massive bronze bell that had marked time for the surrounding community since the church's consecration.

The view stole Claire's breath. From this elevation, they could see not only the church grounds with their ancient cypress sentinels but the sweeping panorama beyond. Rolling hills studded with olive groves, the distant sparkle of Naples Bay, and to the north, the terraced vineyards of the Valenti estate rising in emerald symmetric precision.

"This is where they will come immediately after the ceremony," Father Benedetto explained, his cassock rippling in the morning breeze. "Just the two of them, for a private moment before joining their celebration. From here, they can see both their histories and their future, her family's church grounds, his family's vineyards, the village with Grandma Rosa's trattoria, his parents' villa, the community that shaped them and the home they will build together."

Claire moved to the stone balustrade, letting her hand rest on sun-warmed rock that had witnessed generations of similar moments, newly-weds pausing at the threshold between ceremony and celebration, between sacred promise and lived reality. Below, preparations for the wedding were already visible; workers building a tent in the courtyard, where they would arrange chairs for the overflow of guests who wouldn't fit inside the small church, florists consulting about archway decorations, a musician testing acoustics near the entrance.

"The bell will ring exactly once when they exchange rings," the priest continued, touching the massive bronze instrument with familiar affection. "And then seventeen times after they are pronounced married, representing the average ages at which their grandparents met their respective spouses, an acknowledgment of the family legacy."

Luca joined Claire at the balustrade, as he sketched quick impressions of the view. Standing together in this elevated sanctuary, surrounded by sweeping vistas and centuries of worn stone, Claire felt something crystallizing in her understanding; not just of the portrait they would create, but of the nature of commitment itself.

Marriage wasn't simply a ceremony or a change of legal status, but a vantage point that transformed one's view of the world. From this tower, Gregory and Angelica would see familiar landscapes from a new perspective, unremarkable features revealed in profound relationships to each other, the separate elements of their lives unified into coherent wholeness.

"I think I understand now," she said softly, more to herself than her companions. "What we're trying to capture."

Father Benedetto nodded as if she had spoken her realization aloud. "The moment of integration," he said simply. "When two perspectives become one vision without losing their individual clarity. When common ground becomes holy ground."

They remained in the bell tower for some time, watching the sun move across the landscape, each lost in private contemplation. Claire found her mind filling not with specific images but with emotional impressions; the weight of stone worn smooth by faithful touch, the patient presence of ancient trees witnessing human dramas across centuries, the circular nature of traditions renewed through sincere participation rather than empty observance.

When they finally descended the tower's spiral staircase, emerging into the church's cool interior, Claire felt a profound sense of privilege; not only had they been granted access to sacred spaces, but to the deeper understanding of how spiritual commitment provided the foundation for human love. Their portrait would need to honor this dimension, to suggest the eternal nature of genuine connection even while celebrating its particular expression through Gregory and Angelica's unique bond.

"Before you leave," Father Benedetto said as they approached the main entrance, "I have something for you." From a pocket in his cassock, he withdrew a small cloth pouch, its fabric worn soft with age. "When Angelica was confirmed, I gave her a simple gift, olive wood rosary beads carved from a tree on these grounds. She returned them to me recently with a request."

He opened the pouch, revealing a handful of small, smooth beads gleaming with the patina that comes from years of handling. "She asked that these be incorporated somehow into your portrait, not visibly perhaps, but present within the work itself. A physical connection to her spiritual foundation."

Claire accepted the beads with appropriate reverence, understanding immediately the profound trust this represented. Not merely artistic license but spiritual stewardship; responsibility for incorporating sacred artifacts into their creative expression.

"We'll honor their meaning," Luca said, his voice carrying the weight of genuine commitment.

As they stepped back into sunlight, leaving the church's cool embrace, Claire felt certainty spreading through her like warming wine; they now had all the elements needed for their portrait concept. The vineyard's lesson of roots and renewal, Lucia's demonstration of how the pastries the couple selected can tie traditions to their story, and now the church's testimony to how spiritual foundation elevated human connection.

Walking down the cypress-lined path toward their waiting car, Claire slipped her hand into Luca's, their fingers lacing together naturally. The silver bracelet at his wrist pressed coolly against her skin, a tangible reminder of their own promises exchanged. Above them, the ancient bell waited in patient silence for the wedding day when it would announce new beginnings with its centuries-old voice; continuity and change, tradition and innovation, eternal and immediate all expressing themselves through a single, resonant note.

"We should start painting tomorrow," she said as they reached the car. "I think we're ready."

Luca's dark eyes met hers with perfect understanding. In their shared gaze lived recognition of how this commission had become more than a professional undertaking; it had become an exploration of questions that echoed in their own hearts, an invitation to consider what lasting commitment might mean beyond their own passionate connection.

As they drove back, the Church of San Lorenzo diminishing in the rearview mirror but growing larger in their creative consciousness, Claire held the small pouch of rosary beads in her lap. These humble objects that had absorbed the prayers, hopes, and spiritual seeking of a young woman now preparing to merge her life with another's would find new expression through art; becoming part of a visual testament to love's capacity to transform ordinary existence into sacred journey.

Morning sun entered Luca's studio, painting fluid patterns across the floor that seemed to move with their own intelligence, choreographing a silent ballet of illumination and shadow. Claire sat cross-legged on the worn wooden floor, surrounded by sketches and notes from their meetings over the past two days. Her hair was twisted into a messy knot atop her head, escaping tendrils framing her face as she leaned forward to arrange the drawings into a cohesive story.

"It's all wonderful," she sighed, looking up as Luca who entered with two steaming cups of cappuccino. "But something's missing. The perfect medium to contain all this... meaning."

Luca settled beside her, his knee brushing hers as he examined their collected inspirations. The silver bracelet at his wrist caught morning light, becoming momentarily incandescent against his olive skin. "You're right. Canvas feels too... traditional. Too inadequate for what we're trying to express."

Claire accepted the cappuccino, letting its warmth seep into her palms as she contemplated the challenge before them. Five days remained until the wedding. Limited time to create something that captures not just appearances but essences; the invisible thread connecting two beings who had recognized each other across circumstance and chance.

"I keep thinking about that barrel room," she said pensively, her eyes distant with memory. "How they sat surrounded by aging wine, time itself becoming an ingredient in their connection. How the wood had absorbed decades of transmutation..."

She paused, a sudden clarity washing over her features. Luca noticed the shift immediately, his own expression quickening with recognition of her approaching revelation.

"The wine barrels," she exclaimed, setting down her cup with ceremonial precision. "Not canvas at all, but wood that has witnessed transformation. Wood that has held wine becoming more complex, more nuanced through patience and time."

Luca's eyes widened as he grasped her concept. "The wooden strips from wine barrels? What are they called...? Oh I know it..." Claire could practically hear the wheels in his head turning.

"The..." Claire's brow furrowed slightly, her fingers tracing invisible curves in the air as she searched for the word that eluded her. "Those curved wooden pieces that form the sides of the barrels."

As she was about to reach for her phone to search for the word... "Staves!" Luca announced, remembering what he had learned when he had worked at the Valenti Winery for a summer a long time back. "The staves are those wooden strips that form the sides of a wine barrel. They're cut at an angle, arranged in a circle, and held together by metal hoops." His eyes sparked with growing excitement as he understood the full implications of Claire's vision. "Weathered, stained by years of contact with the very essence of the Valenti heritage?"

"Yes!" Claire was fully animated now, rising to her feet with newfound energy. "Not flat panels but curved pieces arranged to create depth, to suggest the dimensionality of real connection. The burgundy stains inside the barrels become part of the artwork itself...".

"... representing the deeper currents beneath surface appearances," Luca finished, standing to join her in this moment of shared inspiration. "The foundation upon which we make their relationship, their bond visible."

"Claire, you are a genius!" The words tumbled from his lips like an offering, his eyes alight with an admiration that painted her cheeks with the faintest blush.

They stood facing each other, electricity arcing between them as the concept unfurled in their shared creative consciousness. This was how they worked best; each spark from one igniting greater flame in the other, ideas flowing between them like wine between vessels, becoming richer in the exchange.

"We'd need aged barrels," Luca mused, already calculating practical considerations. "Ones that have held wine long enough to be imbued with its essence, but have outlived their usefulness in the winery."

Claire nodded. "And instead of using a single piece or reconstructing a whole barrel, we arrange the staves on the wall in a pattern that tells their story, like a visual poem written in wood and wine memories and paint."

"A three-dimensional portrait!" Luca exclaimed, his artist's mind already visualizing the execution. "Parts raised, parts recessed, creating actual shadows rather than merely suggesting them with pigment."

Claire's hand found his, their fingers intertwining with the same natural harmony as their artistry. "We should talk to Valentis right away. If anyone would have access to retired wine barrels, it would be them."

"We should also reach out to Angelica's parents," Luca suggested. "They might have physical mementos, childhood treasures, family heirlooms, things that have carried emotional weight in Angelica's life. Those could be woven into our portrait too." Claire's eyes brightened at his words, seeing immediately how such intimate artifacts could deepen their creation.

Within the hour, they were back in Luca's Fiat, winding up the now-familiar road toward the Valenti Winery. The day had bloomed into spectacular clarity, the Mediterranean sky an uninterrupted expanse of blue that seemed to make every color beneath it more vibrant, more essential.

Ernesto greeted them with characteristic warmth, though surprise registered in his expression at their unannounced arrival. "Twice in two days? What brings our artists back so soon?"

"We need your wood," Claire blurted in the moment of excitement, then flushed as Ernesto's eyebrows rose at her directness. "I mean, we have an idea for the portrait, but we need materials that only you might have."

Claire's eyes met Luca's in a silent exchange, her gaze imploring him to articulate the concept they had come up with. Luca's voice flowed like aged wine as he wove their concept into words, explaining how barrel staves would become the foundation for the soul portrait. With each sentence, Ernesto's expression changed, surprise melting into something deeper, more profound, as though witnessing the birth of an idea that had always been meant to exist.

"Using our own barrels to tell their story," Ernesto said when Luca's words finally settled in the air between them. His eyes held a newfound admiration, as if seeing his family's legacy through a prism he'd never before considered.

"It was all Claire's idea," Luca said, smiling softly with pride as his gaze found hers.

Ernesto's weathered hands came together in quiet appreciation. "There's poetry in that choice. Come," he beckoned with a gentle wave, his invitation carrying the weight of something precious about to be shared. "Let me show you something."

He led them away from the main villa, down a path that curved behind the winery's production buildings. After several minutes of walking, they arrived at a large structure that appeared older than the surrounding buildings; its stone walls weathered by untold seasons, its wooden doors bearing the dignified patina that comes only from decades of sun and rain and purpose.

"The original storage facility," Ernesto explained, withdrawing an ancient iron key from his pocket. "Built by my great-grandfather when the winery was young. Now we use it mainly for storage and..."

He pushed open the massive door, which moved with surprising ease on well-maintained hinges. The scent there was beyond description; a complex layering of aged wood, lingering wine essence, earth, and time itself. Claire inhaled deeply, feeling the aroma settle into her memory like a photograph being fixed in developing solution.

"...and for keeping pieces of our history," Ernesto finished, gesturing for them to enter.

The interior was dimly lit by narrow windows set high in the stone walls, dust motes dancing in the slanting beams of sunlight. As their eyes adjusted, Claire and Luca found themselves in an unexpected museum of winemaking heritage. Along one wall stood ancient equipment; wooden grape presses with massive screws, hand tools worn smooth by generations of use, bottles from decades past arranged by vintage.

But what drew their immediate attention occupied the center of the space; hundreds of barrel staves leaning against each other in carefully organized groups. Some were relatively new, their wood still showing rich grain patterns. Others bore the unmistakable signs of advanced age, darkened by decades of contact with wine, their insides stained deep burgundy, their surfaces telling stories of patience.

"When barrels can no longer serve their primary purpose, we disassemble them," Ernesto explained, moving to run his hand lovingly across the nearest section. "Traditionally, the wood was burned as fuel. But my father began preserving the staves, believing they contained too much family history to be reduced to ash."

Claire approached with hushed adoration, drawn to a particularly ancient collection. These staves were nearly black along their interior curves, the wine having penetrated deep into the grain. She lifted one carefully, feeling its surprising lightness despite the density of its history.

"These are the oldest," Ernesto confirmed, noting her interest. "From barrels my grandfather commissioned in the 1920s. They held our reserve Aglianico for nearly fifty years before being retired in the 1970s."

"They're extraordinary," Claire gushed, studying how light played across the wood, revealing subtle variations in the wine staining. "So rich with memory."

"For your portrait," Ernesto said with quiet certainty, "you can select from all the generations represented here. The oldest for the foundation, newer pieces for growth and future. A timeline of our family's relationship with the land, echoing Gregory and Angelica's timeline together."

Luca moved through the collection like a curator, his trained eye evaluating each grouping for artistic potential. "We could create something truly unique," he said, excitement building in his voice. "Using the natural curve of the staves to suggest movement, using the wine-stained interiors as shadows and depths..."

"You must take whatever speaks to you," Ernesto insisted, spreading his arms to encompass the entire collection. "Consider it our contribution to the portrait, beyond the commission, a gift from the family."

For the next hour, Claire and Luca moved through the warehouse with growing excitement, selecting staves from different eras that would form the foundation of their creation. Each piece they chose carried its own history; the oldest bearing deep wine memories from generations past, others showing the evolving techniques of barrel-making across decades. Ernesto watched with evident pleasure, occasionally sharing stories about specific vintages that had aged in certain barrels.

"This set held the first wine Gregory ever helped create," he pointed out as they examined a specific set of staves. "We were visiting my parents for summer. He was thirteen, and insisted on participating in every step of the process. The vintage was exceptional, just like the young man himself."

By early afternoon, they had curated a collection that represented not just the vineyard's history but the entire sweep of the Valenti legacy; wood that had witnessed family celebrations, endured hardships, participated in evolutions both subtle and profound. Just as they were preparing to arrange transportation for their selections, Corina appeared at the warehouse entrance, her elegant figure silhouetted against the bright day outside.

"Ernesto, I've been looking everywhere for you," she called, then noticed Claire and Luca amidst the barrel staves. "Oh! I didn't realize you had visitors. I'm sorry to interrupt."

"Perfect timing," Ernesto assured her. "I was about to call you. Our artists have had a brilliant insight for the portrait, and they'll need help getting these materials back to their studio."

As Ernesto explained the concept, Corina's expression shifted from polite interest to genuine enthusiasm. "Using our own barrels, it's perfect," she agreed, moving to examine their selections. "But there's something else you should see that you may like...".

She turned to her husband. "Show them the clock parts," she urged. "From the old tower timepiece."

Ernesto's face lit with recognition. "Of course! I'd forgotten we stored those here as well."

He led them to a corner of the warehouse where several wooden crates stood stacked against the stone wall. With careful movements that belied his enthusiasm, he lifted the lid from the topmost container, revealing a collection of brass gears, wheels, and mechanical components nestled in straw padding.

"The original clock from our tower," he explained. "Installed in 1884, it marked time for the vineyard until 1962, when it became too unreliable to maintain. When the clock was replaced, my father preserved the parts of the old clock."

Claire leaned closer, mesmerized by the intricate craftsmanship. Each gear was a work of art in itself; brass teeth cut with perfect precision, bearing the beautiful patina that comes from decades of faithful service. Some pieces were small enough to fit on a fingertip, while others spanned the width of her palm.

"They're incredible," she breathed, carefully lifting a cogwheel that caught sunlight along its edges like a miniature sun. "And perfect for our concept, actual pieces of time itself."

"The mechanism that measured seasons, harvests, generations," Luca agreed, examining an escapement wheel. "The physical embodiment of how their separate life rhythms found synchronization."

"Take what you need," Corina insisted. "These parts have been waiting for purpose. What better use than celebrating how two lives have found their perfect timing together?"

As arrangements were made for transporting their treasures to Luca's studio, Claire felt a growing sense of rightness about their chosen direction. When they mentioned needing to visit the church again to speak with Father Benedetto, Corina insisted on calling ahead to ensure he would be available. "He's been preparing for the wedding, but I know he'll make time for you. Your portrait has become important to everyone involved."

When they arrived at the church, Father Benedetto was waiting for them at the entrance, his lined face creasing with welcome as they approached.

"Corina called to say you've had an inspiration," he greeted them. "Something about wine barrels and parts of an old clock?"

Claire smiled at his characterization. "Close enough. We're creating a three-dimensional portrait using staves from the Valenti wine barrels and parts from their old clock tower mechanism. But we wanted to ask if you might have any elements from the church that could be incorporated, something to represent the spiritual dimension of their connection."

The elderly priest's eyes lit with immediate understanding. "The sacramental balanced with the temporal," he mused. "Come with me."

Rather than leading them into the church proper, Father Benedetto guided them around the building to a small door set into the side wall. It opened onto a narrow staircase that climbed upward into shadows.

"Mind your heads," he cautioned as they ascended. "This passage was built when people were considerably shorter."

The stairs brought them to the church attic; a vast, timber-framed space beneath the terracotta roof. Dust molecules swirled in the beams of light entering through small ventilation openings, creating an atmosphere of suspended time. Unlike most attics Claire had encountered, this space was meticulously organized, sections clearly labeled, pathways maintained between storage areas.

"The physical memory of our parish," Father Benedetto explained, moving with surprising agility through the systematically arranged artifacts. "Every significant renovation, every historical period represented."

He led them to an area marked "1873-1890" and knelt with remarkable spryness before a large wooden crate. "When I began my service here nearly forty years ago, this attic was a chaotic repository. Everything jumbled together, history and heritage treated with enthusiastic neglect." His voice carried a hint of humor despite the criticism. "One of my first projects was proper preservation, cataloging, organizing, protecting."

As he spoke, he carefully lifted the crate's lid to reveal contents wrapped in aged linen. With ceremonious movements, he unwound the protective covering to expose fragments of colored glass; deep blues, vibrant reds, rich ambers, and emerald greens catching light and refracting it into jeweled poems across the ceiling.

"Original stained glass from the church's first windows," he explained. "Damaged during a storm in 1923 and replaced with the current windows. These fragments were stored rather than discarded, though their purpose for keeping them was never recorded."

Claire's breath quickened as she knelt beside the collection. The glass pieces varied in size from tiny fragments no larger than a postage stamp to substantial sections spanning the width of a small book. Despite decades in storage, they retained mesmerizing vibrance; colors seemingly too pure to be man-made, too enduring to be merely mineral and heat.

"They're magnificent," she enthused, carefully lifting a piece of sapphire blue so deep it seemed to contain the actual night sky rather than merely suggesting it. "The craftsmanship, the color quality..."

"Hand-blown glass from Murano," Father Benedetto confirmed. "The church founders commissioned the finest materials available, believing that beauty itself was a form of devotion."

Luca joined them, his expression reflecting deep appreciation for both the historical significance and artistic potential of the fragments.

"Would it be appropriate to incorporate some of these into our portrait? These pieces that have witnessed countless ceremonies, filtered light for worshippers across generations?"

Father Benedetto considered the question with appropriate seriousness. "The glass was consecrated as part of the original church, yes. But its purpose was always to transform light into something transcendent; to remind people how divine presence changes our perception of the everyday world." He nodded slowly. "Used respectfully in artwork celebrating sacramental union, I believe this continues their purpose rather than diminishes it."

"We would treat them with utmost care," Claire assured him. "Placing them to catch light, just as they did in their original setting."

"Then yes," the priest decided. "Select what you find useful. Just like the barrel staves that have absorbed wine's essence, these fragments have absorbed countless prayers and celebrations. They belong in your portrait of souls joining."

With careful attention, Claire and Luca chose glass pieces that formed a harmonious palette; predominantly blues in varying depths, accented with amber tones that echoed the color of late afternoon seen through the church's current windows. Each fragment was wrapped individually in cloth before being placed in a small wooden box the priest provided.

"These pieces witnessed the first marriage in this church," Father Benedetto told them as they completed their selection. "They were present when Angelica's great-great-grandparents exchanged vows in 1874. Now they'll participate in celebrating her union with Gregory."

"The circle completes," Luca declared, accepting the box with appropriate respect.

"And begins anew," the priest added with a warm smile. "That is the nature of true spiritual connection; never simply ending or beginning, but continuously renewing."

With Father Benedetto's blessing, Luca gathered some small stones from the church garden, already imagining the creative ways they could incorporate them into the portrait.

On their way back, Claire and Luca headed to Grandma Rosa's trattoria. When arranging to meet Angelica's parents, they had gently directed them toward the matriarch instead. "Angelica's spirit belongs more to her grandmother than to us," they had explained. "Grandma Rosa taught her to see beauty in the smallest moments, to find meaning in traditions others had forgotten. If you wish to truly capture our daughter's essence, spend time with the woman who shaped her heart." This wisdom had resonated with both artists. Now the familiar stone building appeared around the bend, promising stories that would illuminate what no photograph could ever reveal.

"Come," Grandma Rosa beckoned, her voice a tapestry of stories waiting to be told.

She led them beneath the sprawling arms of an olive tree that had witnessed generations of laughter and tears. Against its gnarled trunk hung a simple wooden swing, its ropes burnished by decades of eager hands.

"Angelica," she beamed, her fingertips brushing the swing with veneration, "would spend hours here as a child. Even now, when troubles weigh too heavily, she returns." The leaves rustled, disclosing their secrets as the swing swayed in the afternoon light, a silent plea to become part of the story being crafted in the portrait.

Luca's artist's eyes widened with possibility. "The dried branches," he said, trying to contain the inspiration. "We could incorporate them into the framework, an echo of something that has sheltered and supported Angelica through seasons."

Inside once more, Grandma Rosa knelt before an ancient chest, her movements deliberate as she extracted an ornate wooden box, worn at its edges from years of curious fingers. When she placed it in Claire's hands, the weight felt like more than wood and metal; it was a vessel of cherished history being entrusted to her care.

"Angelica's treasures," Rosa explained as Claire lifted the lid to reveal a constellation of childhood wonders. "Stamps from letters she would beg the postman for. Maps she would spread across the floor, dreaming of distant shores. The compass her grandfather gave her when she feared being lost." There were dried flowers, pressed between scraps of parchment. "Wild daisies from the summer she learned to ride a bicycle without falling," Grandma Rosa murmured, her eyes reflecting a memory that lived in her heart as fresh and vibrant as the day it had bloomed.

Claire lifted a childish drawing; a family portrait rendered in crayon, with disproportionate smiles that somehow captured more truth than any photograph. These weren't mere objects but fragments of a soul, collecting in her hands like water from a sacred spring.

"Take the box with you," Grandma Rosa told them, her eyes misting with memories. "Use whatever you need to show who she truly is, then return the rest for safekeeping, for these are the anchors that moor her to herself when storms come."

As they departed, the box tucked safely between them, Claire and Luca walked in silence, aware they carried not just mementos but fragments of a family's existence; a treasure beyond measure for the portrait that now felt less like a commission and more like a sacred trust.

The journey back to Naples passed in charged silence, both artists lost in visions of what they would create. Claire found herself sketching quick studies; arrangements of barrel staves forming flowing structure, notations about which wine stains might best represent different aspects of Angelica and Gregory's connection. Beside her, Luca drove with the focused expression that revealed his mind was equally engaged in creative planning.

By the time they returned to Luca's studio, the small pickup truck with their treasures from the Valenti Winery had arrived and was waiting for them.

The studio hummed with creative potential as they arranged their materials, examining each piece anew. Sunlight slanting through the tall windows caught the glass fragments, sending colored reflections dancing across the floor and walls and ceiling like premonitions of what their finished work might achieve.

"We should test arrangements before committing," Claire suggested, already sketching possible configurations on her pad. "See how the different elements interact with each other and with changing light conditions throughout the day."

Luca nodded, although he had already started thinking of the practical challenges before them. "I'll set up a temporary framework," he agreed. "Something adjustable so we can experiment with different arrangements of the staves."

For the next several hours, they worked in the harmonious rhythm they'd developed over their time together; moving between concentrated individual effort and seamless collaboration without need for discussion. Claire developed the conceptual arrangement while Luca created a support structure that would allow them to experiment with different configurations.

The quiet rhythm of their creative partnership had become a world unto itself; so when the knock echoed through the studio, they both startled like dreamers abruptly woken. Reality had come calling in the form of a server from Caffè Sereno, windswept from his Vespa journey, bearing a package that smelled of home and comfort.

With a polite nod and the package safely delivered, the young man pressed a folded note into Luca's hand before disappearing back into the afternoon.

Luca unfolded the paper, sunlight catching the delicate creases as his eyes traced the handwriting. His voice, when he read aloud, carried Lucia's warmth into the room: "Dear Claire and Luca, I was talking to Corina Valenti earlier and she told me about your plans for the portrait. From what she described, I knew that you had undertaken a substantial project and wouldn't even remember to eat. So I'm sending over some food, my eggplant parmesan and fresh bread, that will help you to stay nourished and energized. I will continue to send you food over the next few days until you are done with the portrait. Love, Lucia."

Their eyes met across the room, a silent exchange more eloquent than words. Something tightened in Claire's throat; this simple act of kindness from a woman who had known her mere days yet cared enough to ensure she wouldn't go hungry. Luca's expression mirrored her own, a blend of surprise and gratitude that made speech impossible.

They savored Lucia's gift together, the rich layers of eggplant and cheese becoming fuel for both body and spirit, calling Lucia to thank her, their voices carrying gratitude that transcended the simple act of sending food, for what Lucia had truly delivered was a reminder that they were not alone in their artistic journey.

As twilight approached, they had assembled a rough prototype;

barrel staves arranged in a flowing pattern that suggested both the terraced vineyard landscape and the human form. The staves alternated in rhythmic succession, newer pieces, bright with untested promise, followed by older ones darkened by decades of wine memory, their harmonious interplay creating a tapestry of time that spiraled outward like the dance of seasons in a vineyard's life.

"It's starting to breathe," Claire said softly, stepping back to evaluate their progress. The arrangement had taken on a life of its own; no longer separate pieces of wood but the emerging skeleton of something organic, something with memory and meaning.

"Tomorrow we'll begin the actual construction," Luca said, coming to stand beside her. "Tonight, we dream."

His reassuring words sent warmth through Claire's entire being. Yes, they would allow their subconscious minds to continue working on the design complexities while they slept. And yes, they would dream together, bodies entwined like the barrel staves they were arranging, connected like the colors merging from separate fragments of ancient glass.

As they closed the studio that evening, locking away the physical elements of their creation-in-progress, Claire felt certainty solidifying within her; this portrait would be unlike anything either of them had created before. It would be more than representation, more than symbolism. It would be actual transformation, the physical materials themselves expressing how love fundamentally changes those it touches, turning separate histories into shared future, individual moments into eternal connection.

The morning sunlight poured through the tall windows of Luca's studio, casting long rectangles of brightness across the wooden floor where their collected treasures lay in careful arrangements. Claire stood before the prototype they had assembled the previous night, her fingers lightly tracing the curve of a wine-stained barrel stave. The wood felt alive beneath her touch, as if those decades of holding wine had imbued it with a consciousness all its own.

"It's speaking to us," she said in hushed tones, not realizing she had voiced the thought aloud until Luca appeared at her side, his presence as natural as the sunlight itself.

"What is it saying?" he asked, his voice low and intimate in the quiet of the studio.

Claire closed her eyes, letting her fingers continue their exploration of the wood's weathered surface. "It's telling us how to arrange the pieces. Look," she opened her eyes and gestured toward their preliminary layout, "if we curve these older staves here, they form something like... a protective embrace."

Luca studied the arrangement, his dark eyes reflecting the same creative awakening she felt stirring within herself. "You're right. The most wine-soaked pieces should form the heart of the portrait; the foundation of their connection."

Together they began rearranging the staves, working in silent communion as the morning hours stretched before them. Each piece found its rightful place in their evolving creation; the oldest barrel staves forming a central core, with newer pieces radiating outward in a spiral that suggested both growth and continuity like growth rings in a tree. The aged wood, stained burgundy from decades of contact with Valenti wine, created a rich, textured backdrop against which they would later incorporate the other elements.

"Hand me those brass gears," Claire said, reaching toward a small box containing the clock components from the winery tower. Luca placed the fragile mechanisms in her palm, his fingers lingering against hers for a moment longer than necessary.

"Where are you thinking?" he asked, watching as she considered the intricate brass pieces.

"Here, where the staves intersect," she replied, positioning a large gear at a junction where several barrel pieces met. "The timepiece that measured their separate lives now marks where their paths converged."

Luca nodded, understanding illuminating his features. "And we could use the smaller gears to suggest the moments still to come, future anniversaries, children perhaps, the steady tick of shared days."

As they worked, the stained glass fragments from the church caught the shifting sunlight, sending kaleidoscopic patterns dancing across the studio walls. Claire arranged them with careful precision, positioning each piece so that it would capture light at different times of day; ensuring the portrait would remain dynamic, never appearing exactly the same way twice.

"Just like a relationship," she observed, watching how a cobalt blue fragment converted a simple beam of sunshine into something otherworldly. "Never static, always revealing new facets depending on the time of the day when you view it."

Luca's smile warmed her more thoroughly than the sun streaming through the windows. "Exactly. And that's what we want to capture, not just how they appear at this moment, but how their bond will continue evolving long after the wedding day."

The hours melted away as they lost themselves in creation. They worked sometimes in parallel, sometimes in tandem; Claire focusing on the arrangement of glass fragments and the branches they got from Grandma Rosa's courtyard, while Luca secured the barrel staves into their permanent positions. Other times they found themselves so closely aligned that their bodies brushed against each other, the contact sending currents of awareness through Claire's skin that had nothing to do with artistic inspiration and everything to do with the man himself.

From Grandma Rosa's collection of Angelica's childhood treasures, Claire carefully integrated select items; the pressed wildflowers became sparks of color between staves, while a fragment of an old map was lovingly incorporated where the wood grain suggested rolling hillsides. The compass found its place near the portrait's center, its needle forever pointing toward magnetic north, a visual metaphor for the constancy of true connection.

By early afternoon, the framework had taken definitive shape. No longer simply materials arranged in space, it had transformed into something that breathed with life and intention. The curved staves created a three-dimensional canvas that seemed to undulate like the Valenti vineyard terraces, while the brass clock components sparkled with surprising brilliance, becoming focal points that drew the eye across the composition.

"I'm so hungry. I didn't realize how hungry I was," Claire admitted, suddenly aware of the hollow feeling beneath her breastbone. They had been working without pause since sunrise, too absorbed in creative flow to register bodily needs.

As if summoned by the very thought, a firm knock echoed through the studio. Luca crossed to the door, revealing the same young server from Caffè Sereno standing on the threshold, bearing a large wicker basket from which emanated tantalizingly complex aromas.

"Buongiorno!" The server greeted them with a bright smile. "Signora Lucia sends her compliments and hopes you enjoy your lunch." His voice carried a newfound warmth, more talkative than the previous day. With a respectful nod, he handed the basket to Luca before departing as swiftly as he had arrived.

Luca carried the basket to a small table near the windows, lifting the checkered cloth to reveal the feast beneath. "Antipasti and ravioli," he announced, his voice colored with appreciation. "Lucia is one of the warmest people I know."

The antipasti platter was a visual poem; paper-thin slices of prosciutto arranged like rose petals, marinated artichokes glistening with herb-infused oil, plump olives in varying shades of green and purple, roasted peppers that gleamed like jewels, and tiny balls of mozzarella nestled among fresh basil leaves. Alongside sat a basket of crusty bread still warm from the oven, and a covered dish that, when revealed, contained ravioli so perfect they might have been sculpted rather than cooked, soft pillows filled with ricotta and spinach, dressed simply with sage butter and a whisper of grated parmesan.

"She included a note," Luca said, unfolding a small piece of paper tucked beside the bread. He read it aloud: "My dear ones, creation requires nourishment of the body as well as the spirit. Eat well, work with joy, and remember that the most beautiful art flows when one is properly fed. With love, Lucia."

Claire felt her eyes grow unexpectedly moist at the simple kindness. "It's a true blessing to have Lucia and Signore Rossi in our lives."

"Yes, I agree," Luca replied, his voice gentle with understanding.

"Once you enter their orbit, you become family. There are no halfway measures with them."

They settled by the window, the wicker basket between them, Naples spread before them like a living canvas. As they savored each perfect bite, the conversation flowed between them with the same ease as their creative collaboration; discussing next steps for the portrait, sharing observations about Angelica and Gregory's connection, weaving plans together as naturally as breathing.

When Luca fed her a piece of ravioli, Claire felt his love infuse the moment as surely as the herbs she was tasting. "The ravioli is incredible," she sighed, closing her eyes to better absorb the flavors dancing across her palate. "How does she make something so simple taste so profound?"

"That's her gift," Luca replied, breaking a piece of bread. "Finding the extraordinary within the ordinary. Taking humble ingredients and redefining them through attention and care." His eyes met Claire's across the table. "Similar to what we're attempting with this portrait."

The parallel wasn't lost on Claire; both they and Lucia were alchemists of sorts, transforming raw materials into experiences that nourished on multiple levels. The thought deepened her appreciation for the meal, each bite becoming not merely sustenance but a lesson in how love expresses itself through creative acts.

When they had finished eating, leaving nothing but crumbs and gratitude, they returned to their work with renewed energy. The afternoon sun now was causing the stained glass fragments to cast different prisms across the evolving portrait. Claire stood back, observing how the changing radiance revealed new aspects of their creation.

"We need to incorporate the rosary beads," she said suddenly, remembering the olive wood prayer beads Father Benedetto had entrusted to them. "Not as visible elements, but woven into the very structure itself."

Luca considered for a moment, then nodded with understanding. "What if we embed them within the framework? Between the staves, visible only in certain lights or from particular angles, present but not immediately apparent."

"Yes," Claire agreed, the concept resonating deeply. "Like faith itself, a foundation that supports everything else without necessarily being the first thing you see."

With careful precision, they began incorporating the smooth, worn beads into the crevices between staves, securing them so they became integral to the portrait's structure while remaining largely hidden from casual observation. Only someone who knew to look for them would discover their presence, a secret dimension of meaning that added profound depth to the work.

As the afternoon waned toward evening, they began applying paint to selected areas of the sculpture-portrait; not to cover or conceal the natural materials, but to enhance and unify them. Claire mixed pigments with the intuitive precision of someone who has found her true medium, creating a palette that echoed the colors of the Valenti vineyard, the Church of San Lorenzo, Grandma Rosa's courtyard, and the Mediterranean landscape that had shaped both Angelica and Gregory.

"I'm thinking we should suggest their physical forms rather than depicting them literally," she explained, a brush poised above a section where several staves converged. "Using line and color to evoke their presence without reducing them to mere appearances."

Luca watched her work, his expression one of profound admiration. "That's perfect. We're not capturing how they look, but how they exist in relation to each other, the space between them is as important as the individuals themselves."

With subtle strokes, Claire began creating abstract suggestions of human forms; not detailed representations but evocative outlines that emerged from and receded back into the wooden structure. The figures were never fully separate from their surroundings but appeared to be emerging from or merging with the very materials that symbolized their shared history and future.

As twilight descended over Naples, casting the studio in lavender shadows, they continued working by the glow of carefully positioned lamps. The artificial light revealed new dimensions in their creation; brass clock components catching the golden illumination and throwing it back as concentrated points of brilliance, stained glass fragments evolving from vibrant daytime jewels to mysterious, glowing embers.

"We should stop for today," Luca finally suggested, though Claire could hear the reluctance in his voice. "Fresh eyes tomorrow will help us see what needs refinement."

Claire nodded, setting down her brushes with the care of someone parting temporarily from beloved companions. She stepped back to observe their progress, and the sight made her breath catch in her throat. What had begun as separate materials, wood and glass, metal and paint, flowers and branches, had begun fusing into something that surpassed its components. The portrait was taking on a presence that filled the studio with quiet power.

"It's alive," she exclaimed, voicing the thought that had been growing within her throughout the day. "Not just a representation but a living artifact."

Luca came to stand beside her, his arm brushing against hers as they contemplated their creation together. "That's what makes it worthy of them," he said softly. "It doesn't just show their connection, it embodies it."

Claire felt a profound rightness settle through her entire being. This was why she had come to Italy, why circumstances had conspired to bring her into Luca's orbit. Not just to rediscover her artistic passion, but to create something that could only exist through their combined vision; something neither could have conceived alone.

"Tomorrow we'll bring it all into harmony," she said, already envisioning the final touches that would complete their work. "Unite all the elements into a single voice."

Luca's hand found hers in the dusky light, his fingers warm against her paint-smudged skin. They stood together in companionable silence, watching how the fading light transformed their creation yet again; shadows deepening, highlights receding, the entire composition shifting into its nighttime aspect.

The third morning arrived with quiet clarity, as if the universe had stilled itself to witness creation's completion. Claire woke in Luca's arms, their bodies having found natural harmony during the night, just as their artistic endeavor had achieved harmony during their days of intensive work.

They prepared for the day's tasks with ceremonial attention; sharing cappuccino in contemplative silence, laying out brushes and pigments with precise care, each movement deliberate as participants in sacred ritual. By the time they reached the studio, morning had achieved perfect quality for painting; clear without harshness, revealing without distorting, illuminating without overwhelming.

Their creation awaited beneath its protective covering, patience embodied in wood and metal and glass. When they carefully removed the cloth, both paused to observe how differently the portrait appeared in this new day's light; subtle relationships between elements changed, certain connections more apparent, others more mysterious.

"It's already changing," Claire exclaimed, circling their work with evaluative attention. "Responding to new conditions, new moments."

"As it should," Luca agreed, selecting brushes with careful consideration. "Like the relationship it celebrates."

They began with the portrait's central core; the oldest barrel staves whose burgundy wine memories formed the foundation of their composition. Rather than covering these rich tones with paint, they applied clear sealant that intensified the natural coloration while preserving its depth and complexity. This treatment emphasized how the wood itself contained history in its grain patterns and wine staining.

Moving outward from this core, they worked with increasingly lighter touches; allowing newer staves to maintain their natural character while adding subtle washes that unified the compositional flow.

The painting process demanded perfect synchronization between them; Claire focusing on chromatic integration while Luca attended to textural harmony. They moved around the portrait like dancers circling a sacred fire, their brushes extending their touch into the creation's deepest recesses, their shared vision guiding each stroke.

"Here," Claire called, indicating an area where several staves created a natural rhythm that echoed the terraced vineyard landscape. "A wash of umber would echo the soil tones, connecting their agricultural heritage with their personal bond."

Luca nodded, immediately grasping her intention. He mixed the precise tone, warm brown with undertones of red earth, and applied it with precision. The color seeped into the wood's receptive surface, enhancing rather than concealing its natural character.

By midday, they had completed the portrait's color integration; establishing the visual pathways that connected separate elements into unified expression, as well as the detailed accents, the final touches that had converted assembly into artistry, construction into creation.

"Look at this," Luca called softly, positioning a small spotlight to simulate afternoon sun.

Claire moved beside him, watching as light passed through the carefully crafted openings to project distinct profiles onto the white cloth they'd hung for testing. The shadow-portraits were unmistakably human yet abstracted enough to suggest essence rather than mere appearance; recognizable as male and female forms while moving beyond specific identity.

"It's them," she erupted with joy, recognition flowing through her. "Not how they look but how they are."

Luca nodded, satisfaction evident in his expression. "And when natural light moves throughout the day, these shadow-portraits will shift slightly, breathing with time's passage, just as their relationship does."

"I think..." Claire began studying their work with critical attention.

"Yes," Luca agreed, understanding before she finished her thought. "It's complete."

They stepped back together, viewing the finished sculpture-portrait with the simultaneous pride and humility that accompanies true artistic achievement. What stood before them was neither wood nor metal nor glass, neither paint nor adhesive nor mechanical assembly. It was a transformation made visible. Separate histories unified, individual elements transcended, materials elevated beyond their own nature.

"Tomorrow we transport it to the winery," Luca said with a voice that carried both satisfaction and reluctance to conclude their creation. "Install it before the rehearsal dinner in the barrel room."

Claire nodded, unable to speak as emotion swelled beneath her breastbone. Creating this portrait had become more than artistic commission; it had become exploration of questions that echoed in her own heart, expression of truths she was only beginning to acknowledge in her deepest self.

They covered their completed work with care, ensuring its protection until morning's transport.

Rather than wait for Lucia's delivery from Caffè Sereno, they decided to surprise her with a spontaneous visit. Claire chose the Vespa over the Fiat, yearning for that exhilarating rush as the wind caressed her face and danced through her hair; a perfect embodiment of the freedom and triumph she and Luca now shared. All they could think was the sweet anticipation to see what tomorrow would bring.

9

WHEN TWO BECOME WHOLE

Dawn painted the eastern sky in washes of pink and pearl as transportation arrived at Luca's studio; a specialized vehicle arranged by the Valentis to carry their creation safely to the winery. The driver brought two assistants experienced in handling valuable artwork, their movements exhibiting the careful precision of professionals accustomed to bearing irreplaceable objects.

Claire and Luca supervised the portrait's preparation with attentive concern; ensuring proper padding surrounded the vulnerable edges, verifying secure attachment to the transport frame, confirming that weight distribution would prevent undue stress during the journey up winding roads.

Once satisfied with these practical precautions, they followed in Luca's Fiat, maintaining visual contact with the transport vehicle throughout the ascent toward the Valenti estate. Claire found herself holding her breath at particularly sharp turns, her fingers tightening involuntarily around the door handle as if she could somehow ensure their creation's safety through physical tension.

"It's well protected," Luca reassured her, noting her anxiety with affectionate understanding. "The Valentis regularly transport much more fragile items."

"I know," she acknowledged. "It's just, we've put so much into this. Not just time and effort, but..."

"Heart," he finished when she hesitated. "We've put our hearts into it."

The Valenti winery appeared ahead, its stone buildings glowing amber in morning light. As they approached the main entrance, Claire saw that preparations for tomorrow's wedding reception were well underway; workers arranging chairs on the lawn, florists creating elaborate displays near the entrance, musicians testing acoustics beside a temporary wooden dance floor.

Ernesto awaited them at the winery's main entrance, his expression reflecting appropriate solemnity for the occasion. "Welcome, welcome," he called as they parked beside the transport vehicle. "Everything is prepared for installation."

He led them through the winery's public areas toward a section Claire hadn't previously visited; a broad corridor connecting the main building with the production facility. This passageway featured stone walls and high clerestory windows that admitted natural light while protecting interior spaces from direct sun exposure.

"Here," Ernesto indicated, gesturing toward the corridor's longest wall. "This is where Gregory and Angelica wished your creation to be installed, the pathway all guests will travel during the celebration."

The location was perfect; an integral position within the family's daily life rather than relegated to formal display. This corridor connected the winery's commercial aspects with its heritage spaces, linking practical production with historical foundation. Light entered from above at perfect angles to activate their portrait's dynamic elements throughout the day.

A team of workers had prepared the installation area according to specifications Luca had provided; reinforced mounting points capable of supporting the portrait's weight, adjustable lighting that could enhance natural brilliance during evening hours, clearance that would allow viewers appropriate distance for full appreciation.

Corina joined them to witness the assembly. "We haven't shared any details about the portrait with Gregory and Angelica," Corina explained as the transport team carefully unloaded their creation. "They also wanted complete surprise, trusting your artistic vision entirely."

This information sent fresh nervousness flooding through Claire's chest. Complete trust carried enormous responsibility; what if their creative choices failed to capture what the couple had imagined? What if their unconventional approach using three-dimensional elements rather than traditional portraiture disappointed expectations?

Luca seemed to sense her sudden anxiety, his hand finding hers with reassuring pressure. "They trusted us because they recognized themselves in our work," he reminded her quietly. "Just as we recognized them in their love story."

The portrait revealed itself from protective coverings like a butterfly from chrysalis; sunlight immediately catching its brass components and stained glass fragments, shadow patterns forming through its negative spaces as morning illumination struck at perfect angle. Even the workers paused in their efficient movements, momentarily captivated by the creation they were handling.

"Magnifico (magnifiscent)," Ernesto rejoiced, his expression displaying genuine awe. "Breathtaking beyond words," Corina echoed the sentiment.

Installation proceeded with meticulous attention to detail; each mounting point secured with redundant protection, every angle verified against Luca's specifications, lighting tested from multiple perspectives. Claire and Luca supervised with the focused intensity of parents entrusting their child to others' care, noting minute adjustments needed for optimal presentation.

By midday, installation was complete. Their portrait occupied the corridor wall with commanding presence; not demanding attention through volume or drama but drawing the eye through inherent harmony, through the living quality that animated its carefully integrated elements.

"Step back," Luca suggested to the group. "Watch what happens as you move through space."

Ernesto, Corina, and the workers followed his instruction, walking slowly past the installed portrait while observing how their changing perspective impacted the viewing experience. From certain angles, the brass clock components shone with particular brilliance. From others, the stained glass fragments projected colored splendor across the opposite wall, creating secondary artwork through reflected light.

Ernesto and Corina approached them as workers departed, their expression containing multitudes; pride in having participated in something remarkable, appreciation for artistic creation fulfilled, looking forward to their son's and future daughter-in-law's response to this unexpected interpretation of "portrait."

"You have created something that will become part of our family legacy," Ernesto said simply. "Not merely decoration but actual presence that will witness generations to come."

"The rehearsal dinner begins at seven," Corina said, consulting her watch. "Gregory and Angelica will see your work for the first time when they arrive. We would love for you to join us for this unveiling."

Claire felt sudden nervousness flutter beneath her ribs once again. Witnessing someone's first encounter with artwork you've created carries a particular vulnerability, especially when that artwork attempts to capture something as intimate as soul connection.

"We would be honored," Luca answered for them both, understanding her momentary hesitation without judgment.

As late afternoon settled over the countryside, they returned to Naples to prepare for the evening's event. Claire put on the dress she'd chosen days before; a deep burgundy creation that echoed the portrait's wine-memory tones. The flowing fabric complemented the organic quality of their creation while honoring the occasion's significance without stealing focus from the true celebration.

When they arrived back at the winery in the early evening, the transformation of the barrel room was complete; the production facility where barrels aged precious vintages had become an elegant space for the rehearsal dinner. Long tables arranged between massive oak containers, subdued lighting creating pools of amber glow that emphasized the room's cathedral-like qualities, wine barrels serving dual purpose as both functional objects and symbolic presence.

Guests began arriving; family members and close friends who would participate in tomorrow's ceremony. Angelica's parents, Elena and Luciano, entered with dignified grace, their eyes immediately drawn to the sculpture. Elena's hand fluttered to her heart as she stood transfixed before it, tears gathering along her lower lashes. Luciano, usually reserved and measured in his expressions, placed a gentle hand on Luca's shoulder, his voice thick with emotion as he thanked him and Claire for capturing the very essence of their daughter's spirit. Claire observed the reactions of others as well, noting with quiet pleasure how people instinctively slowed their pace when passing, how many stopped completely to examine details, how conversations naturally flowed in exalting tones in its presence.

At precisely seven o'clock, a hush fell over the gathering as Gregory and Angelica made their entrance. Conversation paused momentarily, then resumed with increased animation as the couple entered through the winery's main entrance.

Ernesto approached his son and future daughter-in-law with ceremonial formality despite the occasion's intimacy. "Before we begin our celebration," he announced, his voice carrying natural authority that quieted surrounding conversations, "there is something you must see."

Gregory and Angelica exchanged curious glances, their expressions showing the particular harmony Claire had been attempting to capture in their portrait; different features conveying identical meaning, separate faces reflecting unified understanding.

"Your commissioned artwork has been completed and installed," Ernesto continued, gesturing toward the corridor. "The artists are here this evening to witness your first encounter with their creation."

A murmur rippled through assembled guests as Ernesto led the couple toward the corridor entrance. Claire felt Luca's hand find hers, his fingers conveying shared nervousness through gentle pressure. This moment of unveiling carried particular vulnerability; not merely artistic evaluation but deeply personal response to how they had interpreted soul connection.

Gregory and Angelica walked hand in hand toward the corridor, their movements unconsciously synchronized even in this moment of uncertainty. As they crossed the threshold from the main hall to the connecting passageway, carefully arranged lighting activated, high-lighting the portrait with subtle radiance that emphasized its three-dimensional qualities.

Claire watched intently as the couple approached their creation, noticing how their expressions change from curiosity to surprise to something deeper, more profound. They stopped several paces from the portrait, momentarily frozen by unexpected impact, by encountering artistic interpretation so different from conventional expectations yet so perfectly attuned to their unique connection.

Angelica moved first, stepping closer with hand slightly extended as if compelled to touch what she was seeing. Her fingers hovered near the portrait's surface without making contact, following the flow of barrel staves as they created visual rhythm echoing the vineyard's terraced land-scape. Her eyes widened as she recognized materials; her mouth forming silent words of understanding as she identified wood from her fiancé's family barrels, brass components from the winery's historic clock, glass fragments from her family's church.

Gregory joined her a moment later, his movement naturally mirroring hers as he approached from a slightly different angle. His reaction contained simultaneous recognition; eyes tracking the burgundy wine memories that formed the portrait's foundation, hand lifting in unconscious echo of brass gears positioned at junction points, body leaning forward to examine stained glass fragments that refashioned ordinary light into sacred brilliance.

"Look," Angelica called, indicating the negative spaces between staves.

As evening light passed through these carefully preserved openings, distinct shadow-portraits formed on the opposite wall; abstracted silhouettes that captured essential rather than specific character. These shadow forms seemed to breathe with the building's subtle air currents, to shift with passing clouds that momentarily altered illumination quality.

"It's us," Gregory said softly, wonder evident in his voice. "Not how we appear but how we are."

His simple articulation of exactly what they had been attempting to capture sent waves of emotion through Claire's chest. They had succeeded in translating invisible connection into visual language, in making tangible what existed between souls rather than merely recording physical appearance.

"The materials..." Angelica's voice caught as recognition dawned in her eyes. "Wood from Gregory's family barrels, spanning generations of winemaking. Metal from the vineyard clock. Glass from my family's church windows. And..." Her words dissolved into silence as she traced her fingers over the rosary beads she had given Father Benedetto, now immortalized within the portrait.

"The map, dried flowers, compass," Gregory recounted, "from your childhood treasures. I remember you showing me those." Overwhelmed, Angelica rushed forward, enveloping Claire and Luca in an embrace that spoke volumes beyond words. Gregory followed, their collective emotion flowing between them like wine from the same precious vintage.

Their synchronized understanding, their ability to perceive beyond mere appearance to deeper meaning, confirmed for Claire and Luca that they had indeed captured something true about this couple's particular bond. The portrait spoke visual language that Gregory and Angelica instinctively comprehended; not requiring explanation or interpretation but communicating directly to them.

After several minutes of private contemplation, the couple turned toward the barrel room where guests waited with curiosity. The couple's faces held the particular radiance that comes from profound recognition, from encountering external expression of internal truth.

"The artists, Claire Bennett and Luca Castellano" Gregory called, his voice carrying uncharacteristic emotion. "Please come forward."

Luca squeezed Claire's hand once before they stepped forward together. The moment carried exquisite vulnerability. Angelica moved toward them with surprising speed, her usually composed demeanor altered by evident emotion. She enveloped them in an embrace once again, her arms communicating what words could not yet express.

"You saw us," she gushed against Claire's ear. "Truly saw us."

The simple statement contained volumes. It was an acknowledgment that they had perceived beyond surface appearance to essential connection and had recognized the particular current flowing between two souls.

Gregory approached more slowly, his expression containing complexity beyond simple appreciation. He extended his hand to Luca first, then Claire, the formal gesture carrying unexpected weight through his evident emotion.

"You've created something I didn't know was possible," he said quietly. "Not just art but actual presence, something that breathes, that responds, that evolves."

His precise articulation of what they had been attempting to achieve sent fresh waves of satisfaction through Claire's chest. What followed was an unexpected ceremony; Ernesto directing staff to distribute glasses of special reserve wine from barrels that had contributed staves to the portrait. "This vintage," he explained, "had been aging since Gregory's birth, awaiting occasion of sufficient significance to justify opening."

With solemnity that acknowledged the moment's importance, Ernesto offered a toast that celebrated both the couple's imminent marriage and the artwork that had captured their connection's essence. "To relationships that fuse separate histories into shared future," he concluded, raising his glass toward both the couple and the artists. "To love that makes visible what eyes cannot see."

As evening progressed into celebration. Angelica's parents, Elena and Luciano, as well as the other guests continued visiting the corridor to examine the portrait, each returning with expressions of wonder and appreciation. Claire observed how people naturally formed connections through shared experience of the artwork; conversations developing between previously unacquainted family members of the bride and groom, relationships forming through mutual recognition of beauty.

As the evening drew toward conclusion, Claire found herself standing beside Luca in the corridor, viewing their creation in momentary solitude while celebration continued in the barrel room beyond. The portrait glowed with subtle luminescence in the evening's low light.

"We made something true," she said dreamily, the observation emerging from that place deeper than conscious thought.

Luca's arm encircled her waist, drawing her against his side with natural ease. "Truth recognized truth," he replied, his voice containing similar wonder. "Our understanding of connection recognized theirs."

In that quiet moment between evening's crescendo and night's approach, Claire felt completion mingled with a new beginning. The artistic cycle was reaching fulfillment while simultaneously opening doorways to unexplored territories. This portrait had concluded one creative journey while initiating another, and had answered certain questions while awakening fresh curiosity.

"Tomorrow they marry," Luca murmured against her temple. "And our creation witnesses their promises.

The wedding day dawned with pristine clarity, as if the heavens themselves had polished everything to crystalline perfection. The sky stretched above Naples in uninterrupted azure, while morning light painted the landscape in saturated hues that made mundane objects appear newly created, freshly imagined.

Claire woke in Luca's arms, their bodies having found natural harmony during the night, her head resting against his chest where she could hear the steady rhythm of his heart marking faithful time beneath her ear. They lay together in quiet appreciation of momentary stillness before the day's significant events would unfold around them.

"Happy wedding day," he expressed with gentle passion against her hair, his voice carrying the particular quality it held only in these intimate morning moments, rough-edged from sleep yet tender with unguarded emotion.

"Not our wedding," she reminded him softly, fingers drawing phantom drawings over his chest.

"No," he agreed, his arm tightening slightly around her shoulders, "Though we'll witness vows that echo in our own hearts."

His simple observation settled between them like seed finding fertile ground. It carried potential rather than pressure, recognition rather than request. They had not discussed a formal future beyond this present connection, and had allowed their relationship to unfold with natural rhythm rather than predetermined trajectory. Yet in quiet moments like this, awareness hovered between them; recognition that what they were creating together extended beyond artistic collaboration into life's deeper territories.

Early afternoon found them preparing for the ceremony; Claire selecting a dress in deep emerald that complemented the portrait's colored glass elements, Luca choosing attire that honored the occasion's significance while maintaining his characteristic artistic presence. They moved through these preparations with unhurried attention, each moment carrying particular sweetness in its intimacy.

The church appeared as if it was reinvented when they arrived. Its weathered stone façade was adorned with garlands of flowers and herbs gathered from both families' lands, its wooden doors standing open in welcome, its bell tower silhouetted against perfect blue sky like an exclamation mark punctuating heaven's blessing.

Father Benedetto greeted them in the courtyard, his lined face alight with the particular joy that comes from witnessing love's sacred renewal. "Ah, our artists!" he called, embracing them with surprising strength for his advanced years. "Your creation has become the primary topic of conversation, even overshadowing my carefully prepared homily!"

His mock indignation carried genuine pleasure beneath. There was appreciation that their portrait had captured the spiritual essence he himself had observed in Gregory and Angelica's connection. The priest's validation carried particular weight given his depth of experience witnessing human relationships across their complete spectrum.

"Will you sit with the family?" he inquired. "Both Ernesto and Luciano have requested you be considered honored guests rather than regular attendees."

The distinction carried unexpected emotion for Claire; recognition that their brief time spent with Valenti family had established connections that transcended professional exchange, that through artistic collaboration they had become participants in a community that would continue beyond this specific occasion.

298

Inside, the small church glowed with natural light enhanced by hundreds of candles placed in careful arrangements. Flowers adorned every available area; not formal arrangements but wild profusions that suggested nature's spontaneous celebration rather than human design. The effect was one of organic harmony rather than structured decoration, of living participation rather than static ornament.

Guests were already gathering, filling wooden pews worn smooth by generations of faithful attendance. Claire spotted Grandma Rosa near the front, her tiny frame beautifully attired in traditional dress that spoke of respect for heritage. Lucia and Signor Rossi occupied places of honor in the family section, their presence acknowledging the role Caffè Sereno had played in community connection across decades.

Corina Valenti appeared at Claire's elbow, elegant as always in understated formal attire that spoke of quiet confidence rather than ostentatious display. "Come," she said warmly, looking at Claire and Luca. "You'll sit with us."

She guided them to the front pew on the right side, traditionally reserved for immediate family. As they settled into place, Claire observed the church interior with fresh appreciation; noting how her previous visits had informed their portrait's creation, how architectural elements they'd incorporated now appeared in their original context. The stained glass windows that had provided fragments for their artwork glowed with saturated color in afternoon light, casting jeweled patterns across worn stone floors.

Musicians positioned near the altar began playing quietly; not formal processional but ethereal preludes that created an atmosphere of expectant joy. The compositions blended traditional melodies with contemporary interpretations, honoring heritage while allowing the present moment its distinctive voice.

At precisely four o'clock, Father Benedetto took his position before the altar, his ceremonial robes looking like blessed sails filled with divine wind. The music shifted subtly, signaling transition from gathering to formal beginning. Anticipatory silence descended across the assembled community, collective breath held in preparation for what's coming up next.

First came Gregory; not waiting at the altar as traditional grooms often did, but advancing with grace from the side entrance accompanied by both parents. They moved together with dignified purpose, Ernesto's hand upon his son's shoulder conveying generations of support, Corina's arm linked through Gregory's expressing maternal pride. This journey together toward the altar visually represented their approach to marriage itself; family heritage providing foundation for individual choice, parental blessing offered without ownership.

When they reached the altar, Gregory turned to face the central aisle, his expression containing that particular vulnerability unique to moments of profound transition. Claire found herself studying him with artistic attention; noting how emotion rendered him momentarily translucent, inner self visible to attentive observation.

Then Angelica appeared at the church's main entrance, similarly accompanied by both parents, Elena and Luciano, rather than being "given away" by father alone. The symbolic significance of this choice was immediately apparent. It showed equal commitment approaching from equal foundation, partnership rather than transfer.

Her dress defied conventional expectations; not white princess fantasy but subtle cream that complemented her olive complexion, its elegant simplicity speaking of confidence rather than display. She carried no elaborate bouquet but a simple gathering of wildflowers, bound with ribbon woven by Grandma Rosa for the occasion.

As the family trio processed forward, Claire found herself unconsciously reaching for Luca's hand that joined with hers instinctively. The resonance between this ceremony and their own unspoken questions vibrated between them like silent music, asking softly what future might hold, what promises they themselves might exchange in time to come.

The ceremony itself balanced tradition with personal significance; ancient rituals honored through contemporary interpretation, sacred words renewed through present understanding. When Gregory and Angelica exchanged vows, their voices carried perfect clarity despite evident emotion, each syllable weighted with full comprehension of commitment being offered.

Above, the church bell tolled once as rings were exchanged, simple bands crafted from metal with meaningful heritage rather than commercial value. Then seventeen additional tolls followed, marking family legacy through numerical representation, connecting the present moment with generations past.

When Father Benedetto pronounced them married, sanctifying their union with both religious blessing and community recognition, applause erupted spontaneously; not interrupting sacred moments but enhancing it through collective affirmation. This joyful response continued as the newly married couple processed down the central aisle, their expressions containing that particular radiance unique to commitments kept and publicly declared.

Outside, rose petals showered the couple as they emerged into the late afternoon sunlight. The petals from the blooms from both families' gardens, their fragrance released by crushing contact, their brief beauty sacrificed in celebration. Musicians positioned in the courtyard began playing festive compositions that invited movements that reshaped solemn ceremony into a joyful celebration.

Amidst congratulations and photographs, Claire found herself momentarily separated from Luca, drawn into conversation with guests who had learned of her role in creating the portrait. Questions about technique and materials flowed continuously, genuine interest evident in each inquiry. She answered with appropriate modesty while internally acknowledging the artistic achievement they had realized together.

When the celebration began transitioning toward the winery for formal reception, Claire rejoined Luca near the ancient cypress trees that guarded the church entrance. He was deep in conversation with an elegantly dressed older gentleman whose attentive posture suggested serious discussion rather than casual exchange.

"Ah, here she is now," Luca said as she approached. "Claire, may I introduce Marcello Bertini, Director of the National Gallery in Rome."

The distinguished gentleman turned toward her with evident interest, his appraising gaze carrying professional evaluation rather than a social greeting. "Charmed," he said simply, extending his hand with the casual confidence of someone accustomed to moving in rarified artistic circles. "Your colleague here has been describing your collaborative process. Most intriguing."

Claire accepted his handshake, noting the smooth quality of his palm, the subtle calluses at fingertips that suggested he himself worked with materials beyond simply evaluating others' creations. "Thank you," she responded, unsure how much Luca had already shared about their unconventional approach.

As if understanding her question, Luca elaborated, "I was explaining how we incorporated materials with living memory," his eyes holding hers with quiet significance. "How the barrel staves had absorbed decades of transformation, how the clock components had faithfully marked generations of time."

Marcello nodded, his expression revealing genuine engagement rather than polite pretense. "And I was expressing that your approach represents exactly the direction contemporary portraiture needs to explore; moving beyond mere likeness to capture essence, using three-dimensional elements to express what exists beyond physical appearance."

A small crowd had gathered around them, listening with undisguised curiosity. Claire felt business cards slip discreetly into her palm, and saw the same happen to Luca as gallery owners and collectors introduced themselves with practiced ease, their casual gestures belying the calculated networking beneath. The attention carried unexpected weight. It was professional evaluation rather than merely social appreciation.

"Would you consider creating similar works?" Marcello asked, his direct approach suggesting serious interest rather than casual inquiry. "It'll be for a special exhibition I'm curating at the National Gallery in a month from now? 'Reimagining Portraiture' is our working title. I know there is not much time."

The question momentarily stole Claire's voice, its unexpected magnitude requiring mental reordering of her professional landscape. Exhibition at the National Gallery would represent not merely exposure but validation at the highest level, acknowledgment that their experimental approach carried significance beyond personal expression.

Before she could formulate a response, "An intriguing proposition," Luca acknowledged, his hand finding Claire's with natural ease. "Something we need to discuss together, as our artistic partnership requires mutual commitment to new directions."

The casual reference to partnership sent warmth cascading through

Claire's chest. It was not merely professional collaboration but deeper connection acknowledged openly, publicly. The gesture communicated volumes to those observing, establishing their relationship as foundation rather than convenience.

Marcello gave an understanding smile and handed his business cards to Luca and Claire.

Ernesto Valenti approached the group. He clapped his hands once, drawing everyone's attention. "The reception awaits," he announced with characteristic authority. "And I believe our artistic friends deserve refreshment after their spellbinding contribution to this celebration."

The informal procession toward the winery began forming, guests moving with natural flow toward the next phase of celebration. Claire found herself walking beside Luca, their hands still joined as if separation would require conscious effort rather than mere inattention.

"The National Gallery," she exclaimed, the words themselves carrying resonance like bell tones in sacred space. "I never imagined..."

"Why not?" Luca countered gently. "You have pushed what we created beyond just portraiture into new artistic territory. Why shouldn't it be recognized?"

His simple affirmation settled into her consciousness with unexpected weight. It was challenging long-held limitations she'd unconsciously accepted, questioning boundaries she'd believed immovable. Why not indeed? What other artistic territories might they explore together, what other conventional expectations might they transcend through collaborative vision?

As they approached the winery entrance, Claire noticed something unexpected. There was a subtle change in guests' behavior as they entered the corridor where their portrait had been installed. People who had been chatting animatedly fell silent upon encountering the artwork, their expressions shifting from social animation to contemplative appreciation, their pace naturally slowing to accommodate visual absorption.

Gregory and Angelica arrived last, having stayed at the church for private moments together in the bell tower as planned. Their entrance into the corridor carried particular significance. It was their first encounter with the portrait as a married couple rather than engaged individuals, first viewing of the artistic representation of their bond after publicly declaring it through sacred vows.

"It's even more perfect now," Angelica effused, reaching for her husband's hand with unconscious synchronicity. "After going through our wedding ceremony, seeing our vows reflected here in physical form..."

Gregory nodded, his expression containing depths not present during yesterday's first viewing. "It's as if the portrait anticipated what we would become," he observed quietly. "As if it were waiting for us to grow into what it already knew we were."

The reception unfolded with orchestrated spontaneity. Formal elements provided structure within which genuine celebration could expand organically. Tables arranged in the tents next to the barrel room accommodated family groupings while encouraging mingling, seating arranged to facilitate new connections rather than reinforce existing relationships.

Claire and Luca found themselves placed at a table with people they hadn't previously met; art collectors from across Europe, cultural attachés from several embassies. The conversation flowed with natural ease beyond ordinary social exchange, discussions of creativity and artistic purpose developing without self-conscious pretension.

Throughout the meal, courses served with careful attention to regional significance and family tradition, Claire noted the continuous stream of guests visiting the corridor to view their portrait. Each returned with expressions suggesting genuine impact rather than polite appreciation, many seeking them out specifically to share responses.

"Your work has changed how I understand portraiture entirely," one distinguished woman commented, her accent suggesting French heritage. "The way you've captured connection between souls rather than mere physical resemblance, it's revolutionary."

Another guest, identifying himself as curator from a prestigious Milan gallery, expressed similar sentiments. "The three-dimensional quality creates a relationship between artwork and viewer that traditional portraiture cannot achieve," he observed with professional analysis. "One doesn't merely look at this creation, one experiences it, participates in it."

These responses carried unexpected professional consequences. The recognition was extending beyond simple appreciation into potential career redirection. Claire found herself exchanging contact information with significant figures in the European art world, conversations naturally evolving toward future collaborations, exhibition opportunities, commissioned projects.

As soon as the formal dinner concluded, Lucia appeared beside their table, her elegant attire recasting her usual maternal presence into something approaching regal bearing. "It is time," she announced with ceremonial significance. "The millefoglie della promessa (thousand-layer promise pastry). It awaits assembly."

She led Claire and Luca toward a section of the reception area; a dramatically lit preparation station where components for the final wedding pastry had been arranged with artistic precision. Thin layers of perfectly baked puff pastry gleamed with subtle sheen, cream filling waited in copper bowls like clouds captured in vessels, fresh berries arranged by color formed gradients that mirrored sunset's progression. A small crowd of guests who wanted to witness the creation of this cake had already assembled.

"A thousand layers representing a thousand promises," Lucia explained as she started to assemble the layers. "Each one fragile alone yet creating transformative strength when unified." She kept alternating between the puff pastry sheets and the cream filling.

The symbolic parallel to marriage itself was immediately apparent. Individual moments of commitment formed the foundation for lasting union, separate promises combining into cohesive strength. But what surprised Claire was Lucia's next announcement.

"Our artists will assist in the final assembly," she declared, gesturing for Claire and Luca to join her at the preparation station. "As they have captured essence in portrait, now they will participate in creating the symbol of continuous nourishment."

The unexpected invitation carried ceremonial weight. Claire and Luca stepped forward together, quickly washing their hands at the nearby basin before following Lucia's expert guidance in placing alternating layers of pastry and cream, creating structure that rose with architectural precision while maintaining inherent delicacy. With careful precision, they crowned the creation with jewel-toned berries, their fingers brushing as they arranged each fruit to create a tapestry of vivid colors and varied textures.

When completed, the millefoglie stood nearly two feet tall, impressive in scale yet maintaining an impossible quality that suggested both strength and vulnerability. Lucia sprinkled the summit with confectioners' sugar that caught light like fresh snow, then stepped back to allow Gregory and Angelica to approach for ceremonial first serving.

Together they cut through carefully constructed layers, revealing interior structure of alternating elements that created visual rhythm; just as their portrait revealed inner workings of relationship through arranged materials of personal significance. The parallel was not lost on assembled guests, appreciative chatter acknowledging how culinary art that reflected in the visual art that in turn reflected in human connection.

As evening deepened into night, celebration evolved from formal structure to organic joy. Music invited movement, wine encouraged relaxation, shared experience created temporary community among previously unconnected individuals. Claire was continuously sought after; not merely for social exchange but for genuine artistic discussion, questions about technique and material selection emerging from true interest rather than polite conversation.

Claire found herself engaged in an animated conversation with a renowned art dealer who had traveled from Milan specifically for the wedding. The dealer leaned forward, captivated by her passionate articulation, occasionally nodding and offering insights that sparked new tangents in their discussion. So absorbed was she in this unexpected professional opportunity that the celebration around her had momentarily faded into a distant hum.

"Mi scusi (Excuse me)," came Luca's voice from behind the art dealer, his tone apologetic yet firm. He stood there, illuminated by the warm glow of string lights, his dark curls slightly disheveled from the evening's festivities, his white shirt unbuttoned at the collar. "I'm terribly sorry to interrupt what I'm sure is a fascinating discussion about..." his eyes met Claire's with a spark of mischief, "... impasto techniques, perhaps? But I wondered if I might steal the talented Ms. Bennett for a dance."

The art dealer graciously stepped aside with a knowing smile, and Claire felt a blush warm her cheeks as Luca extended his hand. She placed her fingers in his, a current of electricity passing between them at this simple touch.

"As enlightening as that conversation was," she confessed as he led her toward the crowded dance floor inside the main tent where couples swayed to the orchestra's rendition of a classic Italian love song, "I've been hoping for a moment that belonged just to us." Her eyes reflected the golden glow of the surrounding lights and something more, a longing that had been building throughout the evening.

"I've been watching you shine all evening," he lilted close to her ear, his breath warm against her skin, "and waiting for the perfect constellation of notes to bring you into my arms."

His hand found the small of her back, drawing her closer than propriety perhaps dictated, but neither seemed to notice or care. They moved together with unexpected synchronicity, as though their bodies had discovered a language all their own; one that required no translation, no hesitation. The melody wove around them, strings and piano notes binding them together in invisible threads of harmony.

Without conscious decision, their steps carried them beyond the tent's perimeter, away from the laughter and chatter, into the villa's garden where moonlight spilled across ancient stone pathways and cypress trees stood as silent observers. Stars punctuated the velvet darkness above, and the distant music became their private serenade.

Out here, in this intimate sanctuary, Claire felt herself surrendering to the moment completely. Luca's eyes never left hers as they continued their dance, their movements slowing, becoming less about following steps. His fingers traced intricate mosaics against the silk of her dress, each touch igniting new awareness of how perfectly their bodies aligned.

"I feel as though we've created another artwork tonight," Claire whispered, afraid to break the spell with words spoken. "Something ephemeral but no less real."

Luca's hand tightened almost imperceptibly at her waist. "Not ephemeral," he corrected softly, his Italian accent more pronounced with emotion. "Just beginning. Some creations, Claire, are meant to last beyond a single moment."

She couldn't say how long they remained there, moving in slow circles beneath the infinite canvas of stars, their heartbeats gradually synchronizing, their breaths mingling in the cool night air. The world beyond their small circle of two ceased to exist. There was no wedding, no guests, no professional opportunities or lingering insecurities. There was only this: his hand in hers, her head eventually coming to rest against his shoulder, the unspoken acknowledgment that something fundamental had shifted between them, like tectonic plates rearranging to create new landscapes.

"What are you thinking?" he asked softly, his voice carrying that particular quality it held only in their most private moments, vulnerability beneath confident surface, question beneath observation.

"I'm thinking about transformation," she replied with equal softness, meeting his gaze directly. "I'm considering that perhaps Naples need not be a temporary sanctuary," she said simply. "That perhaps what we've created together extends beyond artistic collaboration into life's deeper territories."

The sentence lingered between them, soft as a whisper yet powerful as thunder. Luca's expression shifted from inquiry to understanding to something approaching reverence. It was not a response to a specific statement but acknowledgment of a threshold crossed, of a future opening where previously only the present had been clearly visible.

"For me, Naples is 'home' because you are here," he said quietly. "My studio feels incomplete without your presence. And my home seems empty without you."

The simple declarations settled into Claire's consciousness like stones dropped into still water, creating ripples that expanded beyond immediate impact. Not a grand romantic gesture but honest recognition of what had developed between them, partnership extending into life's fundamental rhythms.

"So perhaps..." she began, then paused, searching for words that wouldn't constrain what was still evolving, still finding its natural form.

"Perhaps we continue creating together," he completed for her. "Not just art but life itself. Not just portraits of others' connections but our own relationship. Not just commissioned works but shared futures."

The suggestion contained neither pressure nor premature definition. It was simply recognition of a direction naturally emerging from what they had already built together.

In the distance, they could see the twinkling lights of Naples scattered like fallen stars, each glimmer a promise of possibilities. But in the winery garden Claire wondered, would the city that had begun as a temporary escape transition into a potential home? Would their journey evolve from a healing retreat into a forward pathway? And ultimately, would their connection deepen from artistic collaboration into life's fundamental partnership? Only tomorrow will tell.

10

THE UNEXPECTED COLLABORATION

Two weeks had passed since Gregory and Angelica's wedding, the celebrations now existing in that peculiar realm between vivid memory and softening nostalgia.

Word had spread about their wedding portrait at the Valenti Winery, drawing art enthusiasts and critics from across Europe who made pilgrimages to witness this unprecedented fusion of mediums. The influential art journal La Voce dell'Arte (The Voice of Art) had published a rapturous review for their dimensional artistry, coining the term "sculptupainting", declaring it an artistic revolution where "the emotional resonance of paint and the tactile truth of form merge into a singular expression that refuses the boundaries of traditional categorization." Though Claire found the term slightly unwieldy on her tongue, their creation had sparked something in the art world that continued to ripple outward, challenging conventions and opening doors.

Now in Luca's studio, the "Confluence" stood complete. Their latest creation was destined for the National Gallery in Rome. Unlike their intimate portrait for Angelica and Gregory's wedding, this piece explored humanity's universal interconnections, a vast composition where sculptural elements emerged from and receded into painted surfaces. Claire watched as Luca gave final instructions to the transportation specialists National Gallery had sent from Rome, their white gloves and measured movements reflecting the gravity with which they approached this pioneering work. Marcello from the National Gallery informed them that, following Luca's instructions, they had constructed an entire room specifically for this installation.

Claire stepped back, observing how their creation was carefully wrapped and secured for its journey. Using elements similar to their wedding portrait, weathered wood, mechanical components, colored glass, they had created something that spoke of human connection in a broader sense. Where the wedding portrait had captured the bond between two specific people, this work explored the universal threads that tied humanity together across generations and cultures.

She felt a familiar bittersweet ache as their artwork disappeared into the specialized transport vehicle. Watching your creation leave was like a novelist seeing their characters take on lives of their own. There was pride mingled with loss, joy tinged with emptiness.

"We've been invited to the opening in two weeks," Luca said, his arm finding its way around her waist as they watched the truck navigate the narrow street. "The Gallery suggested we might discuss a permanent installation in the contemporary wing."

The word "permanent" hung in the air between them, laden with different implications Claire wasn't ready to address. She thought of a permanent commitment to Italy, to a life centered in this country. It represented a decisive choice rather than the balanced ambiguity.

"That sounds wonderful," she replied, her voice carrying a lightness that masked her inner turmoil. "I have that video conference with Susan tomorrow about the Lakeside Properties redesign. I should probably review my concepts tonight."

Luca's expression revealed nothing, but she felt a subtle pulling back that wasn't physical but emotional. He understood what she wasn't saying: that she remained caught between worlds, unwilling to fully commit to either.

"Of course," he said, his voice neutral. "Would you like to work at your apartment or upstairs in mine?"

The easy way they separated when needed had once felt like freedom. Now it sometimes carried undercurrents of uncertainty. There were questions about where this relationship was ultimately headed, whether their lives would ever fully merge or remain in this state of beautiful but incomplete connection.

Back in her apartment now, Claire opened her laptop and forced herself to focus on the Lakeside Properties presentation. The design firm wanted a complete rebranding with logo, website, and marketing materials, that would position them as the premier luxury real estate company in northern Ohio. A year ago, this project would have consumed her, each element demanding her complete creative attention. Now she found herself completing the work with technical proficiency but emotional detachment, her mind repeatedly drifting to the three-dimensional artwork that was currently traveling the two and a half hour journey from Naples toward Rome.

The email notification sound pulled her back from her distracted state. Susan's name appeared in her inbox, the subject line bearing the now-familiar mix of professional patience and mounting concern: "Timeline for Return to Ohio Office?"

Claire's finger hovered over the message. She'd managed to extend her remote work arrangement for a few months now, far beyond what either of them had initially planned. Susan had been remarkably accommodating, but the unspoken question loomed larger with each passing week: Was Claire ever coming back?

The truth was, she didn't know. Her life had split into parallel existences. There was professional designer Claire Bennett with client deadlines and corporate responsibilities, and artist Claire who had discovered her authentic creative voice in Naples, who had fallen in love not just with Luca but with a completely different way of experiencing art and life.

Before she could open Susan's email, her phone chimed with an incoming text from Luca:

"A courier just delivered something to my studio for both of us. Elegant envelope. Intriguing. I want to open it with you. Should I bring it over?"

Her response was immediate: "Yes, please, I could use a break from the screen."

Twenty minutes later, Luca arrived with a cream-colored envelope in hand, the paper so thick it more resembled parchment than conventional stationery. A wax seal embossed with an intricate "EA" monogram secured the flap.

"It looks like a wedding invitation," Claire observed, taking the envelope from him. "But I don't think we know anyone with those initials, do we?"

Luca shook his head, a curious smile playing at the corners of his mouth. "Open it."

The seal broke with a satisfying crack, releasing the scent of subtle perfume, something with notes of bergamot and jasmine. Claire extracted a heavy card stock invitation, bearing embossed lettering in deep navy blue:

"Elisabetta Abianti extends her most sincere compliments to Claire Bennett and Luca Castellano, and requests the pleasure of their company at her Milan atelier on October 10, to discuss a matter of mutual artistic interest."

"Elisabetta Abianti?" Claire looked up, the name vaguely familiar but not immediately placing it.

Luca's eyes had widened, a mixture of surprise and admiration crossing his features. "Only one of Italy's most celebrated fashion designers. Her pieces are walking works of art; she's known for collaborating with painters, sculptors, and architects to create clothing that blurs the line between fashion and fine art."

"But why would she contact us?" Claire turned the invitation over, finding only an address in Milan and a request for confirmation.

"I'm not sure," Luca mused, settling beside Claire on her sofa. "Maybe she was at the wedding? Gregory and Angelica's guest list included several notable figures from the art and fashion world."

A small card had fallen from the envelope, a handwritten note on Elisabetta Abianti's personal stationery, as if answering Claire's question:

Your extraordinary portrait at the Valenti-Lombardi wedding reception captured my attention and imagination. I've not stopped thinking about how you transformed materials with personal history into something transcendent. I believe we might create something equally remarkable together. - EA

Claire felt a flutter of excitement mingled with uncertainty. The fashion world represented yet another direction, another potential commitment. Yet the prospect of collaborating with someone of Elisabetta Abianti's stature was undeniably thrilling.

"Should we go?" she asked, studying Luca's reaction. "It's just 4 days away."

He considered the question with characteristic thoughtfulness. "It would be an honor simply to meet her. Her approach to fashion is revolutionary; treating garments as canvases, textiles as artistic medium rather than mere fabric."

"But it's not what we do," Claire pointed out. "We've never created for the fashion world."

A smile spread across Luca's face, reaching his eyes with a warmth that never failed to move her. "That's precisely why it's intriguing, isn't it? The unexplored territory, the challenge of translating our vision into a completely different context."

Before she could respond, her laptop chimed with an incoming video call. It was Susan, right on schedule for their weekly check-in. The sight of her boss's name on screen sent a jolt of guilt through Claire's system. She'd been so immediately captivated by Elisabetta Abianti's invitation that she'd completely forgotten the call.

"I should take this," she said, wearing her earphones, reluctance evident in her voice.

Luca nodded, understanding as always. "I'll make dinner while you talk. We can discuss Milan afterward."

As he moved toward her small kitchen, Claire accepted the video call, watching her professional world materialize on screen. Susan appeared, her office visible in the background, the familiar environment suddenly seeming like a transmission from another planet.

"Claire! Good to see you. How's Naples treating you?" Susan's tone was friendly but carried the subtle edge of someone who had been maintaining patience for longer than expected.

"Beautifully," Claire replied, shifting mental gears to her professional persona. "I've just finished the preliminary concepts for Lakeside Properties. I think they'll be pleased with the direction."

The conversation flowed into the comfortable territory of deadlines and client expectations, design choices and marketing strategies. Claire found herself responding with practiced expertise, her corporate vocabulary returning with surprising ease. This was the language she'd spoken for years, the professional identity she'd cultivated so carefully.

Yet as they discussed the upcoming projects, she felt an increasing sense of disconnection, as if watching herself perform a role rather than genuinely inhabiting it. From the kitchen came the sounds of Luca preparing dinner, the rhythmic chopping of a knife, the sizzle of olive oil in a pan, his low humming of an Italian folk song she'd come to recognize. Those sounds felt more authentically part of her life now than the corporate discussions filling her ears.

"Claire?" Susan's voice pulled her attention back to the screen. "Did you hear what I said about the Thompson account?"

"I'm sorry, could you repeat that?" Claire refocused, embarrassed by her wandering attention.

Susan's expression softened slightly. "Claire, I think we need to have a real conversation about your timeline. The remote arrangement was meant to be temporary, but it's been extended multiple times now. The team needs to know if they should be planning with or without you in the coming months."

The question Claire had been avoiding now sat squarely before her, impossible to sidestep any longer. "I know, and I appreciate your flexibility. It's just that things here have become..." She paused, searching for words that could possibly encompass the life change she'd undergone. "...more complex than I anticipated."

"What is it, Claire?" Susan asked, her tone knowing but not unkind.

"I've reconnected with a part of myself here, with my art in a way that feels..." Claire struggled to express the profound nature of what she'd discovered in Naples without sounding like she was dismissing the career she'd built with Susan. "It feels essential, somehow."

Susan studied her through the screen, years of professional rapport allowing her to read between the lines. "I understand you better than you might think. But Claire, you can't live in two worlds forever. At some point, you'll need to decide where your heart truly belongs."

The truth of those words resonated painfully. Claire had been attempting exactly that, living in two worlds, maintaining dual identities, postponing the inevitable choice.

"I know," she admitted quietly. "I just need a little more time to figure things out."

"Take the time you need," Susan replied, her tone suggesting this extension of patience had limits. "But remember, clarity comes from decisions, not from avoiding them."

When the call ended, Claire remained at her desk, Susan's words echoing in her mind. The scent of Luca's cooking filled the apartment, garlic, fresh herbs, the distinctive aroma of a sauce that had been perfected through generations. She turned to find him watching her from the kitchen doorway, his expression carrying questions he was too considerate to voice.

"Susan wants a timeline," she said simply.

Luca nodded, understanding immediately. "And what do you want?"

The question hung between them, seemingly simple yet impossibly complex. Claire wished she had an answer that would satisfy them both, that would resolve the tension between her parallel lives.

"I want to go to Milan," she said instead, choosing the immediate decision over the larger one it represented. "I want to hear what Elisabetta Abianti has to say."

His smile held a mixture of pleasure and something more complicated. Perhaps it was an awareness that she was still navigating by increments rather than setting a clear course. But he accepted her response without pressing for more. But he accepted her response without pressing for more.

"Then we'll go to Milan," he agreed, extending his hand to her. "And see what new adventure awaits us there."

Milan existed in dramatic contrast to Naples, its northern precision and cosmopolitan sophistication a counterpoint to the southern city's passionate disorder and ancient rhythms. A city where high fashion wasn't merely displayed but lived and breathed through its very streets. The Italian metropolis stood as a temple to sartorial artistry, where the air itself seemed infused with an intoxicating blend of tradition and daring innovation.

Walking through the Quadrilatero della Moda, Luca felt Claire's fingers tighten around his at the sight of ateliers where dreams were spun into reality by hands that had inherited generations of craftsmanship. Her eyes, wide with wonder, reflected the storefront windows that told stories of passion, garments suspended in perfect stillness that seemed to speak directly to her.

The Milanese moved through the landscape around them with an effortless grace that made Claire feel both out of place and desperately eager to belong. She found herself mimicking their nonchalant confidence, while Luca, born to the Italian streets, navigated them with inherited ease.

Elisabetta Abianti's atelier occupied a renovated industrial space in the city's design district, the exterior maintaining its early twentieth-century architectural integrity while the interior had been recast into a temple of contemporary fashion. Claire and Luca were guided through a series of increasingly exclusive spaces, past design teams working on sketches, seamstresses bent over intricate hand beadwork, and walls displaying fashion photography that blurred the line between commercial imagery and fine art.

"Ms. Abianti will see you now," their guide announced, opening a final door that revealed a vast, light-filled studio.

Elisabetta Abianti stood before an enormous mood board, her petite frame belying her outsized influence in the fashion world. In her early fifties, she possessed the kind of striking beauty that photographers adored, strong facial architecture, penetrating dark eyes, and silver-streaked black hair cut in a severe bob that emphasized her elegant neck. She wore what appeared to be a simple black dress until closer inspection revealed ingenious structural elements that allowed the garment to move like liquid around her body.

"The artists of Naples arrive," she said by way of greeting, her English carrying just enough Italian inflection to remind them they were on her territory. "Your work has been occupying my thoughts since the Valenti-Lombardi wedding."

Direct and without pretense, she gestured them toward a seating area where models of what appeared to be future retail spaces had been arranged on a large table. As they settled into streamlined leather chairs, assistants appeared silently with fancy water bottles, espresso, and pastries before disappearing as efficiently as they had arrived.

"I imagine you're wondering why I've brought you here," Elisabetta continued, studying them with evaluative intensity. "I am not in the habit of working with artists who have no connection to fashion. But sometimes, one encounters work that demands attention regardless of its context."

She tapped a tablet, and suddenly the wall before them morphed into a digital display showing photographs of their portrait installation at the wedding. Someone had documented it from multiple angles, capturing how light interacted with the materials throughout the day.

"What struck me most profoundly," Elisabetta explained, her voice softening with awe as she traced her fingertips along the edge of the table between them, "was how you converted ordinary materials, wood that had served practical purpose for generations, mechanical components that had faithfully marked time, glass that had once filtered light for worshippers, into something that spoke of human connection at its most essential level."

She rose with fluid grace, her silk dress caressed her skin as she moved toward the models of her future stores on the table, each step purposeful yet unhurried. The afternoon light caught in her dark hair, illuminating the passion in her eyes as she continued, "My upcoming Haute Couture line explores the sacred art of upcycling, breathing new life into discarded treasures that the world has forgotten." Her fingers hovered over one of the miniature designs. "I'm reimagining how we perceive value, taking abandoned textiles, weathered metals, and forgotten artifacts that once served humanity, and elevating them to become vessels of beauty that honor their original purpose while transforming it."

She lifted her gaze, vulnerability and determination mingling in her expression. "This collection isn't just about fashion, it's about the intersection of utility and evolution, how functional objects evolve to carry emotional and cultural meaning beyond their practical purpose. Each thread, each fragment tells a story of rebirth, of finding remarkable beauty in what others cast aside as unwanted."

Claire and Luca exchanged glances, both intrigued by the philosophical alignment with their own artistic approach. Elisabetta continued without waiting for response, her creative intensity palpable.

"I am proposing a collaboration, not garments, which is not your medium, but installations for six flagship stores around the world and more coming up in future." She gestured to the miniature retail spaces. "For now it'll be Milan, Paris, New York, Tokyo, London, and Mumbai. Each installation would connect to the location's cultural and artistic heritage while maintaining a visual coherence across all spaces."

The scale of what she was suggesting began to register. This wasn't a modest commission but a global artistic statement, a merging of fine art and commercial fashion at the highest level.

"The project would culminate in the New York installation unveiling during Fashion Week, with all previous installations featured digitally as part of the presentation."

Elisabetta finally paused, her gaze moving between them with keen assessment. "Questions? Concerns? I recognize this may represent a departure from your current work."

Luca spoke first, his artistic integrity compelling him to address the most obvious issue. "Your vision is intriguing, and we're honored by your interest. However, we've never created commercial installations. Our work has been... personal. Intimate."

A smile flickered across Elisabetta's face, appreciation rather than amusement. "Precisely why I want you. The fashion world is saturated with commercial-minded artists who create what they think will sell. I need something authentic, something that emerges from genuine artistic exploration rather than market calculation."

She turned to Claire, gauging her reaction and intuiting perhaps she might be more receptive. "Think of it as translating your artistic language into new contexts, not compromising it."

Claire found herself drawn to the challenge Elisabetta presented. It represented a potential bridge between her professional design experience and her artistic awakening with Luca, a way to possibly integrate her divided worlds rather than choosing between them.

"The timeline?" Claire asked, already mentally calculating how this might fit with her ongoing work for Susan.

"Four months from concept to completion of all installations," Elisabetta replied. "With the New York Fashion Week unveiling in February."

Luca's expression revealed his primary concern. "And our creative control?"

"I wouldn't want artists without strong intuition," Elisabetta stated firmly. "You would have complete creative freedom within the practical constraints of retail spaces. My only requirements are that the installations incorporate elements of the collection's materials and reflect the philosophical core I've described."

She named a compensation figure that Claire found more than satisfactory. The amount that would provide genuine financial security, that would fund years of independent artistic work afterward for her and Luca.

"Consider carefully," Elisabetta concluded. "This is not a decision to make lightly. My team can provide detailed specifications, but I need your answer within the week. The timeline is ambitious."

As they departed the atelier an hour later, armed with elaborate portfolios detailing each location and the collection's conceptual framework, Claire felt simultaneous exhilaration and apprehension. The project represented a unique opportunity but also a significant deviation from the artistic path they'd been forging.

"What do you think?" she asked Luca as they found a quiet café, needing to process what they'd just experienced.

"It's fascinating... and concerning. The scope is impressive, the artistic challenge genuine. But I worry about becoming servants to commercial expectations rather than following our authentic creative impulses."

Claire understood his hesitation. Having herself navigated the commercial design world for years, she recognized the potential pitfalls.

"There's a difference between compromising and adapting your art to new contexts," she pointed out. "The most interesting art often emerges from constraints, from problem-solving within boundaries."

"True," Luca acknowledged, stirring his espresso contemplatively. "And Elisabetta seems to genuinely respect artistic integrity. Did you notice how she discussed the philosophical underpinnings rather than marketing considerations?"

Their conversation continued throughout the train journey back to Naples, weighing pros and cons, exploring potential approaches, and examining their own motivations. By the time they arrived, Claire had mentally constructed an elaborate list, logical considerations on one side, emotional responses on the other.

But lists, she was discovering, rarely captured the complex reality of artistic and personal choices. This decision would affect not just their creative direction but also their relationship, their geographic focus, and potentially Claire's ongoing connection to her career in the US.

That evening, Luca prepared a simple dinner at his apartment while Claire paced the balcony, her internal debate intensifying rather than resolving. The practical benefits were undeniable; financial security, international exposure, the rare opportunity to have their work seen by audiences who might never enter a traditional gallery. Yet Luca's concerns about commercial expectations diluting their creative authenticity resonated deeply as well.

"You're thinking so hard I can almost hear it," Luca observed, bringing two glasses of wine to the balcony. The setting sun painted Naples in warm amber light, the bay a mirror of liquid copper stretching toward the horizon.

Claire accepted the glass gratefully. "I'm torn. Part of me sees this as a perfect bridge between my design background and our artistic collaboration. Another part worries we'd be sacrificing something essential about how we work."

"Tell me something," Luca said, leaning against the railing beside her. "When you think about the installations, do you feel creative excitement? Does your mind start generating ideas about what's possible? Or does it feel like an obligation, a compromise?"

The question cut through her chaotic circular reasoning. Claire closed her eyes, allowing herself to envision what they might create for these spaces, how they could translate their three-dimensional story-telling to each unique location, incorporating cultural elements along-side Elisabetta's materials, creating environments that would transform retail spaces into immersive artistic experiences.

"I see it," she admitted, opening her eyes to find Luca watching her with tender attention. "I'm inspired to see how we could create some-thing meaningful within this framework, something true to ourselves while speaking to a completely different audience."

Luca nodded, something shifting in his expression. "I see it too. But I worry about what happens to artists when they enter the commercial world. I've watched friends lose their voice trying to speak in someone else's language."

"Four months," Claire said softly. "That's all Elisabetta is asking for. Four months to create these art installations, and afterward, we'd have the financial freedom to pursue whatever artistic direction calls to us. If we do not enjoy the experience, we don't need to commit to any more art pieces for her future stores."

As night fell over Naples, their discussion continued, each concern examined, each opportunity weighed. By midnight, they had reached a tentative agreement; they would accept Elisabetta's offer, but with conditions that would protect their artistic integrity and ensure time for their own creative work throughout the project.

The following morning, Claire faced another difficult conversation, explaining to Susan that she needed to extend her remote arrangement further. The video call began with professional updates before Claire carefully introduced the new development.

"An opportunity has presented itself here in Italy," she explained, watching Susan's expression for reaction. "A major fashion designer wants to commission a series of art installations for her flagship stores worldwide."

Susan's surprise was evident, though her professional composure quickly reasserted itself. "That sounds significant. Timeline?"

"Four months," Claire replied, the number suddenly sounding longer when spoken to her boss than it had when discussing it with Luca. "February completion."

Understanding dawned in Susan's expression, not just of the practical implications but the deeper meaning behind Claire's choices. "You're not coming back, are you?" The question carried no accusation, just quiet recognition.

"I don't know," Claire answered honestly. "I'm still trying to figure out how all the pieces fit together. I can continue handling the current clients remotely..."

Susan shook her head gently. "Claire, you're one of the most talented designers I've ever worked with. But you can't build a meaningful career or a meaningful life with one foot on each continent. At some point, you'll need to choose."

The truth of those words landed heavily. Claire had been attempting exactly that, maintaining divided focus, split loyalty, fragmented identity.

"I know," she acknowledged. "I just need to see this project through, to understand if this new direction is truly where I'm meant to go."

Susan studied her with the insight of someone who had navigated her own career crossroads. "I'll extend your remote contract through February. After that, we'll need to either welcome you back fully or wish you well in your new path."

The deadline felt both generous and terrifying. It was a concrete point at which decisions could no longer be postponed. "Thank you," Claire said, with genuine gratitude in her voice. "For understanding, for the opportunity, for everything."

"Just promise me one thing," Susan replied. "Whatever you decide, make it because it's what you truly want, not because it seems like the path of least resistance. You're too talented to settle for anything less than where your creativity can fully thrive."

After the call ended, Claire sat in silence, Susan's words echoing alongside Elisabetta's proposition and Luca's concerns. Three different perspectives, three different pulls on her future direction. And somewhere in the middle, her own voice, still finding its strength, still learning to articulate what she truly wanted.

Later that day, she and Luca sent their response to Elisabetta, accepting the commission with their conditions clearly stated. The reply came within hours, agreement to their terms, contracts to be drawn up immediately, and an invitation to begin preliminary concepts the following week.

The work began gradually at first, then accelerated with each passing week. What started with concept sketches and material experiments evolved into elaborate models, then full-scale prototypes. Luca's studio became command central for the global project, walls covered with inspiration boards for each city, tables laden with material samples from Elisabetta's collection, digital displays tracking progress across time zones.

Milan came first, the prototype installation that would establish the visual language for all that followed. They chose to incorporate floating elements that moved with air currents, representing both the fluid nature of fashion and the invisible connections between people across cultures. Using reclaimed materials similar to those in their portrait installation, they created environments that told stories of transformation, ordinary objects elevated through context and intention, just as Elisabetta refashioned functional garments into artistic expressions.

Paris followed, the installation adapting to the historic architecture of the flagship store while incorporating distinctly French artistic elements. Then London, with its unique blend of traditional and contemporary influences. Each location presented specific challenges and opportunities, each installation building on the foundation established while speaking to its particular cultural context.

Claire discovered unexpected joy in this new artistic direction. The constraints of retail spaces, far from limiting their creativity, seemed to focus it, providing parameters within which their ideas could crystallize with particular clarity. Luca, initially most concerned about commercial influences, found himself energized by the challenge of creating meaningful art for spaces not traditionally associated with artistic contemplation.

"It's almost like the caffè sospeso concept," he observed one evening as they reviewed photographs from the Tokyo installation. "Creating art that waits for strangers to encounter it, offering an unexpected moment of connection in a mundane transaction."

Claire hadn't considered this parallel, but she immediately recognized its truth. Their installations transitioned retail environments into places where customers might experience something beyond commercial exchange, moments of reflection, cultural connection, artistic appreciation woven into the everyday act of shopping.

Then came Mumbai, a city that awakened something primal within Claire. It brought memories of vibrant street markets and the intoxicating scent of spices flooding back from her visit years before. For this installation, they collaborated with local artisans whose hands had inherited generations of wisdom, rendering raw silk into cascading narratives through intricate embroidery and block printing.

The centerpiece became a breathtaking homage to Indian cinema's soul, seven magnificent hanging screens, each crafted from different traditional textiles that told India's story through touch and texture. The first, made of luminous Kanchipuram silk, captured romance in every thread; the second, robust Khadi cotton, spoke to the revolutionary spirit of early Indian films; the third, delicate Chikankari muslin, suggesting nuanced emotional landscapes; the fourth, opulent Banarasi brocade, celebrated the spectacle of musical numbers; the fifth, geometric Bandhani tie-dye, represented the kaleidoscopic nature of Mumbai's street life; the sixth, metallic-threaded Zardozi, reflected cinema's golden age; and the seventh, contemporary raw silk embedded with fragmented mirrors, symbolized how Indian cinema both reflected and fragmented reality.

Visitors wandered beneath this constellation of storytelling, each fabric catching light differently, creating an ever-changing symphony of texture and color. At predetermined intervals, the lights would dim completely, revealing hidden images painted in luminescent pigments. There were iconic moments from Bollywood's greatest films that had remained invisible in the light, now glowing like embers in the darkness.

When illuminated again, the mirrored fragments multiplied these visions across walls and bodies alike, making everyone part of Mumbai's grand cinematic tradition.

"This is where fantasy and reality can dance together daily," Luca beamed. "The artisans there don't just create beauty, they weave dreams into reality."

Claire couldn't speak past the knot of emotion in her throat, overwhelmed by how perfectly the installation captured the very essence of Mumbai, the tension between ancient traditions and electric modernity, all pulsing with an unmistakable heartbeat of human connection.

The New York installation became their most ambitious, a culmination of everything they'd learned through the previous locations. Situated in Elisabetta's flagship Manhattan store, it would serve as the centerpiece for her Fashion Week presentation, the physical embodiment of her collection's philosophical core.

As they worked, Claire's divided existence gradually shifted toward integration rather than fragmentation. Her commercial design skills merged with her artistic resurgence, each strengthening the other. Her work for Susan's clients continued, but increasingly took less emotional energy, becoming professional obligation rather than core identity.

Two months into the project, they flew to New York for initial site assessment and meetings with the local installation team. The city's frenetic energy contrasted sharply with Naples' more measured rhythms, yet Claire found herself responding to its particular vibrancy with unexpected enthusiasm.

"You seem at home here," Luca observed as they walked through Central Park one evening, the autumn leaves creating a golden canopy overhead.

Claire considered this observation. "Parts of me remember American urban energy. But it feels different now, like I'm visiting rather than returning."

"And Naples?" he asked, the question casual but carrying deeper implications.

She took his hand, warmth flowing between their palms in a silent language they already knew.

"Naples feels like," she said contemplatively, "as if it's become part of my artistic DNA now, like I couldn't create the same way anywhere else."

His smile contained multitudes, pleasure at her response, hope for what it might mean for their future, patience with her ongoing process of discovery. The unspoken question of permanence hovered between them. Where would Claire choose when Elisabetta's project concluded and Susan's deadline arrived?

They continued walking, the conversation weaving though the installation details and many other topics.

Time accelerated as Fashion Week approached. January was devoted to finishing the installations, making final adjustments across all locations, and intensive preparation for New York. Video conferences with Elisabetta became daily occurrences, her exacting standards pushing them to refine and perfect every element.

Two weeks before Fashion Week, Elisabetta summoned them to Milan for final consultation and, surprisingly, personal fittings. Upon arrival at her atelier, they discovered she had created custom designs for them to wear at the New York event.

"My collaborative artists should embody the collection's philosophy," she explained, directing them to separate fitting rooms where her team waited.

The experience was unlike anything Claire had encountered, being draped in fabrics so fine they seemed to float above her skin, expert hands making microscopic adjustments, Elisabetta herself evaluating each element with critical precision. The resulting creation was a dress that somehow captured elements of Claire's artistic sensibility while remaining unmistakably Elisabetta Abianti, structured yet fluid, contemporary yet timeless, the color morphing subtly between deep teal and midnight depending on movement and light.

When Claire emerged from the fitting room, she found Luca similarly transformed. His usual artistic elegance had been elevated to stunning effect, a suit that appeared conventionally tailored at first glance, but revealed unexpected architectural elements upon closer inspection. The fabric incorporated subtle textural patterns that echoed elements from their installations.

"Now you're ready," Elisabetta declared, circling them with critical assessment. "The artists become part of their creation."

As Claire studied her reflection, she barely recognized herself. It wasn't because the image was foreign but because it integrated aspects of herself she had previously kept separate. The sophisticated professional, the passionate artist, the woman who had found love in Italy, all these identities coexisted in the person looking back at her.

They returned to Naples for final preparations, spending long days refining the installation's interactive elements. Their creative partnership had evolved through the project's demands, Luca's intuitive artistic approach balancing Claire's structured design thinking, their individual strengths complementing rather than competing.

One evening, with Fashion Week just days away, Claire found herself on Luca's balcony, Naples spread before her in evening splendor. The past months had been so consumed with creation that she'd had little time for the existential questions that had previously occupied her thoughts. Yet now, with the project nearing completion, they resurfaced with renewed urgency.

Susan's deadline loomed just weeks after Fashion Week. The choice could no longer be postponed; return to her career in the US or commit fully to her artistic life in Italy with Luca.

"You're far away," Luca observed, joining her on the balcony with two glasses of wine. The setting sun gilded his features, emphasizing the strong architecture of his face that she had come to love so deeply.

"I was thinking about what happens after New York," she admitted, accepting the glass. "About Susan's deadline."

Luca nodded, giving her the space to continue without pressing.

"Everything has changed since I came to Naples," she said softly. "I've changed. The work we've done with Elisabetta has shown me it's possible to bridge worlds I thought were separate, commercial and artistic, structured and intuitive, American and Italian."

"And what does that tell you about your choice?" Luca asked, his voice gentle.

Claire turned to face him fully, the fading light casting everything in intimate shadow. "It tells me that perhaps I've been asking the wrong question all along. Not which world to choose, but how to bring the best of both into a new way of working, a new way of living."

His expression remained attentive, waiting for her to reach her own conclusion rather than influencing it.

"I don't want to leave Naples," she said finally, the words emerging with surprising clarity. "I don't want to leave what we've created together, not just our art but us."

The smile on his face held such joy that Claire felt her heart expand in response. He didn't rush to embrace her or make declarations, respecting that this was her personal revelation, her own moment of clarity.

"Naples would be honored to keep you," he said simply, raising his glass to hers in quiet celebration.

The New York Fashion Week presentation surpassed all expectations. Elisabetta Abianti's reputation for theatrical innovation was evidenced in her decision to replace the traditional runway show with an immersive journey through the collection's philosophy.

Models moved through Claire and Luca's installation rather than along a conventional catwalk, the environment responding to their presence with subtle shifts in lighting and movement of floating elements. Digital displays showed the installations from other global locations, creating a sense of simultaneous experience across continents.

Claire and Luca watched from seats of honor beside Elisabetta, their custom attire drawing appreciative glances from the fashion elite surrounding them. As the presentation reached its culmination, Elisabetta rose to acknowledge the applause, then gestured for them to join her.

Standing before the international press and fashion industry luminaries, Claire felt a moment of perfect clarity. This world was not her natural habitat, but she and Luca had brought authentic artistry into this commercial sphere without compromising their integrity. They had created something that existed in the space between categories, neither purely fine art nor merely commercial design, but a new territory that incorporated elements of both.

The after-party at Elisabetta's Manhattan penthouse became an unexpected networking opportunity. Museum directors, gallery owners, and collectors approached them with genuine interest, intrigued by how they had translated their three-dimensional narrative approach to retail environments.

"Your work goes much beyond the commercial context," a prominent museum curator told them, his card appearing between manicured fingers. "We should discuss a potential exhibition at the Whitney."

Similar conversations repeated throughout the evening, each one opening doors neither had anticipated when accepting Elisabetta's commission. What had begun as a commercial project had, improbably, elevated their artistic profile within the fine art world rather than diminishing it.

As the evening wound down, Elisabetta found them on her terrace overlooking the city lights. "You've exceeded my expectations," she said directly, never one for false modesty or unnecessary flattery. "I would like to establish an ongoing relationship, annual installations that evolve with each collection."

The offer was as unexpected as it was generous, a guaranteed artistic commission that would provide financial stability while still allowing time for their own creative exploration.

"We're honored," Luca replied, his hand finding Claire's with natural ease and his eyes finding hers for agreement. "And would welcome the opportunity to continue this collaboration."

Elisabetta's sharp eyes missed nothing, her gaze moving between them with knowing assessment. "You work well together," she observed. "In art and, I suspect, in life."

Claire felt a smile bloom across her face, unforced and genuine. "We've discovered that the boundaries between art and life are more permeable than we initially thought."

A rare smile revealed on Elisabetta's usually composed features. "The best art always is."

The day after the Fashion Week finale, Claire and Luca surrendered to the luxurious sanctuary of their Manhattan hotel suite, seeking refuge from the world. Golden afternoon light cascaded through the floor-to-ceiling windows, painting them in warm honey hues as they lounged together in comfortable silence.

"Next time we're visiting the US," Luca said suddenly, turning to face Claire on the bed. "I would like you to take me to Ohio. I would love to meet your whole family. And see where you grew up."

"I would like that," Claire admitted, a sudden ache of longing for her family blooming in her chest. "If we weren't returning to Naples so soon, we could have visited Ohio this time."

Their bodies welcomed the sweet, earned exhaustion that settled into their bones, a cherished gift they embraced rather than resisted, knowing these quiet moments together were as precious as their public victories.

Back in Naples, with Fashion Week behind them and the project officially complete, Claire and Luca found themselves in a moment of unusual stillness. After four months of intense creative output and global travel, the sudden absence of deadline pressure felt almost disorienting.

Their final video conference with Elisabetta concluded with mutual appreciation and concrete plans for future collaboration. The financial security provided by the project's completion, enhanced by unexpected bonus compensation, created a foundation upon which they could build whatever artistic direction called to them next.

"So," Luca said as they sat in his studio, surrounded by the remnants of their global project. "What now?"

Claire studied him in the afternoon light, this man who had reshaped her understanding of art, of love, of herself. "Now I call Susan," she replied quietly. "And make it official."

The video call was brief but emotional. Susan had been preparing for this outcome, and had seen it coming through Claire's gradual transformation over the past months. "I knew when I saw photographs from the Fashion Week presentation," she admitted. "You looked... complete. In a way you never did here."

They discussed practical transitions, Claire would continue consulting on key accounts remotely for a few more weeks, would help train her replacement, and would remain connected to the agency she had helped build. But the decision was final. Her life and work would center in Naples now, with Luca.

"Be happy, Claire," Susan said as they prepared to end the call. "That's all any of us are really looking for."

Later that evening, Claire and Luca rode their Vespa down to Naples harbor. As they walked along the harbor, they could feel the February air carrying hints of approaching spring. The water rippled against ancient stones, each wave a serenade of continuity against Naples' enduring shoreline. Street lamps cast pools of amber light, where the promenade looked like a pathway guiding them forward into their shared future.

"I feel lighter," Claire admitted, her hand nestled in Luca's as naturally as if their fingers had been designed as complementary pieces. "Like I've been carrying two separate identities for so long that I forgot how much energy it consumed."

Luca's eyes found hers in the interplay of shadow and light. "Sometimes the heaviest burdens are the ones we don't realize we're carrying until we set them down."

They paused at a small lookout point, the bay spread before them in darkened splendor, distant lights from boats and shoreline buildings creating constellations against the night. Naples breathed around them, a living entity composed of ancient stone, human passion, artistic heritage, and unending cycles of evolution.

"Originally, I came here to escape," Claire reflected, her voice soft against the backdrop of waves. "To heal from a broken marriage, to find pieces of myself I'd forgotten existed. I never imagined..."

"That you would find a new home?" Luca completed when her words trailed into silence.

Claire turned to face him fully, the city lights illuminating half her face while shadow cloaked the other, perfect visual metaphor for the journey she'd undergone. "That I would find myself. Not the version of Claire Bennett that existed to meet others' expectations, but the artist who had been waiting all along, the woman who could love without fear of disappearing."

Luca's expression held such profound understanding that Claire felt momentarily breathless. He had witnessed her metamorphosis from beginning to end, had provided space for her to unfold without imposing his own expectations, had trusted her to find her way back to both art and love on her own terms.

"Elisabetta wants us to begin concepts for next year's collection in April," he said, his fingers slowly caressing the delicate valleys between her knuckles. "Marcello from the National Gallery told me about possibly having an exhibition at the Venice Biennale. It's one of the most prestigious art festivals that's been running for a very long time."

"And there's that commission for the Milan hospital's new pediatric wing," Claire added, the previously overwhelming options now feeling like exhilarating possibilities rather than anxious choices.

"Also I briefly read the three emails we have received, asking for important events happening with some influential Italian families who saw our art piece at the wedding," Luca mused. "So many paths opening before us. All of them were leading forward together." He said, his free hand gesturing toward the infinite horizon where sea and sky merged in seamless darkness.

As they rode their Vespa back to Luca's apartment, Naples embraced them with a familiar welcome, the scent of night-blooming jasmine mingling with distant cooking aromas, the musical cadence of

Italian conversations spilling from open windows, the eternal presence of history all around them. Claire felt something settle into place within her chest, like the final piece of a complex puzzle finding its home.

The decision had been made. Not in a single dramatic moment, but through the accumulated weight of countless small choices, each one drawing her closer to this city, this man, this life that had revealed itself one layer at a time, like an artwork gradually emerging from the artist's vision.

As Luca unlocked the door to his apartment, their apartment now, in all practical senses if not yet official designation, Claire felt the familiar sensation of crossing a threshold that represented more than mere physical space. Inside awaited not just the comfortable arrangement of furniture and art they had gradually integrated, but the future they were crafting together one brushstroke at a time.

"What are you thinking?" Luca asked as he moved to open the balcony doors, allowing the night air to fill the space with its particular Naples magic.

Claire joined him there, the city spread before them like a living canvas. "I'm thinking about how places change us," she said softly. "It's been ten months since I arrived in Naples. How Naples has transformed me by giving me permission to be myself."

Luca's eyes softened, a tender smile playing at the corners of his mouth. "I have something for you." The weight of his words hung in the air between them, imbued with significance that made her heart quicken. He moved away briefly, crossing to the living room where he pulled open a drawer. When he returned, his palm remained closed, concealing whatever treasure he'd retrieved.

"Open your hand," he whispered, his voice barely audible above the distant melody of the city. When she complied, he placed something cool and metallic against her skin. Claire looked down and her breath caught. It was the key to his apartment.

"Only if you're ready for it," he said, his voice threaded with vulnerability and hope.

Tears welled in Claire's eyes as she closed her fingers around the key, feeling its edges press into her palm, tangible, real, permanent. "I am," she whispered, the simple words carrying the weight of her complete surrender to this love, this place, this life they'd created. "With all my heart."

They stood embraced on the balcony, silent in their tender communion as Naples sparkled below them, its nighttime symphony continuing around them, each component separate yet harmonious, much like the relationship they had built between American practicality and Italian passion.

Tomorrow would bring new projects, new challenges, new opportunities to create together. But tonight was for appreciation of the journey completed, from fragmented existence to integrated wholeness, from temporary escape to permanent home.

In the distance, church bells rang out the hour, echoing through the city like ancient whispers. Claire closed her eyes, letting the sound wash over her, feeling Luca's heartbeat against her back, steady, certain, home.

11

THE ART OF FOREVER

Three months after making the decision to stay in Naples permanently, Claire stood on the balcony of Luca's apartment, watching gray clouds cast over Naples. During those months, she had shared countless video calls with her family back home, her sister Kate, who had initially been skeptical but quickly warmed to the idea; her parents, whose concern gradually transformed into understanding; and her grandmother, who surprised everyone by declaring that "true love and purpose should never be abandoned." The conversations hadn't been easy at first, with her family struggling to understand why she would choose a life so far from everything familiar. But as they witnessed the light in Claire's eyes when she spoke of her new life, the passion that infused her voice when discussing her art, they began to accept that her happiness and sense of fulfillment mattered most. When Claire finally introduced Luca to them, his charm and obvious devotion to Claire had won them over completely. They bonded over stories of Claire's childhood, sharing laughter and creating the first tender threads of connection.

Today, the weather perfectly matched her mood, unsettled yet contemplative, as scattered across the floor around them lay dozens of glossy real estate brochures, each representing another disappointment in their search for the perfect gallery space.

"I can't believe we haven't found a single place that feels right," she sighed, pressing her palm against the cool balcony railings. "Everything's either too sterile, too commercial, or completely wrong for displaying art properly."

Luca looked up from the latest rejection, a space near the harbor that seemed promising until they discovered the humidity issues that would damage their artwork. The afternoon light caught the angles of his face as he pushed aside yet another brochure.

"Perhaps we're approaching this all wrong," he said, rising to join her on the balcony. "Perhaps the perfect space isn't waiting to be discovered in these listings. Perhaps it already exists in our lives."

Claire turned toward him, curiosity flickering across her features. "What do you mean?"

A moment of silence stretched between them as Luca seemed to consider something, his expression shifting through contemplation to something approaching revelation.

"I showed you my grandmother's villa once, remember? It was on a hill." His voice carried notes of memory and hesitation mixed in equal parts.

Claire's expression brightened immediately. "The villa with the terrace overlooking that incredible view! Luca, why haven't we considered it before now?"

The memory unfurled between them. It was the sprawling vintage Mediterranean-style villa nestled into the hillside above Naples, its stone walls weathered by generations of sun and wind, the garden filled with ancient cypress trees and fragrant herbs that released their scents. Claire had visited it only once during their early days together, when Luca had his cousin Marco fill the villa with candlelight. That night, Luca had prepared a sumptuous meal in the rustic kitchen. They had spent the night there, dancing to the melodies of night birds and making love among hundreds of flickering candlelights.

"It's been sitting empty since Nonna passed away a few years ago," Luca explained, running a hand through his hair. "I've been paying someone to maintain the grounds, but I haven't been able to... decide what to do with it."

Claire understood immediately. The villa represented more than property, it embodied memories of the grandmother who had raised him after his mother's death, who had encouraged his artistic pursuits when others had suggested more practical paths.

"Tell me about her," Claire said softly, taking his hand and leading him to the sofa, away from the discarded brochures and disappointments.

Luca's eyes took on that particular distance that appeared whenever he spoke of beloved memories. "Nonna Eleonora was... magnificent. Not in a grand way, but in the details. She noticed everything, how the evening light struck the lemon trees differently than the morning light, how certain herbs complemented each other in both the garden and the kitchen." His fingertips wove unspoken feelings against Claire's forearm as he spoke.

"It was Nonna who first put a paintbrush in my mother's hand when she was just a girl. She saw something in her that others missed. My mother had this ability to capture not just how something looked, but how it felt to be in that moment. Nonna nurtured that gift, spending hours teaching her techniques passed down through generations."

"Our Sunday visits to Nonna's home as a family were my favorite childhood memories, she would sit me on her lap and describe painting, not in technical terms but in emotional ones. She would tell me how a painting makes you feel the ocean breeze on your face. Things like that."

Claire could almost see the scene. There was a small dark-haired boy entranced by his grandmother's stories, the seed of artistic appreciation taking root. "She sounds remarkable."

"She was," Luca continued, his voice warming with reminiscence. "I lost my dad when I was very young. Then my mother passed away when I was a teenager. Nonna became my anchor. She never tried to replace Mamma, but she created space for both grief and joy to coexist." He paused, swallowing hard. "The villa was always filled with visitors, artists, musicians, writers, people who created beauty in different forms. She believed that creativity needed community to truly flourish."

Claire squeezed his hand gently. "Like what we've been trying to envision for our gallery space."

"Exactly," Luca nodded, smiling as the idea took clearer form. "The villa has multiple rooms that"ow into each other, that central hall withthe perfect natural light..." He trailed off.

Luca stood suddenly, renewed energy animating his movements. "We could honor her legacy by transforming it into a place where art and community converge, exactly what she cherished most."

Sunlight pierced through dissipating gray clouds, casting dramatic rays across the city below, nature's own theatrical curtain rising in their new direction. Claire felt a flush of excitement sweep through her as they began planning the villa's renewal unfolding with each passing moment.

"We could visit tomorrow," Luca suggested, his hands gesturing with the passionate emphasis that emerged whenever creative inspiration struck. "We need to see it through new eyes, our eyes, to imagine what it could become."

That night, Claire lay awake beside Luca, her mind racing with thoughts of the renovated villa. She imagined exhibition spaces bathed in that perfect Mediterranean light, visitors moving through rooms where art would converse with architecture centuries old, conversations flowing from gallery to garden as naturally as the air currents through open windows.

More than just a professional space, the villa represented a deeper commitment, to Naples, to their shared artistic vision, and to each other. As Luca slept beside her, his breathing deep and even, Claire realized they weren't just planning a gallery; they were crafting the next chapter of their life together.

The villa revealed itself differently in the morning than Claire remembered. Larger, more dignified, yet somehow more welcoming too. As Luca unlocked the massive wooden door, its ancient hinges protesting slightly, she felt as though they were being granted entry into a realm suspended between past and future.

Inside, sunbeams streamed through tall windows, illuminating rooms that had been waiting patiently for their return. Despite the covered furniture and quiet stillness, the villa didn't feel abandoned, merely paused, as if holding its breath for what would come next.

Luca moved through the space with the curious mixture of familiarity and rediscovery, pulling back heavy drapes to allow more sunshine to flood the rooms. "Nonna always said the villa had its own personality," he said. "Stubborn and proud like all the women in our family."

They spent the entire day exploring, room by room, discussing how each space might transform while respecting its original character. The central hall with its soaring ceiling and marble floors would become the main gallery, its natural light perfect for displaying their three-dimensional works. The adjacent sitting room with its intricate moldings would house more profound exhibitions, perhaps dedicated to emerging artists they wanted to support.

As they climbed the sweeping staircase to the second floor, Claire noticed how Luca's footsteps automatically avoided the places where the wood might creak, childhood knowledge embedded in muscle memory. Upstairs, they discovered bedrooms that could become smaller gallery spaces or studios, each with its own distinctive view of the surrounding landscape.

"And this," Luca said, opening double doors at the end of the corridor, "was my favorite room."

Claire stepped into what had clearly been a library, its walls lined with built-in shelves that stretched from floor to ceiling. A massive desk occupied one corner, positioned to take advantage of the spectacular view through French doors that opened onto a small balcony.

"This is where Nonna would write her letters and manage the villa's affairs," Luca explained. "But for me, it was magical because of what she kept here."

He crossed to one of the shelves and ran his hand lovingly across the empty wood. "Art books. Hundreds of them. Biographies of masters, catalogs from exhibitions around the world, essays on technique and interpretation. When I was a boy, I would sit cross-legged on that rug and lose myself for hours."

Claire could picture him there, a serious child with intense eyes absorbing images that would shape his artistic sensibility. "This should be your office," she said immediately. "Where you can work on commissions and put your own books."

They continued their exploration, finding unexpected treasures; a hidden alcove beneath the stairs, perfect for displaying smaller sculptures; a pantry with original tile work that had somehow missed centuries of renovation; shutters painted in faded blue that precisely matched the distant sea visible from the terrace.

When they finally reached the kitchen, Claire understood why this had been the heart of the villa. Sprawling yet somehow intimate, it featured a massive hearth fireplace, expansive countertops worn smooth by generations of cooking, and a wall of windows that opened onto the backyard, bringing the outdoors in. A long wooden table, clearly designed for gathering many people, occupied the center of the space.

"This wouldn't work as a traditional gallery space," Claire mused, running her hand along the weathered table. "But I can imagine something else entirely."

Luca watched her, curiosity evident in his expression. "Tell me."

"What if we created a café here?" Claire suggested excitement building as the concept formed. "Not just a commercial addition, but a space that embodies the same values as our gallery, community, connection, artistic appreciation."

She moved through the kitchen, gesturing as she spoke. "Small tables here by the windows, the counter along that wall, perhaps displaying Lucia's pastries like edible art beneath glass domes."

A slow smile spread across Luca's face as he caught the direction of her thinking. "And coffee service that honors tradition through execution, not pretension. Signor Rossi would appreciate that approach."

"Do you think they might be interested?" Claire asked. "In establishing a small café here, providing the pastries and training staff on proper coffee preparation?"

"We could ask them," Luca replied, his imagination clearly engaged.

"They've mentioned wanting to expand beyond the original café, but never found the right opportunity. This could be perfect, connected to our gallery but with its own identity."

By late afternoon, they stood on the terrace, the entire villa mapped out in their minds, potential renovations discussed, challenges identified. The sun hung low over the distant horizon, bathing everything in that distinctive Naples saffron haze that had first captivated Claire's artistic instincts.

"What would we call it?" she asked, leaning against the stone balustrade. "The gallery, I mean. It needs a name that honors your grandmother's legacy while representing our art."

Luca considered this, his expression thoughtful as he gazed out over the landscape his family had called home for generations. "Casa dei Sogni (House of Dreams)," he said finally, the Italian flowing from his lips like music.

"It's perfect. I absolutely love it," Claire agreed, the name resonating immediately. "Because that's what art is, isn't it? Dreams made tangible through creative vision."

He kissed her enthusiasm, the broad smile on her lips.

As they locked up the villa that evening, Claire felt a curious sense of rightness, as if the building itself had approved their plans. The universe had delivered not just a gallery space but a home for their artistic souls, a place where past and future could coexist in creative harmony.

The renovation unfolded in stages, each revealing more about the villa's character and history. Workers uncovered original frescoes beneath layers of more modern wallpaper, found handcrafted tiles hidden under mid-century flooring, and restored wooden beams that had been concealed by dropped ceilings installed decades ago.

Claire spent hours each day on-site, directing the flow of gallery spaces, preserving architectural elements while creating contemporary exhibition areas. Her background in design proved invaluable as she navigated the balance between honoring the villa's heritage and creating functional spaces for displaying art.

"The lighting needs to be adjustable here," she explained to the electrician, pointing to the central hall's ceiling. "Art changes throughout the day as the angle of the sun shifts, but we need to maintain consistent lighting for evening events."

Luca handled practical details with local contractors, many of whom had known his grandmother. These relationships proved invaluable; the stoneworker who remembered repairing the terrace steps when Luca was just a boy took particular care with the entrance renovation; the carpenter whose father had built the library shelves crafted display pedestals that echoed their elegant joinery.

"Your nonna would be pleased," the elderly tiler told Luca one afternoon as they uncovered a decorative border in one of the corridors. "She always said this house needed young hearts to keep it alive."

The kitchen overhaul became a particular focus once Lucia and Signor Rossi enthusiastically agreed to establish a small café in the space. They visited regularly during renovation, offering suggestions that balanced operational needs with aesthetic considerations.

"We'll train the staff and I'll personally visit every other day," Signor Rossi promised, his eyes gleaming with excitement as the copper espresso machine was installed. "Every coffee will reflect the same standard as Caffè Sereno; proper extraction, correct temperature, perfect crema."

Lucia, meanwhile, designed a display case that would showcase her pastries while complementing the overall design aesthetic. "Each morning, freshly baked cornetti, bomboloni, and sfogliatelle will arrive from our kitchen," she explained, her hands moving expressively as she described the rotation of offerings. "And special tortes for afternoon visitors, perhaps almond with seasonal fruit, or my chocolate hazelnut that pairs so beautifully with an afternoon espresso."

They developed a menu that celebrated the full spectrum of Neapolitan coffee traditions: velvety cappuccino available only until eleven (honoring Italian custom); robust espresso with its perfect crema;

decadent caffè con panna topped with freshly whipped cream; aromatic caffè corretto with its whisper of grappa; refreshing shakerato for warm afternoons; and, of course, caffè sospeso; the suspended coffee tradition that had first connected Claire and Luca.

One evening, after the workers had departed, Claire found Luca standing in what had been his grandmother's bedroom, now changed into a gallery space dedicated to local artists. Sunset streamed through the windows, casting long shadows across the newly installed wooden floors.

"Are you okay?" she asked softly, coming to stand beside him.

He nodded, wrapping an arm around her shoulders. "Just remembering. Nonna would sit in that corner and tell me stories about Naples when she was young, the artists who visited, the music that played in the piazzas, the way the city rebuilt itself after the war."

Claire leaned against him. "She's still here, in a way. In how you describe the quality of light at different hours, in how you insist on preserving the original door hardware, in a thousand details that might seem insignificant to others but carry her influence."

"That's why Casa dei Sogni feels so right," Luca replied. "Not just as a name but as a continuation. Dreams don't end; they transform and find new expression through different dreamers."

For two months, the old villa had been alive with the sounds of transformation, hammers echoing through marble hallways, scaffolding erected against weathered facades, and the constant murmur of craftsmen debating techniques long forgotten.

Five weeks before their planned opening, the renovation reached a critical phase in what had once been Luca's mother's studio, a small room adjacent to the library that received northern light perfect for painting. Workers had noted unusual acoustics in the space, sound reflecting differently than architectural plans would suggest.

"There's something strange about this wall," the foreman explained, tapping the plaster. "It doesn't appear on the original plans, and the echo indicates a void behind it."

Luca frowned, studying the wall with newfound attention. "My mother remodeled this space when I was about twelve or thirteen. I remember the construction, but I was too young to understand what they were doing."

After careful inspection, they confirmed the presence of a false wall that had been professionally constructed and seamlessly integrated with the original architecture. Luca gave permission to open it, curious to find out what's behind it.

Workers proceeded with careful precision, creating a small opening first to ensure nothing would be damaged. When they widened the hole enough to see inside, their flashlight beams revealed what appeared to be the edges of framed canvases, carefully wrapped and protected.

"Stop," Luca commanded, his voice suddenly tight. "I'll do the rest myself."

Claire recognized the emotion flooding his features, shock mingled with anticipation and a deep, almost reverential caution. This was no ordinary discovery; this was a connection to the mother he had lost at fourteen, the woman whose artistic influence had shaped his earliest understanding of creative expression.

When the workers had departed, leaving tools for Luca to continue himself, Claire stood back, allowing him space for this profoundly personal moment. He worked methodically, widening the opening with careful hands until he could access what lay beyond.

One by one, he removed wrapped canvases from their hiding place, dozens of them, each carefully preserved against time and elements. With trembling fingers, he unwrapped the first painting, and Claire heard his sharp intake of breath as his mother's work revealed itself after decades of concealment.

The painting captured a seaside scene, but rendered with such emotional intensity that it transcended mere landscape. Vibrant blues collided with sunset oranges, brush strokes visible and passionate, creating movement that made the frozen moment feel alive. A signature at the bottom right corner. It read Isabella Castellano. Claire could recognize the distinctive style. The same confident energy lived in Luca's work, though expressed through different techniques.

"She was truly a virtuoso, with talent entering the realm of genius," Claire exclaimed, moved by the artwork. He nodded, unable to speak as he unwrapped another canvas, then another. Each revealed a different subject, landscapes, still lifes, portraits, but all executed with the same passionate approach to color and form. The collection represented a comprehensive body of work that had remained hidden for more than two decades.

As Luca removed the last canvas, something else came with it, an envelope, yellowed with age, sealed with wax and addressed simply: "For Luca, when the time is right."

Claire immediately recognized the significance of this moment. "I'll give you privacy," she said quietly, moving toward the door.

Luca caught her hand, his eyes glistening with unshed tears. "Stay. Please. Whatever message she left... I want to share it with you."

With meticulous care, he broke the wax seal and withdrew several pages covered in elegant handwriting. The paper carried a faint scent of oil paint, preserved within the sealed envelope for all these years.

Claire sat beside him on the floor, surrounded by his mother's paintings, as he began to read the letter, wiping tears away. The words were Italian at first, a private conversation between him and the pages. Then, his voice softened with veneration, he translated for Claire, each word carrying the weight of emotion, his voice occasionally breaking as the grief washed over him.

"My dearest Luca,

If you are reading this, you have discovered the paintings I've hidden behind the studio wall. I sense my time in this world grows short, though doctors speak of treatments and recovery. A mother knows when she must prepare to leave her child, even one as strong and remarkable as you.

These paintings represent my heart's work, not those commissioned or created to please others, but those born from my deepest artistic truth. I've sheltered these pieces as a private testament, meant to reach across time when I no longer can, revealing themselves only when you were prepared to understand their meaning. I made Nonna promise never to mention their existence to you.

My beloved son, art is the language of souls. Through it, we express what words cannot contain. I've watched you drawing and painting since you could hold a pencil, and I recognize in you the same need to translate the world through creative vision.

Trust this gift you have, Luca. It will bring challenges, moments of doubt, periods when inspiration seems to abandon you, people who will not understand why you must create. But it will also bring joy beyond measure, connections that transcend ordinary experience, and a life rich with beauty both seen and unseen.

My greatest hope is that you will someday share your artistic journey with someone who understands your soul. True beauty emerges not from isolation but from authentic connection, when one creative heart recognizes another and together they see the world anew.

The path of an artist is never straight or simple, but it is infinitely worth walking. Know that wherever I am, I watch your journey with pride and love beyond expression.

All my love, Mamma"

When Luca finished reading, silence filled the room, not empty but charged with emotion too profound for immediate expression. Outside, evening birds called to one another, oblivious to the human drama unfolding within these walls. Inside, mother and son communicated across decades through art and written words, the distance between life and death momentarily bridged.

Without hesitation, Claire moved closer, wrapping her arms around Luca's trembling shoulders as they sat amidst the kaleidoscope of his mother's paintings. Her embrace formed a sanctuary where his vulnerability could safely unfurl, her heartbeat a steady rhythm against the chaos of his grief. As tears traced silver paths down his cheeks, she held him tighter, her touch saying what words couldn't, that she was here, wholly present, a witness to his pain and a keeper of this sacred moment between them.

When he finally looked up, his expression had changed, grief still present but accompanied by a profound peace, as if a question long unanswered had finally found resolution.

"She knew," he said with a sort of wonder in his voice. "Somehow she knew someone like you would come into my life."

He handed Claire the letter, his finger pointing to the passage: "My greatest hope is that you will someday share your artistic journey with someone who understands your soul."

"She was writing about artistic collaboration," Claire said gently, not wanting to presume too much.

Luca shook his head, certainty in his gaze. "No. She was writing about love. About finding someone who speaks the same language, not just of art but of the heart. She was writing about you, Claire, even before I knew to look for you."

In that moment, surrounded by his mother's hidden masterpieces and bathed in the evening light she had once loved to capture, Claire understood that the gallery they were creating had gained another dimension of meaning. It would not just be their artistic home but a sacred space where Isabella's legacy would live on, where the son would honor mother through the universal language of creative expression.

"We should create a permanent exhibition space for her work," Claire suggested. "A large room dedicated to her paintings, where visitors can experience her distinct style."

Luca nodded, already envisioning it. "We'll call it 'Isabella's Light' – because that's what she brought to everything she created. Light... and life... and limitless love."

As they carefully cataloged each painting, organizing them by apparent chronology and subject matter, Claire witnessed Luca processing emotions that transcended simple grief or joy. This unexpected connection to his mother, this artistic conversation continuing beyond death, seemed to heal something long fractured in his relationship with his own creative identity.

"I always wondered why I felt drawn to certain colors, certain techniques I'd never been formally taught," he explained as they worked. "Now I see her influence was always there, guiding my hand even in her absence."

That night, as they drove back to their apartment, the car filled with comfortable silence, Claire realized they had received more than paintings. They had been granted another layer of foundation for Casa dei Sogni, a spiritual inheritance that would infuse every aspect of the gallery with authentic emotion and artistic integrity.

Two weeks before opening brought intensifying activity as separate elements began converging into a cohesive whole. Claire immersed herself in curating the inaugural exhibition, selecting works that would establish Casa dei Sogni's artistic vision while honoring the villa's unique character.

Luca divided his attention between gallery preparations and the projects they had already committed to.

Agostina from Bottega dei Colori, the art supply store, became an unexpected cornerstone of their transformation, volunteering to help and arriving each afternoon with her silver-streaked hair twisted into an elegant knot, her expert eyes scrutinizing every surface with the precision of someone who understood the soul of spaces. "Before I sold art supplies, I restored three galleries in Milan," she revealed, her eyes crinkling with memories as she ran weathered fingertips across the villa's walls. "These structures breathe differently than modern buildings, they require materials that honor their history while supporting contemporary art." She advised the renovation team for hours, guiding them in creating custom color washes that enhanced rather than competed with displayed artwork, her whispered instructions creating subtle transitions between exhibition spaces that guided visitors through visual narratives without disrupting their experience. In the room dedicated to Isabella's paintings, Agostina directed them to apply a particular mineral-based finish that responded differently to changing light throughout the day...". Just as her brushwork does," she explained to Luca, who embraced her, tears threatening to spill from his eyes.

In the kitchen-turned-café, Signor Rossi supervised installation of professional equipment with meticulous attention to detail. He tested water temperature, pressure settings, and grind consistency with scientific precision, ensuring each variable was optimized for creating perfect coffee.

"Watch carefully," he instructed the staff he personally selected, demonstrating proper tamping technique. "Too much pressure flattens the grounds and creates channels where water flows too quickly. Too little prevents proper extraction. It must be precise."

His demonstrations transformed routine preparation into performance art; the careful weighing of freshly ground beans, the graceful movement as he distributed them evenly in the portafilter, the practiced twist as he locked it into the machine. Each step executed with reverence for tradition and respect for ingredients.

Meanwhile, Lucia made sure that the display for her pastries harmonized with the gallery's visual language. Elegant glass domes protected precious creations while allowing full visual appreciation of their artistry. Each morning during final preparations, she delivered sample pastries, using the renovation team's reactions to refine her opening day selection.

"Art nourishes the soul," she explained, arranging miniature cannoli with the same precision a jeweler might employ with precious gems. "But the body requires more substantial sustenance. When visitors pause here between gallery sections, they should experience pleasure that engages all senses."

In the final week before opening day, artworks arrived from various collections, pieces Luca had created before their collaboration, works they'd produced together, and a selection of commissioned pieces that represented significant moments in their artistic journey. Each required careful installation, precise lighting, and thoughtful contextual information.

The "Isabella's Light" room received particular attention, with Luca personally overseeing every detail. He curated eleven paintings, his love of prime numbers like eleven, divisible only by itself and one, influencing his selection. These paintings, when arranged chronologically to demonstrate her artistic evolution, represented the full spectrum of his mother's talent. The final painting, a self-portrait Isabella had completed shortly before her illness, occupied the room's central position, her eyes seeming to follow visitors with maternal watchfulness.

Invitations had been sent to key figures in the art world, local community members who had supported their renovation efforts, and friends who had been part of their journey. The response had been overwhelmingly positive, with international critics adjusting travel schedules to attend what was being described as "the most significant artistic opening in Naples this decade."

The evening before their opening, after final preparations were complete and staff had departed, Claire and Luca found themselves alone in the silent gallery. Moonlight streamed through tall windows, creating silver pathways across marble floors and illuminating their artwork with ethereal gentleness.

They walked through each space slowly, imagining tomorrow's unveiling. In the main gallery, their collaborative pieces created visual conversations across the room, three-dimensional narratives that invited viewers to move around them, experiencing different perspectives with each step.

They paused longest in "Isabella's Light", Luca standing before his mother's self-portrait with quiet adoration. The moonlight caught the painting's vibrant colors, somehow enhancing rather than diminishing them, bringing out subtleties that daylight might overshadow.

"Mamma, this is Claire, love of my life," he said softly, putting his arm around Claire's shoulders, trying to keep emotions under control.

Claire felt a tidal wave of tenderness crashing through her. The portrait's eyes, so like Luca's, seemed to see straight through to her soul, weighing and accepting her in a single painted gaze. Her throat tightened as she leaned into Luca's embrace, feeling the slight tremor in his arm, the unsteady rise and fall of his chest against her shoulder. This moment, this sacred introduction across the veil between worlds, felt more profound than anything she had ever experienced.

"I wish I could have known her," Claire said, trying to imagine the woman who had raised such a remarkable son, whose artistic passion had flowed through generations.

"In some ways, you do know her," Luca countered. "Through my memories, through her paintings, through the creative perspective she instilled in me. And I think she knows you too, somehow, through the letter she left, as if she glimpsed you coming into my life long before we met."

They continued their moonlit tour, eventually reaching the café where Lucia's display cases stood ready for tomorrow's pastries and Signor Rossi's coffee equipment gleamed with polished perfection. The space captured exactly what they'd envisioned, not just commercial addition but integral part of the gallery experience, where art appreciation could be accompanied by sensory pleasure.

Outside on the terrace, Naples spread before them, city lights mirroring the star-scattered sky above. The garden below, carefully restored with native Mediterranean plants, released evening-scented fragrances that drifted upward on the breeze.

"When I first came to Naples," Claire reflected, leaning against the ancient stone balustrade, "I was running away, from a failed marriage, from professional constraints, from a life that had grown too small for my spirit. I never imagined I'd find... everything."

Luca stood beside her, their shoulders touching in comfortable familiarity. "And what is 'everything' to you now?" he asked, with genuine curiosity in his voice.

Claire considered this, gathering her thoughts before answering. "Artistic fulfillment, certainly, the freedom to create without compromise, to follow vision rather than market expectations. Professional success beyond what I'd ever thought possible." She turned to face him fully, moonlight silvering his features. "But most importantly, a partnership that enhances rather than diminishes who I am. You've never asked me to be less, Luca. You've only ever encouraged me to be more fully myself."

Something shifted in his expression. There was a deepening of emotion, a certainty taking clearer form. He took her hands in his, his touch warm against the night's gentle coolness.

"Tomorrow," he said softly, "everything changes again. Casa dei Sogni opens its doors, and our private artistry becomes public offering. Are you ready?"

The question held layers of meaning beyond the gallery's opening, nuances Claire couldn't quite decipher but felt resonating through her entire being. "Yes," she answered simply. "I'm ready for whatever comes next."

His smile held secrets and promises as they locked the gallery and headed home, both carrying anticipation for tomorrow's unveiling like precious cargo.

Opening day dawned with perfect clarity, the August sky stretching above Naples in uninterrupted azure. Claire woke early, nervous energy propelling her through morning rituals with meticulous attention. Each choice felt weighted with significance; the dress selected to complement the gallery's aesthetic while remaining comfortable for a day of meeting visitors; jewelry chosen for artistic statement rather than conventional elegance; shoes that would allow her to stand comfortably through endless hours while still harmonizing perfectly with her carefully curated ensemble.

"You're overthinking," she told her reflection, recognizing the familiar pattern of channeling anxiety into controllable details. This was more than a professional milestone, it was the physical manifestation of everything she and Luca had built together, the tangible evidence of choices made and directions taken.

She and Luca arrived at Casa dei Sogni together two hours before the official opening. Despite the early hour, they found Lucia and

Signor Rossi already at work in the café, the intoxicating aroma of freshly ground coffee beans intertwining with the sweet scent of butter and sugar from Lucia's pastries.

"We couldn't wait," Lucia explained with a bright smile, arranging a perfect display of delicate biscotti, a last-minute change from the original miniature cannoli. Her hands moved with the precision of someone creating art rather than food. "This day has been in my dreams for weeks. And we know how important it is for both of you."

Signor Rossi emerged from behind the gleaming copper espresso machine, satisfaction radiating from his expression. "Water temperature and pressure, perfetto (perfect)!" He embraced both Claire and Luca warmly. "First impressions in art, as in coffee, are everything. Today, both will be outstanding."

Claire squeezed Luca's hand, overwhelmed by the dedication of these people who had become far more than business associates. The four of them toured the café space together, Signor Rossi explaining the particular blends he would serve to complement the different exhibition areas.

As Claire and Luca moved through the gallery completing final preparations, Claire marveled at how seamlessly she and Luca worked together, adjusting lighting in certain areas, ensuring printed materials were properly placed, briefing staff on greeting procedures. There was a beautiful synchronicity to their movements, each anticipating the other's needs without words.

"Nervous?" Luca asked softly, catching her hand as they finished the final walkthrough.

Claire considered the question. "Not nervous exactly. More like standing on the edge of something magnificent, about to leap." She gazed around the gallery. What was once intangible had been made tangible through months of work. "Everything feels exactly right."

Luca's eyes held a curious intensity as he nodded. "Yes," he agreed, his voice carrying an undercurrent she couldn't quite identify. "Everything is exactly as it should be."

The first visitors arrived early, art critics eager for privileged first views, followed by local dignitaries who had supported the project, then a steady stream of gallery owners, collectors, and art enthusiasts. Claire and Luca greeted each one personally, moving through the growing crowd with practiced grace, their professional expertise guiding them through introductions and explanations.

"The integration of historical architecture with contemporary exhibition design is masterful," commented a prominent museum curator, making notes as they toured the main gallery. "The juxtaposition creates dialogue not just between artworks but between past and present."

Claire explained their conceptual approach, the choices they'd made to honor the villa's character while creating functional display spaces. Throughout these conversations, she noticed how Luca stayed close, their professional rapport flowing naturally as they completed each other's thoughts and built upon shared ideas.

About ninety minutes after opening, when Casa dei Sogni hummed with appreciative conversation and the steady flow of movement between rooms, Luca gently touched Claire's elbow.

"I'd like to show you something," he said, his voice carrying that same curious undertone she'd noticed earlier. "In Isabella's Light."

Claire nodded, excusing herself from a conversation with a local arts reporter. As they moved through the gallery, she noticed Luca making subtle gestures to certain staff members who responded with almost imperceptible nods.

The room dedicated to his mother's artwork stood apart from the rest of the gallery, not just physically but atmospherically. Isabella's eleven paintings created a narrative journey around the space, culminating in the self-portrait that occupied the central position. Unlike the other gallery spaces, which buzzed with conversation and movement, this room held a hallowed quality, visitors speaking in hushed tones as they absorbed the power of work hidden for decades.

As they entered, Claire was surprised to find the room temporarily empty of visitors. Luca guided her to stand before his mother's self-portrait, positioning her so she faced the painting directly. Isabella's eyes seemed to look through her, wise and knowing.

"This room," Luca began, his voice soft yet somehow filling the space completely, "represents more than my mother's art. It embodies the concept of legacy, how we pass not just objects but emotions through generations. How love never truly disappears but transforms."

Claire turned slightly to look at him, struck by the profound emotion in his expression. Before she could respond, the lights in the room began to dim gradually, not to darkness but to a twilight illumination. Simultaneously, tiny pinpricks of light appeared across the ceiling, thousands of delicate fairy lights that had been hidden within the architecture, now revealing themselves like stars emerging at dusk.

"Luca, what..." she began, but fell silent as the string quartet they had hired began playing from the doorway. The melody unfurled, instantly recognizable, that Italian love song which had accompanied their dance beneath a canopy of stars in the winery gardens during Angelica and Gregory's wedding reception.

With startling clarity, Claire understood that something extraordinary was unfolding. The room had been reborn into a celestial canvas, the twinkling lights above casting gentle radiance across Isabella's paintings and across Luca's face as he moved to stand directly in front of her.

"Claire," he said, taking both her hands in his. "When I lost my mother, I thought certain forms of love were behind me forever, the kind of love that sees you completely, that understands the language your soul speaks without translation."

He paused, his eyes never leaving hers. "Then you walked into my life fifteen months ago, and something changed in the universe. Through suspended coffees and shared canvases, through conversations that lasted until dawn and silences that needed no words to fill them, you reawakened parts of me I thought were dormant forever."

Claire felt emotion rising like a tide within her as Luca continued. "The day after we discovered my mother's paintings, the renovation team found something else in that hidden room, a small wooden box containing her jewelry." His voice softened further. "Among those pieces was this."

With a graceful movement, Luca lowered himself to one knee. The gesture, so traditional yet so unexpected, sent waves of emotion surging through Claire. From his pocket, he withdrew a ring that captured the lights above, refracting them into countless brilliant points.

"This was my mother's ring," he explained, holding it between them. The ring was exquisite, an antique band with intricate detailing that spoke of craftsmanship from another era, centered with a brilliant diamond surrounded by smaller diamonds that seemed to dance with living light.

Claire felt tears forming, her vision blurring slightly as overwhelming emotion welled up from depths she hadn't known existed within her.

"I want to share everything with you, each sunrise and sunset, each moment of brilliant inspiration and creative doubt, each quiet Sunday morning and vibrant celebration. Claire Bennett, love of my life, will you marry me?" Luca asked, his voice steady despite the emotion evident in his eyes.

The question hung in the air between them like the most perfectly composed note. Claire felt as though her entire existence had been leading to this precise moment; every choice, every challenge, every brave decision culminating in this single point in time.

"Yes," she gasped, the word emerging as naturally as breathing. Then louder, so it filled the room entirely: "Yes, Luca. A million times yes."

As he slipped the ring onto her finger, Claire marveled at how perfectly it settled against her skin, as if it had been crafted for her alone. When Luca rose to his feet and drew her into his arms, their kiss felt like the beginning of a new artistic period, one defined not by technique or style but by the fusion of two creative souls.

The sound of applause broke their embrace, slow at first, then swelling to fill the room. As Luca's arm settled around her waist, Claire's thoughts turned unexpectedly to her family. They were thousands of miles away in Ohio. Her fingers found the cool silver of grandma's locket against her collarbone, its familiar weight a bridge between worlds. She wished they could have witnessed this moment, could see the wondrous life she had built, could meet the remarkable man who had just promised to share his future with her.

The thought had barely formed when she felt a tap on her shoulder from behind. Turning, Claire found herself facing an impossible sight. It was her sister Kate, eyes brimming with barely contained emotion.

"Surprise," Kate announced, voice cracking with joy.

Claire stood frozen, her mind struggling to process this reality. And then she saw them, standing just behind Kate were her parents and grandmother, their expressions a beautiful mixture of joy, pride, and barely restrained tears.

"You're all here," Claire managed, disbelief coloring every syllable. "How are you here?"

Kate laughed, the sound bright with affection as she threw her arms around Claire. "We wouldn't miss this for anything in the world."

As Kate stepped back, Claire's father moved forward, his eyes suspiciously bright as he embraced her. "My beautiful girl," he said, voice rough with emotion. "What a marvelous life you've created."

Her mother was next, her familiar perfume, the scent Claire had known all her life, now forever linked with this momentous day. "I always knew you'd find your true path," she said tearfully, holding Claire tightly.

When her grandmother reached her, the older woman took both her hands, examining the ring with approving scrutiny before meeting Claire's eyes. "Magnificent," she declared simply. "Both the ring and the man who gave it to you."

As Claire stood surrounded by her family, a reality she couldn't have imagined possible just moments before, her mind spun with questions. "But how did you know? How did you get here?"

Kate's eyes flickered toward Luca, who stepped forward to join them. "Your fiancé," Kate explained, the new title sounding both strange and perfectly right, "is quite possibly the most meticulous planner in the Northern Hemisphere."

"It started when my phone rang about four weeks ago," Kate continued, her expression alight with the pleasure of finally revealing a well-kept secret. "It was Luca, explaining that he'd found his mother's ring and wanted to propose at your gallery opening."

"You orchestrated all of this?" Claire asked, looking at Luca's face with wonder.

"With considerable help," he replied, smiling at her family. "Kate was invaluable, she told me your ring size so I could get the ring resized, your family's schedules, even what your father might want to hear when I called to ask his blessing."

"You asked my dad's permission?" Claire felt another wave of emotion wash over her.

"Of course he did," her father interjected, clapping Luca on the shoulder with obvious approval. "Two-hour conversation, going through your entire relationship from that first coffee note to finding his mother's paintings. By the end, I felt like I'd known him for years."

"Then he sent pictures of the ring," Kate added, "arranged our flights, booked our hotel rooms, even had a car waiting for us at the airport the day before yesterday. Then yesterday, he met us and took us to meet Signor Rossi and Lucia at Caffè Sereno."

"You've been here for two days?" Claire asked, astonishment compounding with each revelation.

"Hiding us has been quite the operation," her grandmother said with evident delight. "Like something from a spy film."

"When we arrived here at the gallery, Lucia brought us in through the side entrance and then quietly to this beautiful Isabella's Light section. We've been waiting behind that partition," her mother explained, pointing toward a decorative screen nearby. "Watching the whole proposal. I don't think I've taken a proper breath for the last fifteen minutes."

Claire turned to Luca, seeing him through new eyes, not just as her artistic partner or even her lover, but as someone whose capacity for thoughtfulness extended to orchestrating this elaborate, beautiful surprise for her. "You brought my family across an ocean just so they could be here for this moment?"

Luca nodded, his expression serious. "Some moments deserve witnesses who have known you longest, who remember the girl you were before you became the woman I love." He glanced toward her family with evident affection. "Besides, I wanted them to see Naples through your eyes, to understand why you've chosen to make your home here."

The realization of how deeply Luca understood her, how perfectly he had anticipated what would make this moment complete, struck Claire with overwhelming force. This wasn't just a romantic gesture; it was profound evidence of how completely he saw her.

At that moment, staff members appeared with trays of champagne flutes. As those were handed to the guests, Signor Rossi stepped forward.

"In Naples," he announced, addressing the entire gathering, "we believe that true connections must be sealed with proper celebration. To Claire and Luca, may your life together be as perfect as properly extracted espresso, as sweet as the finest pastry, and as enduring as the art you create together."

"To Claire and Luca!" echoed through the gallery as glasses were raised.

As Claire sipped her champagne, she felt the weight of the ring on her finger, not heavy, but present, significant, a physical manifestation of promises exchanged and futures intertwined. Around her, the gallery had transformed from professional showcase to personal celebration, art and life merging into a seamless whole.

The quartet resumed playing, this time a joyful melody that seemed to dance through the rooms. Lucia appeared with a tray of special pastries adorned with edible flowers and silver leaf, insisting that the newly engaged couple sample them first.

"My grandmother's recipe," she explained, watching with satisfaction as Claire took a bite. "Reserved only for occasions of the heart."

Throughout the evening, Claire found herself drawn repeatedly back to Luca's side between conversations, as if some invisible cord connected them even across crowded rooms. Each time their eyes met, she felt the same electric recognition that had characterized their connection from the beginning, the sense that they recognized each other on a level beyond ordinary understanding.

As the night progressed, the gallery gradually emptied of casual visitors until only close friends and family remained. The lighting throughout Casa dei Sogni had been dimmed to create intimate pockets of illumination, changing the professional exhibition space into something that felt remarkably like home.

Later, after even their closest friends had departed and her family had returned to their hotel, having arranged to meet for brunch at Caffè Sereno, a day of sightseeing, and dinner at their apartment prepared by Luca, Claire and Luca found themselves alone on the villa's terrace. The city of Naples lay in the distance, a glittering constellation against the night canvas, each light a silent storyteller promising secrets they would never hear. The night embraced them gently, carrying the mesmerizing fragrance of Claire's carefully tended night-blooming flowers from the garden below, their sweetness intertwining with the faint, primal call of the Mediterranean that caressed against the distant shore.

"I still can't believe you managed all of this without me suspecting anything," Claire said, admiring how her ring, Isabella's ring, now hers, captured the moonlight. "My family, the proposal, everything, it was beyond perfect."

"Perhaps artists develop a talent for creative secrecy," Luca replied, his arms encircling her waist as they gazed out over the landscape together. "Like hiding paintings behind walls or planning proposals."

Claire leaned against him, savoring the solid presence of his chest against her back, the rhythm of his breathing a counterpoint to her own. "When did you know?" she asked softly. "That you wanted this, wanted us, to be forever?"

Luca considered the question thoughtfully. "There wasn't a single moment of certainty," he finally said. "Rather, it was an accumulation of realizations, each building upon the last. The morning I found you sketching on the terrace at dawn, lost in creative focus. Watching you "speak" to my mother through her paintings when we discovered them. How you understood immediately that this villa wasn't merely architecture but memory given physical form."

He turned her gently to face him, his features bathed by moonlight on one side, softened by shadow on the other. "But perhaps most revealing was watching you with Signor Rossi and Lucia, planning the café space. You instinctively recognized that art isn't confined to gallery walls, it's present in the precise extraction of espresso, in the gentle folding of pastry dough, in conversations shared across wooden tables. You understood Casa dei Sogni in ways I felt but couldn't fully articulate."

Claire reached up to trace the contours of his face with her fingertips, committing the moment to memory like an artist studying a subject. "It feels as though we've been creating this moment since that first note," she said serenely. "Each choice, each conversation, each shared canvas leading us here."

"From caffè sospeso to forever," Luca murmured, turning to press his lips against her palm. "Who would have imagined that a suspended coffee would lead to a timeless moment, preserved in platinum and diamond and promise?"

"I think some part of me recognized you immediately," Claire admitted. "Not consciously, but in that wordless place where artistic intuition lives. The part that perceives truth before the mind can articulate it."

Above them, stars gleamed with ancient light, silent witnesses to countless human stories across millennia yet somehow making this particular narrative feel singular and precious. Below, Naples continued its eternal rhythm, the city that had brought them together now forming the foundation for their shared future.

As Claire leaned forward to kiss Luca, she understood with profound clarity that their story, like true art, would continue evolving beyond this moment, beyond this night, beyond even the boundaries of narrative. Their love had become its own masterpiece, eternal yet constantly in motion, creating and recreating itself with each passing day.

As they stood there in an embrace, behind them, Casa dei Sogni stood illuminated against the night sky, no longer merely a gallery, no longer simply a renovated villa, but the physical embodiment of dreams transformed into reality through artistic vision and uncompromising love.

And like all genuine art, its meaning would only deepen with time, revealing new dimensions with each viewing, each touch, each shared breath in the continuing creation of their life canvas together.

EPILOGUE

The Neapolitan afternoon sun streamed through the windows of Caffè Sereno, painting the worn wooden tables in stripes of honeyed light. Claire adjusted her position slightly, the familiar chair conforming to her body like an old friend. Her gaze drifted to her left hand where her wedding ring caught the sunlight, sending tiny prisms dancing across the table's surface.

One year had passed since that magical evening when Luca had proposed amid the breathless wonder of their gallery opening. Eight months since they had exchanged vows in the courtyard of their gallery, Casa dei Sogni. Claire could still feel the whisper of the dusty pink rose petals falling like tender blessings as they spoke promises beneath an archway woven with Naples' most magnificent blooms. Lucia and Signor Rossi had created a wedding feast that made even the most seasoned Neapolitan chefs weep with appreciation, while the string quartet played Vivaldi as the setting sun painted their families and friends in hues of Blush and indigo.

And then there was their honeymoon. Those were transcendent days in Agra, India where they had stood hand in hand before the Taj Mahal at dawn, watching its marble surface shift from ghostly white to blush pink to molten brass as the sun climbed the sky. "This," Luca had professed against her temple, "is what true love creates, something so beautiful it outlives us all." They had sketched together beneath the shadow of the world's greatest monument to love, their artistic souls understanding what Shah Jahan had known centuries before, that some feelings are so profound they demand permanent form.

"What are you thinking about, amore mio (my love)?" Luca asked, his voice still carrying that musical Italian cadence that made her heart flutter. He sat across from her, his espresso cup cradled between paint-stained fingers, his dark eyes studying her with the intimate intensity that never failed to make her breath quicken.

Claire smiled, reaching across to trace the lines of his palm. "I was thinking about," she said thoughtfully, "how Naples has transformed me from the woman who arrived here seeking escape into someone who creates with her whole self."

Signor Rossi approached their table, his face creased with the joy of watching their love story unfold within the walls of his beloved café. His hands carried a plate of Aragostines (delicate pastry shells filled with luscious pistachio cream) that Claire knew Lucia had prepared specially.

"For my favorite artists," Signor Rossi announced, setting the plate between them with a flourish. "Lucia says these are to celebrate the anniversary of your gallery opening, but I think..." his eyes twinkled with mischief, "she just wants to make sure you have enough energy for whatever creative endeavors you have planned for this afternoon."

Claire felt a blush rise to her cheeks even as Luca laughed, that rich baritone that seemed to vibrate through her very bones. Their connection had only deepened with time, each day teaching them new ways to create beauty together, new ways to express with touch what even art sometimes could not capture.

"Grazie (Thank you), Signor Rossi," Luca said, "Tell Lucia her intuition is impeccable, as always."

As Signor Rossi retreated with a knowing chuckle, Claire and Luca took a bite of an Aragostine. Claire closed her eyes briefly as the flavors exploded across her tongue, the delicate crunch of the pastry shell surrendering to velvety pistachio cream, nutty sweetness mingling with subtle hints of salt that intensified the luxurious sensation. When she opened her eyes, she found Luca watching her with an intensity that made her stomach flutter.

"You still look at me that way," she proclaimed, reaching to brush away crumbs of the pastry sheel from his lip.

"What way?" he asked, though his slow smile suggested he knew exactly what she meant.

"Like I'm a masterpiece you're seeing for the first time," she said. "Like you're memorizing every detail for a painting you'll create later."

Luca caught her hand, pressing a kiss to her palm that seared through her body like a flame. "Because you are, my Claire. Every day with you reveals new dimensions, new depths, new reasons to fall in love all over again."

Their gallery had become one of the most celebrated in Naples in the year since its opening. Their combined artistic vision, Claire's meticulous attention to emotional detail complementing Luca's passionate expressionism, had created a body of work that critics compared to the great artistic partnerships throughout history.

The chime above the café door sang its gentle greeting, drawing Claire's and Luca's attention. A young woman stepped inside, perhaps thirty years old, with sun-kissed golden hair cascading over shoulders draped in a silk scarf patterned with Italian motifs. American, Claire could tell immediately, something in the way she carried herself, in the eager curiosity of her gaze that had not yet been softened by Naples' more fluid rhythm.

She approached the counter where Signor Rossi was polishing glasses. Her eyes swept the café with delighted wonder, taking in the cork board with its collage of notes, the ancient espresso machine that gleamed like burnished copper, the photographs of Naples through the ages that adorned the marigold-colored walls.

"Welcome to Caffè Sereno," Signore Rossi said warmly.

"Buongiorno," the young woman replied, her Italian accented but earnest. She hesitated, then continued in English. "I was hoping for a cappuccino, please."

"Of course! I am Signor Rossi, proprietor of Caffè Sereno," he replied warmly, extending his hand. "And this..." he gestured toward Lucia, who was arranging fresh pastries in the display case, her silver-streaked hair caught in the sunlight like rivers of starlight, "... is my wife, Lucia."

"Daisy Fletcher, from California, USA" she replied, her handshake firm and friendly. "It's lovely to meet you both."

"And what do you think of our Naples?" Signor Rossi asked as he began preparing the cappuccino with the ceremonial precision that still captivated Claire after all this time.

"It's magnificent," Daisy breathed, her voice carrying the unmistakable awe of someone encountering a dream made tangible. "Different from anything I imagined. More... alive somehow."

"Naples has that effect," Signor Rossi nodded sagely. "She gets under your skin, becomes part of your heart. Ask those two," he gestured toward Claire and Luca with a knowing smile. Daisy turned toward the couple and offered a gentle wave, her eyes reflecting a wistful curiosity.

As Daisy waited for her coffee, her attention was drawn to the large glass jar sitting prominently on the counter, filled with rolled receipts and marked with a small hand-lettered sign: "Caffè Sospeso." The afternoon light struck the jar at just the right angle, illuminating the paper scrolls within like ancient messages in bottles, each one containing worlds of possibility.

"Excuse me," she asked, curiosity evident in her voice, "what is this... 'caffè sospeso'?"

Signor Rossi's eyes lit up, and he exchanged knowing glances with Claire and Luca, who were listening to this conversation. The café seemed to hold its breath, the ambient sounds fading as if the very walls were leaning in to witness this moment of inception.

Signor Rossi's smile widened with the particular joy of someone about to share a beautiful secret. He leaned forward across the counter, the glass jar between him and Daisy glowing like an artifact of profound magic frozen in time, waiting to be awakened.

"Caffè sospeso," Signor Rossi began, his voice dropping to the hushed tone of a storyteller sharing ancient wisdom, "is a tradition as old as Naples herself..."

REQUESTING A REVIEW

Your Review Matters

If you've enjoyed this book, I would be incredibly grateful if you could take a moment to share your honest thoughts in a review on Amazon. Even just a few sentences about what you liked (or what you didn't) can make a tremendous difference. Your feedback helps other readers discover this work and provides valuable insights that shape my future writing.

The Journey Behind These Pages

As an independent author, I've poured countless hours of research, writing, and revision into bringing this book to life. Without the backing of a major publishing house, each step of the process, from the initial draft to the final edit, has been a labor of love and determination.

For indie authors like me, reader reviews are essential. They increase the visibility of my work, help me connect with my audience, and provide the encouragement needed to continue creating.

Thank you for being part of this journey, and thank you for supporting independent literature.

Seema Shenoy

AFTERWORD

As the last pages of Claire and Luca's story settle in your hands, I find myself returning to my desk, windows open to catch the breeze that carries distant church bells and laughter from the street below, in my imagination. Though I sit thousands of miles away from Naples, writing these words, a part of my heart remains eternally within Italy's embrace.

Creating this novel has been its own form of caffè sospeso, a suspension between worlds, between reality and imagination, between my experiences and the fictional lives that have become so dear to me. Claire and Luca have lived in my mind for so long that sending their story into the world feels like watching beloved friends embark on a journey, their destinies now entwined with yours as reader.

Throughout the writing process, I often found myself transported to moments from my own Italian adventures. The way morning light filtered through lace curtains in Tuscany. The unexpected tears that sprang to my eyes upon first seeing Botticelli's Primavera in Florence's Uffizi Gallery. The pleasure of conversation with local shopkeepers whose kindness transcended language barriers. The transcendent experience of sitting on the Spanish Steps with my husband at sunset, watching Rome transform as golden light gilded ancient domes and the entire city seemed to awaken with newfound life.

Italy taught me to see beauty in imperfection, in weathered facades whose peeling paint reveals centuries of stories, in the unhurried pace that prioritizes connection over efficiency, in the passionate gestures that accompany everyday conversation. This appreciation for the beauty of imperfection found its way into Claire and Luca's journey, their love not despite their flaws and fears, but inclusive of them.

The tradition of caffè sospeso continues to move me deeply. In a world often driven by transaction and immediate return, this simple act of leaving coffee for an unknown recipient represents everything I believe about human connection. It speaks to the best in us, our capacity for generosity without guarantee of recognition, our fundamental desire to reach across the void to touch another soul, our shared humanity that goes beyond circumstance and difference.

As an author, I hope this novel functions as its own form of suspended coffee, a moment of connection between my heart and yours, a bridge across which we can meet despite never having shared physical space. Perhaps some aspect of Claire and Luca's story will remain suspended in your thoughts, waiting for the perfect moment to offer comfort, inspiration, or the gentle reminder that true connection, whether through art, love, or simple human kindness, remains our most profound masterpiece.

With gratitude for sharing this journey,

Seema Shenoy

ACKNOWLEDGMENTS

To Subrao Shenoy, my beloved husband and love of my life, your unwavering support and genuine enthusiasm for my writing have been the cornerstone of bringing this story to life. Thank you for loving me unconditionally and for standing beside me through every triumph and challenge of my creative journey.

To my beloved parents, Dr. Anant and Sudha Bhadri, who taught me the deepest truths about love through their daily lives. Within the walls of my modest childhood home in rural India, they created an extraordinary testament to devotion. My father, a brilliant physician whose kindness reached countless underprivileged souls, and my mother, whose gift for transforming simple ingredients into expressions of affection showed me that wonder exists in life's quietest moments. This book honors their enduring legacy.

Mary De Guzman, the talented artist responsible for the captivating cover that so eloquently conveys the heart of this story. I remain endlessly appreciative of the artistry you've brought to life with your digital palette. Thank you for formatting the book and giving tangible form to what once existed only in imagination.

To Italy, land of timeless beauty, passionate hearts, and sun-drenched inspiration, I owe a special debt of gratitude. Your ancient cobblestone streets, rolling vineyard hills, the melodic cadence of your language, and your unique coffee culture have inspired me to write this story. Your spirit of romance and adventure flows through these pages like wine at a family table; generous, warming, and inviting readers to linger just a little longer.

Seema Shenoy

ABOUT THE AUTHOR

Seema Shenoy is a romantic at heart who believes in the transformative power of love. For forty years, she has called the San Francisco Bay Area home, where she lives with her husband - her pillar of strength, confidant, and the love of her life. Their enduring romance has not only been her greatest adventure but also the wellspring of inspiration for her writing, teaching her that true love shapes not just our hearts but the very fabric of our reality.

Italy has captured Seema's heart in a way she never anticipated. Her passion for the country's rolling vineyards, ancient villages, and timeless romance couldn't be contained within her heart alone, compelling her to create this novel.

A devoted mother, Seema finds immense joy in her relationship with her son and daughter-in-law, filled with love and pride. Her passion for nurturing extends beyond family to her love of cooking, where she believes every meal prepared is an expression of love made tangible. You'll often find her in her kitchen, experimenting with recipes and feeding loved ones, turning ordinary moments into cherished memories.

Seema's understanding of love and sacrifice was profoundly shaped by her parents' extraordinary legacy. Growing up in rural India, she witnessed the beautiful partnership between her father, a dedicated physician who built the area's only hospital, and her mother, whose culinary artistry and nurturing spirit made their modest home a haven of warmth and joy. Their selfless dedication to others and unwavering love for family taught Seema that the greatest romance stories are often written in life's quiet moments of sacrifice and devotion.

Seema writes in the vibrant bustle of local coffee shops, her fingers dancing across her laptop keys as she weaves emotionally rich tales of love that resonate with the human spirit. Surrounded by the aroma of freshly brewed coffee and the soft murmur of conversation, she pours her heart into every word, crafting multi-dimensional characters whose vulnerabilities and passions leap off the page. When seeking a change of scenery, Seema finds inspiration beneath the ancient boughs of redwood trees, their steadfast presence and whispering leaves stirring her imagination as she creates immersive stories that transport readers into the transformative world of epic romance.

Seema Shenoy, Author

www.CreativelySeema.com

instagram.com/creativelyseema

pinterest.com/creativelyseema

facebook.com/creativelyseema

tiktok.com/@creativelyseema